CALL
NO MAN
FATHER

ALSO BY
WILLIAM X. KIENZLE

CALL
NO MAN
FATHER

WILLIAM X. KIENZLE

ANDREWS AND McMEEL

A Universal Press Syndicate Company

Kansas City

ISBN 0–8362–6131–3

CREDITS

Editorial Director: Donna Martin
Associate Editor: Matt Lombardi
Production: Carol Coe
Production Editor: Katie Mace
Book Design: Edward D. King
Jacket Design: George Diggs
Composition: Hillside Studio, Inc.

FOR JAVAN

*My wife
and
collaborator*

ACKNOWLEDGMENTS

Gratitude for technical advice to:

Robert Ankeny, staff writer, *The Detroit News*

Pat Chargot, staff writer, *Detroit Free Press*

Sergeant James Grace, detective, Kalamazoo Police Department

Rudy Reinhard, World Wide Travel Bureau Inc., Troy, Michigan

Archdiocese of Detroit:

Jo Garcia, Theological Library Service. Sacred Heart
  Major Seminary

Roman P. Godzak, archivist/records manager

Sister Bernadelle Grimm, R.S.M., pastoral care (retired),
  Mercy Hospital

Jane Wolford Hughes, Institute for Continuing Education

The Reverend Anthony Kosnik, S.T.D., J.C.B., professor of ethics,
  Marygrove College

Karen Mehaffey, Theological Library Service,
  Sacred Heart Major Seminary

Sister Anneliese Sinnott, O.P., assistant director, pastoral
  ministry, Marygrove College

Detroit Police Department:

Inspector Richard Ridling, homicide (retired)

Inspector Barbara Weide

St. Joseph Mercy Hospital, Pontiac:

Charles Durando, physiotherapist

Thomas J. Petinga, Jr., D.O., FACEP, Chief of Emergency Services

Wayne State University:

Ramon J. Betanzos, Ph.D., professor of humanities

Charles Lucas, M.D., professor of surgery

Werner U. Spitz, M.D., professor of forensic pathology

Irish segments:

Anne Bouch, genealogist

Ray Comiskey, *Irish Times*

Hugh Leonard

Chris and Mary Murray

Harry and Joyce Whelehan

Any technical error is the author's.

Bibliography

Tierney, Brian. *Origins of Papal Infallibility, 1150-1350 (A Study on the Concepts of Infallibility, Sovereignty and Tradition in the Middle Ages).* Leiden, Netherlands: E.J. Brill, 1972.

In Memory of
Anne Zienert

"And call no man your father upon the earth: for one is your father, which is in heaven."

Matthew 23.9
King James Version

> "

PART ONE

PART ONE

God, I hate air travel.

He felt he was entitled to this sentiment. He had clocked tons of hours on airliners, many of them long before some enterprising bean counter had thought up frequent-flier miles.

He easily recalled pleasant trips before deregulation and "hub" cities. Relaxing flights, uncrowded, with room to stretch out, room to breathe, cheerful service. Desirable destinations: Louvain, Tübingen, Rome. Student days. Memories never to be duplicated.

Peripherally, he was aware of being watched . . . studied . . . by a man seated immediately across the aisle. He regretted having worn his black suit and clerical collar.

He was, in fact, a Catholic priest, and the uniform his identification. The only thing that prevented the neighbor from invading his priestly privacy was his open breviary—the book of daily prayer. He wasn't sure how long this ruse would work. But he would stay with it as long as possible.

Meanwhile, he could keep his own counsel.

Nothing, he thought, is as good as it was. Today's music was cacophony compared with the classics of old and the show tunes and popular music of the fifties and before. Cars weren't as sturdy now. Appliances were programmed to self-destruct. Planned obsolescence.

A smile passed quickly. He was becoming a curmudgeon. A little early in life for that. But he didn't mind; as far as he was concerned, it was all true.

To hell in a handbasket. That's where the world was going. And, he feared, the symposium was not going to help.

He didn't want to think about that conference.

He shifted his mind into neutral. He recalled a class he'd taught recently. In analyzing a composition of Palestrina, he had mentioned the musical figure *ostinato*, referring to a motif repeated persistently throughout the composition. To help the students remember the term, he gave them the mnemonic "obstinate." Obstinate, he informed them, derives from the word *ostinato*. And, while the class seemed to absorb all this, years of experience prompted him to check further: Could anybody define "obstinate"?

One confident lad raised his hand: "Obstinate is when you refrain from sexual intercourse."

The kid had confused "obstinate" with "abstinence." But, on second—or third—thought, the young man might just have stumbled onto a shred of confused truth. Surely some people must withhold intercourse out of sheer obstinacy.

His hands grew weary. The breviary fell to his lap, closed.

Instantly, his neighbor pounced.

"Pardon me, father"—the tone carried a measure of urgency—"but are you done with your brevity?"

Brevity, the priest considered. It's not all that brief. But, what the hell, he caught me with my prayer book down. "Not really . . . but, for the moment, yes."

"Vince Weir." The neighbor offered his hand and his name. He did not ask the priest's name, nor was it volunteered. Apparently, he was content dealing with a generic priest. The priest was more than happy to remain anonymous.

Actually, this was Vince Weir's usual means of getting religious questions resolved. If he had a nickel for every "brevity" he'd interrupted on flights . . .

"Father . . ." Weir spoke above the engines' roar but not loudly enough to be overheard by nearby passengers; he was well practiced. ". . . you a parish priest?"

"Not exactly."

"Then what? If you don't mind me asking."

"I teach. At a German university."

"Now that interests me. What?"

"'What'?"

"What do you teach?"

"Oh . . . liturgy."

"That like the Mass?"

"Uh-huh." The priest hoped this wasn't going to lead into one of those sick jokes. Like the one he'd heard last week:

What's the difference between a liturgist and a terrorist?

You can reason with a terrorist.

"I've been wondering, Father: Whatever happened to all that good music we used to have in church? It's all gone. How come we don't hear it anymore?"

Appreciation for the sublime Church music of the past! The priest had not expected as much from Mr. Weir. "Sad, isn't it?" the priest commiserated.

"Yeah! Hymns like 'Holy God,' and 'O Mother of Perpetual Help' and 'Bring Flowers of the Fairest,' and 'O Lord I Am Not Worthy,' and 'Mother, I Could Weep for Mirth.' Why can't we get them back?"

The priest's sensibilities wilted. "Tell me, Mr. Weir, where do you live?"

"Milwaukee."

"Perfect."

"What?"

"Your archbishop—Rembert Weakland—is a gifted musician. Try to get an appointment with him. Or write to him. I'm sure he'd be glad to clear up all your questions."

"Gee, thanks, Father. Here, lemme give you one of my cards. . . ." Weir presented the priest with a business card, tapping his line of business with a finger. "I'm in ladies' wear."

There was humor there somewhere. But the priest did not wish to explore it.

Their conversation, such as it was, was shattered by the loudspeaker, as the attendant's singsong fought a battle with static: "Ladies and gentlemen, we are beginning our approach to Dublin Airport. We ask that you make sure your trays are stored and that your seat backs are in an upright position, and that all items of baggage are securely stowed under your seats or in the overhead bins. We will be on the ground in approximately ten minutes. The local time is 11:43 A.M. The weather is clear and the temperature is four degrees Celsius.

"At this time, we ask that you fasten your seat belts and extinguish all smoking materials."

His seat was upright and his tray had disappeared into the armrest. He hadn't unbuckled his seat belt since fastening it. He did not smoke.

But he did hold on. His knuckles were white. Taking off and landing; those were the most dangerous moments in air travel. For all he knew, this plane could well be of a certain age. The mechanics who serviced this craft might not be knowledgeable, conscientious, reliable. They might have been poorly trained, slipshod, unconcerned. The plane might touch down only to find a tire going its separate way while the wing scraped the tarmac, throwing sparks that could ignite God knew what. When it came to air travel he had come to trust no one and nothing.

For all his anxiety, the landing was almost picture perfect. The plane did not even bounce.

They taxied directly toward the terminal. He could recall flights—lots of them—where they'd spent more time sitting on the strip waiting for an available gate than they had in the air. His mood eased up. Perhaps this trip would not be as nerve-racking as he had feared.

However, he reminded himself, he still faced a layover before the departure of his connecting flight—then, including the stop at Shannon, some eight hours to Boston, where he would have another two-hour layover, then another two hours to Detroit, where, as travel jargon had it, he would terminate.

The plane rocked to a standstill. By this time, most of the passengers were standing, pulling themselves together and extracting luggage out of overhead bins and from under seats. All a bit premature and all in disobedience to the crew's orders.

But since it was now time to deplane no one was any longer making an issue of remaining in seats, buckled down until allowed to rise.

He was seated in the first row of the tourist section. He looked back at all the poor trapped souls who now would be set free at least for a while. There were so many. Today's jetliners seemed to have been designed with the sole purpose of packing in a maximum quota of passengers while still being capable of becoming airborne.

It was like a scene from hell. Or, since it would end sometime, purgatory.

There was no cause for haste; he had a layover of some two hours—longer, should there be a problem with the next flight. Nonetheless, he was eager to get out of here. So, valise and hat in hand and coat draped over arm, he managed to be the first tourist passenger to reach the first-class compartment, where the exit door yawned.

But barring his egress was an attendant. That was no accident, as he discovered when he attempted to step around her. She moved to block him again. "Let's let the first-class passengers go first." Her tone was that of a petulant grammar school teacher. She didn't even bother looking to see whom she was addressing.

For the first time during this flight he really felt like a second-, perhaps third-class passenger. He hadn't envied first class their menu; it wasn't that much better than tourist. As for spaciousness, first-class passengers had barely more legroom than he had in his bulkhead seat. But, forced to stand and wait while the elite made their leisurely departure—well! It was such treatment that engendered revolutions.

Eventually the front cabin cleared and the class-conscious attendant stepped aside.

He and Vince Weir parted company, with Weir expressing added gratitude "for your help, Father." The priest was the first of his group to descend the stairs to the ground. Didn't Dublin Airport believe in the extending ramps that protected deplaning passengers from the elements? Fortunately, the weather was clear and not terribly cold. And shuttle buses were waiting to carry them to the terminal.

The Dublin terminal was—or appeared to be—practically empty. He credited that to the fact that it was Sunday. Many shops were closed. Perhaps shop owners in this overwhelmingly Catholic country believed they should not do business on the Lord's day?

After going through customs, he looked about for the reporter from the Irish paper. God knows when the man had phoned he'd been eager enough for an interview. And after the priest had cooperated and given his flight number, the reporter had promised that they would meet at the customs counter. But, where was he? No one in sight.

The priest shrugged, then sighed and made his way to the main part of the terminal, where he checked in for his transatlantic flight, which, he was assured, would depart on time. He was free till then. The café was open, but he decided not to try it. For one thing, he wasn't very hungry; for another, he had already exchanged his money for U.S. currency. And he didn't want to be weighed down with change in the form of Irish punts. In short, it simply wasn't worth the bother. Besides, they'd be serving a meal of sorts on the upcoming flight.

He strolled, stretching his legs, mindful of the confinement ahead. Many of the people he passed were uniformed Aer Lingus personnel. In addition to the pilots, attendants, and clerks, there were the terminal's maintenance people in their distinctive basic blue with orange stripes.

In a remote section of the terminal he came upon a bank of unoccupied seats. He reasoned that he couldn't continue walking aimlessly until the Boston flight, so he took a seat in the middle of the row.

Several moments of blessed peace were his. Then he spotted coming toward him, without the slightest uncertainty or hesitation, a small girl, well bundled. She regarded him for several moments. If either was made to feel awkward and apprehensive, it was the priest. He looked away from her several times while she gazed at him unblinkingly. He looked about imploringly. *Where were her parents?*

She took several steps toward him.

He wanted to say, with compelling vigor, Go away, little girl! But an image kept intruding on his mind of Jesus saying, "Let the little children come unto me."

Finally, she clambered onto the chair to his immediate right. He offered no assistance whatsoever.

He did not know how to talk to a child. He never thought about children. Why did people think priests like children? Priests don't have any of their own. Perhaps children were like cats—inexorably drawn to people who don't like them . . . people who are allergic to them.

Whatever. The two of them sat side by side for several moments in uncompanionable silence.

He was reminded of the story that a priest friend told. The friend, early on in his priestly career, had been assigned to a Manhattan parish. One Saturday afternoon, while he was hearing uncounted confessions, the curtain at the entry to his confessional was suddenly pulled aside, and a little blonde girl called out in a loud, clear voice for every one in the church to hear, "Mama, there's a man in here, and he's going potty!"

The moral of that story was that little girls are not as reserved as people think they are.

But now he had his own urchin. The moppet sitting next to him took a small, toy baby carriage out of her pocket. Then she began running the carriage up and down his right arm.

He did not know what to do. So he just sat there and watched the carriage go up and down his arm.

Finally, he managed, "So . . . you are a little girl."

At that, a shriek filled that area of the terminal, and, advancing on him like the sea of doom, a wrathful mother hen screeched for the child to COME AWAY FROM THERE!

Which the girl promptly did. Casting a look-that-could-kill at the priest, the woman dragged the little girl away.

Now, the priest thought, what could have brought that on? Then he flashed on the scandal of child abuse so infamously involving priests and religious, especially in the States. The woman must have grossly mistaken his intentions. He was embarrassed. The few people in this section of the terminal seemed to be looking at him as if he were an ogre.

No matter how tired he might be by the time his Boston flight left, he decided he'd better keep moving. Especially away from those disapproving eyes.

Eventually, the walking stirred something within; he began looking for a men's room. He found one hidden away in one corner of the main floor. It appeared meticulously clean. There were six stalls and six urinals and only one other man using the facility. He seemed to have completed his business and was washing his hands.

He surveyed the room. It was more than merely clean, it was spotless. Besides the stalls, urinals, and washstands, there were two dispensary cabinets on the wall. Each offered condoms. Specifically, MATES™, which seemed to be the trade name. The condoms advertised a series of choices and advantages: Natural, Ribbed, Coloured, Spermicidal, Lubricated; eight for three punts, five for two punts.

God Almighty, he thought, what is this civilization coming to!? What does a casual visitation to a men's room afford? Breath mints? Band-Aids? Shaving or toothbrushing equipment? A shoe-polishing machine? Evidently, something far more practical, useful, and needed than any of those. Somehow, modern man must be protected from venereal disease and fatherhood.

Again, these thoughts led back to the coming conference. And he didn't want to think of that until, in the course of events, he had to.

The other man, business completed, departed.

He was alone.

Privy matters attended to, he left the stall and moved to the bank of washstands. He leaned in to get a better look at himself in the mirror. No doubt: He could use a shave. The heavy shadow that overlaid his cheeks and neck and circled his mouth seemed incongruous in contrast to the formality of his clothes. Though the black suit was a bit rumpled, it had been cleaned and pressed just before he left; it still held its creases. Then there was the roman collar and clerical vest. No white plastic insert at the neck of his black shirt; his was the full starched linen collar, buttoned at the nape. Old-fashioned, yes. But that's the way he was.

Someone entered.

A terminal maintenance man, apparently. Clad in coveralls with the distinctive colors, he was trundling a cart of cleaning supplies and equipment.

The priest glanced briefly at the man, who had begun to dust mop the floor. As far as the priest was concerned, nothing in this restroom needed immediate attention. But it was good to know that the Irish cleaned things that were already clean.

He opened his valise and removed shaving equipment and a dry washcloth. The greater part of his adult life, he'd had problems with shaving, especially with a fresh blade. Either he would cut himself or he wouldn't press hard enough to remove all the stubble.

Until, that is, in Cologne a German barber gave him the secret of prepping his face with moist heat.

He removed his collar, vest, and jacket, turned the hot water on and drenched the washcloth, wrung it out, bent low over the sink and pressed the cloth to his face, holding it there as long as he could bear the heat.

When he straightened up, so intent was he on getting a clean shave that he hardly noticed that the maintenance man was now directly behind him. Nor had the priest more than a split second to comprehend what followed.

In one fluid motion, from the rear, the man cupped the priest's chin in his right hand while his left hand grasped the priest's head. With a powerful wrenching motion, he twisted around and down until the priest's chin was well beyond his right shoulder. The shattering of his spinal cord made no sound. Nor was there any blood. The priest slumped dead to the floor.

The killer nodded once in quiet satisfaction. Everything was going perfectly.

He stripped the victim, gathered the dead man's garments, emptied the pockets, and stuffed the clothing into a large duffel bag. He then removed his own coveralls and added them to the bag. He was attired in a suit and roman collar identical to the dead priest's uniform.

He dragged the now-naked corpse into a stall, lowered the legs into the toilet bowl and propped the body on the seat. With a length of rope, he tied the body to the wall pipe. Satisfied that the body would stay put, he locked the stall door from the inside and lifted himself over the partition and out of the stall.

He paused to look about. Perfect so far. He hadn't even had to resort to a ruse to get the priest off by himself.

After transferring the contents of the victim's wallet to his own, he added the empty wallet to the duffel bag. He removed a black overcoat and hat from the interior of the cleaning cart.

Finally, he retrieved the black-on-yellow sign—OUT OF ORDER/TEMPORARILY CLOSED—from just outside the men's room, where he'd placed it before entering. He placed the sign in front of the locked stall.

Now dressed as a priest, he left the men's room, carrying the valise and the duffel bag. He went directly to an outside bin he knew would be emptied within the hour.

Twenty minutes later his flight was called. The security people had no problem with his carry-on valise, nor with the contents of his pockets. The forged passport passed muster.

He found his seat in the tourist section, loosened his clerical collar, and settled in for the first leg of his twelve-hour trip to Detroit. By the time he had mentally run through his agenda for the next few days, lunch was being served. Later when the movie began, he took a cassette from his pocket, inserted it into a compact player, and connected the earphone. It was a book being read by an actor with Midwest American roots. He shut his eyes and, as he had done so many times before, silently moved his lips as he practiced an accent that was not his.

Sometime later he drifted off to sleep.

He needed the rest. He had business in Detroit.

2

The body was discovered late that afternoon.

The maintenance man was puzzled when he saw the OUT OF ORDER sign in front of the stall. A defective toilet was not on his repair list. But there it was. He would have to try to fix it.

The next puzzler was the locked door. Why would anyone lock a stall door from the inside, whether the toilet was working or not?

Crawling beneath the door, he glimpsed the body grotesquely positioned on the toilet. With a quick intake of breath, he scrambled awkwardly back.

Nor would he reenter. When the Gardai arrived, one of the officers had to climb into the stall and unlock the door. This was not the United States; the Gardai were shocked at what they found.

Soon, homicide detectives arrival, along with technicians. The crime scene was studied, recorded, and analyzed with great care.

Standing at the rear of the gents' room somewhat apart from the immediate action were Sean O'Reardon, Superintendent Garda Siochana from the headquarters in Phoenix Park, and his chief detective, Sergeant Thomas Carty.

O'Reardon warmed his hands on the still-hot bowl of his pipe. Out of consideration for the others in this restricted space, he would not puff. "Well, then," he said, "quite a sight."

Carty rubbed his fingers over his chin stubble. "It is." He cleared his throat. "Can't say that I've ever laid eyes . . . maybe in the north . . ."

O'Reardon's eyebrows lifted.

Carty hesitated. He didn't want to seem to be lecturing. "Um, you know, the symbolic sort of thing. Kneecapping . . . uh . . . like that. Sort of a significant punishment short of death. Like what God might do to you for a venial sin—short of a mortal sin."

"Ummm." O'Reardon pondered that. "So, that's what you're thinking, Tom. Then what do you suppose it is somebody's trying to tell us with this caper?"

Carty dug a little deeper in his stubble. "Damned if I can guess it, Sean."

"Nor I. If it's the Provos, they surely ought to make themselves more clear. In this case, they should've written it out in detail and attached it to the poor man's forehead. Do you know, did they find the clothing?"

"Not yet. We're going over the whole terminal. Nothing so far. We're checking the pickup schedule. Maybe something will turn up."

"Well, he didn't walk in here naked." Pause. "Did he?"

Carty smiled. "Nothing out of the ordinary today. And there's plenty would notice a man walkin' around with no clothes on. That's one puzzle we won't have to solve, please God. No, he lost his britches in here. And that's for certain and sure."

"Ah," O'Reardon agreed, "and more than his britches. Everything! Even his drawers. Who the hell would want his drawers?!"

Recognizing the question as rhetorical, Carty merely shook his head. "'Then the hobo drooped his weary head / And breathed his last refrain / His comrade swiped his shoes and socks / And hopped an eastbound train—'"

A deferential young Garda interrupted the sotto voce solo. "The coroner is finished, Super. He says the man's neck was broken. And that'd be the cause of death . . . at least until they get at a complete autopsy."

O'Reardon nodded. The Garda returned to his duties.

O'Reardon and Carty approached the corpse that now had been stretched out on the lavatory floor preparatory to being inserted in a body bag. "The boys?" O'Reardon wondered softly.

Carty shrugged. "Sort of depends on who the victim is. I can't place him. You?"

O'Reardon shook his head. "Rings no bells with me. Got a bit of stubble there on his chin."

"Could be a tramp. Maybe the song rings true . . . the part about the comrade swiping his shoes and socks—and, in this case, his drawers as well—and skipped."

O'Reardon said nothing. Then, "There's something . . . something that makes me think he was more than a tramp . . . although I couldn't say what. Any one of us naked and dead would be reduced to common clay. But there's something . . .

"What do you think about the cause of death?"

"What?"

"Broken neck."

"Odd, yes . . ."

"No blood anywhere. Looks as if there was no struggle . . . like somebody just up and broke the poor sod's neck."

"Have to be pretty strong, wouldn't he . . ."

"And," O'Reardon added, "confident of his own strength."

"Right. If the first twist doesn't do the job, the killer's in for a fight, sure enough."

O'Reardon flexed his shoulders and nodded to the Gardai. They removed the body and began packing their equipment.

"Well," O'Reardon said as the two detectives left the men's lavatory and walked through the terminal, "it's a small country. Somebody must know him. If, indeed, he's from here. Maybe we can get an IdentiKit picture on tonight's late news. Maybe somebody will identify him."

"I'll see to that," Carty said. He had to force himself to slow his pace. Normally, by this time, he would've been far ahead of his colleague. O'Reardon seemed almost totally lost in thought.

"The *who*'s important, all right," O'Reardon mused. "And then we've got all those *why*'s. Why the air terminal? Why the broken neck? Why remove all the clothing? Lots and lots of questions."

"One thing: There won't be much pressure."

"Hmm?"

"The type of crime," Carty said, "that attracts some popular attention for just a bit, then they move on to something else. They'll probably think the nakedness a bit crude. In a few days the public'll lose interest entirely. And, once the public loses interest, so does the media. And when the media loses interest, so does the government. So . . . the pressure on us is not going to be very intense, I'll bet."

"There's a good bit of truth in what you say, Tom. But I won't forget this one soon. There are just too many odd little things to bug me. I can see it coming. We're going to need a lot of luck—or guidance from above." O'Reardon tried to hide a pixieish smile. "No doubt about it, Tom: We'll need help from the good Lord. And did you remember to go to Mass today?"

"I did not."

"Oh? Herself didn't grab you by the ear and drag you off to church?"

"No. In point of fact, she didn't go at all."

"Mary? Mary didn't go? Of a Sunday, she didn't go to Mass? She's not ill, now, is she?"

Carty stopped and turned to his superintendent. *"In ainm an Athar agus n Mhic agus and Spioraid Naoimah."* It was the sign of the cross.

O'Reardon chuckled. "Said Mass in the Irish, did he?"

Carty nodded. "And what with the missus waitin' for the return of the Latin, it's all too much for her, I'm afraid."

"His Reverence had better not pull that again. If I can't count on you—and I can't—I've got to depend on Mary's prayers."

3

This was Wanda's "once-a-year day."

Each year, just before Christmas, Inspector and Mrs. Koznicki hosted a small dinner party for a few of their closest friends. Traditionally, as was the case tonight, the entrée was standing rib roast—a treat normally considered somewhat beyond their ordinary budget.

Wanda very much enjoyed cooking these meals and she gave their preparation exquisite care. As she put the finishing touches on the meat, the potatoes and the gravy, the vegetables and salad, her husband was attending to their guests: Father Robert Koesler and Father Paul Smith, Lieutenant Alonzo Tully (known to his confreres as "Zoo"), and his recent bride, Anne Marie.

Tully and Koznicki worked together in the Homicide Division of the Detroit Police Department. Father Koesler was pastor of "Old" St. Joseph's parish in downtown Detroit. From time to time in the past when a measure of expertise in Catholicism was needed in a police investigation, Koznicki and Tully had called upon Koesler.

It was December 11, the third Sunday of Advent—earlier than usual for the Koznicki Christmas dinner. But an unusual and momentous event was about to occur in Detroit. It would have been awkward this year to schedule their holiday dinner at its customary time, for it would have conflicted with the pope's visit to Detroit.

The Koznicki home was located in a once-wealthy neighborhood of Detroit no longer populated by *hoi aristoi* but still a well-kept area. The house was large, though, since their children were adults and out on their own, mostly empty. But the kids and the grandchildren would soon be home for the holidays and the house would again be happily filled.

Koznicki and Tully, with their long history of police work, had countless interesting if occasionally grisly stories to tell. But neither was close to being garrulous. So the priests, whose peculiar lifestyle was a story in itself, carried the brunt of tonight's conversational ball, with an occasional assist from Anne Marie, who taught in a Detroit public school.

16

Father Paul Smith, officially retired, or, "given the status of senior priest," helped out in the parish the Koznickis attended. Smith's oval face, rimmed by thick glasses, was crowned by a bald head that reflected the chandelier's light. A tall man, Smith seemed a mere shadow of the vigorous priest that Koesler had known in past years.

Father Smith was concluding a story about a funeral he had presided over. As he related the details of the wake, he described how the deep faith of the bereaved family was able to transcend the sorrow of the loss of a husband and father. At one point, the widow called her children together in the viewing area of the funeral home. She wanted to make sure that they realized that their father lived on in eternity and that the body in the casket was now merely the empty shell that once had housed his soul.

"Remember," she said to her children as she gestured toward the bier, "that is *not* your father." One of her daughters, gifted with a high level of black humor, replied, "Gee, it's a dead ringer for him!"

Everyone laughed. Smith gave Koesler an it's-your-turn-to-carry-on glance. With all the experiences logged by these two clergymen, it was not difficult to pick up the flow in the wake of each other's stream of consciousness.

Koznicki added a quartered log and some kindling to the fading fire. Those seated nearest the fireplace felt the increased warmth as new flames sprang to life.

"I'm afraid I haven't had any spritely funerals lately," Koesler said. "But one of our priests—a seminary professor—did mention one he had recently that might fit the category. It seems he was called to help out at one of the inner city parishes—St. Patrick's, near Orchestra Hall."

His listeners nodded. Actually, Father Smith was the only one who knew exactly where St. Patrick's was. But everyone was familiar with "acoustically perfect Orchestra Hall" as it was routinely described on WQRS-FM, Detroit's classical musical station.

"The pastor," Koesler continued, "was in one of those dilemmas where the only solution was bilocation. So he asked the priest-professor to take the funeral.

"Funerals and weddings," Koesler explained, for the benefit of his lay listeners, "are particularly hazardous to a pinchhitter. These are rather intimate occasions, and it doesn't help if the presiding priest doesn't know anyone in the assembly.

"On top of that, the pastor asked this priest to try to involve the mourners in the eulogy.

"Now, some priests can carry off such a liturgy. Unfortunately, the seminary prof was one of those not at ease enough to generate an atmosphere where this sort of audience participation might work. But, to help out the pastor, he said he would try.

"The deceased was a woman in her mid-nineties. Added to that, St. Patrick's is in the middle of Cass Corridor. What with her advanced age, and the deterioration of the neighborhood, there were few mourners. When it came time for the eulogy, the priest tried, really tried—perhaps too hard—to get someone—anyone—to say something—anything—about the deceased.

"But they all just sat and looked at him. He kept telling himself that it might take time for someone to loosen up. Seconds crept into minutes. Finally, in response to his now almost desperate urging, an elderly woman stood. 'Well, for God's sake, I thought the old fart died ten years ago.'"

The laughter was interrupted by Wanda's announcement of dinner.

The group filed into the dining room, where the table almost groaned under steaming dishes.

Tully moved to seat Anne Marie, then realized that the others had remained standing for the grace—which Father Smith, after a nod from Koesler, led.

"Bless us, O Lord, and these Thy gifts which we are about to receive from Thy bounty, through Christ, our Lord." Which was followed by a resounding "Amen."

The next several minutes were occupied with serving dishes being passed from one to another, and murmured appreciation as plates were filled.

As he helped himself to each dish passed, Koesler reflected on the personalities of those gathered for this feast.

Wanda Koznicki. Hers was a marriage made in heaven. The word was hardly ever used nowadays, but Wanda was the perfect "helpmate." She had borne the inspector's children and had done more than her share in raising them. She was totally content to make this home her sanctuary and Walt's castle. Her cooking was not Cordon Bleu, but, then, neither her husband nor their children were gourmet eaters. And no one had ever been served a poor meal at the Koznickis.

Walter Koznicki. Inspector, in charge of the Detroit Police Department's Homicide Division—one of the busiest in the nation, if not the world. A thorough investigator and a competent officer, well able to instill confidence in his staff.

Koesler and Koznicki's paths had first crossed almost twenty years before, during an investigation into the serial murders of priests and nuns in Detroit. Purely by chance, Koesler had discovered one of the bodies, was drawn into the case, and had been instrumental in solving the crimes. As a result, two things had happened: Koesler's acquaintance with Inspector Koznicki had grown into a deep friendship as the years passed; and Koesler had been called on to lend his expertise in a number of succeeding murder cases involving the Catholic community.

Alonzo Tully. Lieutenant in charge of one of the seven Homicide squads, he had entered Koesler's life a few years ago, in much the same fortuitous manner as had been the case with Koznicki. Though Koesler had no way of gauging Tully's professional standing, it was clear that Koznicki had complete confidence in the lieutenant's ability and competence as an investigator and leader.

Koesler had been vaguely aware that Tully's previous marriage had ended in divorce, and that his ex-wife had remarried and, with their children, lived in Chicago. Koesler was also aware that the sole cause of the divorce was Tully's total dedication to his work. The same held true for the breakup of Tully's more recent significant relationship with a social worker. In the face of these failures, hope was not high in Koesler for this second marriage.

Anne Marie Tully. Koesler as yet knew her only slightly. It was his understanding that she came from Cleveland and that she had not been previously married. Tully surely would test her patience and forbearance. Anne Marie was a teacher and, more interesting to Koesler, a Catholic. In view of Tully's previous marriage, Koesler wondered what, if any, accommodation might have been made. It was always possible that Tully had been granted a declaration of nullity. Or maybe someone other than a priest had witnessed the second Tully nuptials. In which case, the Catholic Church would not recognize it as a valid marriage.

In any case, Koesler would never intrude. He would, if requested, try to help. Maybe Anne Marie would answer some of Tully's questions concerning Catholicism, should any arise. On the other hand, questions concerning Catholicism could be so complex that even experts often needed help.

Finally, Father Paul Smith. At age seventy, Smith was about five years older than Koesler and, as such, he was in a bit of a time warp. Perhaps in all of Christian history, Catholic priests had never retired as a matter of course. Then came the Second Vatican Council and it seemed right and proper to the hierarchy to join the rest of civilized society and permit—even encourage—priestly retirement. The initial reaction among elderly priests was to resist any sort of retirement, particularly compulsory. Then, following the Council, the drastic changes, initiated mostly by young priests who were formed by Vatican II, soured many older clerics. In effect the seniors were saying, "Okay, it's *your* Church now. You can run with it. I'm out of here."

The third and current development brought another—apparently unavoidable—option: The Church found itself running out of priests. Those leaving the priesthood surely were part of the problem. Much more significant was the near-empty-seminary syndrome. And while parishes tried to make do with a fraction of the priests that had once staffed rectories and schools, there were all these healthy and experienced priests marking time in retirement. So, those "retired" priests were now encouraged to help as much as they could or would.

Such was the case with Father Paul Smith, as with many of his vintage. He was "in residence" at St. Gregory's parish, which happened to be the one in which the Koznickis were members. He helped with the Mass and other sacraments. He counseled by appointment only. He had pet projects. But he never ever met with the parish council or bothered with any administrative business. And, by and large, he was happier than he would have been in retirement.

As for Father Koesler himself: Despite the problem areas he had encountered in his nearly forty years as a priest, he felt fulfilled in his ministry. He was open to learning new things. He enjoyed helping people. He saw his Church with all its warts, and still basically prized it.

If only he could escape this periodic involvement in police investigations.

4

Wanda was not one to dissemble. She accepted her guests' praise graciously. She had learned—from Father Koesler, in fact—that humility was truth. She lived by that principle. It *was* a good meal.

"It's too bad," Wanda said as the compliments segued into appreciative gustatory sounds, "that we couldn't have had this dinner closer to Christmas. But I suppose most of us are going to be all wrapped up with the pope's visit. Certainly our two Fathers will."

"Speaking for myself," Father Smith said, "I think I'll just be a spectator. They don't want old geezers like me around cluttering up big shindigs like this. But I'll be watching. Wouldn't pass up a spectacle like this for the world." He turned to Koesler. "How about you, Bob?"

"Just window dressing," Koesler said. "I think I'm supposed to be on some panel or other. And then I've got some routine duties at the Mass.

"But I would imagine that you two"—he addressed Koznicki and Tully—"would be busier than we will."

Koznicki nodded as he swallowed a bite. "We will be busy enough. We will have a total of 3,241 officers covering various duties."

"Hmm." Tully made an interested sound. "I didn't know. That's almost everybody."

Smith grinned. "Who'll be protecting *us?*"

Koznicki chuckled. "The three thousand figure is an overall one. Not all those officers will be on full-time duty with the Holy Father. Most of them will have, oh, perhaps some traffic duty. After that they will go back to their regular assignments. And some"—he looked pointedly at Tully—"will not be involved at all."

"I appreciate it." Tully's smile was relaxed.

"You didn't tell me," Anne Marie said.

"You didn't ask," Tully replied. "Walt was able to exempt my squad from special duty."

Koesler knew that Koznicki considered Tully's squad the most effective in handling homicides, and that, undoubtedly, was the reason they would be permitted to escape this papal detail.

"But why so many?" Anne Marie asked Koznicki. "I know the pope is a celebrity guest, but he's just one person and he's only going to be here a couple of days. I don't see why you need so many officers."

"The Holy Father," Koznicki explained, "is not only a celebrity guest, he is also a head of state—the Vatican. So, not only will more than three thousand of our people be on the detail—at least from time to time; the Wayne County Sheriff's Department and the state police will also share in the responsibility. And, because of the pope's chief-of-state status, the U.S. Secret Service will be here also."

"I'm afraid I share Anne Marie's puzzlement," Smith said. "It seems like an awful lot of layers of protection for just one man. Unless you're expecting something . . . ?"

"Expecting something? More like being prepared," Koznicki said simply.

"Like the Boy Scouts?" Smith joked.

"More like the military. *Semper Paratus.* Very serious business," Koznicki replied.

"Oh, I didn't mean . . ." Smith was embarrassed.

"We have a list of trouble spots in previous incidents—"

"Eat, Walt," Tully interjected. "I can handle this one. I was in on the initial briefing—" He turned to Anne Marie. "—before the inspector exempted me.

"Back in 1979, the American Secret Army for the Liberation of Armenia claimed responsibility for three bombs that exploded in the Trans-World and British Airways offices in Spain, to protest the pope's visit to Turkey.

"In '80, in Zaire, seven women and a couple of children were trampled to death at an open-air Mass. Later, in Brazil, crowds trying to see the pope broke through a barrier, and several women were crushed to death.

"In '81, there were three incidents. First, in Pakistan, just twenty minutes before the pope arrived, a man was killed at the entrance to a stadium by a bomb he was carrying.

"Then, in St. Peter's Square, an assassin named Ali Agca shot and wounded the pope.

"And in St. Peter's Basilica, a man carrying a bomb was apprehended just minutes before the pope was scheduled to appear."

It was obvious, as Tully spoke, that he had committed a lot of information to memory.

"Two in '82. In Nigeria, two men and a woman were arrested just after the pope's arrival. They claimed the pope was trying to introduce European ideas into black Africa.

"Also in '82, a former Roman Catholic priest attacked the pope with a bayonet in Paris.

"Then three in '83: Just before the pope's arrival, a religious statue was blown up in Lourdes. Also, on this same date, telephone lines went dead under suspicious circumstances in a town about twelve miles from Lourdes. Later that year, in Italy, the stage where the pope was supposed to speak from was blown up by a Molotov cocktail. Still later that year, a Vatican workman's daughter was kidnapped as a hostage to be exchanged for Agca, the guy who previously shot the pope.

"And finally, in 1987, Chilean troops used a water cannon and tear gas to chase antigovernment demonstrators at an open-air Mass that the pope was offering.

"And that's about it," Tully summed up, as he returned to his meal. Anne Marie wore her Nancy Reagan gaze of adoration.

"What a remarkable performance," Smith enthused. "You aren't even assigned to the pope's security detail and you have all these facts at your fingertips."

Tully shrugged. "It's a police matter. And I'm pretty good at those. Besides, you never know, we might get called in. Anything's possible. The important thing is to be ready so if we do get called, we can hit the ground running."

"As you can plainly see from what Alonzo has cited," said Koznicki, "it is possible—indeed, it has happened—that violence of various kinds can visit the appearance of the Holy Father.

"The problem can be as ordinary as crowd control, as was the case in Zaire, or as deadly as the attempt on the Holy Father's life, as in St. Peter's Square. Whatever the thrust, it will be a challenge to provide absolute security for His Holiness even though he is here for only a short time and even though an impressive number of local and federal officers will be on hand."

"Yeah," Tully added, "it was Kennedy who said if they want to get you, and especially if they are willing to pay the price, they'll get you."

"But," Koznicki said, "we will do everything humanly possible to make sure nothing happens to him here."

"It would be interesting," said Smith, "to get an idea of what sort of measures you're taking. Is there . . ."

". . . anything in writing? There sure is," said Tully. But it's top secret. If we let outsiders in on our arrangements, they wouldn't be a secret anymore. And if they're going to be effective, they've got to remain a secret."

"Oh, yes, of course." Smith shook his head. "Stupid of me."

"I wonder though"—Tully turned to Koesler—"outside of some nut who wants to become famous by killing somebody famous, why would anyone want to off the pope?"

"Well, dear," Anne Marie said banteringly, "we've already ascertained that you are not exactly a religious fanatic."

"I'm afraid there's no scarcity of people who at least have a bone to pick with the pope," said Koesler.

Koznicki and Tully were the only diners still working on the main course. The others, who had been listening to the officers' explanations, were anticipating dessert.

"Yes," Smith added, "there certainly are enough 'causes' that have some people all stirred up. Optional celibacy for priests, women in the priesthood, situation ethics, abortion—you name it and there's a group of Catholics on the fringe agitating for it."

"Sounds like a small army," Wanda said.

Tully shook his head. "With all that brewing, why in the world is he coming here just before Christmas? Sounds like he wants to turn a happy holiday into one helluva lot of contention."

"It's birth control, isn't it?" Anne Marie asked softly. Her gaze alternated between the two priests, who looked at one another seeking silent agreement on which of them would field the question.

"Birth control!" Tully exclaimed. "What's that got to do with it?"

"I've been reading," Anne Marie said. "The local press hasn't gone into this very deeply. But some of the magazines, especially the religious ones, have been speculating on the birth control issue as being the real reason for his visit. . . ." Her statement seemed to be a question aimed at either priest to answer.

Finally, Koesler spoke. "I think the secular press has, by and large, decided to pass on that aspect, because it may be too complex a concept to explain to their readers in any coherent way."

"It's that complicated?" Tully wondered.

"Only if you're not more familiar with the history of it than the average reporter," Koesler explained.

"First, that the pope plans to make some sort of statement about birth control seems no more than a rumor. He hasn't yet made it clear just what he plans to do during his stay here. And that—the nonspecificity—is unprecedented, at least in this pope's style.

"It's just that there are some indications that bolster the hypothesis that he may be going to make some statement on family planning."

"That's what has me confused," Anne Marie said. "I thought the Church had said everything it's going to say about birth control. Unless the pope is going to change his mind," she added thoughtfully. "But then, he doesn't do that, does he?" she concluded.

"Not often." Koesler smiled. "I think it was the Protestant theologian Robert McAfee Brown who said that if the Catholic Church were ever to change its stand on any doctrine, the statement would have to begin with the words, 'As the Church has always taught . . .' Because our Church doesn't have 'oops' in its vocabulary. And this pope doesn't seem like he's going to be the first to say 'We blew it!'"

"Well, then," said Wanda, "if he's not going to change anything, what's the big fuss?"

Koesler sighed inwardly. Interpreting Church scuttlebutt, politics, the convolutions of dogma, or merely everyday goings-on to the laity was rarely easy or simple. And when trying to explain things to outsiders, i.e., non-Catholics, Koesler felt like Einstein trying to explain the theory of relativity in German to listeners who understood only English.

But for the sake of Lieutenant Tully specifically, and to some degree for those besides Smith, Koesler decided to essay a brief explanation and history of the official Catholic stand on birth control from when the moral doctrine began to change to the present moment.

Wanda, waving Anne Marie back into her seat, began clearing the table.

"Let me try to explain," Koesler said, "and maybe it will become clear why there's not much about this in the secular press."

"Talk loud so I can hear too." Wanda propped the kitchen door open.

"To begin with, there's the stereotype of Catholic families with an awful lot of kids. That's because until relatively recently, there was only one morally acceptable way for Catholics to avoid conception: abstinence. And no sexual expression was permitted except intercourse."

Even in the simple narration of how things used to be, Koesler felt—and not for the first time—a degree of embarrassment. "And that's the way things stood until the early fifties, when Pius XII delivered a famous—to Catholics anyway—address to Italian midwives. The pope reflected on a then new awareness that not only is there a time in a woman's cycle when she is infertile, but it is possible to pinpoint that exact time. So the pope in that speech gave official approval to use this 'rhythm method' for family planning.

"During much of a woman's cycle the egg is not in position to be fertilized. Thus, having natural intercourse during this time, while abstaining during the fertile period, was unobjectionable. The rhythm method became known as Catholic birth control. And because in some women the cycle was not all that regular, making it impossible to pinpoint the precise infertile period, it became known as Vatican roulette."

That Tully had heard of.

"Then," Koesler continued, "came the birth-control pill. With a success percentage in the high nineties, the pill might literally be an answer to prayer. But the official Catholic position was that it was morally objectionable.

"Once again, in order to be faithful to official Church teaching, Catholic couples had to go back to relying on the frequently unreliable rhythm method.

"Then, brought to the fore by grass-roots pressure, the question was seriously raised as to whether the Church would actually admit new opinions and possibly change its position."

At this point, Wanda suggested they move to the living room where the discussion could continue in more comfortable accommodation. She also accepted Anne Marie's offer to help serve dessert and coffee.

5

Pontificating was not Father Koesler's style. After everyone was resettled, he suggested that Father Smith finish the tortuous history of Family Planning According to Rome.

"Well," Smith picked up, "there really isn't very much more to it. The grass-roots pressure that Bob mentioned surfaced about the same time the birth-control pill become popular.

"Pope Paul VI removed all discussion of family planning from the Second Vatican Council, and instead appointed a committee to study the matter and report its findings to him.

"And so they did—after leaking their majority report to the media. Hopes—at least liberal hopes—were high that the pope would accept the committee's findings and change the Church's stand. But . . . he rejected his own commission's conclusion and issued perhaps the most controversial encyclical of all time. It was called *Humanae Vitae* and the sentence in it that most people remember is, 'Each and every marriage act must remain open to the transmission of life.'

"The trouble was that most of the Catholic laity had already made up their mind. They were convinced the pope was wrong. And they had been brought up to believe that the pope is never wrong. That's why this encyclical was controversial. It was pivotal. And that is pretty much where we are now," Smith concluded.

"That's it?" Tully said after a few moments. He had been following the explanation with some interest. Odd for him, since religion—as well as anything else that did not pertain to his work—did not particularly concern him. "It looks like you've got Catholics between a rock and a hard place."

Smith gave no indication he intended to respond.

Once more unto the breach, Koesler silently exhorted himself.

"Well, at this point, another consideration comes up. When this encyclical was published in 1968, Pope Paul went out of his way to assure everyone that this document was not in the realm of infallibility." Koesler hesitated, taking a mental breath. "And here again it gets complicated. But the complication now doesn't involve birth control or family planning; it has to do with Church teaching. Typically, the Church teaches from the top down."

"That makes sense." Tully was used to getting orders from superiors.

"Sort of," Koesler agreed. "But what we've been tinkering with since Vatican II is some way to get the entire Church in sync—a system whereby the pope, the bishops and clergy, as well as the laity, move as one entity. But so far the pope has kept a firm hand on the reins.

"And even in that context, the pope has two vehicles he can use for teaching purposes. One is when, as head of the Church, or ex cathedra, he teaches the universal Church on a doctrine of faith and morals. Such a pronouncement is considered infallible. And that happens far less than one percent of the time.

"The much more common teaching office is called the Ordinary Magisterium. And that—the Ordinary Magisterium—is what Pope Paul was referring to when he issued *Humanae Vitae* and specified that it was not an infallible doctrine.

"The difference between the two teaching devices is how they affect the rest of the Church."

Noting his listeners' deepening expressions of less than total comprehension, Koesler, once more sighing inwardly, moved further afield. "See, an infallible statement is supposed to be received with what's technically called 'an assent of faith.' Which probably means you'd be a heretic if you denied it. And, by the way," he digressed still further, "according to most observers, there has been only one expressly unequivocal infallible statement since the doctrine of infallibility was defined in 1870. And that was Pius XII's pronouncement that after her death, Mary, the Mother of Jesus, was bodily assumed into heaven. And"—he smiled—"no one I know wants to go to war over that.

"But"—returning to his main theme—"what we are dealing with all the rest of the time is the Ordinary Magisterium. And Catholics are supposed to give this sort of teaching—again technically—'a religious assent,' in effect, a respectful hearing and prayerful consideration.

"Now to be fair, there is a divergence of opinion here. Some think the only difference between the two teaching offices is that while you are not a heretic if you disagree with the ordinary teaching, you *are* wrong and must eventually get yourself in line with the pope." He looked about at his listeners. "I myself belong to the 'religious assent' school."

"Wait a minute," Wanda objected. "I know this gets down to nit-picking and male in-house jargon, but I don't see an awful lot of difference there. What was it you said, Father: The reaction to infallibility was . . . what?"

"Assent of faith."

"And that means pretty much what we grew up learning about infallibility. I mean," Wanda pursued, "'If you want to be a Catholic, you'd better believe this.'"

Koesler chuckled. "Pretty much. At least that's the way it is with a sizeable majority of Catholics so far."

"And then," Wanda continued, "the other thing—the, what—Ordinary . . . ?"

"Ordinary, day-to-day pronouncements of the pope and the bishops—the Ordinary Magisterium," Koesler said. "The jargon term to describe the called-for Catholic reaction is 'a religious assent of soul.'"

"What it comes down to, Wanda, is that Catholics are supposed to give the ordinary teachings of the Church a respectful hearing."

"I always wondered what the difference was," Wanda confessed. "I mean, between an infallible pronouncement and any other papal edict. So, what you're saying is that most things the pope says aren't infallible?"

Koesler nodded affirmation.

"But how many Catholics know that or believe it?"

"Probably not very many. And that, as a matter of fact, is exactly what this discussion this evening has been about."

"It has?" Tully was trying to hang in.

"Yes," Koesler said. "We were speculating about why the pope was leaving the Vatican, especially so close to Christmas, and coming here. And, while the pope has not seen fit to come right out and say, there are lots of rumors. By far, the most popular guess is the one that Anne Marie suggested: that he's going to make a major statement about family planning and birth control. And, if that's it, coming as he is at this time, that statement is likely to be revolutionary."

"Revolutionary!" Tully's full attention had been captured.

Koesler sipped coffee. "Well, as Anne Marie said, it does seem as if the Church has said just about everything it's going to about birth control. Paul VI discarded the findings of his own commission and issued an extremely definitive statement in that encyclical. And we know how that encyclical was received by, especially, the laity. According to every study I've seen, the Catholic laity are indistinguishable from everyone else when it comes to using what is generally termed artificial birth control."

"So," Smith contributed, "the Church, in the person of the pope, has spoken. Once upon a time, that would have been it."

"But," Koesler continued, "remember that Pope Paul specified when he published *Humanae Vitae* that this was *not* an infallible statement. Which means that Catholics are bound only to . . ."

". . . give a respectful hearing!" Tully was beginning to understand that this "Catholic" infighting might well involve him professionally.

"Exactly," Koesler said. "And, ever since Paul issued his teaching a little more than twenty-five years ago, it has remained the last word on this matter. So, if it is true—if the popular rumor is accurate, if the central issue of this visit is to state something about family planning and birth control—it is not likely to be a restatement of *Humanae Vitae.* Everyone—Catholic or not—knows all too well this official position, So, what could it be?"

"Is it possible," Anne Marie said, "that he would take the stand that Pope Paul refused? Could this pope find any rationale for allowing artificial birth control?"

Smith shrugged and chuckled. "He's the pope, Anne Marie; he can do anything he wants."

"Yes. It's possible." Koesler was deadly serious. "But it's the old dog-bites-man story; we're not likely to find that on the front page. But if it's man-bites-dog, that's different." Noting his listeners' knit brows, Koesler knew he had to make himself more clear.

"By now, we've considered a few ifs. *If* the pope is using this occasion to make a significant statement; and *if* this statement has to do with family planning; and *if* something about this peculiarly Catholic position is going to change—then it's more likely to be in the man-bites-dog category. This pope has never given an inch on Pope Paul's encyclical. On the contrary, he has taken every opportunity to reinforce that stand. So . . . what's left?"

"I would suppose," Anne Marie said slowly and with a touch of regret, "the only thing left is to upgrade."

Smith nodded. "And that's what most of the priests are talking about. We think it . . . likely that he will raise the ban on artificial birth control to an infallible pronouncement."

There was silence as each weighed what, if any, effect such a pronouncement might have on their lives as well as on the rest of the world.

Tully broke the silence. "This may be an awkward question, but who gives a—uh, who cares? It's the pope's business, and it affects Catholics. The rest of the world solved this problem long ago without having to fiddle with anything like 'rhythm.'"

"Well, yes and no, Lieutenant," Smith said. "All over this world countless unwanted babies are born every day . . . even in developed countries like this one."

"Yes," Koesler echoed, "let's just suppose for a moment that the pope has come here and has made such a pronouncement. And let's say he has left no possible doubt that he intends this as an infallible pronouncement—and that he intends to end any debate whatsoever on this matter. And now he's gone back to Rome."

"Our job is finished." Tully smiled. "We've protected him and he's out of our jurisdiction."

"But," Koesler said, "what a turmoil he has left behind him!

"Catholics will be divided—disunited, conflicted—as never before in history—except possibly during the schism and the Reformation—in any case, more split than at any time in our memory.

"Some will try to remain in the Church, even though they cannot in conscience give the pope that 'assent of faith' that he demands.

"Others—a relative few, I think—while happily anticipating the departure of the liberal wing of the Church, will be impatient to force out those moderates who are trying to remain 'in' even though they are unable to profess what the pope demands.

"And still others—many, I fear—will accept the pope's ultimatum and leave the Church, some in fury, some in sorrow.

"Now I know what you're thinking, Lieutenant: Whatever the consequences, this remains a 'Catholic' problem. But, consider this: American Catholics have been and, to a degree still are, a force to be reckoned with. Once upon a time, there was a sizeable 'Catholic' vote that could be swayed, if not delivered, by bishops. That's probably defunct now—and rightly so. But still and all, in our brighter moments these days, a great number of Catholics can and do unite over such important issues as peace, justice, violence, promiscuity, and environmental preservation. And Roman Catholics now constitute the most sizeable religious body in this country. That will be no more.

"Besides, in those countries, especially in South and Central American nations, where the population is most explosive you can find the heaviest concentration of Catholics. It's anyone's guess as to why the Catholic countries of Latin America are overpopulated and why the population explosion is continuing like an epidemic. A lack of education—especially for women—poverty, life expectancy, infant mortality—all of those are unquestioned reasons.

"But no one can overlook the firm, repeated, and forceful teaching of their Church on family planning. In Latin America, the numerically small upper class has little or no problem with family planning. Nor would I expect them to pay any attention to what the pope says on this—or, for that matter, on any subject.

"There being hardly any middle class, it's the poor who have all the children. So you would expect them to be untroubled by an infallible doctrine. But that's just the problem: Much of the world is trying to put a cap on this runaway population explosion. They could use some help. But, particularly should the pope speak 'infallibly' against birth control, those who are trying to curb population growth will simply have a more difficult time of it.

"The bishops of Latin America, by and large, will be championing the pope's pronouncement. This will put them on a collision course with most of the area's priests. And the priests who are on the firing line down there will spend a good deal of their time battling the bishops.

"The poor don't realize that the intelligent planning of their families is one of the necessary steps they're going to have to take in order to achieve a more tolerable existence and a better life. Such a contrary infallible papal stand is, to say the very least, not going to help."

"Then," Tully said reflectively, "it's not just the conservative crackpots we've got to protect the pope from."

"Definitely not," Koznicki said. "But the number of those in disagreement with the Holy Father, for whatever reason, in no way affects our commitment to protect him. The officers—federal, state, and local—will form a protective shield around him. We learned a lot from the pope's previous visit. And we intend to be even more circumspect this time."

Tully rubbed his brow. "I don't know, Walt. I'd expect our guys and the feds would have a pretty good list of nuts—religious and otherwise, pro-choicers and activists. But now we're talking about . . . what? Just Catholics who don't agree with the pope? Pretty substantial . . ."

"I know." Koznicki nodded gravely. "We all know. But we intend to make it as prohibitive as we can for anyone to break through the circle of participants. And the legitimate participants will be wearing credentials. It will be virtually impossible for anyone not accredited to approach the Holy Father and his entourage."

Wanda's husband was about to become involved in a duty fraught with danger. It was by no means the first time. But the frequency of risk did nothing to lull her concern for his safety. If anything, time was becoming an enemy. Walt was slowing. This was not perceptible to the casual observer. But she knew. And she also knew him well enough to be convinced that if duty demanded a fearless response, Walt Koznicki would not send someone into that peril without going along himself.

All this was the result of the pope's coming here, to Detroit. Of all the nations in the world . . . of all the cities of those nations, why Detroit? Any other choice and she could have spent a comparatively quiet and secure Christmas with her husband and their family. *Why Detroit?*

"Why Detroit?" Her anger and frustration were obvious.

"'Why Detroit?' may be the most pertinent and revealing of all questions," Father Smith responded. "Insiders and wannabes are pretty much in agreement about this. And their assessment is a further indication that the centerpiece of this papal visit is the birth-control issue.

"The seed for this was sown during the Second Vatican Council. It happened during the development of one of the Council's sixteen documents. Specifically, the one titled 'The Pastoral Constitution on the Church in the Modern World.'"

Father Smith was unaware that Wanda was only half-listening. Concern for her husband's safety was uppermost in her mind; all she could think of was Eliza's, "Words, words! . . . Is that all you blighters can do?!"

Oblivious, Father Smith pressed on.

"I would venture to guess that most of today's old-time Catholics are quite familiar with one of the Church's most venerable teachings. And that would be 'The primary purpose of marriage is the procreation and education of children.' Every couple who were going to be married in the Catholic Church in those days inevitably would be asked, 'Do you realize that the primary purpose of marriage is the procreation and education of children?' And unless both partners indicated the affirmative, official wedding plans ground to a halt right there.

"That single teaching set the tone for marriage Catholic-style. It stated clearly that the first purpose of marriage, the prime reason people got married, was to have kids—as many as 'God sent.' And the Church demanded assent from the engaged couple. Catholic couples were expected to have children as the consequences of having intercourse—"

"In fact, if I can interrupt for a moment, Paul," Koesler said, "when medical science came up with the rhythm method of birth control, and when the Church okayed it, theologians established three prerequisites for the 'lawful' use of rhythm. The mnemonic was WAR, and it stood for: Both parties, husband and wife, were *willing* to abstain from intercourse during the fertile period. Both parties were *able* to use this method without, say, falling into some sin like adultery. And the couple had to have some positive *reason* for not wanting children. It could not be a selfish reason.

"We learned all that in the seminary. And then came real life. And I came to realize that selfishness is the best reason in the world not to have children. If a couple are going to be successful in being parents, they *must* be generous to a fault. Selfish parents need all the things a child needs—like care, attention, selfless love, and unstinting generosity.

"But excuse me for interrupting, Paul. You were talking about the Church teaching on the primary purpose of marriage. I think I know where you're going on this. I hadn't thought of it in these terms, but I think you're right."

"A point well made, Bob." Smith resumed his narration. "Anyway, as I said when we came in here for our postprandials, Pope Paul removed the whole topic of birth control from discussion in the Council.

"But something happened when the Council was writing its document on 'The Church in the Modern World.' It was in the section on 'Harmonizing Conjugal Love with Respect for Human Life.' It was tricky language, but, without getting too technical and to make a long story a bit shorter, the 'Primary Purpose of Marriage' simply disappeared. There was no longer a 'primary purpose.' Or, to put it another way, the love, affection, and support of a married couple for each other was at least as important as having children. It was, or could have been, a lead-in to the change in teaching that Paul's commission would later recommend. A change that Paul suppressed in favor of his own teaching in his encyclical, *Humanae Vitae*.

"The relevance of this bit of history is that Detroit's archbishop, Cardinal Mark Boyle, was largely responsible for that Conciliar language.

He is the one who most helped do away with the concept of the 'prime purpose of marriage.'

"So, now, you see, if all of our guesswork this evening is correct, and the pope does intend to make this unprecedented statement on birth control, then there is good reason for picking Detroit as the place where the statement will be made.

"The pope will enter the den to beard the lion. It was Mark Boyle's intervention that made it difficult for the Church to emphasize the almost infinite obligation of having children. It is into Mark Boyle's jurisdiction that the pope comes to make what can only be the final definitive statement on birth control. This doctrine will more than make up for the discarding of a 'prime purpose' for which excision Detroit's Cardinal Mark Boyle is largely responsible."

The evening was wearing thin. The shifting in chairs, the stacking of dishes and cups heralded the end.

"Well," Koesler said, as he stood and stretched, "it seems we have once again addressed some universal problems and not exactly solved them."

"Nonetheless," Koznicki said, "I am glad we aired all this. For me, it has added new dimensions to the Holy Father's visit to our city. We have more concerns than we supposed."

"Still and all, Walt . . ." Tully spoke in hopes that these "added dimensions" would not drag him into this duty, ". . . you shouldn't have much trouble. You've got a small army once everybody gets assembled."

"That is true," Koznicki admitted. "No outsider should be able to get to the Holy Father."

"That's reassuring," said Father Smith.

6

He knew something was wrong. All these years together had made it possible to communicate without words; gestures and sounds sufficed.

Now that their guests had gone, he was scrunched into his favorite chair near the fireplace. Ordinarily, if Walt Koznicki were to offer to help clean up, he would be shooed away. So he seldom volunteered.

He had not yet read the Sunday paper and was now trying to catch up. But there was something about the sounds coming from the other room. . . .

He sighed, dropped the paper next to the chair, and headed for the dining room. He could hear the dishwasher pumping as the first of tonight's loads neared the drying cycle. Most of the dinner dishes had been cleared away. He gathered the few pieces left and carried them into the kitchen.

There was no reaction from Wanda. She neither thanked him nor discouraged his help. She seemed unaware of his presence.

All the signs were in place. He knew it. "What is it, dear?"

Wanda was startled. She really had been deep in thought. At several inches taller than six feet and approximately 240 pounds, Walt was a formidable figure, the type regularly described as bigger than life. Wanda had to be profoundly preoccupied to be startled that he was standing only inches away.

She looked up at him, then back at the food she was placing in the fridge. "Oh, nothing."

"Something," he insisted.

"Oh, I was just thinking of the children . . . and the grandchildren. It's so close to Christmas. They should be home soon."

That seemed credible. But somehow it did not jibe with what Walt's sixth sense told him. However, for the moment, he would follow her lead. "Yes, they will be home soon, and the house will be filled and noisy again. Are you getting anxious to see them?"

"Of course. I miss them."

"You don't look particularly happy."

She folded the dish towel and snapped it across the rack. She swiveled abruptly to face him. "It's not the kids. That's not what's upsetting me. It's the pope!"

His eyes widened. "Our Holy Father! Why should he make you angry?"

"Because he's coming here! Because he's coming just before Christmas! Because he'll be here in just a few days! Because—if the Fathers were right tonight—because he's going to cause turmoil."

"Not to us." He smiled indulgently. "Family planning is over for us. It was something we handled and, thank God, we were able to do so in keeping with the Church's teaching."

"Because you could set the clock by my periods." Her blood pressure was not going down.

"Yes." The rhythm method had worked for them like a charm, but only because of her calendar-like regularity.

"But what about our kids?"

"What about them? We have no way of knowing about their private lives."

"I do."

"What?"

"I talk to them. They talk to me. You've got to remember, Walt, I was the one who was with them *all the time* when they were growing up. I'm not saying anything about your role as their father. God knows you were—you *are*—the best father and husband God could make. But you had a career. And you lived it. To the fullest. You tried to be with us for all the important things. You were with us just about every moment you were free.

"But you were a policeman all the time, whether you were on duty or off. There were lots of things the kids couldn't bring themselves to tell you. They felt awkward sometimes . . . like it would be your duty to arrest them if they did something bad, or even questionable."

"But—"

"I was with them *all the time*. They told me everything. They still do. I can talk to them about everything. They can talk to me about everything. So, we've talked. We talk every time they come home. We will talk when they come home for Christmas. I know how they feel. I know what they're doing."

This conversation was surprising Koznicki. And he was not easily surprised. "And what are they doing?"

"What are they doing? They've got jobs. They've got kids. They even go to church—most of the time."

"Most of the time!"

"*That* they don't talk to you about. In fact, that they go at all is mostly out of loyalty to you."

Koznicki was truly shocked. "I was not aware of that. They all attend Mass when they are with us."

"And sometimes when they're not with us. But only sometimes. And not with a lot of conviction."

"I must speak to them—"

"Not unless you want them to stop confiding in me. That you know now is only because I've told you. They don't want you to know."

"But . . . but what has this to do with our Holy Father?"

"They have no confidence, no faith in him whatever. It is with them as the Fathers were saying tonight . . . and I'm thinking mostly of Anthony." She slumped into a chair at the kitchen table.

Anthony? Anthony was his father's pride. Anthony the miracle baby. Conceived at the time when Wanda thought she was physically beyond fertility.

It had been a difficult pregnancy. Several times she almost miscarried. The last two or three months she'd spent mostly in bed.

Anthony was Wanda's lone difficult pregnancy. He fought to remain growing in the uterus. He fought for life after he was born.

He was the last of their children. With his uncertain coming into the world, Anthony was especially favored by his mother, and particularly by his father. Walter and Wanda, as is usual with parents, would immediately affirm that they loved each of their children equally. And, indeed, they did love all their children. But silently, in their hearts, they had a special affection for their youngest.

Koznicki sat across from his wife. "Anthony!"

Wanda was close to tears. She choked them back. Koznicki waited.

"Tonight . . . tonight I was so startled . . . I thought the Fathers knew Anthony. It was as if they were describing him." She paused. "Anthony was born years after the Vatican Council. That attitude where Catholics pick and choose what they believe was a part of Anthony's formation."

"But we sent him to parochial schools—even high school and college," he protested.

"And that's what they were teaching."

"I didn't know."

"I did. But what was the use of bothering you with it? The schools he went to instillled discipline and were excellent academically. They were better than anything the public schools could offer. But they weren't the schools you and I went to. The Sisters were gone. The *Baltimore Catechism* was gone. We did the best we could. Your job was important and took most of your time and just about all your concentration."

Koznicki was stunned. "Anthony . . . Anthony does not attend Mass?"

Wanda shook her head. "He's about the only one who goes all the time . . . even the holy days of obligation."

"Then . . . ?"

"Anthony is the one the Fathers were talking about tonight. He and Cynthia had two kids their first three years of marriage. We love our grandkids and we just took it for granted that Anthony and Cynthia wanted a big family. Things were tough for them financially. But they were making do. . . .

"It took Anthony a long time, but he finally told me what was going on. They tried rhythm but it failed them. The kids decided they would use a more dependable method of birth control."

"But the Church—"

"It was just as the Fathers said, Walt. Anthony was very much aware that the pope said this was not an infallible teaching. In fact, Cynthia didn't want to try rhythm from the beginning: Her periods were not that regular.

"But Anthony wanted to give the pope a 'respectful hearing.' Oh, he didn't use exactly those words; but that was the idea. It was obvious the pope preferred rhythm, so Anthony talked Cynthia into trying it. But not the third time. He felt he'd given the pope's opinion all the respect the opinion deserved.

"Obviously, Walt, Anthony relied on the pope's own word that the doctrine had some latitude. Otherwise, Anthony would be torn between following the pope's teaching blindly, or destroying his marriage. He was—and he is—at peace with his and Cynthia's decision to use artificial birth control." She left off, seemingly spent.

After a few moments, Koznicki asked haltingly. "Does he . . . mention this in his confession?"

Despite the depth of her emotion, Wanda could not help smiling. "It must have occurred to you, dear, that people don't go to confession like we used to . . . especially young people."

Actually, even as the question left his lips, he recalled the crowded churches of his past. Saturdays, and particularly at Christmas and Easter time, priests had spent countless hours hearing individual confessions. Nowadays, it was as Wanda pointed out: Few people went to a priest for confession anymore, and certainly not with any frequency or regularity.

"Besides," Wanda said, "Anthony and Cynthia don't consider what they're doing sinful. They listened politely to the pope, and gradually—even reluctantly—decided they could not follow his direction. As far as they are concerned, they are acting in good conscience." She leaned forward in deep concern. "But now, Walt, what's going to happen to Anthony and Cynthia and how many more just like them if this pope comes over here and tells the world—or at least the Catholic world—that there is no longer any option? It doesn't take much to figure that out. People like Anthony will be driven from the Church in anger and frustration—if not outright disgust. They will be lost to the Church . . . probably for the rest of their lives.

"And," she continued after a moment, "what about their children? What affect will their parents' departure from the Church have on our grandchildren? Do you think they'll keep going to Mass if their parents don't?"

The long silence that followed was disheartening. Unknown to the other, each of them was reliving Anthony's life. They had come so close to losing that beautiful little boy so many times. But he had braved his way into adulthood. If only one of their children could still be close to the Church of their tradition, it was not suprising that it would be Anthony.

"Maybe the priests are wrong," Wanda said finally. "Maybe . . ."

But Koznicki shook his head. "To be truthful, I would be willing to admit that perhaps Father Smith might be a bit eager to pass on some unfounded opinions. But when Father Koesler corroborates . . . well, I think this is far more than idle speculation."

"What can we do . . . ? What can anyone do?"

Koznicki shrugged. "Pray?"

"Pray against the pope!? Somehow that doesn't sound as if it could work."

They fell silent again.

"There isn't anything we can do about it, dear," Wanda said softly. "Why don't you read your paper, or go to bed? It's getting late. I'll just do another batch of dishes."

Koznicki glanced at his watch. It *was* getting late, and he would have to be fresh for work tomorrow.

He went to bed aware that it would be difficult to fall asleep. He could not put their conversation on a back burner. He knew his son. Anthony would never be able to rationalize his way around an infallible pronouncement of a pope. Nor would he be able to risk his marriage. If these priests were correct—and Koznicki was quite sure they were—what course would Anthony choose? Would he abandon his strong faith? Would he lose Cynthia? For Koznicki was certain that having solved a major problem, she would never return to the uncertainties of the rhythm method. Would Anthony and Cynthia agree to live as "brother and sister"? What sort of relationship would that be?

All of this tempest was the result of the decision of one man.

Strange, this was the first time Koznicki had ever envisioned the bishop of Rome as a single, solitary individual. Heretofore he had taken for granted the pope's predilection for referring to himself in the plural. He had no idea just when a pope had first decided to use "we" instead of "I." But he was sure it had been going on a very long time. And so, when hearing or reading of the pope's "we," Koznicki had quite naturally taken it as God speaking through the pope's voice.

Now something vital and personal was going on.

For Koznicki the pope had suddenly lost his divine aura . . . at least in the present case. Now Koznicki's cherished son was threatened. Instinctively, Koznicki the father searched about for some way of defending Anthony. It was as if the pope were somehow attacking the boy.

For the very briefest of moments, the thought of attacking the pope crossed his mind. The notion was so outrageous that he almost laughed aloud. It had to be an animal instinct.

His next thought was not that preposterous. What if his reaction to some threat to the pope were to be passive? Almost criminally passive . . .

He thought of two movies he had seen. He'd found them memorable not because they centered on police work as such. Actually, they were about the Secret Service. Both movies had to do with protecting the president of the United States.

One was *In the Line of Duty,* wherein Clint Eastwood played an agent who had been on duty in Dallas when President Kennedy was assassinated. The agent had been slow to respond to the first shot fired in Dealey Plaza. If he had been a step faster . . . if he had been a step faster, he might have saved the president's life. He might have "taken the bullet" that had been the fatal shot. The agent had never been able to forget, or to forgive himself.

The other movie was a comedy, *Dave*. Kevin Kline played a double role. He was president of the United States, a cruel, manipulative, self-centered, arrogant bully, and also a shameless womanizer. His top advisers found a look-alike, a wannabe actor. Dave, the lookalike, a kind, thoughtful, loving buffoon, is coached to stand in at ceremonial functions while the president is woman-occupied.

Physically, they are identical. Morally they are each other's antithesis. Much was made in this film of the solemn duty incumbent on members of the Secret Service to protect the president at the risk of their very lives. The agent assigned to Dave, the impostor, is at home with his responsibility to the real president. He is not nearly that sure that, should an emergency occur, he would lay his life on the line for the impostor. Eventually, Dave proves himself so courageous and good that the agent—at the very end of the tale—tells Dave, "Yes, I would take a bullet for you." It is the ultimate gift of faith in a person of worth.

Take the bullet.

It was not a virgin concept to Koznicki. He had been on many a protective detail for important personages visiting Detroit. The duty was, for him, a sacred trust. Never could that trust be more sacred than when the visitor was His Holiness the pope. This he was aware of to the very marrow of his Catholic bones.

But now . . .

Now this pope was coming to this city.

And he was coming to . . . destroy Anthony. No, that was melodramatic. But Anthony's Catholic belief probably would not survive the pope's mission to Detroit.

However, he, Inspector Walter Koznicki, had been assigned to this protective detail. And he would fulfill his duty.

Besides, what were the odds that anyone would actually attack His Holiness? The very proliferation of officers—federal, state, and local—had to discourage nearly everyone, even professional assassins. Anyone foolhardy enough to attempt an assault on the pope would likely not escape with his own life.

Beyond all that, even if someone were determined enough to try to kill the pope, what again would be the odds that one Inspector Walter Koznicki—out of all the thousands of guardian officers—would just happen to be *the* one called upon to take the bullet?

But what if he were?

Never mind the odds. The time for such an assault would be chosen by the assassin. At whatever time he planned it, some few officers would be close enough to the pope to have the immediate responsibility of ensuring his safety. Very likely, in this scenario, someone would be called upon to step into danger's way. To hell with the odds; he could be the one!

And if he were?

Police instinct, training, professionalism would take over. Koznicki very well might find himself responding to the instant with professional instinct.

But, to be totally candid, he could not guarantee how he would respond. Not now. Not anymore.

In the dark, he could feel Wanda crawling carefully into bed. Obviously she thought he was asleep. He pretended sleep; he didn't want his freshly conceived misgivings to upset her.

Shortly, her deep, regular breathing told him she was asleep. He would stay awake most of the night battling his choices.

How could he save the life of the man who might destroy Anthony's faith? How could he not respond to a duty that was second nature to him?

And so the silent debate continued through the night.

7

Zoo Tully had no clue anything was wrong. He and Anne Marie had not been together long enough for either to have developed that sort of spousal sixth sense.

She had been silent on the ride home. That was not unique, not even rare. In fact, it was one of the characteristics that Tully treasured in their relationship. He liked that they could be together in silence. That conversation could become *necessary*, he felt, was a sign of awkwardness in a relationship.

So they returned home in silence.

Tully's thoughts were in neutral as he pulled into the underground garage of the building known only by its address: 1300 Lafayette. Here in one of the cheaper, lower-level apartments, Anne Marie had lived before she married Tully.

Tully, in turn, had sold his house and moved in with Anne Marie just before their wedding. His home had housed his first wife and their children before the divorce. Thereafter, she and the children had moved to Chicago, where, later, she had remarried. Shortly after that he had shared the home with Alice, his significant other. Alice had thought that she could accept the fact that his work came first, second, and third in his life. Eventually, fourth place was not enough and she left him.

This building—1300 Lafayette—was almost directly across the street from the school in which Anne Marie taught. It was only a few blocks from another 1300—1300 Beaubien, police headquarters, home of Detroit's Homicide Division and Tully's squad of homicide detectives.

So far, the Tully relationship was working well. But both were painfully aware of his blighted marital record. He was resolved that this time it was for keeps; she hoped it was.

Once home, they exchanged a few inconsequential remarks about the evening as they prepared for bed.

He checked the answering machine. Most of the messages were for him; none was urgent. Meanwhile, she slipped into bed.

Only lately, since she had become Mrs. Tully, had Anne Marie become friends with the Koznickis. That was natural since, over the years, Walt and Zoo had bonded. Both Walt and Wanda were pleased to learn Tully's new wife was Catholic. Aware that Zoo had been married before, the Koznickis were diplomatically tactful concerning the form of the Tullys' wedding. Aware that Anne Marie took Communion regularly, they assumed that somehow this marriage was Church blessed.

That was not precisely the case.

Anne Marie attended one of the many core-city parishes whose pastors on occasion dodged much of the red tape that entrammeled Church law. Having discussed with Tully his first marriage, Anne Marie's priest determined that, one, it had been an honest effort on both parts, but simply had not worked; and, two, Church law, in its cold heart, would never grant an annulment to clear a path to a canonically correct marriage for Alonzo and Anne Marie.

So their marriage had been witnessed and blessed by the priest and probably God, but not by the official Church.

That was enough for Anne Marie and more than enough for Tully.

Which is not to imply that Anne Marie had rejected the official Church. By her own lights, she cared enough about her Catholic faith to do almost anything to remain in good standing with her Church. Her priest had made that choice easier for her. She trusted him. He did not appear to be troubled by the counsel he had given her.

It was, in fact, her allegiance to and regard for her Church that prompted her anxiety over the evening's topic of conversation.

Anne Marie was disturbed at all the possible consequences of the pope's looming visit. If he were indeed to do what the priests thought he intended, her Church would become a laughingstock to most of the world. Of perhaps greater impact, the Church would be decimated. So many, particularly those who respected and generally followed the directions of the hierarchy while liberally interpreting their faith, would be torn away from their Church, their tradition.

And, as had been intimated this evening, the pope could be walking out on an extremely flimsy branch. Someone might well try to sever that branch. Someone might well try to kill him.

No matter what, she would never wish anything like that on the pope. Moreover, even a mere attempt on the pope's life would draw her husband into the picture. His squad had been spared the assignment of protecting the pope. Yet if there were a homicide—or even an attempted homicide—Zoo's squad undoubtedly would be the first to respond. And Zoo suddenly could be in danger's path.

The bathroom light was extinguished. Only the night light provided any sight lines.

She felt the mattress give as Zoo slid into bed. Usually they welcomed each other with an embrace. But tonight Anne Marie didn't turn to him. He wondered about that. He snuggled close to her and gently stroked her breast. Her breasts, like the rest of her body, were firm and rounded. As the song went, "lovely to look at, delightful to hold, and heaven to kiss." But tonight there was no response.

Tully did not now need a seasoned sixth sense to know something was wrong.

Propped on one elbow, Tully asked, "Something wrong, babe?"

Anne Marie turned onto her back. "I can't get tonight's conversation off my mind."

"Tonight's—that? You mean about the pope? Shoot, that's got nothing to do with us, honey. No need to trouble yourself. He'll be in and out of town before you know it."

"But I *am* troubled—worried. What if what those priests were saying actually happens?"

"They're just guessing, hon. Educated guesses, I s'pose, but still just nothin' more than guesses. Anyway," he said reassuringly, "whatever happens's got nothing to do with us." Silence. "Has it?"

This Catholic stuff could get into a person's bloodstream. Not his. But possibly his wife's.

Anne Marie's concern was twofold. She was troubled for her Church. She did not want to experience what might prove to be the second great schism. Also, she was worried about her husband's role in the upcoming drama.

There was no point going into the first of these concerns. It would make no sense to Zoo. Privately she thought he was as apprehensive as she about the danger inherent in this papal visit. "What if the priests tonight are right—about the kooks out there who want to get to the pope?"

"About that, they've got to be right on target." He rolled onto his back. Under the covers he held her hand.

"That is one of my main worries—about you . . . and the danger you'd be in."

He chuckled softly. "Homicide cops don't get in trouble . . . at least not usually. We're the whodunit gang. I'm not in any trouble, hon. All the while the pope's here, I'll be off doing my thing. And I won't be running out of work. We got a backload of cases crying to be solved. That's why Walt got us excused from the protection detail; he knows better than anyone how much there is for us to do. He left my squad intact just for that."

"But what if someone attacks the pope? What if someone . . . actually kills him?"

Tully shook his head. She could hear the pillow rustle. "It'd be our jurisdiction all right. But he's a head of state. All hell'd break loose. I don't even want to think about *that*.

"Of course," he mused, "all hell's gonna bust loose anyhow. He couldn't have picked a much worse time to come here. Just days before Christmas. There'll be strike forces and special agents all over the place. Whole areas of the city'll be cordoned off. And people are still gonna be doing their last minute shopping. No, I don't wanta think about it.

"The only good thing"—he continued to think about it—"is that this isn't gonna be one of those multination conferences where the heads of state from around the world get together. All we have to protect is the man in white. So, there *is* a silver lining."

Anne Marie felt somewhat reassured, at least with respect to one, and perhaps her predominant, concern.

She turned to him, sliding her arms around his neck.

It was an invitation to which he readily responded. Now this, he thought, is more like it!

8

Father Koesler removed his boots before opening the door and starting on what for him had become a mad dash to deactivate the alarm system. In actuality, he had ten seconds from the time he opened the door before the alarm sounded and, as the salesman had accurately described it, all hell broke loose. But such was Koesler's concern for the residents of this sparsely populated neighborhood that he wished neither to disturb them nor rob them of sleep.

Old St. Joseph's, Koesler's benefice, was only a few blocks north of the Detroit River and a few blocks east of the city's prime avenue, Woodward. Once, many years ago, it had been a bustling parish, but time and migration had taken their toll.

Now, the complex of rectory and church stood quite alone. High-rise apartments and columns of condominiums stood apart as if challenging the old parish to become at all relevant to their fast-lane lifestyle.

Koesler had been attempting to do just that in the few years he'd been pastor of St. Joe's. Gradually he was gaining a bit of ground. The number of weekend liturgical participants was growing, sometimes imperceptibly. But he was counting.

This marked the end of a busy Sunday. He had presided over two morning liturgies and had several scheduled appointments in the afternoon. Then there was the Koznicki party this evening.

Koesler had always enjoyed visiting with these longtime friends. His friendship with Lieutenant Tully was cordial. And Anne Marie's gregarious personality would make her welcome in any gathering.

As for Paul Smith, this was another example of the tight fraternal ties that bind priests in a virtually universal companionship. The "universal" aspect of this connection had suffered somewhat since Vatican II. Prior to the Council, the Catholic clergy had little to debate. At least into the twentieth century, development of doctrine was minimal and tortoise-like—while moral theology lay entrapped within 2,414 Church laws.

Then, as the Vatican bombshell hit, some priests raced ahead of the vanguard, some stood still, hoping it would all go away, and some were destroyed.

Koesler liked to consider himself eclectic, picking and choosing his way through the ecclesial debris, preserving what seemed best to serve his people, and disregarding what might harm them. Though he would not describe himself as "liberal," that label would be pinned on him as an epithet by traditionalists.

Their motto could have been popularized as, "The Church: Love It or Leave It." Of course, by loving it, they must accept totally all that is commanded by Rome. Various categories of ecclesial philosophies are claimed by or attached to today's priests. Where once there was near unanimity, now there are sharp and deep divisions.

The mere fact that Paul Smith was just entering his seventies did not automatically place him in some foreordained slot. But Koesler was at a loss to pinpoint exactly where in the ecclesiastical spectrum Father Smith fit in.

Smith was only five years older than Koesler but, even though they'd been ordained to serve in the same archdiocese of Detroit, they'd never been close. Which is not to say they were unfriendly in any way, only that they seldom traveled in the same social or fraternal circles.

Koesler naturally was aware that Smith had been a high achiever in the seminary and that he'd been selected to study abroad just before and after ordination. Seminarians like Koesler who had what might be described as an unexceptional school career—completing their studies in the states as was the normal course of events—knew that those who were sent to Rome, Louvain, and the like were being groomed for special offices . . . teaching, officiating in the Chancery or Tribunal, or becoming bishops.

Not everyone sent abroad to prepare for special ministries scaled the ladders of promotion. Smith was in this group. Filled with promise as a seminarian, he seemed to lose his fire after ordination. Thereafter he lived a normal, fairly prosaic priestly life. He was an assistant—or as later titled, associate—pastor; then pastor in several different parishes; and then came retirement.

Some of those who retired did so in spades, to homes they had prepared for themselves in Florida, California, or even Hawaii. Some stayed in harness, but worked at their own pace in parishes they chose.

Some of these migrated south for the winters. They were now, compared with their years of parochial assignments, masters of their fate.

Paul Smith had chosen in retirement to work in St. Gregory's parish. Nor did he go south for the winter. Since Smith happened to work in the Koznickis' parish, Koesler figured to be drawn more close to Smith in the foreseeable future. Koesler had no problem with this. Smith seemed a friendly, knowledgeable priest and, blessedly, had a sense of humor.

Sleep beckoned. It was a bit early for Koesler's bedtime, but he'd had a busy day and tomorrow would be even busier. Besides his regular parochial duties and appointments, there was that blasted symposium panel he was supposed to moderate. And there was the rehearsal scheduled for tomorrow morning. Tonight he was trying to rationalize his way out of preparing for said rehearsal. Surely there would be time for that early tomorrow. Surely, as moderator, he would have need of little or no preparation.

Surely he was kidding himself.

He poured a few fingers of Scotch into a tall glass, adding ice and water. Just enough liquor to taste but not anywhere near enough to impede concentration.

He went to his office and took from a desk drawer an official-looking packet. The packaging was impressive. It looked as if it contained highly sensitive materials reserved for the eyes of a few of the elect. But appearances can be deceptive.

He knew that almost any priest in the archdiocese could get a packet like this . . . and without pulling all that many strings. But, on to his homework.

There would be six panel discussions in all. Each would be held in various large meeting rooms in Cobo Hall. This huge structure, named after a former mayor of Detroit, was located just west of Woodward at the edge of the Detroit River. Both underground and roof parking were available. The hall itself could be set up to accommodate almost any size gathering from a gigantic auto show to a relatively small meeting. Depending on the configuration, one might be looking merely at four walls or one might enjoy a breathtaking view of downtown Detroit, the glorious river and/or downtown Windsor in Canada.

Tomorrow—Monday—was sort of an orientation exercise: get to know your fellow panelist and moderator. The six conferences were labeled: Dogmatic Theology, Moral Theology, Canon Law, Liturgy, Evangelization, and Stewardship.

The purpose of these conferences was anyone's guess. Papal visitations were a relatively new wrinkle. During the reign of Pius XII in the thirties and forties, the pope was known as the prisoner of the Vatican. If he was a prisoner, the confinement was self-imposed. The beloved John XXIII also stayed home. But beginning with Paul VI, popes began amassing air travel miles.

Even so, when a pope came to town, he just arrived, visited, said what he came to say, and departed—all with the maximum hoopla.

However, consensus held that this visit to Detroit was going to be unique in a number of areas. And staging panel discussions as a prelude to the pope's arrival was just that—unique.

Koesler paged idly through the booklet he'd been sent. It had been prepared by several experts in various ecclesial fields: seminary professors, chancery personnel, and assorted other bureaucrats. The identity of these scholars and officials was not disclosed. Rumor had it that some contributors were women. Rumor had it that this—women contributors—was the reason for this wholesale masking of identities. The pope, in effect, seemed to think that women's place was in the laundry, the kitchen, the bed, or at prayer.

It was thought that there was no point in disturbing the pope needlessly. Thus there was no need of publicizing the scholarly contributions of local women. So there were no bylines. Some of the male contributors were not pleased. There was nothing they could do about it. This was Cardinal Boyle's territory. And that's the way he allowed things to operate.

The anonymous authors of the day-to-day and hour-by-hour agenda reminded Koesler of malpractice-worried physicians. Every item, every second seemed carefully and totally scheduled.

For example, the panel discussions themselves were covered by the following "key elements":

List of those to be credentialed; pre-event timeline; event timeline; clean site; security; staffing; lighting (with technician); sound system and backup (with technician); standby generator (with operator); decorations (curtain with logo, flags, other decorations, platform); steps to platform (12"); plantings (floral, greens); chairs (2); stool (1); podium; box lunches; check temperature control; stage hand(s); first aid station(s); post-event cleanup; list of volunteers to be thanked.

That, thought Koesler, ought to do it.

The two chairs undoubtedly were for the panelists, the stool for himself.

The item that most caught his eye was the first: "List of those to be credentialed."

Fanning through the booklet, he noticed photos of some of the participants in this papal affair. But these were big shot Church functionaries. A smattering of Cardinals, some archbishops and bishops. Koesler thought these worthies would be "credentialed," though he was uncertain exactly what the word denoted.

While he was looking over the list of bishops, it occurred to him that there were precious few Europeans. Mostly Americans and a smattering of Orientals and Canadians.

The top-heavy listing of Americans was to be expected. Those especially who had been made bishops most recently would be lemmings should the pope gesture toward a cliff edge. So loyal were they.

Koesler wondered at the absence of representatives from European and Second and Third World countries. Was this a statement? Were they voting with their feet—staying away in protest of what the pope was expected to proclaim?

Koesler thought that hypothesis held considerable water.

Next he turned his attention to the panelists in the various conferences.

Somebody had a sense of humor.

Koesler did not personally know any of them. But he had heard of all of them. And he was familiar with their work as well as their conservative or liberal platform.

This is where all the opinions about this papal visitation came together.

The prime projected guess as to the raison d'être for this convocation was, of course, that the pope was going to bump the doctrine on birth control as established in *Humanae Vitae* from Ordinary Magisterium to infallible pronouncement.

That was the supposed bombshell.

But adding weight to that supposition were these preparatory conferences. Koesler bet that these panel discussions were aimed at setting the scene for what the pope would do once he took center stage here. The panelists were supposed to prepare the ground for the seeds of dissension that would follow, (thus theoretically neutralizing all such opposition and quashing any such dissent).

Probably the topics were prepared in Rome, maybe by the Curia—the top bureaucratic Church agency. But obviously, either Rome had not picked the participants, or the people Rome had picked had been artfully waylaid. The participants listed were more apt to ruffle feathers than make smooth the path.

Without exception, each and every panelist and moderator was American. European hotshots such as Bernard Häring, Hans Küng, Edward Schillebeeckx were conspicuous by their absence.

All those listed were American citizens. Many were teaching or otherwise functioning overseas. While they were not the big guns, they were probably just as learned and informed. They merely had not been packaged and marketed. They represented both conservative and liberal camps . . . although the conservatives preferred the appellation "orthodox" (not to be confused with the Orthodox Church).

It was the liberal faction that most interested Koesler.

For the pope's purpose, it would have been more advantageous to have the liberal wing represented—but *not* strongly. Church spokesmen who favored the individual instead of the institution were needed, but as a sort of window dressing.

It seemed obvious to Koesler that these panel discussions were intended to lead into the most conservative pronouncement in recent memory. To achieve this, the liberal camp must be set up as a straw man whose only purpose is to be knocked over.

But the liberals who would be streaming into town even at this very moment were not by anyone's lights weak or ineffectual opponents destined to deliver a token opinion before obediently falling on their swords.

These gentlemen would give battle.

All of this, to Koesler, portended an interesting couple of days. And it indicated to him that, as far as Rome was concerned, something had gone very wrong. He had no way of telling where the glitch had occurred. But unless he missed his guess, somebody, buried perhaps in Detroit's bureaucracy, had thrown a wrench in the Vatican's works. That somebody, even now, was scurrying to protect his rear.

And well he should.

The next two—or even three—days might just be a lot of fun!

The only fly in that ointment of merriment would come if someone were to actually attack the pope.

Koesler consoled himself with the memory of Inspector Koznicki's assurance that no one not credentialed to the inner sanctum of these events would be able to approach the pope.

In a sense, these layers of priests and bishops, added to the considerable covering provided by federal agents, county sheriffs, and Detroit police, would shield the pope from almost any conceivable successful attempt to harm him.

No one not credentialed could get close to the pope. And no one in the inner circle would want to harm him. That seemed certain.

9

The story is told of a priest who was head of Detroit's Tribunal, or marriage court. He began each working day with the words—intended solely for the ears of his fellow priests—"Let the perjury begin!"

Admittedly, it was a jaundiced view. But it was an indication of how frequently he heard, or thought he was listening to, lies told under oath.

A similar cynical attitude was common among journalists, especially the investigative variety. They would follow leads, rumors, gossip, innuendo. That was part of their job. But all the while, their experience indicated that a lot of what they uncovered was deceit—bald-faced, straight-out lies.

Patricia Lennon had heard the stories, the rumors, the gossip. Her background as one of Detroit's premier reporters had taught her to doubt them. More than that, she didn't want to believe them.

Once, many years before, she and Joe Cox had worked at the *Detroit Free Press*. The newspaper was lucky to have the two of them. They were superior reporters, who gave the *Freep*, as it was colloquially called, a virtually unbeatable one-two punch.

As is all too common, the paper did not appreciate its good fortune until it lost its advantage. That was when Lennon moved the couple of blocks down Lafayette to the *Freep*'s arch-competitor, *The Detroit News*.

But even though they no longer worked for the same paper, their love affair did not suffer in the least. Not that their relationship didn't have its hills and valleys. For one, Cox found monogamy, even without benefit of clergy, an unnatural state.

It was as if they were bound by elastic. Cox, straying, would seem to come to the end of the rubber band and snap back to Lennon. Sometimes, slowly, often reluctantly, she would leave the door ajar and, gradually, they would resume almost at the point of their latest parting.

Then, responding to an offer he felt was irresistible, Joe moved to Chicago and the renowned *Tribune*.

Absence, in this case, made the hearts grow forgetful and the passion tepid. It didn't happen all at once. But in small ways they lost a personal interest in each other.

A little more than a year ago, Joe Cox had accepted yet another enticing offer.

Dan Darlton, his editor at the *Tribune*, had wooed and won a sufficiency of backers to finance a slick city magazine that could take on the established and highly successful *Chicago*.

This wet-behind-the-ears publisher offered Joe Cox the position of editor-in-chief of the new magazine, *Chicago Monthly*. It was a journalistic function Cox had never had the opportunity to try his hand at.

The pay would be only slightly higher than at the *Trib*. But Cox found the challenge intoxicating.

Leaving behind hard feelings on the part of the *Trib*'s executives, and moving into the gun sights of the long-established and financially powerful *Chicago*, Joe Cox launched on his new career.

He enjoyed the competition *Chicago* provided. He continued to be captivated by this fascinating city. He was overjoyed to be able to direct the thrust and policy of a splashy magazine.

For a while.

After a few months, Darlton began to invade the magazine's editorial realm. The invasion was insidious in its beginnings. He started dropping in on, then gradually taking over, the planning meetings.

Next he demanded that all manuscripts, whether assigned, submitted "on spec," or over the transom, be run by him. These he would notate—notations that were at best unkind, but more usually nasty, hurtful, and humiliating to the writers.

Cox was careful to blot out or erase all notations before either processing the pieces or returning them to their authors. Cox was a writer; he knew how thin-skinned they frequently were. He knew how tactful one must be, especially with work that has been sincerely and hopefully submitted. At that moment the writer is at his or her most vulnerable.

Little by little, but increasingly, Darlton began meddling in editorial ground.

He had a monthly column in the magazine. That was not unusual. Many publications carried their publisher's opinions. But this publisher's column usually arrived on Cox's desk in scribbled longhand at the blueprint stage and regularly overran the page reserved for it. Which obliged Cox to find something in the otherwise print-ready magazine that had to be killed for the publisher's column. However, should anyone else not write for space, Darlton would go berserk.

Even then, Darlton's unprofessionalism might have been tolerable had he not taken every opportunity to undermine Cox's position at the magazine.

Cox faced a many-sided conundrum. If he challenged the publisher, in all likelihood he would be fired and made to look incompetent. If he continued in this position, he would soon be psychologically emasculated. If he quit, where would he go? The print world—which was Cox's world—would assume he had failed and might well be reluctant to take him on.

At long last, swallowing a lot of pride and not a little gall, he contacted Nelson Kane, celebrated city editor of the *Detroit Free Press*. Darlton had once worked for the *Freep*; Kane, from personal experience, knew what an obnoxious prick he could be. He also knew that Cox had been deflated to a shell of what he'd once been.

Kane was willing to gamble that Cox could come back. So it was with mixed emotions that the two resumed their former relationship.

That Cox had signed on with the new magazine, that this was his first crack at being editor-in-chief, that *Chicago Monthly* was beginning to lose in its challenge to *Chicago*—these were facts.

When it came to the inner workings of the new magazine, rumor ran rampant. Gossip had it that Cox had been given a free hand and had blown it, that his promiscuity had brought about his downfall, that he could no longer cut the mustard in either arena.

Many Detroit area newspeople had lost many a page-one story to Cox's journalistic cunning and doggedness. Some still harbored bitterness. Now that he seemed to be slowly swinging in the breeze, they used him for target practice.

Pat Lennon had known both men when they worked at the *Freep*. Darlton had been one of her pet peeves. She knew what a fourth-class human being he was. In fact, when Cox had been offered the magazine position, she had warned him of what probably would happen.

Her instincts—which were superb—enabled her to see through the lies, the innuendo, the rumors, and the gossip. She hoped Cox would succeed against all the odds that faced him. She felt sorry for him. That's about all she felt for him.

Earlier this Sunday, Cox had had to call on his vaunted investigative skill to locate Lennon. So out of touch were they that he knew neither

her current address nor her unlisted number. Once and present colleagues were not cooperative.

Finally, he did nail her phone number, only to be greeted by an answering device. Her voice, even recorded, still bore that provocative mixture of strictly business with a touch of seductiveness.

By early evening he was about to resign himself to spending another lonely night, when she returned his call.

He sensed her deliberate distancing from him. He wanted to meet her for . . . anything. Dinner would be fine. She offered excuses. He persevered. They agreed to meet at Carl's Chop House. The food was good, and it was one of the few restaurants that still would be serving Sunday dinner at this hour.

He waited for her in the lobby. Their meeting was awkward. He leaned to kiss her cheek. She offered her hand. They had lived together for more than ten years before their what then seemed final breakup. The memories were like heartburn.

The huge restaurant was nearly empty. They sat in a booth. He ordered a double scotch straight up. She ordered warm water. He ordered a steak. She ordered a small salad. She claimed she had eaten earlier. He wondered.

He carried the verbal ball almost single-handedly, narrating the chronology of his time at the *Tribune* and *Chicago Monthly*. She listened without comment.

He did not overly badmouth the magazine's publisher. But she knew Darlton well enough that chapter and verse were unnecessary to document his essential evil.

As Cox talked, he could not help but reveal his present state of life. She saw clearly through his conscious and unconscious defenses.

He had not once mentioned his social life in Chicago. Knowing him as she did, she was willing to credit the scuttlebutt about his prolific dalliances. As sailors were reputed to have a girl in every port, so Cox was rumored to have one in every neighborhood. Probably an overstatement in a city with as many neighborhoods as Chicago. But not total exaggeration.

By the time he ordered pie à la mode and she orange sherbet, she was pretty much up to date in The Life and Hard Times of Joe Cox.

All the while she had viewed him in an unreal sepia sort of light. *What had she seen in him?* He was, as the song in *Show Boat* went, ". . . an ordinary guy." Certainly neither a hunk nor debonair. In short, nothing extra-special to look at. However, appearances had never been high on her desirability list.

He *had* been fun. Imaginative, with a good sense of humor. Self-confident to the point of overconfidence. It had not been his looks that had attracted her; it had been his personality.

And now that personality was all but shredded. His eyes, which she had always found warm, lively, and interesting, now had a hangdog cast to them. She felt sorry for him, genuinely sorry. But nothing more.

As he spun his latter-day autobiography, his mind virtually in neutral, he studied her.

Some women, he considered, start out being attractive and grow more beautiful as the years progress. That was Pat Lennon.

Her hair was flecked with gray. Obviously it didn't bother her; she had done nothing to disguise it. She had put on just a tad of weight. With that, she had become voluptuous. She wasn't trying to be anyone else. She was who she wanted to be.

And she no longer had strong feelings for him. His purgatory at *Chicago Monthly* had not completely impoverished him. His instincts were still operative even if he did not trust them as he once had.

Dinner was over. But Cox would continue to ask for coffee refills to postpone the inevitable parting.

Pat was willing to extend the evening. She genuinely wanted to help him; she just did not know how. "So, Joe, where're you living now?"

"Southfield. In a high-rise on Nine Mile near Greenfield. Here . . ." He handed her a small, neatly folded piece of paper. ". . . my address and phone number. Just in case . . ."

"Sure." She tucked the paper in her bag after briefly scanning it. "Any contact with any of the guys?"

"Tried. Not much luck. Doesn't seem to be much enthusiasm out there for the prodigal son."

She didn't doubt that. He exuded dark depression and pessimism. Nowhere near close to the Joe Cox of happy memory. She was even willing to believe that he had no *belle du jour*. And good old Joe sans a woman in hand and at least one in the wings was almost a contradiction in terms. "Have you checked in at the *Freep* yet?"

"A few days ago."

It was near closing time; the waitress was showing signs of wanting to wrap this up. She didn't want to have to clear their table and settle their tab on her own time. Cox smiled at her with what he hoped was irresistible charm. "I'll have another decaf." With a forced plastic smile, she refilled his cup.

Lennon caught the message. She felt as trapped as the waitress. Whatever business she and Cox had this evening had to be concluded here in the restaurant. She did not want to go through "your place or mine" or "maybe we can drive around for a while." She wanted to wrap things up within the protective walls of Carl's. And soon. "How's Nellie Kane?"

"Seems the same as always." Cox sounded surprised. "Don't you ever bump into him? I mean it's only a matter of a couple of blocks. There's the Press Club. . . ."

She shook her head. "Downtown was pretty dead even before you left. It's a little deader now." Pause. "You did talk to Kane, didn't you? About the job?"

"I talked to a *lot* of people about a job. Nellie's the one who came through for me. I won't forget that."

Lennon felt even sorrier for him. At one time, and not all that long ago, Joe Cox could've written his own ticket anywhere. Now in order to get a job, he had to rely on what was in reality a favor from a former employer. Cox *was* down. Lennon would not kick him.

"Well"—she tried to sound bright and upbeat—"at least you're settled. I assume your apartment is comfortable . . . and you're certainly familiar with your workspace and the job." No sooner had she mentioned the apartment than she regretted it. It opened the door to a potential invitation.

Cox's libido flirted with the idea. But he was fairly sure such an invitation would be rejected out of hand. Moreover, the evening had gone better than he had hoped. It was obvious that her feeling toward him approximated something a benevolent person might harbor toward a frightened, abandoned pet. He decided not to press his luck. "The apartment's okay," he said, "for starters anyway." Pause. "Starters! That's about what I'm doing . . . starting all over. About one step up from copy boy."

"Oh, come on, Joe, it can't be that bad. The *Freep* is still an important paper. Part of its past glory was yours. No," she insisted, in response to his expression, "I'm not trying to pour it on. You really had some major stories while you were there. They can't take that away from you."

"Joe?"

Cox grimaced. "They can't take that away from me, huh? Well, guess what Nellie has me covering."

Lennon shrugged.

"How about the pope's visit?" His smile was half sneer.

"What the hell's wrong with that?" She was animated for the first time this evening. "We've only had one previous papal visit. There'll be dignitaries from all over the world. Likewise the media. My God, Joe, you'll be sitting on top of one of the year's major stories!"

He deliberately held her gaze. "Lemme ask you something: What are you working on now?"

She hesitated. "A Recorders Court judge on the take."

"How close are you to breaking the story?"

"Maybe tomorrow," she replied almost guiltily.

"And then?"

"Well, I'm working with Bob Ankenazy on a nursing home scam."

"Are you still top gun in the Detroit media?"

"Well . . ."

"Don't bother: You are. So how come *you're* not doing the pope story."

She had no good reason for the embarrassment she felt. "It's . . . it's not my kind of story."

Cox was triumphant. "Remember when we were working this city on our separate but equal beats? The pope coming to town was not my kind of story either. The pope is coming to town! So is Santa Claus. I'd rather be good for Santa's sake."

"Joe, you're not being fair. Not to yourself. Not to Nellie Kane. You've only just got back in town. *I've* never left it. You know as well as I that you've got to build these stories. One lead gets you to another. Pretty soon you've got a string of leads. You know how that works. For all Nellie knows, you *do* have to start over to build, or maybe *re*build your sources. In the meantime, the pope is one helluva goddam good story!"

He flipped his napkin to the center of the table in disgust. "One helluva goddam good story to whom? The Catholics get out their rosaries and get them blessed. Daddy told me never to take seriously men who go to work wearing dresses!"

"Come on, Joe, don't exaggerate for my benefit. I don't have to tell you it could be a major piece. There's plenty of speculation on why he's coming to Detroit, of all places. And just before Christmas. It's just possible that his message is going to affect not only Catholics, but maybe the whole world."

"And where would you expect to see that story? The AP? Reuters? One of the news services? This isn't my kind of story. You know that, Pat."

She snapped her pocketbook closed. Dinner and the evening were definitely drawing to a close. "Maybe not, Joe. Maybe not. But you'll be on the beat again, I'm sure of that. Nellie knows what you can do.

"And meanwhile this is a big story . . . maybe lots bigger than you give it any credit for."

Cox scrutinized the bill, figuring the tip. "Remember the guy who used to be the *Freep*'s religion writer? Long time ago . . . Harlen . . . Harley something . . ."

"I know who you mean."

"I didn't agree with much he said or wrote. But one thing I thought carried a lot of weight: He said something about religion being basically dull and he didn't want to touch religion stories unless there was something that made them sensational."

"Yeah . . . it rings a bell."

"And good old Harley was not above being personally responsible for injecting that sensational element. Well, that's the direction I'm leaning in just now." He left enough on the table to take care of the bill plus a generous tip.

Lennon was reapplying her lipstick. Suddenly what Cox had just said sank in. "Joe! What the hell are you talking about? You wouldn't . . . you couldn't—"

He smiled, but his eyes refused to meet hers. "You never know. You just never know."

He stood, shrugged into his coat, and waited. Lennon was staring at him in disbelief. *What was he thinking of?*

He couldn't mean that he might actually . . . She tried to push this thought from her mind. When it came to journalistic integrity, Joe might step on the line, but he'd never cross it; she knew him well enough to be certain of that. But . . . this was not exactly the same Joe Cox she had known a few years ago.

What might he do, how far would he go now to regain his former eminence in Detroit journalism?

What sort of mayhem—figurative or literal—might he be capable of to achieve a page-one breakthrough?

10

He had been asked to pray for the pope not once but four times.

He'd been asked to pray that the pope would have a safe and fruitful trip to Detroit. At the 5:00 P.M. Mass yesterday and again at the 8:00, 10:00, and noon Masses this morning, a lector had read, "Let us pray for our Holy Father, that he may travel safely and that, while here, he may continue to lead us, directed by the Holy Spirit. Let us pray to the Lord." And presumably everyone responded, "Lord, hear our prayer."

Everyone, that is, except Dave Wallace.

But no one paid any attention to the movement or nonmovement of his lips. Besides, he was virtually hidden behind the organ console.

In his conscience, he could not make this petition his prayer. If he had prayed for anything, it would have been that the pope's plane would go down in flames on the way here. However, should that not be the pope's fate, David Wallace had another contingency in mind.

Dave Wallace was organist and choirmaster of St. Waldo's of the Hills in an extremely wealthy suburb of Detroit. He liked to refer to himself as *Kappelmeister*. His choir humored him with the title.

Wallace, in his early fifties, was tall and lean, with an ability to grow heavy facial hair almost on command. At the moment, he was clean shaven. His full head of dark black hair was barely flecked with gray.

He was unmarried, and thereby hung a tale.

It was 1960 when David Wallace and Abigail Quinn, both from strict Catholic families, were married.

Wallace, of Holy Redeemer parish, had spent four years in a Redemptorist seminary in Kirkwood, Missouri. It took him those four years to fully grasp what life would be like without a wife and family. So, having spent his high school years preparing for the vocation of priesthood in a religious community founded by St. Alphonsus Liguori, he continued his college career at the University of Detroit.

Dave inherited from his mother a keen musical ability. Quite naturally that talent expressed itself in his interest in Church music. Along the way to a Ph.D. in music, he joined Palestrina, an institute that trained Church organists and choir directors.

It was as a rather poor but dedicated organist that he met Abigail Quinn, a very pretty but delicate young lady whose fair complexion bespoke her Irish heritage.

Abigail had been frail from birth. An only child, she was carefully and lovingly nurtured by two devoted parents.

At age six she fell deathly ill with rheumatic fever. She was diagnosed as having endocarditis, a respiratory infection involving the heart muscle.

After a prolonged recuperation, she was discharged from the hospital. The doctor advised regular checkups for her heart murmur. Otherwise, she seemed quite healthy. However, in the strongest terms, the doctor warned Abby and her parents against any heavy physical activity for her. Her heart, to mix a metaphor, was her Achilles' heel.

Even being most careful, at age sixteen she had a heart failure incident. She was hospitalized again, with an overwhelming bacterial infection and pneumonia. She recovered but this time even more slowly. It was no longer a suggestion: She was required to see her doctor periodically.

Her parents did everything they could to protect her, short of enclosing her in a protective glass bubble.

Abigail learned to live with her physical limitations. And, as she grew into young adulthood, she was vivacious, intelligent, accomplished—and beautiful.

Their chemistry was copacetic from the first moment Dave and Abby met.

She mentioned only in a peripheral way her heart problem. He understood that there were limitations as to physical activity. And he made allowances.

Finances forced them to postpone what to them was an inevitable and long-desired marriage. Then Dave got two jobs: one teaching at his alma mater, and another as music director at one of the larger city parishes. As Church law would put it, *omnia parata*—all was ready for the marriage.

But before marriage, Abby made an appointment to see her doctor. This was not her regular interval, but in her condition, it seemed to everyone a good idea. When asked, "How are you?" by anyone anytime, she had a difficult time replying. Her "fine" was another person's "poorly." But lately, despite the fact that she had been following her doctor's instructions scrupulously, she had begun to feel worse instead of better.

The examination revealed little physical change. Her heart remained the problem: It was functioning, but it was weak.

At the conclusion of the examination, her doctor, knowing that she was soon to be married, cautioned, "By the way, I know this will be no great surprise to you, but don't even consider pregnancy."

Despite his supposition, Abby was indeed surprised by this radical advice. She told him so.

He explained that during pregnancy the heart has to work at a different rate because of vast hormonal changes. In any normal pregnancy, there is significant physiological stress. In her case, with her condition, this could precipitate potential heart failure.

With great apprehension, she shared this prognosis with Dave. They had, of course, discussed children, and planned to have a large family. The shock was deep and mutual.

Birth control, until now, had not been a consideration. Gladly would they have accepted "all the children sent to them by God." Now, this was a new ball game.

To make certain they had access to every possible method of family planning, they read everything the public library carried on the subject. They talked to Abby's doctor. They went to see her parish priest who would plan with them and witness their marriage.

And so they learned about the variety and dependability of condoms and diaphragms. They read about the success ratio as well as the dangers of the IUD. They were instructed in the rhythm method, then virtually in its infancy. A friend suggested withdrawal before ejaculation. The friend also warned that withdrawal was by no means foolproof. Somewhere they read about "amplexus reservatus," which demanded the rather Herculean effort on the part of the male in intercourse to stop and suppress orgasm at the last possible moment.

About this time the pill made itself both known and popular. The success rate was, perhaps, the highest of all the methods. Not completely known, and troubling because of this, were any possible side effects.

Armed with this vast array of information and suggestion, they went to consult again with their parish priest.

He was an older priest who tried to keep up to date. At least he knew the names of all the devices and procedures that this young couple had researched. He also knew the mind of Mother Church and what ecclesial law permitted and forbade—mostly forbade. He sympathized with the couple and he was agreeably impressed that they had come to him to get the final and definitive word. "Church law is most clear on this matter, my dear young people."

All these years later, Dave Wallace could recall this interview verbatim.

"All these methods of contraception you've mentioned," he continued, "all of them are intrinsically immoral. They are *in se mala*, which just means that these actions *in themselves* are sinful to their roots. *Mortal* sins. And no good intention can rescue them. The end does not justify the means, you know."

He told them nothing they hadn't known. They had hoped something in Church thinking had changed. They were not surprised that it hadn't.

As they had studied, there was one glimmer of hope. That was the pill. In the journals and sources they had used, there seemed to be no official Church stand on the pill. This, they rightly surmised, was due mostly to its relatively recent discovery.

"Father," Dave asked, "does what you say apply to the birth control pill?"

There was a little song and dance going on behind the priest's eyes. His reading had been so up-to-date it even included the pill. "To some extent, the jury's still out on the pill. Couples have a right to feel uncomfortable about the possible medical consequences—side effects—of using that pill. But morally—*morally*—I've got to tell you that I haven't found a single recognized theologian who thinks the use of the pill is justified. Not a one!"

Abigail had been twisting a handkerchief in and out of her fingers. "What are we going to do, Father? We've talked it over and we're *going* to get married. That's all there is to that—"

"Well," the priest broke in, "there's the rhythm method!"

The priest, for some disconnected reason, felt rather proud of the rhythm method . . . almost as if he personally had discovered it. He had been on board when there was no alternative to Catholic family planning but abstinence. How he had hated to hand down that restrictive ruling! He had experienced that gigantic collective sigh of relief when rhythm had been discovered by medical science and Pope Pius XII had blessed its use!

Even then, it had not solved everyone's problem. But it was a life-saver for many who had reason to more carefully structure their families yet desired to stay in the good graces of Mother Church.

"Now," the priest continued, "you said you talked to your doctor about rhythm?"

They nodded.

"So you know how it works—medically, that is." The next bit of business was to check on whether they were morally qualified. He knew his mnemonic: "Are you both willing to practice the rhythm method?"

Dave and Abby looked at each other. They knew the three conditional qualifications as well as did the priest. But the way the priest was presenting them, he made it seem like some sort of final exam.

"Yes, Father," Abby said. Dave could no more than nod. Making love to Abby by a calendar was only a slight improvement to not having her at all.

"And," the priest said, "the use of rhythm isn't going to lead you into other sin, is it?"

"No, Father," Abby responded.

"Like what?" Dave asked.

The priest was immediately uncomfortable. He had not wanted to go into this matter in any detail. Dave suspected that would be the case; he wanted the priest to squirm a bit. It was feeble revenge, but it was all that was available. Dave felt the Church had painted him into a corner.

"Well, like adultery, masturbation, impure thoughts . . . you know." The priest thought that small list pretty well covered the matter. "So"—he looked at Dave sternly—"do you think that abstaining from intercourse for a few days each month will cause you to fall into other sins?" This was a bit more authoritarian a challenge than necessary, but he wanted to maintain his role as teacher.

"No," Dave answered simply.

"Then," the priest said, "I don't think we'll have to go into your reason for regulating your family . . . not since the doctor has told you you could risk your health—"

"Life," Dave corrected. "We're talking about Abby risking her *life* by getting pregnant."

"Yes, you're right, of course. It *is* a risk to life, if that's what the doctor said."

68

"There is one more problem," Abby said almost apologetically. "My periods are not all that regular." She felt awkward and embarrassed bringing up "female" problems to this celibate and otherworldly gentleman.

"Meaning," the priest said, "that you probably will have to allow for a little leeway—a small margin for error. I understand. I have dealt with many couples who have that problem. Which brings up something I wanted to mention but haven't had the opportunity until now." Pause. "Faith!"

"Faith?" Dave and Abby said simultaneously.

"Yes, indeed. Faith!" the priest proclaimed. "Faith that moves mountains. First you must include the success of your enterprise in your prayers. And then you must have faith." He leaned back in his chair with an expression that would be matched only when he would, in the next life, behold the beatific vision. "I don't mind telling you that many others who have sat in the chairs you're in now have put their fate in the hands of God with great confidence. I wish I could tell you the miracles—yes, the miracles—that faith has wrought! Just take my word for it.

"Read your Bible. See how Jesus castigated His chosen Apostles when they faltered. 'Oh, ye of little faith!' he would say."

He looked at them intently. "I don't want to give you the impression that what we've been talking about is just a lot of rules and regulations. Of course moral judgments must be made. But what we're really about here is so much more than mere laws. God knows it will not be easy for you, especially as you begin your married life with the use of rhythm. But you must have faith. That will see you through. Mark my words: You will come through the stronger for having done God's holy will."

That was about it.

They spent a few minutes more filling out papers, answering the fundamental questions addressed to all who would marry in the Catholic Church. They confirmed the date of their marriage. Dave and Abby had been careful to pick a date that would coincide with her infertile period. At least they would begin their marriage in a celebratory mood.

Things went well during their first year. Dave was awarded a raise in pay for each of his jobs. It was unnecessary for Abby to work outside the home. Her health was stable, neither noticeably improving nor degenerating.

They began the process of adoption through the Catholic Charities organization. They were at the end of a long line of couples seeking a child.

Then it happened. She missed three periods. During those three months, she had not felt well. But that was not particularly unusual.

With great trepidation she went to her doctor. He confirmed it: She was pregnant.

Her doctor was not the sort to berate them or even consider that there was any "blame" to place. He knew they had used rhythm from the outset. And of course, he was aware of her menstrual irregularity. At that time, these two conditions existing in the same marital relationship constituted a miscalculation waiting to happen.

The important thing now was to help Abby through to a successful delivery. Little thought was given to the possibility of an eventual cesarean. At that time, with Abby's condition, the C-section was not a sound option.

Rest was the first, second, and third prescription.

Dave did everything in his power to insure that the most exercise Abby got was walking slowly from bed to couch or chair. He managed to get a leave of absence from both his jobs, an allowance that was extremely rare in those days.

Even with this tender, loving, and constant care, Abby was not trouble-free. She was tired and short of breath nearly all the time. She gained considerable weight and her feet and ankles swelled.

With Dave's loving care and attention, home was the better choice for Abby. The hospital could do little beyond what Dave was providing. So Abby stayed home until her weakened condition caused fear for the life of her child.

Dave moved into the hospital with her. He was holding her hand when, with quiet dignity, she seemed to struggle for one last breath. Then, almost biblically, she breathed forth her spirit.

At that point the scene of quiet dignity gave way to frenzied activity.

Abby's body was rushed to the operating room. There, as medical personnel tried routinely to resuscitate her, the C-section was performed and a seven-pound, one-month-premature baby was delivered.

This baby had been in trouble since it was a zygote.

Dave, with the hospital chaplain, was waiting outside the OR when the doctor confirmed Abby's death and the critical condition of the baby.

After consulting with Dave, the chaplain baptized Antoinette Wallace. By the following morning, little Toni had joined her mother: congenital and congestive heart failure.

The final crutch of hope taken from him, Dave spent the next few days just existing. He could not console his father- and mother-in-law, nor they him.

Fortunately, he was sufficiently stoic to schedule the funeral service in the parish where he was employed. Abby's parents had wanted the Mass in the parish where Dave and Abby had been married, with the same priest who had witnessed their wedding presiding at her funeral.

Dave could not have survived that. He might have punched the priest if he had mentioned "faith."

The Church had been in control of a "Catch-22" situation: If you have sufficient faith, all that you wish will come to be. If you don't get what you pray for, obviously you didn't have enough faith.

They had tried. They had prayed. They had believed.

Had they enough faith?

Who could say?

Not a priest.

Not theologians.

Not a pope.

But that is exactly who had said so.

Because these men who spoke for God could see no exceptions to their uncompromising man-made laws, a priceless young woman was dead.

If these men had the floor, they would blame Dave and Abby. Evidently, the young couple had insufficient faith. Or, knowing that they would be unable to drum up enough faith, they should have lived as brother and sister.

How considerate of them, Dave thought, sharing their lives of celibate chastity with newlyweds!

Granted, none of the methods of birth control was foolproof, particularly when one considered possible side effects. Nonetheless, rhythm used by a woman with irregular cycles and for whom pregnancy threatened death was preposterous.

The point was, the Church had given them no-win alternatives.

If anyone were to blame for Abby's death, it was the Church—at least in David's mind. And by the Church he meant the pope.

71

It was the pope who blessed rhythm as—and opened the door to—an alternative to abstinence . . . at least for those whose metabolism lent itself to the system. Or those for whom another child would not spell either catastrophe or death.

This concept of papal responsibility was powerfully strengthened later when another pope appointed a representative commission to study whether, in the light of the knowledge explosion, Church teaching should be modified. After the majority of this commission stated that, yes, the teaching should be updated and changed, this same pope who appointed the commission dismissed its findings . . . and then wrote the definitive encyclical cementing the flawed doctrine.

Nothing had changed.

Even today, a young couple—mirror images of himself and Abby—would be condemned to the same frightening fate. Any one of the shrinking number of obedient young Catholics could have their lives ruined because a series of popes had remained—and continued to remain—closed to reason and medical knowledge.

And now, another pope was about to make things worse.

In the years since Abby's and Antoinette's deaths, David had retreated from a social life that might be expected of a single young man. His time was spent either alone or in the company of several priest friends. From them, he had heard all the rumors surrounding the coming papal visit. Of those of his friends who believed these rumors, some were indifferent. To them the matter had been settled long ago and not in accord with papal thinking. Others were outraged that the pope would apply this added pressure.

Some priests of course were in total agreement with the pope. None of these were among David's friends.

Clearly, the bitterness that filled Dave's soul had grown rather than faded over all these years. As far as he was concerned, his beautiful young wife had suffered a completely unnecessary death. Her death was a festering wound that, in itself, programmed his current life.

He had had many opportunities to date women. He accepted few of them. He never allowed himself to become serious with any woman. In effect, he was neither a widower, nor was he single; he was married to a dream.

His emotions were volcanic and ready to erupt. This papal visit was becoming the spark that could cause chaos.

Without being bid entry, plans were beginning to form in his conscious mind. At first they had seemed harmless daydreams. But now he was testing them for feasibility.

Through his priest friends, David had become familiar with the scheduled events that would culminate in the pontifical Mass.

As a prelude to this Mass, to be celebrated in Cobo Arena, one of the largest indoor structures in the city of Detroit, several related conferences were to be held. The thinking of his clergy friends was that these conferences would be geared to smooth the pope's path.

But at the time these meetings were to be held, the pope would not yet have left Rome.

When the pope actually arrived in Detroit at least the first phases of his arrival would be a carbon copy of the previous papal visit.

His plane would land at Detroit Metropolitan Airport and taxi to the General Motors hangar. There he would be met by Cardinal Boyle, and all of Detroit's auxiliary bishops, of course. All the civil dignitaries that could be rounded up would be present, including Michigan's governor and other state officials.

The pope would no sooner hit the ground than he would be surrounded by a ton of security, federal, state, and local.

David's best guess was that it would be next to impossible for anyone to breach that security. Some of them would be fawning. Some would be delirious with celestial joy. Some—particularly Boyle—would be cool: They had met a pope before. In Boyle's case, he had helped elect the pope.

A goodly number of those physically close to the pope in concentric circles would be heavily armed. They would not hesitate to shoot to kill should anyone attempt to attack the pope.

In any case, if the pope survived Metro Airport, he and the other bishops, and as many priests as could fit, would board a helicopter and, with a heavy air escort, travel to Sacred Heart Major Seminary in almost the heart of Detroit. The spacious grounds of the seminary had formed one of the borders of the brutal '67 riot. With a huge, completely fenced-in playfield, and with the principal players inside a circling shield of protectors, things should be pretty secure.

When, next, the papal motorcade traveled the short distance to Blessed Sacrament Cathedral, security would have to break down to some degree. For the occasion, the cathedral would be filled with clergy and Very Important Catholics. This would be a relatively short stopover.

With the pope entering from the rear of the cathedral and proceeding down the middle aisle, he would be quite near to those closest to the center of the church. While an attack would not be anticipated from anyone in this gathering, still there were all those angry and alienated priests. An attack here? Unlikely, but still possible.

In any case, if he survived to this point, the pope would then retire for the night, surrounded by maximum security.

However, the next day was a different matter.

There was the public pontifical Mass in Cobo Arena. No one could provide fail-safe security to match the size of that crowd.

Here, actually, David thought, was the ideal place and moment for an attack. To strike just before the pope was scheduled to make his dogmatic declaration—that would give maximum meaning to the act.

Throughout this scenario, David had not identified the person who might level this assault. Obviously, it would have to be someone who was able to draw near the pope—ideally someone with the credentials that would gain him or her access to the man.

As conductor of the combined choirs, David would be so accredited. In that capacity, he would be only several yards from the pope, with no one between them.

He had identified the best place and time for an attempted murder. Now: Who would do it?

Whoever did it probably would not survive the deed. Whoever did it would have to leave behind some document explaining the motive as well as the necessity.

In the calm of this Sunday evening, David realized that if by the time the pope was about to make the promulgation, no one had acted to prevent it, he himself would be the last best hope.

The thought made him tremble.

The deed would make him a murderer.

And it would make him a victim.

He did not want to die.

Could he die for this cause?

David thought again of Abby. How different his life would have been if she had lived.

He thought of Catholics of a strict observance. Somewhere out there was another Abby—undoubtedly more than one.

He did not want to kill anybody. The very thought was repugnant.

But if the pope were to promulgate such a restrictive doctrine, a lot of innocent people would have their lives shattered.

He would have to center his imagination on Abby. But, yes, if pressed, he could do it.

So little time, so many preparations to be made: He'd better prepare the document, his apologia.

He started toward his desk, when another thought occurred. Perhaps there was a way to accomplish this goal without killing the pope. Perhaps there was a way to dissuade the pope from pursuing his course.

It was well worth some serious thought.

11

The dictionary defines "gang" as "a group of persons working toward unlawful or antisocial ends; esp: a band of antisocial adolescents."

Detroit had a frightening number of gangs. But so too did many large particularly industrial cities in the United States and other countries.

One of the most disturbing of Detroit gangs was the group that called itself the Young Boys. For this is what they were: very young African American boys. Too young to be sentenced to a traditional prison, their lockup was more likely to be some form of reformatory. And, due to their tender age, they generally were not held for any significant period.

The Young Boys were controlled by slightly older young men, who, if convicted of any of the crimes for which they were responsible, would be in Jackson State Penitentiary—"Jacktown"—for a very long time, if not for life.

But the Young Boys were by no means the only local group of antisocial adolescents, merely, for their time of ascendancy, the most troublesome. There were many other gangs. Some destructed by attrition as members were murdered by rival gangs or even by those in their own camp.

Among the most active recruiters were the proliferating Latino gangs. The bottom line for most of these groups was to force prospective members into a position of either being "for us" or "against us"—with an early death the likely outcome of either choice.

The group of young people now gathered in the Vanderwehl basement by no means fit the general profile of a modern gang. But by definition, "a group of persons working toward antisocial or unlawful ends," this was a blue ribbon gang.

At this moment, they were in their own self-described mode of a "cooldown." In a sense, they were not unlike the Jets of *West Side Story*.

Near the end of that musical, the Jets have had a "rumble" with another New York City gang, the Sharks. Both gangs thought this would be a fight, quite probably bloody, to establish territorial rights. Things got out of hand, however, and there were two killings.

The scene of the Jets in an abandoned building immediately after the deaths is arresting. The now-leaderless gang is so frenetic it is all they can do to keep from exploding emotionally.

The group presently gathered in the Vanderwehl basement was in an emotional state almost identical to that of the fictional Jets. Except that the "Golds," as this gang called itself, were or appeared to be too cool to let the explosiveness express itself. There was no pacing or finger snapping or shouting. But their eyes were wildly out of focus.

Until this evening, this had been a routine, even boring, Sunday.

Most of the day had been spent cruising the Birmingham-Bloomfield suburbs. They had been ready, eager for action. But, seemingly, no one else was.

In late afternoon they had returned to the Vanderwehl estate. The owners of this mansion, and parents of Rick Vanderwehl, were in their winter retreat in the Virgin Islands. Usually they stayed in their Bloomfield Hills residence until after Christmas. But this year winter had become serious early on and Mrs. Vanderwehl particularly grew tired of the snow. So Mr. and Mrs. V had staged an early escape.

They left Rick behind. There was school and his friends and all. But, today being Sunday, school was out and Rick's friends were in.

Rick's friends were four in number—all, like Rick, high school seniors. In tow were the boys' steadies. There being nothing better to do, they ordered pizzas delivered. That was followed by group grope, group sex, and gang bangs. After which the young women were casually dismissed.

Since there was no consensus for evening activity, Rick decided to return to cruising. Something had to develop.

It did, on a lonely stretch of Franklin Road.

A lone driver, a woman, in a silver BMW traveling at the speed limit. On a rise in the road, none of the Golds could spot another vehicle either ahead or behind.

Rick moved his Jaguar up slowly but steadily until it was almost touching her car. At that point he bumped the BMW gently.

Her head shot up and around. Obviously she had been unaware of the vehicle behind her. She sped up. So did Rick.

He bumped her car again, this time harder since they were going faster.

Then she made a serious mistake. She'd read it in the papers. She'd heard it on the radio. She'd seen it on television. When something like this occurs, drive to a well-lit, crowded area. Or, better yet, drive to a police station. Under no circumstances stop your car.

She stopped her car and got out.

She was furious.

A second later she was terrified.

Rick's entourage descended on her. Before she could step clear of her car, they picked her up and threw her into the backseat of the BMW. Three of the young men crowded in with her. The fourth got behind the wheel and drove off. Rick followed.

They headed for a parking lot behind a series of shops on Telegraph Road. Since the shops were closed, the lot was only dimly lit.

By the time the two cars reached the lot, she had been stripped. The gang rape had begun.

When the third young man began to mount her, her screams took on one coherent word—his name.

He immediately lost his erection. He scrambled backward out of the car. "She knows me!" he screamed to Rick.

"Shut up!" Rick frowned. "Are you sure?"

"Sure I'm sure! *I* know *her*. She lives in our neighborhood."

"You could have told us a little earlier, you know." Rick was covering rage with his usual flippancy.

"No! I didn't know! I was driving. I didn't get a look at her till she saw me. She recognized me, okay!? What the hell are we going to do?"

Rick pondered that. Then he took a small-caliber pistol out of his jacket. He offered it handle-first to the other, who shrank in horror. "What the hell is this?" he exploded.

"A gun," Rick said calmly.

"I know it's a goddam gun!" He stopped, stuttered. "Y-you . . . you d-don't expect m-me to—oh, no! That's murder one!"

"It's murder one if they *catch* you. Let that bitch live and you'll be in Jacktown until you're old enough to be her grandfather."

"There must be . . ." But he began to see the situation clearly. It was exactly as Rick stated it: If she lived, he probably would spend most of the rest of his life—or at least the best part of it—in prison. And if he tried to take any of the other Golds with him, he'd be a dead man.

"Look at it this way," Rick said calmly, "we're lucky we've got a gun. This way it's not messy. One shot, maybe two, and it's over. You don't have to hit her or strangle her or knife her, nothing like that. No muss, no fuss. Simple for everybody—including the bitch."

It sounded so reasonable, so logical. It was inevitable. He was the one she'd recognized; he was the one who had to do it.

But killing someone! He'd done a lot in his young life, but he'd never killed anyone. Animals, yes; but a human being . . .

"How should I do it?"

Rick laughed. "Pull the trigger, you jackass."

"I mean, where do I shoot her? Where do I point . . . where do I put the bullet?"

"Well, don't shoot her in her big toe. Put it in her brain."

"How . . . ?"

"Look, get back in the car. When she sees you, she'll probably open her mouth. She'll probably start begging. It's even money she knows that IDing you was a king-size mistake. So she'll try to talk her way out of this. When she opens her mouth, just put the barrel of the gun in it and fire. That's it. Easy."

With a shaking hand, he took the gun. Slowly he crawled back into the car where the other three were holding her down. Just as Rick had predicted, she was pleading for her life.

When she saw him, her eyes grew wide, as if he alone could save her. Her mouth opened . . .

While Rick stood guard, the others worked diligently; no print or clue must be left.

When they were done, Rick checked it all over. Clean.

They returned in the Jaguar to the Vanderwehl home.

Had they been the Jets, by now they would be nervously pacing up and down the basement. They would be acting out their disorientation, their gnawing fear.

But they were not the Jets, misfits and castoffs of society, "depraved on account of we're deprived."

No, they were the Golds. Their problem was not poverty, but affluence. Most of them came from extremely wealthy families. Since, in their experience, everything in life had a price, and money was the answer to everything, the parents reasoned that they could buy a present and a future for their children.

The children's response to life on a silver platter was boredom.

However, this Sunday evening they had chanced upon a remedy for boredom: murder.

So, while they were not engaged in choreographed rage, as the Jets had been, the Golds were every bit as much on the breaking edge.

The Golds were cool. The Golds could take everything in stride. If all else failed, their parents could always buy them out of trouble's way.

Were they really cool?

The silence of the oversize rec room was broken by sobs. At first quiet and restrained, then racked and agonized. It was the young man who had pulled the trigger.

The others, except for Rick, were first embarrassed, then troubled by the realization that they shared Ronnie's guilt. Outside of the sobs, which were growing into cries of self-torture, the room was deathly silent.

"Okay, okay . . ." Rick's voice was as commanding as it was sympathetic. He would have been a leader no matter what course his life had taken. "Let's put a cap on this. We haven't got a thing to worry about. We covered our tracks."

"Covered our tracks!" Ronnie, red-eyed, was breathing irregularly. "We just killed a woman! We just killed a goddam woman!"

Rick looked at Ronnie as if he were an interesting but foreign insect under the microscope in a biology class. He was always surprised that he was so far ahead of everyone else in seeing what the future held. "Hey, it's not like we never killed before."

"Killed before!" It was John's turn to be surprised. "You mean animals! We killed animals! Dogs, cats, birds, 'coons . . . like that. Just animals. This was a woman! A human being, for God's sake."

"Dog, cat, mouse, woman, man . . . what difference? That's what it's all about," Rick said. "We're born, we live, we die. That's it. That lady could be in some hospital right now telling the cops what happened to her. She'd be a little worse for wear, but she'd still be hangin' on. She had the tough luck to know Ronnie.

"Even then, if she'd pretended that she didn't recognize him, she'd've made it. Tough luck. But that's the way the witch burns."

Somehow he was making sense. It wasn't their fault. They'd just been out for some kicks. They'd had plenty of sex with their girl-friends. But that couldn't touch the thrill of doing it to somebody who resisted.

Somehow it made sense that the whole thing was *her* fault. *She*'d done everything—stopped her car, got out, fought them every step of the way. Yeah, she'd done it all just right until she let on she knew one of them.

So they had no alternative. It was like she put the bullet in her own head.

So, instead of getting treated and released from the hospital, instead of being able to tell her country club girlfriends about her exciting ex-perience, instead of being alive and recovering, now she was gonna be on a slab in the fridge in the morgue waiting to be identified.

Too bad. Not their fault. *Her* fault. What next?

Rick could tell from their expressions that his gang was going along with his reasoning. Time to chart the next step.

"So, what next? We could stay right at this level. If we do, we'll be hanging around automatic tellers waiting for some poor schmuck to take out a couple of hundred. Then we step up and take the wad and the car, maybe put a slug in his head. Or, we just get in the carjacking scene and if the driver looks at us cross-eyed, we off him. Or maybe we give the 'burbs some drive-by action. So far, nearly all the drive-bys are by the blacks and for the blacks. The lily suburbs haven't had that thrill yet . . .

"How does all this grab you guys?"

Rick looked around. Ronnie was reduced to sniffling. He seemed to be trying to follow Rick's premise.

The others gave every indication that carjacking and drive-bys might be just the ticket. Rick would have to burst this bubble. "Come on, you guys!" His voice dripped with ridicule. "That's penny-ante stuff! We passed all those plateaus tonight. This very night. If they caught us for what we did tonight we'd be in the slammer for the rest of our lives—no parole. Hell, if we did it in some other state, they'd snuff us. Don't you get it: We can do this over and over again! We can off guys and broads because they don't want to give us their car—or because they're scared shitless, but don't get out of their cars fast enough. Or we can cruise and pick off some people just because they're standing on their porch, or on their front lawn, or walking down the street—or just be-cause we don't like their haircut.

"But—and this is the important part—whatever we do to people like this, we can't beat what we did tonight. See?"

The others looked at one another, bewildered. "So, what then . . ." John asked finally, ". . . we retire undefeated?"

They all laughed, even Ronnie. After a few moments, Rick joined in. When the laughter waned, Rick said, "No, buddy boys, what we do now is we go to the top—or as close to the top as anybody's going to get."

They looked uncomprehendingly.

"Let me put it this way. Who's coming to town?"

After a minute, John said, "Santa Claus?"

"Yeah," Leo said, "we better be good."

The laughter was less forced this time. Rick joined in heartily. Laughter was helpful. They'd have to put tonight's killing behind them so he could lead them on to new contests. And laughter helped. "Okay, you morons, don't any of you guys read the paper . . . or even watch TV?"

"Wait a minute . . . the pope? My God"—John was horrified—"you mean the pope?!"

Rick simply smiled.

"What about the pope?" Leo asked.

"Don't you get it?" John said. "Rick's talkin' about takin' out the pope!" There was awe in his voice.

The rec room became as silent as an empty church.

"The pope."

"The pope?"

"The pope!"

"*The* pope!"

One by one each member of the Golds demonstrated comprehension.

"The pope," Rick confirmed.

"You must be out of your effin' mind," John said with solemn conviction. It was not a frivolous comment, but a statement, every word of which John fully intended.

"The pope!" Leo still did not grasp this as reality.

"Why fool around with the same old thing time after time?" Rick picked up a pool cue and began twirling it. "Everything the ordinary human being could think about right now would be in the same category as what we pulled off tonight. The same thing over and over again. Put a bullet through a bitch's head. Put a bullet through some asshole's heart. It hits the papers for a couple of days. The cops come up dry—no arrests, no leads. The same thing all the time." The only way to enhearten them was to make them think it was nothing; give them something else to think about. "Hell, I'm giving us a chance to change history. To become more famous than you ever dreamed.

"Try it this way, when I say Abe Lincoln, whaddyou think of?"

"The Civil War."

"A tall guy with a weird hat, a beard, and a huge zit on his cheek."

"He got shot."

"John Wilkes Booth!"

"That's it," Rick said. "John Wilkes Booth. The guy who assassinated Abraham Lincoln."

"Only one problem," John said, "Booth didn't live too long after that. They got him."

"Right," Rick agreed. "They got him because he made some lousy plans and because the team he put together turned out to be a Mickey Mouse gang."

"The pope!" Leo was in a daze.

"You got a better plan?" Ronnie asked.

"What you got in mind?" John demanded.

"Okay." Rick pulled an armful of newspapers out from behind the wet bar. He spread them over the pool table, the Ping-Pong table, and every flat surface he could find. "See . . ." He pointed to the first of his series of papers. "The pope leaves Rome in his comfortably outfitted plane, which flies nonstop to Metro. That's where our opportunity begins—at Metro."

He moved to the next set of papers. "Now, see, here's the layout at Metro. If he goes through any of the regular gates, we got a great chance. There'll be TV cameras and reporters, the priest guys and a zillion sightseers, along with all those cops. Easy for us to squeeze into this mob.

"But he ain't going to a regular gate. His plane goes to the GM hangar, where there's a real tight space. And look . . ." He pointed to a sidebar. "Everybody in that hangar has to have special credentials to even be in there."

"So that's not a good place," John said.

"That," Rick said, "is a first-class lousy place.

"But we move right along. The whole bunch—or most of them anyway—get into helicopters for the next stop. And by the way," he said, "they got choppers guarding the choppers. Get the idea of how much they want to secure the whole area the pope happens to be in?"

The others nod. They are impressed.

"That," Rick said, "just shows you what a fantastic caper this is. You got feds, state, county, and local cops. You got the best security money can buy and this country can provide—and a bunch of high school kids beat it!

"Man, when we are like 103 and if, by then, we're dying, we can give the press our names for history. We'll be among the most famous bad guys of all time."

The others began to get into the spirit of the thing.

"Now . . ." Rick pushed several papers together to form a montage. "These choppers set down on a big fenced-in field at this seminary. I've seen it. It's humongous.

"But this'll be in the late evening and, at this time of year, it's gonna be awful dark. They plan on having powerful searchlights around the area where the pope will set down. but there's no chance in hell that they'll ever be able to light the whole shebang. That gives us an in.

"Three, maybe four, of us will cause one hell of a disturbance in the dark, just outside the lights. When the security people start toward the ruckus, one of us moves into range and pops the pope." He looked from one to the other to gauge their reception.

"Wait," John said, "how do we get in there in the first place?"

"There's a wire fence around the place. They're not gonna have the heat at every inch of fence," Rick explained. "Now you're thinking, 'Sure, but they'll spot five guys climbing over the fence.' But I've already been there . . . and I cut through one section of the fence and I put it back together with wire hooks that we can pull away easy. I checked: There's no moon that night. We'll be through that fence in no time. Once the pope is shot, everybody'll be running every which way. We head back right where we came from. Our fence entry is dead up against some heavy bushes. It'll be a snap.

"So, how 'bout it? Whatddya think?"

Silence.

"How come we gotta get so close to the pope?" Ronnie asked. "John here is pretty good with a rifle. We could be a mile away—whatever range John is comfortable with—and not run the risk of getting close."

"A point," Rick admitted, "but the cops have got that angle pretty well covered. You guys ever see that movie, *Day of the Jackal?* Well, this professional assassin is trying to take out de Gaulle. He gets a dead bead on the guy and he squeezes the trigger—just as de Gaulle bends over and the shot goes over his head.

"It'd be even tougher to get a bead on the pope. Security's all over him all the time, and they keep moving. From a distance, no matter how good you might be, you're more likely to bag a cop than the pope.

"No, whoever gets the pope is gonna hafta do it up close and personal."

"So," John asked, "which one of us is it gonna be?"

Rick looked from one to the other. Each seemed enthused. Good! Great! They're in it. He'd done it; he'd got this frazzled bunch of wealthy delinquents to agree on the greatest caper in history . . . or at least one that would rank.

Why there was any doubt as to who would pull the trigger? He would, of course. But . . . one thing at a time. They were in; enough for the moment.

Rick, Leo, John, and Ronnie, as if on cue, looked to Andrew. Through this entire episode he hadn't said a word. He seldom did. They called him Harpo. Not because he had curly blond hair, but because he was virtually mute. He looked back at them. He nodded and smiled. He was in.

"We got one more thing to plan," Rick said. "We got to cause some kind of diversion . . . some kind of distraction that'll make it easier for us. Now I got just the thing we're looking for—I think you're gonna go for it."

The plotting, the questions, the answers went on into the wee hours. The gang's enthusiasm crescendoed as the details became more specific.

Completely and oddly forgotten was the unclothed body of a socialite who would be found about 2:30 A.M. Police on patrol would spot the pricey car and investigate.

Her purse and identification were in the car. In a few hours her husband would be notified and would go with the police to identify his wife.

The husband, the children, the family, relatives, and many friends would be devastated. She had been very active in many charitable causes. The obituaries would be lavish; the funeral, from Christ Church Cranbrook, impressive.

Those reading about it or seeing the story on TV would wonder again what this world was coming to. The usual cast of characters would reawaken the fight for tighter gun laws. The other usual cast of characters would remind everyone that guns don't kill, people do. Besides, there is the Constitution to defend.

Rick, Leo, John, Ronnie, and Harpo would be tickled by all the publicity they have engendered. It would give them courage and incentive to forge on in their plot for the ultimate media event.

12

He'd never played the part of a priest before. First time or not, everything seemed to be going well.

He sank into the upholstered chair, exhausted as much by tension as the discomfort of air travel.

He took stock of his surroundings. By his standards, this was more than adequate, it was luxurious.

He was seated in what might be called a living room, or perhaps a den. Three walls were almost totally bookcased; the fourth wall was almost totally windows—three large ones that looked out on the courtyard. The bedroom had two similarly sized windows, the lavatory a smaller one—all again overlooking the courtyard.

What pleased him most was having his own loo, with cabinet, washstand and—think of it!—a shower.

Indeed, as far as he could tell, things were moving along flawlessly.

Not a shred of trouble at customs in Ireland or in Boston. But that was due to his meticulous planning, not deferential treatment bestowed on a clergyman. Undoubtedly there had been a time when "Father" was waved through inspection zones. But no longer—not with international terrorism so prevalent.

The flight—his first long journey ever—was confining and uncomfortable. The food was slightly better than he'd expected. He was able to listen to his tapes of TV and radio newsreaders without interference, though he sensed that at least a couple of people would have liked to engage him in conversation. When he wasn't eating or practicing his accent he was grateful for the privacy a nap afforded.

He was met at Detroit Metro by a man in a driver's uniform and cap, holding a sign bearing the name of the priest whose identity he had taken. When they got into the limousine, the driver handed him an envelope that read, "Preliminary Information." He noted that on checking in at the seminary he was supposed to present a photo of himself to be given to the police for identification and security purposes. Fortunately, he had two extra copies of his passport photo in his wallet.

On the trip into the city, he tried out his borrowed accent. It went over fine; the driver made no comment about his pronunciation. They chatted a bit about the weather, which, with the dusting of snow, was quite Christmassy. But mostly they talked about what for metro Detroiters was, after Christmas, the most discussed topic—the pope's visit.

He was grateful for the limo. This way he'd have to converse with as few people as possible. Once at the seminary he would try to keep to himself. After all, he wasn't sure what to expect—and there was always the possibility that somebody there could have met the real priest. But he'd cross that bridge when and if . . . For now, he'd take it one step at a time. His luck had held so far.

When they finally drove through the entrance of Sacred Heart Major Seminary, he noted that it was not very well guarded, and the guards did not look like professionals. Obviously the major security was being reserved for the pope's arrival.

He checked in at the seminary's back entrance hallway, which had become the entry foyer when what had been the building's main entry in front was virtually sealed off many years ago—for security's sake.

He handed over the requested photo and watched carefully. No comment was made; it was put with a stack of other priest photos, which he assumed would be turned over to the police. He was given his room number and directions on how to reach it. He was also given a packet containing information on and a diagram of the seminary, including the chapel, the dining hall, snack bar facility, and the like. The packet also contained the agenda for the symposium and the main event—the Pontifical Mass in Cobo Arena.

He was not surprised—he had taken it for granted—that the dining room was closed. It was now quite late Sunday evening. He was grateful that the snack bar was open around the clock. In good time he would eat, more to keep up his strength than because he was hungry.

But first he wanted to familiarize himself with this building. He hoped he would not meet anyone in the hallways. If he did, he would try to appear in too much haste to stop and talk. He didn't know how anyone he might meet would be dressed. He'd already noted that it was quite warm in the building; attire could be anything from pajamas and robe to more formal garb. He quickly decided to wear the traditional black suit with clerical collar and vest. That way there'd be no question but that he belonged.

Everything had gone so smoothly thus far, he was beginning to relax somewhat.

He left his room, locking the door behind him. He smiled; the chance that someone might try to rob or attack him was ludicrous; would a hungry rabbit stalk a lion?

The building's layout was simple and easy to grasp, but he wanted to walk it through.

The centerpiece was the Gothic chapel. Everything else revolved around it. Unfortunately, only a few lights had been left on so he wasn't able to properly appreciate his surroundings. Because of the half-light his steps were cautious as he made his way down the middle aisle.

Looking from side to side he was able to make out some three or four small chapels against either wall. From his recent study, he knew that private chapels such as these were probably not used nowadays. At one time—he could almost see it in his imagination—these altars would have been busy with priests and their servers saying "whisper" masses, so as not to distract each other.

The pews in the body of the chapel seemed farther apart than usual. If ever these were occupied by laity accustomed to parish churches, he thought, there must be many an embarrassing moment when, kneeling, they tried to rest their fannies on the seat . . . only to find that kneelers and seats in this chapel were too far apart for this customary convenience.

The sanctuary had been modified to comply with the post-Conciliar liturgy that did away with the ornate "high" altars where the priest was far removed from worshipers and, for the most part, kept turned away from the people. Now a table covered with altar cloths was set as close to the pews as possible.

In the subdued light, he could not make out much more in the chapel.

He was able to examine the diagram of the building by the light of a miniature flashlight on his key ring. Thus guided, he located classrooms, study spaces, parlors, lockers, the gymnasium, the main dining room, libraries.

Basically the seminary was a three-story building with a rectangular outline, the chapel cutting through the middle of the rectangle, and appendages at each corner. The extensions were an auditorium, residence halls, a recreation building, and a one-time convent, now used by various diocesan departments.

He was almost at the end of his tour when, dead ahead, a bright light blinded him momentarily. "Hold it!" The voice carried a naked warning.

He stood stock-still. He was afraid of nothing but a gun. And from all that he'd read and heard about Detroit—hyperbole and fact—he believed that for many inhabitants of this city a gun simply was the extension of a hand.

The figure behind the light came close enough to see that the man he had challenged wore clerical attire. He reversed the light, aiming it first at his badge, then up to his large, amiable black face. "Sorry if I scared you, Father," the guard said. "Can't be too careful in this neighborhood."

"That's okay. Actually, I'm glad it was you."

The guard lowered the beam. "Anything I can help you with, Father?"

"I guess not. I was trying to get my bearings. I'm new to this building—to this city."

"Kind of late," the guard observed.

"I know. I just got in a little while ago." This Midwestern manner of speech was his primary concern. But his accent must be okay as the guard made no comment except to reiterate, "Anything I can help you with?"

"Now that you mention it, I haven't come across the snack bar."

The guard chuckled. "Hungry?"

"All I've had today is what they served on the plane."

"We gotta get you some kind of antidote for that. You're lucky you ran into me. I got the keys to the *big* box."

He accompanied the guard, not certain which way they were headed. He tested his grasp of the configuration of the building by checking the landmarks he had already become familiar with.

They were headed toward . . . yes . . . the main dining room and, thanks to the guard's keys, the kitchen with its walk-in fridge.

He took the chair indicated by his guide. In short order, the guard placed glasses, plates, bread, cold cuts, condiments, and milk on the table. Then his host sat down across from him and gestured toward the food. "Dig in," he said, and proceeded to do so himself.

"I'm sorry to put you to all this trouble. I could have survived with the snack food."

A low rumble of laughter came from the other side of the table. "Tell you the truth, Father, this just about perfect for me. This about the time I come down here every night to get me through till morning."

He caught the implication: This late-night spread was definitely not in the line of duty. Why was the guard confessing this to a total stranger? A stranger who could very well report this breach to the supervisor?

Then it came to him: *He thinks I'm a priest. He's banking on a priest's discretion if not kindness not to tell anyone. He has no doubt he can trust me.*

The guard hadn't thought twice about including the priest in this petty infraction. There were, of course, priests who approached law with a literal observance. But the guard fancied himself a good and intuitive judge of character. This priest could be trusted. And this judgment was made after the exchange of just a few words. Remarkable.

He bit into a chicken sandwich. "This is a big building. I can hardly believe you guard it alone."

"You walked the whole building?"

"Yes."

"All the floors?"

"Far as I know."

"And you didn't see any other guard?"

He shook his head.

Then the guard shook *his* head. "Do tell. Well, you shoulda seen two or three others on duty. I don't know . . . God knows where they're off to." He seemed genuinely distressed by his colleagues' shirking of duty. Apparently he was not at all concerned that, at this moment, he too should have been patrolling the halls.

"Well, that makes sense," the man said. "Seems to me a place this big should have at least four or more guards. Come to think of it, with the po—His Holiness coming in just a couple of days, I would have thought there would be lots of guards patrolling these halls."

The guard laughed aloud. "I sure hate to be the one breaks this to you, Father, but they ain't gonna beef the security till The Man gets here. I mean"—he chuckled—"I don't want you to think that you—me—the people here are just small potatoes. The folks runnin' this show jus' figure, I guess, that ordinary security is good enough until the real big shots show up."

His listener wiped his mouth with his handkerchief and finished his milk. One sandwich was sufficient. "Ordinary security," he repeated. "Does 'ordinary security' include the guards I didn't find?"

The guard swallowed a bite that should have been chewed. Had he made a mistake? Would this priest report the missing guards—plus the one who had just admitted a nightly breach of duty? "Now, now," the guard managed, "just 'cause you didn't find them don't mean they weren't on duty. This could be just a coincidence. And we've been here eatin' in the kitchen for jus'—" He checked his watch. "—fifteen minutes or so. Not enough time for anything to happen . . . don't you know."

"Just the same . . ." The man's tone was righteous. ". . . I'd feel a lot better if I had some idea of how we're being protected." He waited.

The guard hesitated. He wasn't supposed to discuss specifics about his tour of duty. Too many people know your routine and pretty soon that element of surprise that's part of the routine vanishes.

But . . . this priest could cause trouble. Better to humor him. "Look, Father, you got no cause to worry. It's years since anybody broke in here. Practically every inch of the outside of this building is lit by floods. The whole building! The property is all fenced in. The whole property! Believe me, Father, nothin' and nobody can get in here. Nobody's even gonna try. The automatic security's been set up by experts. You got nuthin' to bother yourself about."

Whether or not the man was worried, it was clear that the guard was disturbed.

"Well," the man said, "that's all very nice, but can you absolutely guarantee that nobody who wants to get in here *can't* get in here?"

Somehow, the guard saw some kind of lawsuit in the offing. What if he were to stick to his boast that the building was impregnable? He knew better; nothing is foolproof. So, what if someone does get through?

He had painted himself into a corner and saw the need to get out. "Be reasonable," the guard pleaded, "it's like the security they give the president—or the pope!—if somebody wants to get in someplace or wants to get somebody, they probably can find a way no matter how much protection they is. But I can tell you this without doubt: You're pretty damn safe in here . . . pardon the language."

"Well . . . all right," the man reluctantly allowed. "But I am not impressed with the internal security. I know it's unlikely, but what if? What if some criminal does manage to break in? Then what?"

"Look Father, I'm not s'posed to give this information out, but . . . look: We got to check in all the time when we're on duty. All the guards here got the same routine. Maybe you didn't see 'em when you was walkin' around, but they here. Ever' fifteen minutes they got to check in from a different station. Ever' hour they patrol their whole section. I prob'ly—um, whatchamacallit—overre*act*ed when you said you didn't see nobody till we come across each other. They're around; you count on it. It been workin' fine for long time now."

"Okay," the man said. "Now, if I understand you, you make your complete rounds every hour. And you check in at fifteen-minute intervals . . . is that it?"

"That's it okay. You got nothin' to be concerned 'bout. We'll take care of you and the other Fathers jus' fine . . . you see?"

"Okay." He leaned forward to focus on the guard's name badge.

The message—that his identity had been noted just in case there was a foul-up—was not lost on the guard. "Can I get you back to your room, Father?"

"No, thank you. I can make it very well myself."

They parted company.

That's the last time I go out on a limb for a priest, thought the guard, as he continued on his tour. Ordinarily, he had this snack time carefully timed so he would check in promptly. He would be a bit tardy now, due entirely to having to spend time reassuring this nitpicking priest that he was adequately protected. But he would not use this as an excuse. If his supervisor were to confirm this excuse with the priest, it would only open a can of worms. Better to get a demerit point on his record and get docked a little pay than have to go through all this again with the priest.

He used to think, If you can't trust a priest, then who? From now on, he thought he might just not trust anybody.

The man found his way back to his room without difficulty. Now that he'd followed the building's diagram by actually making his way through it, he felt much more sure of himself.

Running into this guard tonight was a distinct bit of luck. Now he knew the building's security setup. And he knew that should he pinpoint a guard's presence at a specific check-in area, the guard would not return to that point for another hour.

Invaluable information.

13

Zoo Tully lay very still.

He found it impossible to sleep. He couldn't forget the conversation earlier this evening. The conversation at Wanda's party as well as the ensuing one with Anne Marie.

If he were alone he would have risen from bed and done something—anything: read, watch TV, work a puzzle—anything. He knew from the testimony of others as well as from his own experience that it is counterproductive to remain in bed when sleep is elusive.

But he also knew from experience of his wife's sensitivity. The few times he had gotten out of bed for any length of time, Anne Marie invariably would sense his absence, come looking for him, and insist on keeping him company until he could sleep.

So he just lay there, not daring either to get out of bed or even to toss and turn.

But slowly Anne Marie became aware that her husband lay awake. It was his breathing: It wasn't the deep, rhythmic breathing of a deep sleep. There was no doubt: He was awake. "What is it, hon? What's wrong?"

"Nothing. Go back to sleep."

"Something. You're wide awake."

"I've just been thinking . . . you know: can't turn the brain off."

"Want to talk about it?"

Silence. Then: "I was just thinking . . . do you know how many people want to kill the pope?"

"What?!"

"You know how many people want to kill the pope?"

"I give up: How many?"

"Just about everybody."

She shook her head. There were times when she thought homicide was a disease he had caught. "That's silly. You just had a nightmare. Go to sleep." She turned on her side again, but snuggled close.

I wish, he thought, it *was* just a nightmare.

PART TWO

PART TWO

14

Not surprisingly, Zoo Tully would have overslept had not Anne Marie awakened on time.

It had been well after midnight when Tully finally drifted off into sleep. It was Anne Marie's "silly" that had reached him. At length he'd had to agree: That everyone wanted to kill the pope was ridiculous, an irrational concept that sometimes comes unbidden in those ghostly hours of the black night.

Most metro Detroiters were delighted by this return visit. At worst, they wished he had decided to come at some other time—any other time. Everyone was preparing to celebrate either the holy day, the holidays, or both.

The pope was an extra added attraction that might better have been postponed.

Once reality had lit Tully's somnolent consciousness, he was able to slip into untroubled sleep. His metabolism tried to even things by borrowing time this morning. Thanks to Anne Marie's more faithful inner clock, they would both get to work on time, but with little to spare.

Tully arrived at his squad room having neither read the morning *Free Press* nor caught a complete radio newscast. On arrival, he immediately began to review cases, some he had been investigating and others that had come in after he had gone off duty.

While he reviewed these investigations, two of his detectives arrived. Phil Mangiapane and Angie Moore, both sergeants in Tully's homicide squad, exchanged cursory greetings.

Their room, like the other six squad rooms, was strictly utilitarian, without a frill in sight. Old wooden desks and chairs occupied the otherwise uncluttered work space. The bile-colored walls added a depressing note. The sole exception to the drabness, decals of Santa, his sleigh, and reindeers, had been plastered on the dingy windows by Angie Moore.

"You catch the murder-rape in Bloomfield last night?" Mangiapane asked of no one in particular.

"No. Was it in the paper?" Moore asked. "If it was, I missed it."

"Nah; too late for the paper," Mangiapane said. "I caught in on the radio."

Tully had also heard the sketchy radio report, but had not given it his undivided attention. If it happened in the 'burbs, it was out of his jurisdiction. He had plenty to keep him busy here at home.

Mangiapane, having aroused Moore's interest, said no more.

"So," Moore said finally, "what was it? What happened?"

"A woman in her forties. Wife of a doctor. I didn't catch the name. Found in her car in a parking lot behind a strip of shops on Telegraph. Looks like rape, maybe by more than one guy. Then a shot to the head. The news broadcast didn't have all that. But that's what I got out of it."

"Any suspects?"

"Not yet. It'll probably get played up big by the afternoon *News*." Mangiapane shrugged. "Funny, it's not all that rare in the city. But this was Bloomfield. A white woman, a doctor's wife. It's gonna get plenty of ink."

Moore halted in her desk work. She was overcome with a rush of sympathy for the dead woman. Angie could not blot out the atrocity that ran like a movie through her mind.

It happened too late for the morning paper. She was found in her car. Someone got in that car. Maybe the killer was waiting inside her car and she was unaware until she got in. Maybe it was one of those bump and jump attacks when she stopped her car after the killer rear-ended her.

Moore shuddered; she could feel the woman's terror. What was it Mangiapane said: Maybe more than one guy? The added agony of being overwhelmed by a bunch of goons. A gang rape. The humiliation. The only hope, that she could somehow get out of it alive. The ultimate horror when she saw death in the form of a gun.

It took Moore several moments to pull back from the impotent rage she felt. It wasn't an appropriate thought for a law-enforcement officer, but she gladly and willingly would've thrown the switch electrocuting those animals.

Zoo Tully also was distracted by Mangiapane's news.

Without moving his bowed head, Tully shut his eyes as he recalled the first time he'd met Anne Marie.

It was late last spring.

He'd been headed for his bank to withdraw some cash from the

ATM. As he pulled into the parking lot he saw her: an African American woman, stylishly dressed—class, elegance. Watching her leave the bank and walk toward her car he almost forgot what he'd come for.

Ordinarily, he would have noticed immediately the young white male headed toward her. But he was so taken with her that his normal observant police faculty was clouded.

Tully spotted the guy only seconds before he reached the woman. He had been walking briskly at an angle that would intersect with her path to her car. Abruptly, he broke into a dead run.

Tully hit the accelerator and his car leaped forward. No way could he reach her before the assailant.

Only a few yards from the two, Tully jammed on his brakes, threw the gear into park and jumped out of the car. All he could think was: Let go the purse, lady; *let go the purse!*

But she wouldn't. Her assailant had grabbed it and as the strap slid down from her shoulder, she caught the strap before he could get away. He was a tall, powerful kid and, as he tried to flee, he pulled her off her feet and began to drag the now-shrieking woman across the asphalt paving. Her body spun from side to side as he fled. Then he saw Tully coming full tilt.

The thief had a choice. He could release the purse and try to get away. Or he could flatten this black guy and maybe get away with the purse as well.

It was an easy choice; Tully was not an imposing physical specimen. He dropped the purse and the clinging woman and turned to face Tully. He swung a roundhouse right. Tully ducked, then drove his fist deep into the young man's midriff.

A whoosh came from the man's gaping mouth. He doubled over, gasping for breath. Tully chopped with his rigid right hand at the meeting point of neck and shoulder. The young man dropped as if gravity had doubled its pull.

Tully turned toward the woman, who was pulling herself away from him. For all she knew, he was going to pick up where her erstwhile assailant had left off.

He realized what she was thinking. Quickly he showed her his badge. Next he held the badge out for the benefit of the gathering crowd.

Seldom had he seen a woman so disheveled. Both shoes were lying at the spot where she had been attacked. Her stockings were torn, as was her dress. Her hair was a mess. She had picked up a coating of dirt. She was shaking from the shock of the attack.

Tully knelt by her side. The neck of her dress was ripped, exposing lace at the top of her slip. In other circumstances he would have found this sexy. She was fighting back tears. Somehow withal she retained class.

She looked into Tully's eyes with gratitude. He looked into her eyes protectively. It was what the French, those masters of the language of amour, call *coup de foudre*—the thunderbolt that is the basic beginning of love at first sight. For both of them.

After a minute, she tried to stand, mostly to be sure nothing was broken. He assisted her to her feet. Everything seemed in working order. He told her to stay right there till he had taken care of the stunned would-be thief.

Within minutes after his call, two uniformed officers arrived. They got the necessary preliminary information and took statements from eyewitness bystanders.

Once the excitement was over and the groggy attacker packed off, the crowd quickly dispersed. Finally just the two of them were left. Could he take her home? There was a good chance that shock could set in once the adrenaline slowed.

She was sure she could make it home okay. However, she was a teacher and she would appreciate it if he would tell her principal what had happened so that a substitute could be called in.

Could he call on her later—say, this evening? Just to make sure all was well.

That would be fine.

So from that action-filled meeting, an occasional dinner would be shared. Then dates. Then romance. Then a love affair. He made no secret of the fact that he had gone through a wife, then a significant other. He also made no secret of the reason that neither had found it possible to maintain a conjugal relationship with him.

She tested this relationship until she was satisfied that it was working and would continue. She was an extremely attractive woman who had been pursued by other men. She had never allowed herself to make a lasting commitment. Until now.

Yes, she was sure.

And, without his quite understanding how she had arranged it, they were married in an east side Catholic church.

Saving a woman from a mugger was by no means a first for Zoo Tully. But it was the first time he'd saved a woman who would become the love of his life.

From that time on, anytime he heard of any sort of similar attack on a woman, it became a personal thing with him; at such times he would relive his experience with Anne Marie.

Tully lifted his head from the reports. "Manj, check with the Bloomfield cops. See where they are on that rape-murder."

"Right, Zoo."

More members of the squad trickled in while Mangiapane was on the phone. When he hung up, he took his notepad and approached Tully. Angie, who had so empathized with the victim, joined the two men.

"They're still putting things together, Zoo. But so far, they think they've got a multiple rape—real violent. The vagina is pretty well torn up. A single bullet. She got it in the mouth. Real rough."

Moore shuddered. Tully grew grim.

"They think somebody bumped her car. They figure she stopped and got out. And that's when they got her."

Tully shook his head. "She got out!"

"Yeah. That bump was more like a ramming. The vehicle was hit twice. Her husband said the car was in perfect shape before. Now it's got a couple of benders in the rear. One of 'em is a heap of damage."

"Any make on the perp's car?"

"Not yet. They found some black paint chips. Figure it's at least a black body and considerable damage on the grill, maybe even on the hood or fenders."

"Have they got it on LEIN?"

"They're getting it on now." Mangiapane, notepad in hand, started back to his desk. Then he turned. "I was just thinking . . . if the guy does a lot of his driving in the Bloomfield-Birmingham area, that car'll stick out like a sore thumb. Here, it would just be one more smacked-up heap."

True, Tully thought. But not quite a needle in a haystack. The perp's car might very well be one of the high-price ones. If, that is, the perps were from one of those northern suburbs. A Mercedes or something like that might well draw some attention in Detroit.

But if it's a clunker . . . well, there was no dearth of rattletraps and battered vehicles on Detroit's streets.

It was undoubtedly the best clue available right now.

Before returning to his case study, Tully had one parting thought. He'd give a lot to find the bastards who'd done this. After Anne Marie's brush with serious injury at the hands of a mugger, it was too easy to imagine something like this happening to her.

Oh, yes, Tully would indeed like to be the one who found those SOBs.

15

The list of things Father Koesler took on faith grew longer as the years passed.

As, for instance, his part in an upcoming panel. He had not volunteered, he had not even agreed to it; he had simply accepted the assignment.

Just as in the "good old days" when, periodically—every five years ideally—priests received from the Chancery letters directing them to some parish where they would serve until they got another such letter.

These letters were never, or at least very seldom, challenged. They were, for most priests, one slight notch below "God's will."

Actually they were a pseudo-scientific labor on the part of those priests who made up the assignment board. In the fifties and sixties and earlier, tons of priests were moved about the diocese each June and September. It was the job of the assignment board to direct their fellow priests to parishes or special work without making any spectacular blunders, such as returning a priest to a parish he'd already served, or mixing languages, such as assigning an Italian-speaking priest to a Polish parish and the like.

Once the list of assignments was made up, the bishop might check it over. More likely not. But since the bishop had appointed his priests to the assignment board, and since the bishop was the administrator of God's will in the Ordinary's diocese, by extension the assignments *were* God's will.

Thus when the priest received a letter, which invariably began: "For the care of souls, I have it in mind to send you to . . ." he went.

For the most part, that routine no longer had much if any impact. Generally, parochial openings were listed and priests were free to apply or not. However, there were exceptions. Father Koesler's position as moderator of the panel on dogmatic theology was very definitely a case in point.

He had of course studied dogma in the seminary, some forty years ago. Since then he had tried to stay current. That had not been difficult during the period between his ordination in 1954 and the Vatican

Council in 1962–65. The seminarians of that era in the final four years of their training enjoyed an excellent theological education. And things developed with all deliberate sluggishness.

After the Council, change became the coin of the realm. The race was on to come up with the latest biblical interpretation, the most relevant liturgy, a morality whose direction shifted at credentialed whim.

It was all too much for Koesler. He could not completely abandon a treasured and classically formed past, nor unreservedly embrace an untried present and future.

And so he became what he had always been at the core—an eclectic, choosing what he carefully and prayerfully considered to be the best of those two worlds: pre– and post–Vatican Council II.

All of which, as far as he was concerned, hardly qualified him to moderate a panel on dogmatic theology.

But then his opinion on this assignment was not asked. Someone downtown was counting on his spirit of obedience. Someone downtown knew him pretty well.

Besides, the subject was not the complete field of dogmatic theology. That, indeed, would have been well beyond his capability—even as a mere moderator.

No, the subject had been narrowed to a discussion on papal infallibility.

The very fact that this topic was going to be publicly treated gave weight to the rumor as to what the pope had in mind for his trip to Detroit.

Was he going to raise the doctrine of *Humanae Vitae* to the status of an infallible pronouncement? Why else would the very topic of infallibility be scheduled to be debated as a prelude to the papal visit? But, even then, what good would discussing it do?

As Koesler proceeded through his morning ritual—breakfast, reading with greater or lesser attention the morning paper, shower, shave, etc.—he decided he might as well let infallibility rattle around in his head.

At the outset, he had to admit he seldom if ever even considered the concept. It was symbolic of the aforementioned gap that separated the pre- and post-conciliar Church.

Before the council, infallibility for Catholics in general was a given. However, oddly enough, it seemed that this peculiar power had been used only once. Since the doctrine of infallibility was defined at the

First Vatican Council (1869–70), only the dogma that Mary, the Mother of Jesus, after her death was assumed bodily into heaven had been proclaimed in 1950 by Pope Pius XII.

So, as infrequently as he ever thought of it, Koesler always wondered why in the nearly two thousand years of the Church this awesome concept had been invoked only once.

Additionally, after Vatican II, all sorts of what hitherto would have been fairly ordinary pronouncements became tagged with the stamp of infallibility—for example, the proclamation of someone being named a saint.

Still, for the vast majority of Catholics, the Assumption of Mary remained the least-common denominator. While other pronouncements of the pope, with or without the consent of the world's bishops, might be argued over, virtually everyone agreed that the Assumption doctrine bore the stamp of infallibility.

And it was exceedingly difficult to get very worked up about that. Whether or not Mary's body and soul were in heaven would not have anything to do with war, famine, pestilence, or the destruction of our environment.

If it had not been rumored that the present pope intended to introduce infallibility to a teaching that would have far-reaching consequences, no one would be giving infallibility a second thought.

Now, even the rumor of such a papal act could, on the one hand, cause most serious problems for an already-overpopulated world and, on the other, further fragment an already tortured Church. In addition, such a proclamation would drive deeper the wedge that divided Christian churches.

And so Father Koesler was involved. Not by his choice but through fiat of some ecclesial bureaucrat.

He was dressed, groomed, and ready to go. The only question was how to get there.

Mass transportation was unreliable. There was his car. But considering the Christmas rush as well as preparations for the pope, he figured he would drive that short distance only to have the devil of a time trying to find convenient parking.

He decided to walk.

The temperature hovered between thirty-two and thirty-three degrees Fahrenheit so the snow on the ground as well as that which was now gently falling was turning to slush. He would need boots.

And, because the wind was blowing across the river, he would have to bundle up.

When finally he was ready, he resembled a little boy whose mother has wrapped him like a mummy only to find he had to go to the bathroom. Thank God, he thought, that wasn't the case.

He left the rectory via the front door, and walked the few yards down Jay Street, noting the marker designating his church as a national monument. Then he went south on Orleans toward the river, turning off at Lafayette. He decided to walk through Greektown. There was always so much traffic on those cluttered streets that it seemed warmer than it actually was.

He turned south again on Randolph and reached Jefferson. He was only five uneven blocks from Cobo Arena. But he was also only a short distance from the river with nothing to block the windchill as the breeze whipped around the RenCen complex.

He was a little more than halfway across Woodward, the main thoroughfare of downtown Detroit, when it happened.

He heard the acceleration, a motor suddenly racing, roaring. He half turned his head in time to see a car bearing down on him.

Instinctively he tried to roll his body out of the vehicle's path.

It was that turn that saved him. The car brushed him with little more contact than a bull might have on a sidestepping matador. But he was down in the slush.

The car didn't even brake, but spun left on Jefferson and headed east. A woman screamed and afterward thought it was her cry that saved the priest. In reality, the car was past him by the time she'd reacted.

Koesler felt a fool lying in the muddy slush. He tried to get up, but strong arms held him down. "Better stay still, Father, till we find out if you're hurt." The voice belonged to a well-dressed pedestrian.

The woman, who—mercifully—had stopped screaming, dug his glasses out of the slush. Koesler tried to clean them with his coat sleeve. No improvement.

A policewoman who had been directing traffic a block away came running.

Koesler insisted on standing and, with help, he did. Nothing broken. A little tender here and there.

The officer, after being assured the victim was not seriously injured, sought eyewitnesses. As usual, the majority of the bystanders didn't want to get involved. But the two who had come to Koesler's aid stayed the distance.

"Did you see the vehicle? Get a license number?"

"Not very good. When I heard the motor roar, I glanced at the car but I was more interested in staying out of the way," the man said.

"'Staying out of the way'?"

"Yes. I'm quite sure he was headed straight for the priest. Father was in the street—with the light, I should add. I was on the median. I was mostly concerned that the car wouldn't jump the median and hit me."

"License?"

"No way."

"How about make and color?"

"Dark. Black or dark blue. An expensive model—BMW or Jaguar or something like that. Sorry, that's about the best I can do."

The officer took down the witness's identification and urged him to call if he remembered anything else.

"How about you, ma'am?"

"Is he all right?"

"The priest? He seems to be. My partner will see to him. What can you tell me about the accident?"

"Well, we were crossing the street, Woodward, when this car raced forward. I screamed. I think that's what saved the Father. I'm Catholic," she added, uncertain whether her religious preference was relevant.

"Did you get a—uh, do you know what make car it was?"

"Dark. Black, I think."

"But the make? Chevy? Plymouth? . . ."

"A big expensive car, I think. Maybe one of those Lincoln Town cars or maybe the big Mercury." She knew she wasn't being helpful. But she had been frightened.

"Yes, ma'am. Is there anything else you can think of? Anything at all?"

"Well . . . yes . . . The front of the car—what do you call it . . . the grill . . . ?"

"Yes, ma'am?"

"It was sort of smashed in . . . like it had been in an accident before and hadn't been fixed."

"Are you sure of that? A damaged grill?"

"Yes. I'm certain. I remember thinking how odd that was." She looked at him. "You know, the rest of the car looked so new and expensive, I wondered why anyone who owned such a nice car wouldn't have it repaired right away. Of course, if he drives like this all the time, the car's going to be a wreck in no time."

"Yes, ma'am. Anything else?"

"Uh . . ." She thought for a moment. "No, I don't think so. Are you sure the Father is all right?"

"Yes, ma'am. We'll see to him. But, about the car: Think now, did you see anything else? Anything at all? You said, 'If *he* drives like that': Did you see the driver . . . or any passengers?"

"Oh . . . yes, yes, I remember now: a couple of young people, I don't know, maybe in their teens . . . or early twenties. A boy and a girl . . . a man and a woman . . . but young. And he was driving."

"Do you think you might be able to recognize him—or either of them—if you saw them again?"

"I don't know . . . it happened so fast. Maybe . . ."

"I see. Would you wait here for a moment, please. I'll just see about Father. Then maybe you could come to headquarters and look at some photos. Maybe you could help us come up with a couple of composite pictures."

"Oh . . . I don't know. I haven't got a lot of time . . ."

"It's for Father."

"Uh . . ." She took another look at Koesler. He was beginning to look like a poster captioned, SEND THIS KID TO CAMP. "Well . . . all right. If it'll help . . ."

The policewoman turned her attention to Koesler, who was being interrogated by her partner, who was about out of questions. No, the priest had no idea who the driver might be or why the car had seemingly been aimed at him. No known enemies. No clue whatever as to why this had happened. But, and by all means dominant in Koesler's mind, he had not been injured. He had just been turned into a mess.

"Funny thing," Koesler mused, "I think I owe my life to my father."

His father is still alive! The policewoman thought that amazing.

"When I was a kid," Koesler explained, "I once walked right into a moving streetcar. . . ."

"A what?"

"You don't remember streetcars, do you?" Koesler smiled. "Anyway, I wasn't hurt then. But I hardly ever left home, even when I was an adult, that my dad didn't remind me, 'Keep your chin up.' In other words: Don't walk into moving vehicles. I looked up this morning and just barely got out of the way. It was, I must say, close."

"Did you have business downtown, Father?"

Koesler looked forlornly at Cobo Arena. So close and yet so far. "I was trying to get there." He nodded toward the huge building. "I'm supposed to be part of a program . . . uh . . ." How to explain it in the least cluttered terms? ". . . welcoming the pope. It's really quite important that I get there. I gave myself a little extra time this morning." He looked down at himself. "Looks like I'm going to need it." He resembled a soiled snowman.

"We can help you, if you'll help us," said the officer. "Where's your parish?"

"Old St. Joe's . . . on Jay and Orleans."

"Okay. We'll take you there and you can change. Then you can come with us to the station and fill out a report. Then we'll get you to Cobo. How 'bout it?"

"Fine with me," Koesler said. "Just in case we run a little late at the station, could you let the panelists I'm supposed to be with know what happened?"

"Sure. We've got so many cops downtown today, we could almost relay the message by word of mouth."

They flagged down a blue-and-white and loaded Koesler and the woman in. She spent most of the short drive asking Koesler if he hadn't heard her scream. And wasn't it that very scream that had alerted him to the danger? And wasn't it this sequence of events that saved his life?

Koesler honestly could not recall a scream. But he allowed her the benefit of his panic. Undoubtedly she had screamed if she said she did. She was thrilled that she had been given the opportunity to tell him that it was she who probably saved his life.

Saving the life of a priest seemed to her an extremely appropriate immediate preparation for Christmas.

16

Bonnie, mouth hanging open, sat half turned toward Rick. "I can't believe you did that!"

Rick smirked.

After running down Father Koesler, he completed the left turn onto Jefferson. He was going so fast, and with the wet, slippery pavement, he fishtailed, just missing another pedestrian who had stepped off the curb in anticipation of a green light. Hearing the roar of the engine, the man had looked up to see the car seemingly out of control.

It was a miracle he wasn't hit. It was amazing luck, if not a miracle, that Koesler was not seriously injured, and that the careening auto managed its illegal turn against traffic. With the extraordinary police presence downtown that no officer was at that corner at that moment was the final unlikely event.

The police gathered quickly and tried to turn up witnesses. Of course the majority of motorists and pedestrians had seen nothing clearly. It was not unusual; frequently eyewitnesses became momentarily "blind."

Rick had no right to that much luck. The secret was that he couldn't have cared less. He was out for thrills on a grand scale. Damn the torpedoes! Anyone with the slightest hesitation, or concerned about the slightest margin of safety, probably would not have made it through all those obstacles.

He was on a roll. He piled all his chips on blind luck. And, at least for now, he'd won.

"You almost killed two people back there!" Bonnie shrieked.

"Yeah!" Rick regained control of his car and aimed it down the ramp onto the Chrysler Freeway North. He stayed in the fast lane, which wasn't moving all that fast on this miserable, snowy morning. He dangerously tailgated one car after another until they successively gave way and moved out of his path. With each psychological victory, he became more convinced something, somebody, was making him invulnerable.

"Slow down! You'll get us killed!" Bonnie protested.

"Didja see that first guy?! He was wearing one of those collars—whadyacallem, religious. I think he was a priest! I didn't know that when I headed for him. Didja see what happened to him? I didn't get that. D'ya think I got 'im? The bump didn't sound so solid. I don't think I killed him."

"Killed him?! Killed a priest?!"

"It's like somebody up there—it can't be God, must be the devil—somebody's telling me it's okay. Go ahead. Wow, this is really somethin'! I've never been pumped up like this! Woweee!"

Bonnie studied him. She was beginning to believe.

When he'd told her what had happened last night, she hadn't quite known how to react. Her first inclination was to credit him with an over-vivid imagination. She expressed her disbelief.

In response, he tuned the car radio to a newscast. Sure enough, there was the story, at least in skeletal form. Rick had included rich detail that the newscaster didn't touch. He turned off the radio.

What did that prove? Only that Rick had already heard the news account of the killing, adapted it as his own, and embellished it.

Probably it was as much to convince her as to satisfy his growing hunger for danger and violence that he'd performed those daredevil stunts just now.

But . . . if he could commit attempted murder with the car, maybe he could have been responsible for the brutal murder of that woman. The dawning truth sent a shiver through her. "You really did it, didn't you?"

"What?"

"Last night. That woman. You and the Golds. You raped and killed her."

He was giddy. "What gave you the clue?"

"What you just did back there."

"You didn't answer me." He brushed aside her act of faith. "What happened to that priest back there? I couldn't see."

She took a moment to collect her thoughts. "I don't know. Last I saw, he was on the ground. I was too shocked to pay all that much attention."

"I don't think I offed him." Rick shook his head. "The hit just wasn't solid enough. I think he was spinning away when I hit him. Pretty good for an old man. Hey, turn on the news. Maybe there'll be something about it on the radio."

"Come off it, Rick. It just happened, for chrissake!"

"Okay. See if you can get some metal—"

"No! We gotta talk!"

He reached for the radio button. She grabbed his hand. Fury suffused his face as he glanced at her. Then, unexpectedly, he softened. "Okay, babe. But don't ever do that again." He concentrated on the road. Those ahead of him continued to give way as, barreling ten miles over the limit, he hung on their rear bumpers. He would have gone faster, but the other drivers were adjusting their speed to the worsening road conditions.

Bonnie could do little about his breakneck driving. In fact, she admitted to herself that she was enjoying the way her man was having his way on the highway. "What's got into you, lover? You're like a different person. And, hey, could you get off the freeway, please. This traffic is driving me nuts!"

He had to agree it was time. No one was on his tail. He had continually checked his rearview mirror for flashing lights. None appeared, though he might have been pursued by police as much for his driving as for the hit-and-run back on Jefferson.

He slid the Jaguar over two lanes merely by flipping on his right turn signal and moving to the right. A cacophony of angry horns protested this dangerously inconsiderate maneuver.

Once back on the surface street, Bonnie repeated, "What happened? How come, all of a sudden, you're like this?"

He grinned. "I didn't have any idea it could be like this! We've done every drug on the market, haven't we?"

She frowned. "Well, I haven't done horse."

"This is better. Imagine you had an unlimited line of coke or an unlimited supply of crack. Imagine the high you could get just going from one to the other! Imagine!"

She imagined.

"Well," he continued, "this is better!"

"What?"

"Murder! It's the ultimate high! There can't be anything better than this!"

"Rick!"

"I mean it!"

She thought that over. Maybe there was something to this after all. He had never yet led her down a barren path. And he was good about it; he always tried everything himself before presenting it to her. From grass to crack, he had led the way. He even warned her that heroin could be a downer. It had been for him, though he still did it from time to time, mostly as a change of pace. And that was the explanation for her never having tried horse.

Rick was telling the truth, at least subjectively. Throughout his young life almost nothing had been denied him.

His father, a partner in one of Detroit's most prestigious law firms, led a socially active life. So did his mother. They had "people" to clean, to cook, to fix things, to arrange for parties, to send cards. Although now vacationing in the Virgin Islands, Rick's father had taken a pile of files along, and kept in regular touch with the office by phone and fax. He would return to Detroit far sooner than his wife.

Thus had the Vanderwehls' married life proceeded. Along the way, they'd had Rick. That was incontrovertible; he was there for everyone to see.

His father would be hard pressed to explain why they'd had him. An accident, partly. The thing to do, partly.

In any case, it was as painless an event as they could make it. Outside, of course, of the birthing process. Pregnancy had been excruciatingly inconvenient. And that could not hold a candle to actually delivering the squalling little package.

But, that was life. The good with the bad.

The thing to do was to hire someone to raise the child. Which was more of a challenge that they'd anticipated. The brat had a knack for attracting crises. Illnesses, sleeping disorders, childhood diseases, a reluctance to go to bed, get up, go to school, go out, stay in . . . Froward was his middle name.

Then there were the home repairs needed almost every time he touched a household item.

As one might guess, the parents were forced to hire an almost endless series of nannies, custodians, counselors, jailers. All in an effort to have as little parental contact with this child as possible.

One way of ridding themselves of the lad, his parents soon discovered, was to fulfill his every desire and cave in to his every demand. It was so much faster and unproblematical, wasn't it?

Rick's problem lay in trying to come up with new things to want.

Gradually, through his years in school, he'd gathered a tight circle of friends who were assailing the seasons in much the same way as Rick.

Since he was left as alone as he cared to be, Rick's home became headquarters for the group of five who called themselves the Golds. The name described the lifestyle to which they had become accustomed and which they intended to continue.

Rick was by no means stupid. He might have amounted to something substantial. But with his background, that would have been a moral miracle to challenge such conversions as that of Paul, Augustine, and Francis—either Assisi or Xavier. For Rick, such a metanoia was not in the cards.

He and the Golds and their camp followers stumbled down so many avenues of novelty that their search for fresh depravities was drying up.

Then came last night.

What a thrill!

Better than any drug Rick had ever tried. Instantly—he was not stupid—his plans for the immediate future were crystal clear, fitting snugly into his quest for higher and higher highs.

Along with his plans for homicidal thrills came an unreasoned feeling that some sort of inexorable destiny was guiding him. It was as if nothing, no power, could reach him, stop him.

And each new episode only reinforced the conviction that he had become invulnerable.

Largely, this morning had been a test.

He had left himself open for instinct and inspiration to take control. Who could have done what he did and expect to get away with it?

But he had. He had just let a force greater than himself take over. And he had come out of it totally unscathed.

As he grew in confidence—and, at this moment his confidence was absolute—he wanted to pass on, to communicate this self-assurance to the Golds. And to Bonnie. Nobody was closer to him than Bonnie. She had followed his every lead. She had gone through the drug culture never once doubting him.

Now he wanted "his people" to scale the heights with him. And they would if only they would place their trust, unreservedly, in him. It was as if, as far as authority was concerned, he was invincible. His people would share in all this with him. All he needed was their blind obedience.

He pulled into a supermarket parking lot, found an empty space near the street, parked, and turned off the engine. He turned to Bonnie. "Look, have I ever let you down or steered you wrong?"

"Umm . . . no. And I was just thinking that."

"Well, I told you what went down last night. That means I trust you. I trust you with my life. 'Cause that's what would happen if you told anyone. I could be stepping into life in the slammer."

Sincerity beamed from her face. "I know that, Rick. I would never tell. You've got to know that."

"I do. And you won't have any doubt when I tell you what comes next."

"What comes next! How 'bout a hit-and-run in downtown Detroit, then breaking every traffic law on the books?"

Rick waved that away. "That was nothing. Just a test drive. You saw how it worked. Nothing can happen to you while you're with me. I know 'cause nothing can happen to me . . . understand?"

She nodded enthusiastically.

"We are going to . . ." Rick paused. The enormity of what he intended to do engendered awe even in him.

Bonnie was deeply impressed. This must be really big if Rick couldn't bring himself to just come out with it.

"We are going to . . ." He tried again. "Well, let me put it this way: What very important person is about to come to Detroit?"

Bonnie turned her head and looked out the windshield without seeing anything. Slowly her eyes widened as she gradually looked back at Rick.

"Not . . ." She halted.

"Say it!"

"The . . . the pope!"

"You got it."

"The pope! Honey, you gotta be out of your mind!" No sooner were the words out than she regretted them. He grabbed her wrist roughly and squeezed so hard she gasped. "Don't ever—*ever*—say that again."

Tears of pain and confusion ran down her cheeks.

"You got me?" he said roughly. "Never, *never* . . ."

"Okay! All right! Rick, you're hurting me," she wailed.

He released her hand. *"Do you understand?"* he said quietly but firmly.

"Yes. Yes!"

"Okay. Now: Remember everything I told you. You're safe with me." He looked deep into her eyes. "It doesn't matter what I do or what the odds are: Nothing can happen to you as long as you're with me."

"Yes, honey. Oh, yes!"

115

"All right. Now, I've got everything planned for the greatest high any of us have ever had. It's foolproof. So what I want to know: Are you with me?"

She hesitated. It seemed so insane, so pointless.

But how could she call herself his friend, his lover, if she wouldn't trust him completely, unquestioningly? He had proved he was truly extraordinary. She *had* to trust. She *had* to believe. "I'm with you, darlin'."

He relaxed. The last brick was in place. "Okay. Okay. But you're going to have to warm up for the big one."

"'Warm up'?" Doubt crept back.

He started the car, slipped it in gear, and pulled out of the parking lot. Suddenly, for Bonnie, the moment of truth seemed to have arrived.

Agreeing to join Rick and the boys in the assassination of the pope had been like promising to accompany him on a trip to Mars—like killing a pope it was no more than a fantasy . . . something they would get serious about sometime during the next century—or, perhaps, the one after that.

"Warming up" for that put everything in the present tense. It was scary.

Rick reached across to the glove compartment and pulled out a packet. He felt under his seat and came up with another, which he handed to her. "Take the mask out."

It was a standard ski mask, the sort that people wear when skiing or otherwise out in bitter cold. Or when needing a disguise.

It was going to happen. Something was going to happen. "What are you going to do?" Her voice quavered.

"What are *we* going to do?"

She stared at him blankly.

"We are going to rob a store. Maybe one of those little convenience stores."

"But why? We don't need money."

"You need the experience. The Golds are a couple of violent crimes ahead of you."

It was useless to argue. She knew she was going to do what he wanted. At this point, all she could wish was for this episode to be over, with no one seriously hurt.

Bonnie had never heard of Patricia Hearst, kidnapped and brainwashed by a terrorist gang. At one point during her captivity, she was filmed participating in a bank robbery. The argument over whether she had collaborated willingly continues to this day.

But now Bonnie knew that she would go along with Rick even if it wasn't of her own volition.

"That looks good," Rick said as they drove by a small store on Detroit's northeast side. It appeared to be open for business, but no cars were parked in front or on the side lot.

As they finished circling the block for the second time, Rick said, "Get your mask ready."

Adrenaline racing, Bonnie obeyed. Rick was right: This was a very definite high. But not of the desirable sort.

As they pulled their ski masks over their heads, Rick leaned past Bonnie. He took a gun from the glove compartment.

"Rick! You're not going to use that!"

"What are we gonna do, honey—go in there with our hands open and say, 'Trick or treat'?"

"But you're not going to use it!"

"Not unless I have to. Now, we can't sit here with our masks on forever. Let's go!"

They quickly moved from the car to the store. Rick's gun was in his hand and visible.

As they entered the store they were greeted by a whoosh of heated air and the mingled aroma of fruits, vegetables, and meat so characteristic of small markets.

Behind the counter stood an elderly clerk, presumably the owner. There was one customer, a young black man. Their eyes widened and their mouths dropped when they saw the masked duo, one brandishing a gun.

Bonnie froze just inside the door.

Rick advanced, waving the gun at the customer. "Down! Get down! On the floor! Face down! Now! *Now!*"

The man dropped to the floor as if struck, his groceries rolling around his prone body.

Rick turned his attention to the clerk. "The money! Put it in a paper bag! Now! Don't try anything! Don't even think about it!"

The man carefully took a paper bag from the counter. Under no circumstances did he want to give the impression he was doing anything but cooperating. He began taking money from the register and stuffing it in the bag.

"Faster! *Faster!*" Rick shouted.

"Let's *go!* Come *on!* Somebody might be coming," Bonnie pleaded.

Rick shot a jittery glance at her. As he returned his attention to the clerk, the man was holding the bag toward Rick. However, his other hand was inside the register. Unhesitatingly, Rick fired. A small hole appeared in the man's forehead. He stood very still for a moment, then crumpled to the floor, the bag still in his hand.

Without bothering about the bag, Rick shouted at the terrified customer, "Count to fifty, sucker. Don't get up till you hit fifty. And count real slow!"

Rick had to push Bonnie out the door. She was glued to the spot just inside the door from which she had not budged since entering.

They jumped into the Jaguar and gunned away, kicking up slush and broken bits of asphalt in their wake.

Inside the store all was deathly quiet. The customer, still on the floor, heard the car race away. But he was taking no chances. One of the robbers might've stayed behind. As unlikely as that was, the young man was counting his blessings—principal of which was that he had escaped with his life. He wasn't about to meddle with that.

The door opened and somebody entered the store.

The prone customer intensified his fervent prayer that they had not returned to finish him off.

"What's happenin'?"

The voice belonged to neither of the robbers. One customer shakily got to his feet to greet the second customer. "They shot him! They shot Mr. Abdoo! Call 911! Maybe they killed him! Didja see them?"

"Uh-uh. All I seen was two guys in masks runnin' outta here. I seen 'em get in a car. It was still runnin'. They whipped out right by me."

"You see what it was?"

"A Jag. Late model. Black. Didn't make no plate . . . bad grill."

"Call 911! Call 911!"

"Okay! Okay!"

Once clear of the neighborhood, Bonnie and Rick whipped off their masks. Bonnie, sobbing, buried her face in her hands.

Rick would have paid more attention to her had he not been so busy evaluating his own emotions.

This was different—vastly different—from what had happened last night. Last night he had provided the gun. He had ordered the outcome. But Ronnie had pulled the trigger.

Now, it was he—Rick himself. He—no one else—had taken a human life.

Once again by his peculiar rationalization process, clearly it was the victim's own fault. All he'd had to do was hand over the money. He would be alive now if he had just done what he was supposed to. Just as it was that bitch's fault last night: If she hadn't recognized Ronnie, she'd be at her garden club meeting right now.

Their fault!

It took Rick no time at all to reach this point.

Now he was testing his appreciation of what he'd done. It wasn't quite the thrill he'd expected. If anything, he merely felt numb. He wondered about that.

Next he thought of what he'd told the Golds last night: Once they'd done it—once they'd killed—things had to escalate. Now, hell, if anything, he was retrogressing.

Last night the victim had been a cultured, wealthy woman. Her murder would have to be a very high priority for the police.

That was one level—a high level.

But he'd just killed a relative nobody. Maybe the guy owned the store. So big deal! In Detroit something like this happened by the day.

That must be it . . . why this was almost a downer for him. And he had it figured out. He knew what had gone wrong.

They had to move ahead. Aim high.

He relaxed behind the wheel. He would take Bonnie home—to his house. He would quiet her, convince her. She would come around. She always did.

Meanwhile he had learned a valuable lesson.

His plan was nearing completion.

They would act soon. Very soon.

17

It started in the shower.

He had been pretty well composed as the police had returned him to his rectory. The woman, who had volunteered her eyewitness statement on the near fatality, had chattered incessantly. That had proven a distraction.

The police were solicitous beyond question. They almost seemed to need reassurance that Koesler was all right. He reassured them.

He did not wish to impose on either the police or the woman witness. He assured the police that he could make it to Cobo on his own and that he would stop off at 1300 Beaubien en route to the arena and file his report on the hit-and-run.

On entering the rectory, he encountered Mary O'Connor, secretary and general factotum. She had arrived for work just after Koesler had started out for Cobo Arena.

Mary was shocked. He was a mess. She could not recall ever having seen him so disheveled. She needed to be reassured that he was not hurt. He reassured her. Also, he explained that he had no time for an explanation, but that he would explain after he finished his business at Cobo for which business he was already late.

In his room he decided that at very least his overcoat and trousers needed the cleaners. Fortunately he had been wearing his second-string suit and coat. There had better not be any further mishaps; there was no backup suit and coat in his closet. One more messy accident and he would have to give serious thought to a sweat suit or a barrel.

Under the strong, hot shower spray he began to feel the stiffness and pain. At one point, he feared he might pass out. No matter how late he would be for his appointment, he would have to take the rest of this morning more slowly and gingerly.

While dressing, he buzzed Mrs. O'Connor on the intercom and asked her to call a cab. No more slogging through the slush this morning for him. She asked how he was doing. He reassured her again.

After a stop at headquarters, the cab discharged him in the circular drive outside Cobo's main doors. He walked stiffly into the building. It was as if he were discovering muscles he hadn't used in a long while. Actually, he was reacting to the bruises inflicted by his fall.

He found the room where tomorrow two scholars would debate the doctrine of infallibility. A debate he was scheduled to moderate. A debate that was supposed to have been rehearsed this morning—beginning some forty-five minutes ago. Koesler was unsure what he might find at this time. He peered tentatively around the door.

The room was much larger than he had anticipated. But there were fewer folding chairs than a room this size would seem to call for. He assumed more chairs were available if the crowd were larger than expected. It was difficult to estimate in advance.

At this time there were no plans to accredit or even distribute tickets to the audience. As of now the debate was simply open to the public.

Nor was there much evident security. A few guards here and there, but he couldn't find even one Detroit police officer. If law enforcement people were here—city, county, or federal—they must be be in plain clothes.

On a dais at the front of the room were three chairs, a cut above the audience's folding variety, and a lectern.

While technicians and maintenance people were were busy checking the electrical equipment, the thermostat, and the public address system, the two priests in animated conversation on the dais paid them no mind. It seemed that the two must have pulled their chairs together on the same side of the dais.

Koesler surmised that they were the scheduled presenters at this conference on dogmatic theology. He had read some of their articles in theological journals, but he had never met them.

One had to be Father John Selner, a Sulpician (a society whose choice it was to teach seminarians). Koesler recalled a photo from his days as editor of the *Detroit Catholic;* Selner was the one to Koesler's right.

John Selner was heavyset with a full head of dark hair. He wore a cassock that should have gone to the ragbag long ago. Probably it had been purchased during one of Selner's abstemious periods. Now it stretched across Father's midriff tortuously trying to hold on to the buttons. The upper edge of his clerical collar was buried under the folds of fat at his neck. Maybe, thought Koesler, that was why Selner's face was so red. Perhaps the blood ascending from the powerful pump that was his heart could get through his pinched neck, but had a lot of trouble getting any further.

There, thought Koesler, was a stroke waiting to happen.

Further, Koesler thought that when he had the opportunity to get up close and personal he would find that much-used cassock would have a generous measure of food stains. Perhaps some cigarette burn marks as well.

Here was a man consumed by matters theological and totally unconcerned with personal appearance. If he were correct in identifying this gentleman as Father John Selner, S.S., then Koesler had found the conservative proponent in this debate.

Surely by accident, the liberal spokesman was to Koesler's left. If he was correct so far, the other participant was Father Daniel Hanson.

As if to accentuate their philosophical differences, the two experts were worlds apart physically.

Father Hanson, while not pencil thin, was spare. His oval head was bald except for a white fringe above the ears and around the back. Unlike Selner, Hanson wore glasses. As Koesler recalled from photos he'd seen of Father Hanson, the priest usually wore civilian clothing, including a tie—all very businesslike, of course. Now, perhaps in deference to what would not be an academic setting, he wore a plain black suit and clerical collar.

The two priests were so wrapped up in their private conversation, they seemed oblivious to the hubbub around them.

Slowly, gingerly Koesler approached them. When he came within a few yards of the dais they noticed him and immediately became aware of his halting gait. They both stood and came to assist him. As they did, Koesler noted that Selner, in addition to being overweight, was packed into a compact body. He couldn't have been more than five-foot-six or -seven.

Hanson, on the other hand, was much taller, perhaps five-foot-ten or -eleven.

Koesler felt like a relic as the two priests assisted him to a chair on the dais. As he hobbled along, introductions were made. Koesler had been correct in his tentative identifications. The two men had recognized Koesler since they had heard about what had happened to him; he was the only priest they had encountered who appeared to have been hit by something like a car.

"Sorry . . ." Koesler eased himself into the chair. "I'm afraid I'm really terribly late. That is not my m.o. at all, believe me."

"My poor man," Selner said, "don't think of it. The police told us what happened to you. Are you sure you're all right? Shouldn't you be home in bed or something?"

Koesler chuckled. At least *that* didn't hurt. "No, no, I'm okay. A little stiff, that's all. I don't usually play Dodgem this early in the day . . . any time of the day, for that matter.

"But I saw you talking to each other. Were you rehearsing your presentations?"

Hanson smiled. "No, my dear man." He looked at Selner. "Shall we confess, John?"

Selner shrugged good-naturedly.

"We were," Hanson said, "arguing the relative merits of our soccer teams."

"Your soccer teams?"

"Yes. You see, John and I have been out of the states for the best part of our priestly lives. With John, it's been teaching in several seminaries in France. While I've been virtually exiled from my diocese, and wandering—on assignment of course—around Europe lecturing, writing, eluding the Church authorities as much as possible."

"You see," Selner continued, "we've been away from stateside distractions like football, baseball, and basketball for all these years. But you have no idea how absorbing soccer is over there. So *that*, we confess, is what we've been discussing—not arguing about. *Ignosce mihi.*"

"You're forgiven," Koesler responded. "But what about the rehearsal? This conference is scheduled for tomorrow. And again, I'm so sorry to have kept you waiting all this time. Can we do something about that now?"

The two men looked at each other.

"There's no real need," said Hanson.

"Daniel," Selner said, "maybe we ought to explain. We take it all too much for granted. Father Koesler here—"

"Bob," Koesler suggested.

". . . Bob here would not be in a position to know what we do from time to time over there."

"What you do over . . . where?"

"Oh," Hanson said, "various places in Europe. Usually as part of seminars or conferences. Very much like this one, only not at all on such a grand scale. We've never been an opening act for the pope before."

"You see," Selner added, "both of us are basically dogmatic theologians. And one or another topic in this field has been a subject for us to chew over in the past."

"Believe me," Hanson said, "we've been over the topic of infallibility more than once."

"Dozens of times."

"You mean," Koesler said, "that you just update your material as the years go by?"

"There's really not much to update, to be perfectly frank," Hanson said. "It's all pretty much rooted in history." He winked at Selner. "As a matter of fact, after all this time, we probably could switch sides and argue against each of our own convictions."

"Without actually changing our own positions, mind you.

"But, come to think of it, we *are* so familiar with the arguments as they develop in these debates, we probably could switch roles just to relieve the monotony."

With an impish grin, Hanson said, "Should we, John? Should we argue the other side for Bob here?"

"Uh . . . I fear it would be a bit confusing for the dear man. But I think we should let him in on what will happen tomorrow. We certainly don't need the rehearsal. But, since he's never heard us before, we ought to cue Bob into what we'll be doing tomorrow."

"Righto," Hanson agreed. "First off, after you go through the curricula—"

"I'm suffering a distraction already," Selner said. "Haven't we worked out the plural for a résumé? Is it curricula vitae, or curriculum vitarum, or curricula vitarum?"

"Or curriculums," Hanson offered.

"Horrors! Well, continue."

"After you finish the backgroundings—which, by the way, you should have already . . ." Hanson looked expectantly at Koesler.

"Yes, I have them."

"Then," Hanson continued, "it would be best to give me the floor first . . . wouldn't you agree, John?"

"Oh, yes, by all means. You see, Bob, the way this will develop in context is that infallibility is a given, a datum. We Catholics—and most non-Catholics—are familiar with the concept of infallibility. So it makes little sense for me to begin by explaining what infallibility is. Catholics, by and large, believe in it. Non-Catholics of course wouldn't believe, but at least they'd be familiar with the concept.

"So, since Daniel will deny the existence of that particular doctrine, it is more practical for him to lead off . . . at least, that has been our experience."

"Dan denies infallibility!" Koesler exclaimed. "You mean you claim there is no such thing as infallibility?"

"Exactly," Hanson said. "In a nutshell, that's about it."

"I think I can see why you try to avoid the hierarchy."

"Well," Hanson said, "I don't go around shouting from the rooftops, you see. So the institutional Church does not have to confront me most of the time. That"—he scratched his head—"is why both of us have wondered why we've been invited to this particular convocation. This is going to draw an awful lot of media coverage. And while John is a dear soul, a brave colleague, and a brilliant theologian"—he winked at Selner—"he hasn't a leg to stand on in this matter."

"Thank you, Daniel, for the extravagant adjectives. But I wouldn't agree."

"Of course not. Where, then, would be the debate?"

"So . . ." Koesler shifted uncomfortably in his chair. ". . . I call on Father Hanson to give the opening statement."

Hanson chuckled. "Yes, then pretty much hang back. We will shift into our debating gear . . . and we'll be off."

"Is this," Koesler asked, "at all related to that old wheeze about the orchestra conductor who mounts the podium and finds a note telling him to pick up the stick and begin waving it? 'Beautiful music will start. Keep waving the stick until the music stops. Put the stick down, turn around, and bow.' Is that sort of what I'm supposed to do—introduce the two of you, then get out of the way?"

"No, not at all," Selner said. "You *are*, after all, the moderator. If one or both of us gets out of line—starts to hog the stage as it were—you step in."

"It has happened," Hanson admitted.

"In that case," said Koesler, "I'm a bit embarrassed. You ought to have an expert sitting in with you as moderator.

"Don't get me wrong," he added, "I'm honored to be with you. I probably would've attended this conference anyway. But I think I'll be learning things from your talks. I may not know if or when you are out of line."

"Actually," Hanson said, "we'd rather have . . . uh . . . a general practitioner—if you don't mind that description. I mean it in the best sense of the term."

"I don't mind. Especially in a situation like this, with experts in their field conducting the program, what better way to describe a parish priest than a general practitioner."

"Okay," Hanson said. "Again, you introduce us and call on me as the first speaker. And, with Father Selner's permission, I'll begin by dropping my bomb."

18

"Your bomb?" Koesler wondered.

"That," Hanson continued as if Koesler had not spoken, "there is not now, nor has there ever been, such a thing as infallibility for anybody except God."

That *is* a bomb, Koesler silently agreed. Hitherto his idea of a bombshell would have been that for all of its controversial history, infallibility had been explicitly used only once.

Selner was shaking his head. "Dan, that's the weakest part of your argument."

"What?" Koesler was fast approaching bewilderment.

"The part about beginning," Selner said.

Hanson nodded. "That is a strong point in your argument. But not entirely defensible by any means."

Their disagreement, to Koesler, seemed in the most amiable of spirits. There appeared to be nothing personal intended; each was arguing facts as he saw them.

"To begin," Selner said, "there's Luke's account, when Jesus says to Peter, 'I have prayed for you that your faith may never fail. You in turn must strengthen your brothers.'"

"Granted," Hanson said. "But almost all the early Church fathers commented at great length on that passage. Not one of them interprets that text to mean that Peter or his successors were infallible."

"That comes under my 'argument from silence.'"

"Ah, yes," Hanson addressed Koesler, "his famous 'argument from silence.' About which we will hear more later, unless I'm mistaken."

"Let's cut to the chase, as they say nowadays," Selner said. "I think it unnecessary for the people who will be at tomorrow's symposium to remind them that it's Peter we're talking about."

Hanson shrugged assent.

"But," Selner continued, "it may be important to point out that Peter was the only one of Jesus' followers whose name the Lord changed. The Apostle's real name was, of course, Simon—"

"And the change in his name is your strongest argument," Hanson interrupted.

"One of them," Selner stated affably. "It happened when Jesus singled out Simon and told him that henceforth he would be known as 'the Rock'—Petrus in Latin, Cephas in Aramaic—the language they spoke. The pun was perfect in Aramaic. 'You are Cephas,' Jesus said, 'and upon this Cephas I will build my Church. And the gates of hell will not prevail against it. I will give you the keys of the kingdom. Whatever you bind on earth will be bound in heaven. Whatever you loose on earth will be loosed in heaven.' *The keys of the kingdom!* What more clear statement could the Lord make!"

In his mind's eye, Koesler could see the huge inscription on the inside of the dome in St. Peter's Basilica: *"claves regni coelorum."* The keys of the kingdom of heaven.

"All well and good," Hanson responded, *"if* Jesus actually said it."

"Really, that is unworthy of you, Dan. If you can't refute a statement, you claim it never happened."

"Not so. And not so cavalierly. You know as well as I that textual criticism compares exhaustively all of the so-called quotes of Jesus. Some are accepted by nearly all scholars. Others . . . not.

"When you read on," Hanson continued, "Peter's place in the early Church is pretty plainly spelled out. He was indisputably first—but first among equals. But *infallible?* Hardly. Remember the confrontation at Antioch. It had to do with Jewish dietary laws—which were and, for the most part, still are extremely strict.

"Peter was guided by a vision to cut through these laws. All of the earliest Christians were Jews, of course. But the new faith was to be open to all.

"However, Peter was waffling. When he ate with the Gentiles it was as if there were no dietary laws. With the Jews he ate kosher.

"Then came the confrontation at Antioch, when, as Paul tells it, 'I directly withstood him because he clearly was in the wrong.'

"Peter and Paul in Antioch is one of the reasons scholars and critics doubt the 'keys' statement. First among equals, as I've said; but infallible . . . ?"

Selner began to pace in a small rectangular perimeter, as if he were in a tiny cell. "Peter in Antioch was on the horns of a dilemma. He knew Jewish law would have to be reconsidered in most if not all ways. He was with Gentiles in Antioch and had no reservation about eating with them. Then the Jewish Christians came to town. If he suddenly insisted on Jewish law, the Gentiles would have been confused at best. If he continued to eat with the Gentiles, the Jews would be scandalized.

"He decided in favor of tact and diplomacy. Paul thought that was a bad call and that Peter was 'in the wrong.' But it was not a doctrinal matter. It involved little more than good or bad manners."

"Bravo, John," Hanson said. "You've refined that argument since our last go-round. But and however . . . the word 'infallible' hasn't yet been mentioned by anybody. There's when I begin looking around in history for the first mention of the concept.

"And I don't find it until about 1300—the beginning of the fourteenth century! And then the idea was to *confine* the pope's powers, not to broaden them.

"You know"—he turned toward Koesler since Selner was basically familiar with the argument—"religious orders, such as Franciscans and Dominicans, routinely take vows—usually three: poverty, chastity, and obedience. You'd think their meaning would be obvious. But, in practice, they mean what the religious order says they mean. And this is particularly true of 'poverty.'

"Now, in about 1300, Pope Gregory IX declared that poverty as practiced by the Franciscan order meant giving up *all* worldly goods 'singly and in common.' In other words, Franciscans were not only to own nothing, they were to live dirt-poor as did their founder, Francis of Assisi.

"Now, enter an otherwise unknown Franciscan monk, Pietro Olivi. He couldn't have agreed more with Pope Gregory. But he was fearful that some future pope would come along to undo this evangelical poverty. So he came up with in effect the concept of infallibility.

"Originally, the infallibility invented by Olivi gave no 'sovereignty' to popes. Instead, it severely limited them to everything taught by all preceding popes.

"For instance, if Pope Gregory's teaching on the total poverty of the Franciscans were infallible—guaranteed by God to be free from error—then should any future pope attempt to water down the doctrine, such pope would ipso facto disqualify himself from the papacy. He would be a false pope since he denied a previous pope's infallible statement. So, Franciscans would live dirt poor forever and ever. And Olivi would be happy and a peace forever and ever.

"Naturally, the popes of that time would not permit themselves to be restricted by everything ever taught by all their predecessors. In fact, Gregory's successors, Nicolas III and John XXII, condemned the doctrine. And nearly all the early defenders of that doctrine were declared heretics.

"So that's it. Not only was infallibility unheard-of, not even dreamed of, by the early Church, it was invented at the beginning of the fourteenth century by a monk who wanted to make sure his order would live as poor as its founder, Francis of Assisi, until the end of the world."

"Nice," Selner said, "but I would change 'unheard-of' to 'taken for granted.'"

"His 'argument from silence,'" Hanson said to Koesler.

"And valid," Selner rejoined. "Take the Eucharist—the Mass. The Synoptic Gospels of Matthew, Mark, and Luke, when they tell of the Last Supper, each quotes Jesus, 'This is my body. This is my blood.' These words are the basis for our belief in the changing of bread and wine into the body and blood of Christ. Yet though John's Gospel treats the Last Supper in great detail it makes no mention of the transubstantiation of bread and wine.

"Now some have argued that since John omits these vital words they were never said. But the concept of what the Synoptics record would be incomprehensible without John's sixth chapter wherein Jesus promises and explains the Eucharist.

"The simple explanation is that by the time John wrote his Gospel the Eucharist was familiar to all Christians.

"And simply, that's what happened to the doctrine of infallibility: The concept that Jesus taught through Peter and his successors was a given. The Church from its earliest times simply took the doctrine as a fact.

"Granted, it had to develop over the years, just as did every other Christian doctrine. It had its ups and downs until it was specifically defined by the First Vatican Council back in 1870."

"Well," Hanson said, "*half* defined."

"All right," Selner conceded, "infallibility was to proceed from a consensus of bishops and laity. It wasn't any of their fault that war forced the bishops to leave Rome before the role of bishops and laity could be defined. But that was corrected in Vatican II."

"John"—Hanson's tone was impatient—"for the past century or so, Cardinals become popes and Cardinals are made from bishops. And the prime qualification for the office of bishop is loyalty—as blind a loyalty as can be imagined—to the Holy See. How difficult can it be to reach a consensus from a bunch of clones armed only with rubber stamps?"

"You exaggerate!"

"A little. But I think the word we're looking for here is *indefectibility*—that no matter how many mistakes and blunders we make, somehow, by the intervention of the Holy Spirit, we will muddle through till the end of the world."

"But . . . uh . . ." Koesler, who felt like a spectator at a verbal Wimbledon, hesitated to interrupt, but the two men seemed to welcome his question. ". . . how did we get from that Franciscan monk to here?"

"How?" Hanson leaped in. "Simple: Infallibility became a handy tool that popes used against Gallicanism and the Protestant Reformation. And finally it became like the atom bomb: The mere threat of it became a powerful weapon popes could use to get their way. And they have been very clever in hardly ever using it.

"Frankly, you have to suspend logical thought to agree with the present interpretation of infallibility. But with this as an extraordinary teaching tool that is scarcely if ever used, they have created the 'ordinary' magisterium. And the 'ordinary' teaching office of the Church is so closely related to the 'extraordinary' that to deny something 'ordinarily' defined is to be, simply, wrong.

"What a marvelous weapon! How we got from there to here is that we have discovered a device so powerful we just can't lay it aside. It's more intoxicating than the possession of atomic power. The last few popes, with the exception of John XXIII, have been threatening to 'infallibilize' just about anything that's near and dear to their hearts.

"And"—he turned back to Father Selner, who was obviously eager to get his licks in—"let me tell you this, John: If this pope comes in here to raise *Humanae Vitae* to an infallible level, you can cross the 'One' out of 'One, Holy, Catholic and Apostolic.'"

Hanson, with a smile, turned back to Koesler. "As for me, I say, with the late John Henry Cardinal Newman, 'I will drink to infallibility. But first, I will drink to conscience.'"

"Dan," Selner said in all seriousness, "I think you've gone—"

A surge of sound brought further discussion to a sudden end. The ruckus seemed to be coming from the corridor. Neither of the doors to this room was closed, so the noise could be heard quite clearly, though not intelligibly.

"What the hell is that?!" Hanson exclaimed.

No one bothered answering because no one knew. But they all hastened to the doors and out into the hallway.

There they found two men, one casually dressed, the other in shirt, tie, and jacket, shouting at each other. Push was rapidly coming to shove.

Two guards were trying, not very effectively, to separate them.

Finally, two police officers, a male and a female, both black, got between the combatants. No blood had yet been spilled, and the officers seemed determined that the altercation not exceed verbal abuse.

But there had been enough commotion to cause a general emptying of the various conference rooms into the hall.

Hanson slipped over to one of the security guards, who was visibly relieved that real police officers had taken charge. "What was that about?"

"Damned if I know," the guard replied.

Letting Hanson lead the way, Koesler and Selner listened in.

"Did it start out here in the hallway?" Hanson asked.

"No, not here. In that room over there . . ." The guard indicated a conference room directly in front of them.

Hanson squinted to read the small sign posted on the wall next to the door. It read: FAMILY PLANNING: A MORAL PERSPECTIVE.

"Wouldn't you know it?" Hanson shook his head. "One more war fought over morality. Let's see what the damage is."

19

The three priests entered the conference room.

To Koesler it seemed a duplicate of the one he'd just left. The dais with its three chairs, the lectern, the mike and speakers, the floral decorations, the folding chairs.

The difference was that several of the metal folding chairs were overturned or scattered helter-skelter across the room. Koesler wondered whether any of the chairs had been thrown or if they'd just been stumbled over and toppled. He recalled the memorable photos of Indiana basketball coach Bobby Knight hurling a folding chair across the floor. That could hurt.

The three priests still standing at the dais, apparently the participants of this conference, seemed dumbfounded. A police officer was questioning them.

Another priest was coming toward Koesler. For a moment he could not place the man.

It was Father Paul Smith, who had been at the Koznickis' last night. Why hadn't he recognized Smith immediately?

The problem was that Koesler had not expected to see him here. It must have been that Smith had plainly said that he planned on being merely a spectator at this whole affair.

Of course spectators could attend these rehearsals. But Koesler had assumed that a merely casual observer might limit attendance to main events.

Father Smith looked pale. Of course that could be due to the muted, indirect lighting that gave the room a grayish tint. But, now that he thought about it, Koesler had noticed the same pallor last night.

"I didn't expect to see you here, Paul. Are you feeling okay?"

Smith frowned. "It's nothing. Just Michigan's winter crud. It gets to you earlier the older you get."

"Don't I know." Koesler introduced Smith to Hanson and Selner, identifying everyone comprehensively.

"How did this mess get started, Paul?" Koesler asked.

"The pot was simmering for quite a while," Smith replied. "I believe it was brought to a boil by that gentleman right there, talking to Monsignor Martin. Do you know him?"

Koesler gazed at the man dressed in Salvation Army discards, He was busily taking notes. It was the notepad that gave him away.

"'Less I miss my guess, he's a reporter . . . for the *Free Press*, I think. Name is Cox or Box or something like that. It's been a long while since I've seen him. How did it start?"

"Well . . . first, do you know these three guys—the ones who are giving this conference?"

Selner and Hanson said their paths had occasionally crossed with those of the two speakers. They were unfamiliar with the moderator. Koesler, on the other hand, knew the moderator but not the presenters.

"The moderator," Smith explained, "is Monsignor Martin, a pastor here in Detroit. The shorter of the other two is Norb Rasmussen. From Milwaukee. Teaches at Tübingen in Germany. The tall one is Bill Palmer. Belongs to Boston, but teaches at the North American Seminary in Rome."

Rasmussen was built squarely, somewhat like a smaller version of a sumo wrestler, Koesler thought. His hair was in a brush cut, in itself a statement. Palmer seemed quite tall, but that may have been due to the contrast in height with Rasmussen. Palmer's elongated head probably was bald. His thin white hair seemed combed from the side over his pate. In wire-rimmed glasses he looked every inch the scholar.

Koesler wondered briefly at the casting for this conference. The personnel of the two panels he had seen so far mirrored each other to a striking degree. One short and stocky, the other tall and thin. He'd have to check out the other panels as this program moved forward.

"Actually," Smith said, "I intended to try to attend your rehearsal, Bob, but you weren't there and you weren't there . . . did something happen?"

"Later." Koesler didn't want to get into that, especially since it was old news to the other two priests in this foursome.

"Anyway, that's why I was a trifle late for this conference. It was already under way when I got here. But I doubt that I missed much. On the matter of family planning we had one conservative and one liberal. You two," Smith indicated Koesler's companions, "already know these two presenters. Let's see if Bob can sort them out."

Koesler smiled. "Too easy. If Father Palmer teaches in Rome, he's apt to be on the conservative side. Otherwise he'd be courting martyr-dom. That leaves Father Rasmussen a liberal. Otherwise Tübingen would have introduced him to Hans Küng."

"Congratulations," Smith said. "Really, all they seemed to be doing was rehashing *Humanae Vitae*. It was getting quite tedious. There's a limit to how many ways there are of stating that every act of inter-course must be between the validly married and must be open to the production of new life. I must say that Father Palmer was rather inven-tive in finding a whole bunch of duplicate statements. And he had quite a few popes who agreed with his views. Not a bad bench."

"So?" Koesler prodded.

"So?" Smith responded.

"So how did this turn into a donnybrook?"

"Oh, yeah. Well, a couple of men seated in the audience began ask-ing the panelists questions. At first they were unwilling to take ques-tions. But after a short while—when it became obvious that those two weren't going to desist—the speakers began trying to address the ques-tions. Then, the two gentlemen began pretty much talking to each other.

"The main problem seemed to turn on natural family planning.

"Palmer and one of the gentlemen argued that natural family plan-ning—or NFP, as Palmer called it—was more effective than any other form of birth control, including all the devices and methods con-demned by official Church teaching.

"Rasmussen and his constituent made the point that maybe NFP was, indeed, better and more effective than the rest of it. But that wasn't the point. The point—or at least Rasmussen's argument—was that the only moral decision that had to be made was whether a married couple should try to have a baby. If they decided, for whatever reason really, that they should not have a child, the moral decision was made. After that, any form of birth control was all right, including NFP."

"What I'm interested in," said Selner, "is how all these people got in here. I was under the impression that security would be tight."

"I didn't have any trouble getting in at all," Smith said. "There *is* a security station just inside the doors. You fellas must have had to go through it to get in this morning."

"But we had to show our credentials," Selner protested.

"I don't think so," Smith said. "I mean I don't think you *had* to show them. I just showed the guard my driver's license . . . come to think of it, he didn't ask for any identification. Of course, I *am* wearing clericals."

"Anybody can buy clericals," Selner protested. "I want to know where this promised security is!"

"We are, as they say in Washington, outside the loop," said Koesler, remembering last evening's conversation with Koznicki and Tully. "The real security kicks in when the pope gets here. And even then the bulk of security is going to be aimed at protecting him and those closest to him. We'll still be little fish."

"Maybe they'll tighten security after what happened to you, Bob," Hanson said.

Koesler laughed. "Oh, I don't think so. That appears to have been a couple of crazy kids. Maybe he was trying to show her what a big man he was. It didn't have anything to do with this event."

"Well, they certainly ought to do something about it after this outburst this morning. I know they were only scuffling, but this *is* the 'Murder Capital of the World,'" Selner noted.

"I know we get a lot of bad press about being a city where casual, random, aimless murder happens," Smith said, "But it isn't always true. Remember after the Gulf War back in, I think, '91, when a young soldier returned here and was shot and killed. The media made a huge thing about how this kid got all the way through the war without a scratch, but then he comes back to Detroit where he's murdered for no apparent reason.

"The contrast did a lot more damage to this city: You can go through a war and emerge with no harm done, but you can't load up a car in Detroit without getting gunned down.

"Then, a day or two later, it came out that his wife had paid someone to kill the soldier to collect something like a hundred—or a hundred and fifty thousand dollars in life insurance."

Smith realized that he was painting himself into a corner. "I know that soldier was just one more murder in this city. But it was different than the image of Detroit where drive-by kids shoot at each other instead of honking their horns. This was the cold, calculated murder-for-profit that can happen anywhere. It's sort of like the hypochondriac who comes down with a real, genuine illness."

"It's still a scary city," Selner insisted.

At this point, Monsignor Martin joined their group. Again, Koesler made the introductions, not including Smith, whom Martin, of course, knew.

"Wasn't that something!" Martin clearly was still in an excited state. "Did you guys see it?"

"I did," Smith said. "The others were in their own conference."

"Those guys should never have been permitted in here," Martin said. "I'm going to see about that. Tomorrow's the real thing. And if something like that were to happen—why, all hell might break loose." He turned to Koesler. "Bob, you're in with the cops; why don't *you* talk to them?"

"You've got that wrong, Marty. I don't tell the police how to do their job, and in return, they don't tell me how to preach."

"Even though those people shouldn't have been there," Martin said, "I think we might have gotten through without the violence if it hadn't been for that reporter—Cox, he said his name was . . . from the *Free Press*."

"Cox, Joe Cox, that's it," Koesler confirmed.

"What did he do?" Hanson asked.

"It wasn't so much what he did or even what he said," Martin said. "It was his smartass demeanor. When the presenters got around to natural family planning, Cox asked if that wasn't just an updated version of rhythm that had been discarded as impractical and unreliable long ago. And how are you going to teach a method like that to the illiterate and impoverished of the Third and Fourth Worlds, and a majority of them Catholic?

"Well, that got the conservative gentleman arguing with Cox. Then the liberal guy started defending Cox, and that's how the altercation began.

"About as soon as I got those two quieted down, Cox was on his feet again with the Church's attitude on condoms. He laid heavily on O'Connor's opposition to condoms even when they're used by gay men not to prevent children but to avoid AIDS.

"That started those two yelling at each other about homosexuals, or, as the conservative preferred, 'faggots.' Too bad; before that, the debate was moving along pretty good. I particularly liked Father Rasmussen's saying that the pope was likely to issue an encyclical entitled, 'Epistle to the Fallopians.'"

"Speaking of that," Hanson said, "did you hear about the second-grader who told his teacher that his mother wasn't going to have any more babies? The teacher was foolish enough to ask why not. The kid said, 'Because she had her boobs tied.'"

"You heard that joke in Tübingen?" Koesler asked, in a non sequitur.

"'In German it rhymes,'" Hanson replied.

"Well," Smith broke in, "I heard what's supposed to be a true story about kids. I think it involved the bishop of Saginaw—I can never remember his name. Anyway, he was taking these kids through a Q and A session before confirming them. He asked one boy, 'What does a bishop do?' And the kid said, 'Moves diagonally.'"

As the laughter subsided, Hanson said, "I think it took a lot of episcopal guts to ask that question."

"Even more guts if he had asked a bunch of priests," Koesler noted.

"This," said Martin, "doesn't involve kids, but the priest who told me about it thought it did. This priest had a wedding, confessions, and the regular parish Mass, in that order, on a Saturday. He witnessed the wedding, then headed for the confessional. There wasn't any business at all, which didn't surprise him—"

"These days," Smith interrupted, "almost no one goes to confession. Certainly not like the good old days." This was said for the benefit of the two presenters, who, buried in academe, might not know what was going on in the real world.

"Anyway," Martin continued, "there being no penitents, the priest just sat in his box and thought about the sermon he would preach at the coming Mass.

"Then, he heard someone enter the confessional on the blind side. He waited for the penitent to start the confession, but there wasn't any voice, only awkward sounds like perhaps a youngster fumbling around trying to get comfortable on the kneeler.

"Finally, the fumbling sounds stopped. But still there wasn't any voice. So, after a reasonable time, the priest leaned over to the curtain and whispered, 'All right . . . go ahead.'

"Now there wasn't the slightest sound. After another pause, the priest leaned over again and whispered, a little louder, 'All right . . . go ahead.'

"A voice on the other side of the screen said, 'Who *are* you?'

"'I'm a priest! I'm hearing confessions! Who are *you?*'

"'I'm the photographer!' came back the voice. 'I'm changing my film.'"

Koesler was always gratified at how easy it was for priests, generally, to slip into casual camaraderie. Some of these priests were poles apart philosophically and/or theologically. But they respected their shared priesthood. And they could enjoy each other's humor even at initial meeting.

They were now joined by the two speakers at this conference. Monsignor Martin made the introductions. Fathers Rasmussen and Palmer were slightly acquainted with Fathers Hanson and Selner, but were so shaken by the fracas that it took a while for the dawning of recognition.

Everyone knew everyone else well enough to know that the speakers on each team at the conferences were poles apart from each other.

"In the name of God's green earth," said Rasmussen, "who arranged for this symposium? Who picked the participants?"

With uncontrollable good humor, Monsignor Martin said, "I did."

With mouths ajar and similar expressions of surprise, they all regarded Monsignor Martin. It was as if someone in a crowd had asked who was king in this country and one in the group claimed the title.

"Marty! You? How come?" Koesler asked. "You aren't part of the administration. You're a pastor, for God's sake."

"Well, I exaggerated slightly," Martin admitted. "I didn't do it entirely by myself. Paul here helped."

"Not very much," Smith demurred.

"Nonsense," Martin insisted. "You were a great help in locating some of these scholars. Fortunately for me, Paul has kept current on modern theologians."

"But you made the final selection, as well as picking the topics," Smith insisted.

Koesler, recalling Smith's promise in the seminary, had to silently applaud his continuing interest in theological development.

However, none of this really addressed Koesler's original question. "But how did either—or both of you get this assignment?"

"An oversight, I think." Martin grinned. "The idea of having a symposium came from Rome. It was supposed to be a prelude to the pope's visit." He grinned again. "I think this idea was not completely thought out or planned. I think Rome just took it for granted that the local boys—that's us—would work it out satisfactorily.

"However, our local administration got wholly into the papal presence. They're falling all over themselves booking residences, planning music, making sure the pecking order—secular, profane, and religious—gets observed—things like that.

"The symposium was a minor event to them. Just think: When the pope gets here, everybody who is anybody will want to shake the papal hand, get in the same photo with him. Practically the entire Detroit Police Department will be providing security, along with state police and federal agents.

"We, on the other hand, get so little security that our audience can and did get into a fight.

"In the absence of any great interest on our chancery's part, the symposium was dumped on me. And when he heard about it, Paul, good man that he is, volunteered to help.

"Then we, Paul and I, decided we would have a little fun. So we didn't set up any straw horses that the pope could rely on to prepare the way for him. Instead we will have an honest symposium.

"This little thing we've set up may mean that neither Paul nor I will become bishops. But we can live with that."

"But," Koesler said, "what about Cardinal Boyle? He's the host for this event. He must know what you've done!"

"I think you're right," Martin said. "But if the pope doesn't say word one about *Humanae Vitae*, this symposium isn't going to hurt very much. If, on the other hand, the rumors are accurate, and the pope's going to drop his bomb on Detroit to spite Boyle and punish him for his intervention during the Council . . . well, I think Boyle is laughing behind his hand at what we're doing."

"Besides," Smith said, "I don't think this symposium is going to make much of a splash in the media. The cameras and pens and pads will be aimed at His Holiness. They will little note what we do here."

"I don't understand, Paul," Koesler said. "Last night, you said you were going to be just a spectator at this conference. Now it comes out you've helped plan it."

"I didn't think that mattered much. My part in this event is over now. Now, as I said, I'm a spectator."

"I'm not so sure something isn't going to hit the fan over this," Palmer said.

"What do you mean?" Koesler looked concerned.

"This event," Palmer replied, "has a lot of similarities to that youth convocation a few years back in Denver."

"Despite the fact that it's the Christmas season, this event certainly is not for kids," Martin said.

"Not the audience," Palmer said. "The progressive routine. The Denver program was a papal event here in this country with world-wide consequences. And, most of all, it was to be followed by a papal encyclical that was touted as being close to infallible.

"That's what we've got here: not a carbon copy of Denver, but the same progression. Denver produced some statements that laid the groundwork for that very conservative encyclical, *Veritatis Splendor*. Granted it wasn't termed 'infallible,' but it was a very strong position paper.

"I think—and I'm sure I'm right on this—that this symposium was supposed to be set up, as was the Denver thing, as an introduction to whatever the pope is going to say. And whatever that is, it's a lead pipe cinch that it will be extremely conservative.

"And, with all due respect, this symposium doesn't have a beeswax candle's chance in hell of turning out any kind of consensus. It will not come close to producing a statement that the pope—given his conservative bent—can use as a springboard for anything he may say."

No one spoke for several moments. Everyone was weighing Father Palmer's statement.

"Well," Martin said finally, "I certainly don't want to get anyone else in trouble, especially not with the pope. The other conferences, with the exception of the one on canon law, are not stacked with conservative versus liberal presenters. So, I'll go talk to those speakers and tell them about the chance they may be taking.

"For now, I'll put it to you, Father Rasmussen, Father Hanson: How do you feel about what Father Palmer just said? It would be awkward, to say the least, if you were to back out at this stage. Although, in a pinch, I guess we could come up with a couple of experts whose opinions were much, very much more moderate than yours.

"The option's yours. You could agree to tone down your statements." He smiled. "But I don't guess you'd consider that. Or, you can opt out, no questions taken or answered. Or, if you want, we can proceed as scheduled."

They all looked at Rasmussen and Hanson, who looked at each other for several moments. Finally, the two broke into laughter. "Damn the torpedoes," Hanson said.

"Full speed ahead," Rasmussen rejoined.

"Okay." Martin smiled. "Is it all right with the others? Father Palmer? Father Selner?"

Selner snorted. "It's *their* heads, not ours, that are going to be mounted on the bridge."

"Actually"—Palmer looked ready and eager to do battle—"it's refreshing to have such a worthy opponent."

"Then," said Martin with finality, "it's done. I'll just go and sound out the canonists."

As Martin departed, Koesler drew near Hanson. "Are you certain?" he asked, in muted tones. "Are you certain? I really feel you're taking a big chance challenging the very concept of infallibility. Don't mistake me; I think you're on solid ground historically. But . . . this could have breathtaking consequences."

Hanson smiled. "Thanks for the concern, Bob. But for one, I don't agree with Palmer's conviction that we're going to make that great a splash. The people who attend this symposium more than likely will be scholars who more or less already have their minds made up. Oh, there'll be a few zealots like the ones provoked to fight this morning. But let's hope the security will be at least slightly superior to what we've seen today.

"The media—and that's about the whole thing as far as most of the populace are concerned—are going to be all over the pope and the other big shots. We won't make a ripple."

"I confess," Koesler said, "that I'm of two minds. I wish everyone could hear you and think about the practical consequences that have to flow from your research. On the other hand, I wonder if the majority of the Catholic world could handle such a theological bombshell. I really don't know what to think. But my instincts go with you and the truth of the matter."

"We'll just have to wait until tomorrow and trust in God," Hanson said.

"Seems, at this point, literally all we can do." Koesler almost made the statement a prayer.

20

Nelson Kane, city editor of the *Free Press*, stood near the photostat machine talking with one of his reporters, Alva Depp. They were discussing the continuing saga of the papal visit. "I've got very reliable sources," Depp said, "but nobody seems to know."

"Does that strike you as strange?" Kane always spoke as if it were difficult for him to breathe and almost impossible to move his mouth enough to form the words.

"It sure as hell does. He's not coming here to celebrate Christmas with us 'cause he's lonesome in Rome. But nobody seems to know for sure what he has in mind. Actually, one of my best sources is one of Cardinal Boyle's secretaries. Even *she* doesn't know."

"What's so odd about that?"

"What's odd—or different—is that the Cardinal usually lets his secretaries in on things like this. He feels they ought to be able to answer questions competently when people—especially the media—call. But he's playing this one tight-lipped. So, not only does she not know what the pope is going to say, she doesn't know why she doesn't know."

"Then we'll have to go with the rumor. But make sure you use all the words, 'alleged,' 'reportedly'—you know, the disclaimers."

"Okay for now. But I'm gonna find it. There's gotta be a chink somewhere. Somebody knows. And somebody's gonna tell me."

"'Atta girl. Go get 'em." Kane wished more of his people had Alva's tenacity. There was a day when reporters were a combination of bulldog and magician. Lately, a closed door was a sealed passage.

And, with the thought of the blend of magician and bulldog, out of the corner of his eye Kane spotted Joe Cox entering the long, white, rectangular room from the elevator. Cox made a beeline for his desk, dropping coat and scarf on a nearby chair.

Kane poured a cup of coffee and returned to his desk in the epicenter of the city room.

Kane was the closest thing to a revered newsman still functioning journalistically in Detroit. He was among those who were living proof that one could reach the top on talent alone—no dirty tricks or special favors.

Odd for bosses in this era, his people respected him. A tall, heavyset man, nearly bald, with arched eyebrows, he could on occasion resemble the late Otto Preminger.

As he fingered through wire copy, Kane kept track of Cox as the reporter pumped words into the computer. As he did so, Kane remembered the youngster he'd first hired almost twenty years ago.

Cox had come to the *Free Press* with few technical skills. He could type at an acceptable speed using from two to six fingers. He had insatiable curiosity. He feared no one. He wrote lean prose almost instinctively.

He had to be trained to verify sources, to be scrupulous about accuracy and thoroughness. These and other lessons required patience. Kane was *not* the patron saint of forbearance. But he recognized Cox's potential. So they played acknowledged games with each other until Cox became a premier reporter in metropolitan Detroit.

Then came Pat Lennon from the *Cleveland Plain Dealer*. Pat was a native of Michigan and a graduate of Marygrove, then a women's Catholic college in Detroit.

Lennon had it all. She interviewed with the personnel director. He counted his lucky stars that she had chosen the *Free Press* over the *News*. He sent her to Kane, who managed to keep a straight face while being near overwhelmed by her accomplishments and ability while noting also that she was definitely less than ugly.

It was like having Ruth and Gehrig in the same lineup. Lennon and Cox, Cox and Lennon. Two of the best in the same city room. They were golden years even when the two reporters began sharing everything but their bylines, muddying the situation.

Then Lennon, victim of a couple of managerial blunders (not Kane's) moved down Lafayette Boulevard to the *Detroit News*.

For a long while, Cox and Lennon improved and refined as they fought each other for page-one leadership. Until Cox was wooed from Detroit to Chicago and the *Trib*. Then there was that debilitating experience with the magazine, which led first to unemployment, then to a return to the *Freep*.

Kane was aware he was out on a limb in rescuing Cox. No one else in management agreed wholeheartedly with the decision. The force of Kane's clout alone proved decisive.

So Kane brought Cox back into the city room, where the hostility was near overpowering. Some of the younger reporters knew Cox only by reputation. There were chips on shoulders daring Cox to live up to that one-time fame.

Cox's contemporaries at best pitied him. As far as they were concerned, he'd lost it in Chicago where he'd been a failure. Cox had never competed for the congeniality award. He now paid a price for that oversight.

Cox finally sat back from the computer. Finished with his piece, he hit the button that would compute the length of his story.

Kane called up the story through the reporter's name.

On their separate machines, both Kane and Cox read the story, a follow-up to Cox's original piece on the symposium. "Cox!" Kane barked.

Cox braced, then relaxed with a smile. In a split second almost twenty years dropped away. How often Cox had answered Kane's summons with apprehension! Suddenly, it was like the good old days.

Then, equally as suddenly, it was not. Not by a long shot.

Cox looked around the sparsely filled room. Those faces he could see sported smug smiles, as if hoping Kane's invitation was a command performance on a carpet that was not red. Cox felt like rising from his chair and loudly announcing to the assembled players, "Get a life!"

Wisely, he thought better of it. Instead, he walked casually to Kane's desk.

"You wanna get yourself some coffee?" Kane said.

"Oh, it's gonna be that way." Cox took the chair next to Kane's desk. "Thanks, but no blindfold."

It wasn't clear whether Kane was suppressing a smile. "You got any idea why the pope's coming here?"

Cox shook his head. "No . . . and frankly, I don't give a damn."

"That's what I was afraid of."

"What's that mean?"

"The story you did yesterday . . ." Kane gestured toward the morning edition lying open on his desk.

Cox looked at it blankly. "Uh-huh?"

"The assignment wasn't to cover rehearsals for a symposium that nobody'll attend anyway."

"It was more exciting than anything else going on with the pope's one-night stand."

"So I was told."

"Huh?"

Kane ran his palm across his head, compressing some fine hairs. "The manager of Cobo called." Kane waited for a response.

There was none.

"It seems the excitement was *your* contribution to the proceedings, by and large."

Cox straightened up. "How does he figure that? He wasn't even there!"

"Not when the fracas started. But right after, when security called."

"Look, okay, so there was a ruckus. But I wasn't in it."

"No. But wasn't it a lucky thing you were there when it started."

The sarcasm did not elude Cox. "I asked some questions!" he protested. "That's what I've been doing since before I met you."

"According to the manager, it was your questions that set off the fight."

"That's his opinion. And remember, he wasn't even there.

"Look, Nellie, let's cut the crap. The pope has an interesting history and heritage, I'm sure. He's the good guy all in white. Only he could ride in a popemobile. But let's face it: He's about as exciting as a box of corn flakes."

"Cox, don't be an idiot. When the pope comes to town, that's news! How many things can you think of that could bump the pope off page one?"

"That's the kind of story that you find on page one with Veronica Lukashewski's byline. Hell, you know I wasn't crazy about this assignment in the first place—"

"You mean it's not worthy of your investigative talents? Look, Cox, I gotta level with you: It *used* to be beneath your best efforts at investigative reporting. Now, we don't know. You've been out of this for a while. Your best effort on a magazine ran along the line of the Ten Best Places to Eat an Ice Cream Cone.

"Now, this is a damn fine assignment, Joe. Don't blow it. I expect a workmanlike job on this. Then maybe we'll talk about the investigative pieces."

"Anyway"—Cox nodded toward the morning edition—"what's wrong with that? It's damn readable, no?"

"Oh, it's readable, okay. It's also contrived."

"And it's a scoop!"

"Let's hope it stops with that."

"Say what?"

"Let's hope the *News* and/or one of the TV or radio stations doesn't pin you up on their bulletin board for everyone to see: 'How Not to Cover News: Manufacture It.'"

"It's arguable that I caused it. It's more like it happened because the only security there was some Cobo personnel. No cops."

"The cops weren't there because the arena told them they wouldn't be needed until the pope makes his appearance."

"No bull! Even after what happened to Nancy Kerrigan, they didn't learn!?"

"That's one positive thing you're responsible for, Cox: Now they're going to put some uniforms on duty even before the pope arrives. Not many, but some. Most of the force is already allocated."

Kane leaned forward and fixed Cox with what, over the years, city roomers had come to call The Look. "As for you, Cox"—Kane enunciated deliberately—"I want you to take a goddam interest in what the pope's going to say and just why he's saying it here and now."

He sat back. "That's the story, and I want you to get it without causing any more saloon fights."

Cox nodded. "I'm on it. Late this afternoon a Cardinal . . ." He flipped through his notebook. ". . . yeah, here it is . . . Schinder—Cardinal Dietrich Schinder—is coming into Metro on Northwest."

"Schinder? Like the guy who saved the Jews?"

"That's Schindler. This is Schinder, no relation. This guy is numero secundo in the Vatican. German, from Cologne. They tell me he's been the pope's right-hand man—also hatchet man—for a bunch of years. I'll nail him the second he gets off the plane. And this is *exclusive*, Nellie."

"What's your source?" The question was mostly just curiosity.

Cox smiled. "A chancery secretary."

It never fails, thought Kane. Cox still had sources no one else could match. A good eight-tenths of them were female. Victims of Cox's charm that mostly attracted, occasionally repelled. Instinctively, Cox always knew who was which; he hardly ever wasted a bead of charm on anyone who would not succumb.

"What time's the plane due?"

"Schinder? Not till 5:00."

Kane nodded brusquely. "You'd better get your ass in gear."

Cox nodded and wordlessly returned to his desk, keyed his story to copyediting, picked up his coat and scarf, and headed out.

He left Nelson Kane wondering and just a whit worried.

During his absence from the Detroit and Chicago newspaper scenes, some traumatic things had happened to Joe Cox. Was he still the same gifted reporter he had been? Was his self-confidence as firm and true as Kane had known it once to be?

Already, Cox was getting into roiling waters. Worse, he was the one roiling those waters. Was he covering this story, or was he creating—steering—the story?

From all appearances, the latter seemed more likely.

Cox had taken a fairly meaningless event—a rehearsal for a symposium—and escalated some differences of opinion into a free-for-all.

He'd been the only reporter on the scene. His story was exclusive mostly because he had created the story. Was it possible that he was less interested in the story than he was in regaining the measure of fame he had once had?

So far, he had sparked a fight that was at the very least violent, and easily could have led to bloodshed or serious injury.

Kane found it disturbing that not only had Cox done this, but that it had seemingly been deliberate. Was he setting a pattern?

The bottom line was: How far would Cox go?

Kane had to admit, he wasn't sure.

21

She was busy. But no matter how occupied or preoccupied, she did not want to neglect Joe.

In fact, Pat Lennon was worried about him. So she returned his call.

He asked how her story on the nursing home scam was coming. She and Bob Ankenazy were just about ready to go with it, she told him. They couldn't hope to name every home that was ripping off its patients, but they had gathered enough to stir up the animals and get the reform machinery moving.

Cox did nothing to conceal his basic uninterest in the story. At the root of it, he lived for the present and, at most, the immediate future. He never adverted to that inevitable time when, if he lived long enough, he would grow old. That necessarily meant that he would no longer be young. And this, while not being beyond his imagination, was an eventuality he just never considered.

If he had given aging serious consideration, he would have had to acknowledge that, with his track record, he probably would end his life alone. No wife, no family, no one to care for him. Very likely he would be headed for a nursing home.

This certainly was not the case with Pat.

Like most women, Lennon was aware of and sensitive to changes that marked phases of life. Puberty rings no bells for boys. For them it is a state something akin to the demarcation of seasons. Gradually, one sees a change in sun patterns as the energy star seems to dip away from its position directly overhead. A subtle chill sets in and leaves turn color. Some time later, it is time for snow. But all these changes occur almost imperceptibly.

So it is with male puberty. The bodily and psychic development is a quiet evolution. Step by inexorable step changes take place and nature whispers its new powers and demands.

Menarche strikes young girls with the abruptness of a suddenly open wound. They may or may not have been prepared for menstruation. That doesn't matter: One day the periodic flow begins. And nature tells them that now, this moment, they may nurture life. And so series of phases begin and pass until menopause announces the end of that life-giving potential. Woman's life then may continue for many years. But the warning of a new transition has been delivered. No matter how many earthly years remain, the promulgation has been made: This life will end.

Men, however, at least theoretically, can—no matter what age they happen to be—sire children at any time.

It was easy for Pat Lennon, though still a young woman, to empathize with the broken bodies and spirits of the elderly. She, and her sisters, knew that old age was yet another phase to be faced and dealt with. She felt for the helpless elderly whose stories she recounted. At least some of those who unconscionably took advantage of the least of God's children would be exposed through the stories reported by Lennon and Bob Ankenazy.

Aware of Cox's disinterest, Lennon abbreviated the nursing home report. She was well aware that the reason he'd phoned originally was to bring her up to speed on *his* story.

He went over the morning program, including the part of the symposium directed to family planning. He knew she had read his published piece, but now left out no detail, including his role leading up to what he still would not admit any responsibility for, the fisticuffs.

She chose not to comment. She was certain that he was steering the story, manipulating it for its shock value. But he had not asked for her opinion. Time enough for her advice or suggestion when he was in a more receptive mood. Which clearly was not now.

Next he recounted his just-completed interview of Cardinal Dietrich Schinder. Unstated in his account of that meeting was an admission that the interview was not a categorical success.

"Did you have any problem recognizing him in that crowd?" Lennon asked.

Cox snorted. "Are you kidding?"

Lennon bridled. "Listen, I know what Metro is, especially around the holidays. It's wall-to-wall people. All I'm asking is how you were able to spot him in that crowd."

Cox realized his remark had been patronizing and he backed off a bit. "It wasn't so difficult picking him out. He's a tall guy; every inch aristocratic; with a full head of white-on-white hair; dressed all in black of course—no hat."

"Impressive," Lennon said. "No red? No red at all?"

Cox recollected. "Yeah, now that you mention it. There was a little splash of red in front, just under the roman collar. I don't think I would've noticed it—it was such a small bit—but it was an eye-popping red."

"That's the Cardinal color. It's the most brilliant red imaginable."

"While we're at minutiae, there was a chain of some kind—I could just see it across his chest under his coat."

"It holds a crucifix. Called a pectoral cross. Another sign that he's at least a bishop."

"Always good to talk to a Catholic."

"Glad to be of service. What did you get from him?"

"Not a lot. I was pretty much walking backward. He wouldn't stop. He kept right on walking. So the only way I could get to talk to him was to walk backward."

Lennon chuckled quietly. "I didn't know you could do that, Joe."

"Necessity is the mother of it all. Anyway, I was just trying to get him to commit on whether the pope was going to outlaw birth control infallibly. Hell, I couldn't even get him to admit the damn pope was even coming to Detroit!"

"The language of diplomacy, Joe."

"About all I could get out of him was history. He was willing to say that as far as he knew, that encyclical . . ."

"Humanae Vitae?"

"I guess. That is, according to Schinder, still in effect. That the only one on earth who could alter, suppress, or strengthen it is the pope. And that was it. He said whatever course the pope would take was entirely up to the pope—subject of course to the Almighty's passing the word along to His Holiness. And he hadn't the slightest idea which way the pope might move—if he would move at all. He used lots and lots of words, but basically that was about the extent of it. I think the guy could think of a million ways of saying 'No comment.'"

"So it was a washout?"

"Not totally. I did get a few usable quotes. Not much, but something. Actually, there's only one thing that keeps it from being a total washout."

"And that's . . . ?"

"Mine was an exclusive interview."

Lennon laughed. "What good's that if he didn't say anything worthwhile?"

"Some of the things he said *to me alone* would work in nicely in a story on him."

"Hmm?"

"You know . . . say, if something were to happen to Schinder. I might be the only reporter to have talked to him since he landed here. You know, something like the value of a painting multiplying after the painter dies."

"After the painter dies! What the hell are you talking about, Joe? Nothing's going to happen to Schinder . . . or do you have some info you're holding back?"

"Holding back? Nothing important. They're going to house him at the seminary . . . the, uh . . ." He didn't want to dig his notebook out just for a name.

"Sacred Heart Seminary," Lennon supplied.

"That's it."

"Kind of odd," Lennon observed.

"How's that?"

"Well, I'm not sure what kind of facilities they may have gotten since I last visited there, but most of the rooms are kind of primitive . . . at least by the standards I would suppose a Cardinal would be used to. Especially the number two man in the Vatican."

"Sacred Heart is what he said."

Pause.

"Joe . . . are you leveling with me?"

"What do you mean?"

"This talk about death . . . implying that the Cardinal might die and your interview might be worth more because you got an exclusive . . . What's that supposed to mean? Why should anything happen to the Cardinal?"

"Nothing *should* happen to the Cardinal. But you know as well as I do, anything can happen. I mean, he's going to stay in the heart of the city. And the heart of this city can be a pretty dangerous place. What the hell! You didn't think I was going to do something to Schinder?! Good God, Pat, I'm a reporter, not a hit man!"

Cox's laugh rang hollow to Lennon. "Joe, it's still early. You want to meet for dinner?"

Pause for several long moments. "I . . . I don't think so. Geez! No . . . no, I can't. Not tonight. There's some stuff I gotta get done. Maybe tomorrow. Can I have a rain check?"

"Sure, Joe. A rain check. See ya."

She hung up and wondered and worried.

Somehow, Joe Cox did not seem to be the same person she had once known—known very well.

Something had changed. Joe had never treated a story so cavalierly. Now he gave every indication that he was steering, manipulating.

How far would he go? What might he do?

She wondered and she worried.

22

He had been chauffeured back to the seminary in a limo. A nice touch. "Nothing's too good for Father."

Never before had he impersonated a priest. He had studied the mannerisms of this singular way of life just as he had steeped himself in what was supposed to be his field of religious expertise. He was confident that he was carrying this masquerade forward successfully.

Everyone he had associated with so far this day had been cordial, with that special courtesy extended to a fellow professional.

But this symposium was no more than a distraction. Necessary, but a distraction nonetheless.

Now, alone in his room, he lay, fully clothed, on the bed, hoping for the merciful release of a nap. As these days progressed, he would need to call on his every reserve of alertness, caution, aggressiveness, drive, dedication, and, yes, luck.

It would be good if he were to be able to utilize every opportunity for some much-needed rest. But if it was not to be, well, so be it.

He had been in training for this task for a long time now. And he had planned most meticulously as well as precisely. He had only to carry out these plans and the deed would be done.

But it was similar to dying: One got only one chance to do it. So it was of greatest importance that he extend his every effort to the maximum. How did they put it in sports terms over here? Oh, yeah: "He came to play!" "He gave 120 percent!"

Not a bad way of describing what lay ahead.

So he would rest until it was time to at least put in an appearance at dinner.

Meanwhile, he would go through the mental checklist again and again.

He would have only this one opportunity. It had to be perfect. He could not countenance failure. Not now. Not after having come so far.

So near.

No. He could not fail.

*   *   *   *

Being selected as music director for that most rare papal appearance was, as David Wallace was discovering, not an unmixed blessing.

For one, there was the rehearsal schedule. The earliest they could get to it was late afternoon. Most of the choir members were working people. And, as rare as this papal event certainly was, there was the economy to keep in mind. And how far from the mind could the economy stray at the height of the Christmas season?

For example, toy stores and toy departments faced almost a singular challenge: how to keep the inventory up. And if one could guess what item was going to be *the* blockbuster toy, game, or doll of the season—and should that person somehow corner a market for said item—he or she could almost retire.

Independent toy stores had to make it big at Christmas. It was a long time between Christmases, and some part of this revenue had to tide the stores over.

And so it was with so many businesses and financial enterprises.

The marketing of Christmas began earlier almost every year. But all that packaging came to term as the day itself arrived. This was the season to be jolly. And, as much as the choir saw the need for perfection as part of a liturgy celebrated by the supreme pontiff, a liturgy to be telecast internationally, business was business.

Wallace had to keep reminding himself that his choir was a volunteer group. They were not hired to sing. Those who were employed were attorneys, sales personnel, architects, and so on. Others made care of house and children full-time work.

Some of the musicians were professionals, and the difference between them and the unpaid was telling. Beyond their superior abilities, the pros needed but a raised baton to ready their instruments. Making music was their work, and they were professionally serious about it.

For the others, while they enjoyed singing and playing, doing this was a sideline. It was a difficult challenge to keep them concentrated on the business at hand.

Further, it was a convivial setting. Many of these people had not seen each other since the previous visit of the pope, and some of them felt the need to clear up missing history. So, as they wandered into rehearsal there was a good amount of chatter.

They're volunteers! They're volunteers! Wallace kept telling himself. The sotto voce repetition helped. The director smiled as frequently as he could make himself do so. It also helped him hold his temper—no mean trick at this stage of the affair.

In addition to the present and predictable problems, there was the matter of the program. In large part, Wallace had no idea what music would be performed. That determination was supposed to emanate from the liturgical panel of the symposium. That discussion wasn't scheduled until tomorrow. And tomorrow would be one scant day before the pope's arrival.

For this abbreviated rehearsal, Wallace had complementary aims: to get these performers used to one another and to establish himself as the leader. To do this, he decided to rehearse *something.* It wasn't necessary that the music practiced actually be used in the papal liturgy, only that they become accustomed to their unique *sound.*

Mainly because almost the entire contingent of musicians was present, he decided to run through a playing of Copland's "Fanfare for the Common Man." As Wallace had hoped, the pros pulled the amateurs along. All in all, it was close to an inspired rendition. About the only evident flaw was the continued merry, mirthful light chatter from the singers.

They're volunteers! They're volunteers!

He held both tongue and temper.

As the orchestra concluded the "Fanfare," another singer arrived.

Sally Forbes had a crush on David Wallace. Just about everyone who knew them knew that. About the only one who hadn't yet tumbled was David Wallace. He had many private and secret concerns. He gave little or no heed to interpersonal relationships, let alone a love affair.

Once Sally had parked her packages, bundles, and outer wear, she casually approached Wallace. He had nothing specifically planned for the next few minutes. As soon as a few more essential members of the choir showed up, he would run them through a hymn and/or a motet or two. So he didn't mind Sally's interruption.

"Any word yet from the liturgical panel?" she asked.

Setting his jaw, Wallace shook his head.

"How do they expect us to perform if we don't know what the program will call for?" Sally persisted.

"We've got enough of a core group of good performers that we should be able to handle whatever they throw at us." Wallace smiled. "But I must admit this is pretty nerve-racking."

Sally directed at him a Nancy Reagan look of adoration. "The only reason we're any good at all is because we've got all this confidence in you."

Had he taken her seriously, he would've been embarrassed. As it was, he merely shrugged and began to arrange the music on his stand.

Sally switched her weight to the other foot. "What do you think, David: Is the pope going to do what everybody's been talking about?"

"Introduce infallibility into the family planning debate? Beats me. We're just here to render the liturgy as best we can."

"What do you think will happen if he does?" she pressed.

A slight shudder passed through David Wallace. "I don't really know. I don't even want to think of it."

Sally looked around the vast arena. The main floor was empty save for the maintenance people who ranged among the seats in a final cleaning effort.

Almost absently she walked slowly toward the newly constructed altar. The altar that had been used for the previous papal visit had been used at the Silverdome in Pontiac. In any case, the original altar had been destroyed shortly thereafter. No one had envisioned a repeat papal visit to Detroit so soon.

Wallace looked up from his music to see Sally standing at the impressive raised pulpit from which the pope would address the crowd. Wallace had lost track of her as he concentrated on which selections he would use as a warmup. "Sally! What do you think you're doing?"

She looked over at him, smiling. "Come on over here, David. It's quite a sight. It's the same view the pope's going to have."

"Get back here!" He couldn't really be angry with her. He admired her buoyant youth and spirit of adventure.

"No, come on, silly," she urged. "Just for a minute."

At that moment there wasn't anything going on. Nor would there be till the rest of the choir arrived. For now, those present were chatting among themselves or simply drinking in the far reaches of this immense arena. So he followed in Sally's tracks.

He found himself counting his steps. Fifteen strides from his podium to the pope's pulpit. A short distance indeed. Others might be awed at the proximity to so famous a personage. His thoughts were on how accessible the man would be—the man who, if the rumors were true, would make a mockery of Abigail's sacrifice. It was this old, tattered doctrine sharply limiting the means of family planning that had led to her death.

Fifteen strides.

Wallace didn't own a gun. He'd never fired one. He did own a knife. He'd checked: It fit snugly in his baton case.

Fifteen strides and he could cut down this pompous prelate before the man could enshrine this dangerous, deadly "moral" teaching in the powerful cloak of infallibility.

Wallace didn't want to do it. God knew he shrank from the notion. He had prayed that it would not come to this. But, to date, there was no assurance whatever from Rome that the scuttlebutt wasn't true. And, so far, there was no indication that anyone intended to challenge the man.

Of course, the pope was not standing at this pulpit yet. Maybe something would happen, maybe somebody would do something. . . . Maybe David Wallace would not be the one last hope. His prime prayer was that this responsibility would not be his. But if it was . . . if it was . . .

He had never killed anyone or anything. He didn't actually know if the dread moment arrived what he would do, how he would react.

One thing was for certain: If he attempted this murder, he would forfeit his own life. His proximity to the pope would make the deed possible. He was in the inner circle. That was where all the security was gathered—

"Are you going to stand there all night?"

"No . . . no. The view is mesmerizing, isn't it?"

"Sure is."

Wallace, now fully returned to the present, looked back at his choir and musicians. Most of them were smiling as they studied the one-and-a-half lovebirds.

"Come on," he said, "we've got enough to have a decent rehearsal. Let's get on with it."

They walked, not hand in hand, back to the stage.

"I was just thinking, David," Sally said, "do you have anything on for this evening?"

"What?"

"I mean, I'm not doing anything. And it's awful close to Christmas to be alone. I thought maybe you could come over to my place. I can whip up a pretty decent dinner if you don't mind a sort of vegetarian meal."

Wallace hesitated as he continued walking. "I . . . "

"Please. It would make me very happy."

His smile was a shrug. "Seven?"

"That would be great."

Sally settled into her chair and fiddled with the music stand.

The other choir members continued to smile. All the world loves a lover . . . especially at Christmastime.

"Let's try the *Panis Angelicus*," Wallace said. "It's a fairly safe guess to be included in the program." He smiled. "Anyway, it'll get us started."

He raised the baton. This would be *a capella*. The musicians rested. The choir members were slow in readiness.

They're volunteers! They're volunteers!

Actually, once they began, they sounded quite good.

Finding it unnecessary to concentrate on this most familiar hymn, Wallace's thoughts drifted toward an evening with Sally Forbes.

Just what the doctor ordered, he thought. Left to his own devices this evening, he would only torture himself over and over again.

Could he do the deed? Would he do the deed, if push came to shove? Was he willing to put his life on the line?

Only the moment of truth, if it should arise, would tell.

For now, it would be good to take his mind as far from these questions as possible.

An evening with Sally. Yes, just what the doctor ordered.

23

"I can't believe it!" Leo said.

"You better believe it. Wanna hear it again?" Rick flipped on the radio. It was tuned to WWJ-AM, the all-news station. As luck would have it, reporter Ed Breslin was narrating once more what had become the day's top story: A couple—at most a small group—of young people were rampaging through the Metro area causing injury and death in seemingly random fashion.

Sunday night it was a suburban socialite, gang-raped and shot to death execution-style. Monday morning, it was a Detroit priest who was fortunate to escape with his life in a hit-and-run incident. Shortly thereafter, it was the proprietor of a convenience store—shot and killed without provocation.

Police were certain, from physical evidence, that more than two males had participated in the rape. Eyewitnesses to the other two crimes agreed that there were only two, again probably young people, involved. Police state that the vehicle used in each of these crimes may have been a black, late-model Jaguar with a damaged front grill. Anyone with any knowledge of . . .

"Believe it now?" Rick's face glowed with uninhibited glee.

The others shook their heads in uncomprehending belief.

"But why?" John inquired.

"Bonnie . . . hell, Bonnie *and* me needed the practice. Sunday night Ronnie had all the fun. We had to catch up."

"Well . . . what about the rest of us?" Leo said. "We haven't got any-body!"

"Too late for that," Rick said. "Besides, things are getting too hot for us to fool around. The cops are looking for us. And they're getting close—too close. For one thing, we can't use the Jag anymore."

"How about if we get the front fixed?" John said.

"By who?" Rick replied. "Every dealer and bump shop in and out the area is lookin' for a black Jag with a busted grill. Tell ya what," Rick challenged, "I'll take the Jag into a bump shop if one of you guys pick it up with the front fixed and a couple carloads of cops waitin' for us." He waited a moment, but none of the four took him up on that.

"So," he continued, "anybody got another set of wheels till this blows over? If it ever blows over?"

The others seemed lost in searching thought.

"How about you, Harpo? Haven't you got a jalopy?"

"Well . . . yeah," Andrew reluctantly admitted. "But it ain't anything you guys would ride around in. It's just a bucket a bolts."

"It runs, doesn't it?"

"Yeah, it runs, okay. But it looks like hell."

"Just what we want. The last thing the cops'll be lookin' for will be a heap like that. If you can tool with a Jag, who's gonna ride in a jalopy?"

"Sounds good to me!" Ronnie said.

Throughout this conversation, no one paid any attention to Bonnie, who crouched in a corner of the Vanderwehl rec room. Tears coursed her cheeks in unrestrained abundance. Her body was shaking uncontrollably. She said nothing and nothing was said to her. She might as well have been elsewhere—anywhere. Bonnie was in mild shock. None of the boys cared. She could have been a tragic ornament.

"So it's settled: We use Harpo's jalopy." Rick looked around for the expected unanimous approval.

He got it from everyone except Ronnie. "Before we risk our lives in this rattletrap, does anybody know if we can depend on it?"

"Yeah, right." Without Ronnie's expressed doubt, John never would have come up with a question on his own. "So the cops won't be looking for innocent lookin' kids like us in Harpo's boneyard. What the hell good is that if our getaway car can't get away?"

Rick froze them with a single glare. Thus they knew their objection—any objection—was thoroughly out of place. Then Rick mellowed. "Come on, you guys know better than anybody what a good mechanic Harpo is. He can fix anything. Who do we all go to when something's busted?" The question hung rhetorically. "If Harpo says the crate runs, the crate runs . . . no?"

After a moment, Leo spoke. "Okay. While you and Bonnie were makin' your own crime wave, we were checking through your plan. We cased the grounds back of that seminary. We walked it all through. We're ready to go. So, when do we go?"

"*When do we go? When do we go?*" Rick spoke in mocking imitation. "We don't go until we take care of one more bit of business." He was about to tell them when it occurred to him to put it in the form of a quiz. "Anybody know what has to happen?"

Bonnie knew. But Bonnie wasn't talking to anybody.

"Wait," Ronnie said, "we got to . . . oh, yeah . . . we got to get the cops to loosen the knot."

"What?" Leo looked bewildered.

"Ronnie's right," Rick said. "Right now, the cops'll be mainly concerned with security for the pope. They'll be tight in on him. We can't get a clear and sure shot unless we go close. So we gotta do something that'll make them have to protect a wider circle of people. That way there'll be more holes in their protection screen.

"That's what comes next."

"Uh . . ." Leo jerked his thumb in the general direction of Bonnie. "What about her?"

For the first time in a long while the boys became aware of Bonnie.

"Gimme a few minutes." Rick walked back to Bonnie's corner of the room. The others gathered around the pool table, occupying themselves with offhand talk, or fooling with the billiard balls. None of them attempted to listen in.

"Hey, babe, come out of it, willya?" Rick said softly.

Bonnie just looked at him. In her eyes was an emotion he'd never seen before.

"What is it? What's the matter? Take your time. But talk to me. C'mon now." He rubbed his hand along her arm. But she shrank from him. She tried to talk, but her teeth were chattering.

Rick had been playing off an emotional high. Now for the first time he experienced fear. The fear was about Bonnie and, if she did not pull out of this, what he might have to do.

If she came totally unglued, she might feel compelled—an inner compulsion—to rat. He couldn't sacrifice the guys. What a dilemma! Before he would let her harm him or his friends . . . well, the only way he might be able to stop her would be . . .

But he loved Bonnie! How could he kill the one he loved? He tried to recall: There'd been something about that in school. He had almost been paying attention. For some reason, the words had stuck. What were they? Something about . . . you always hurt the thing you love, something like that.

So somebody before him had had to think about the necessity of killing a loved one.

Somehow the idea was not as threatening once he realized he was not alone in thinking such a terrible thought.

He continued to stroke her arm. She stopped pulling away. That was a good sign. "Babe," he said softly, "babe, say something. You're scaring me. C'mon, what is it?"

"Honey . . ." At last she spoke. ". . . you . . . you killed that old guy. You killed him. Why'd you do that?"

"Is that all it is?" Rick's relief was obvious. "Hell, he kept his hand in the register. You saw him. Or maybe 'cause you stayed back by the door, maybe you didn't see it. He wouldn't take his hand outta the goddam till. He probably had a gun in there. You didn't want him to get a shot off at me! At us! You didn't, did you!"

She seemed a bit calmer. "N . . . no. No."

"Well?"

"You sure he had a gun in there?"

Rick snorted. "I coulda asked him. 'Excuse me, sir, but do you happen to have a gun in that register? And do you intend to shoot me and my loving companion?'"

She smiled nervously.

"I don't know for sure. How could I know for sure? All I know is he wouldn't take his hand out of the till so I could see his hands were empty. If he had raised his hands so I could see he didn't have anything, he'd be eating ice cream now and telling his friends all about the exciting armed robbery he *lived* through. But . . . as it is . . ."

Once again Rick tortured his rationalization to blame the victim for his own death.

But once again it seemed to be working. "You gonna be okay, babe?"

"Yes. I think so. But, honey, do I have to . . . you know . . . with the pope?"

Rick grimaced. He had very definitely planned on her being with them all the way. What other reason could he possibly have had in taking her with him on their dangerous crime spree? But now, clearly, it was not to be. He could not possibly depend on her in an attack on the pope. "No, babe, you don't have to do it. You sit this one out. Tell you what: I'll bring you the pope's head complete with white beanie."

The image sickened her. But she managed a smile.

"Why don't you sack out for a while? You look like you could use it. We'll get busy with our plans."

Gratefully, she stretched out. Though she couldn't imagine herself napping, let alone sleeping.

Rick returned to the Golds. He was glad he did not need to kill Bonnie. Because now he knew he could if he had to.

Zoo Tully was following developments very carefully.

The link between the three crimes was tenuous at best. The three events shared only one element—a black, late-model Jaguar with a busted grill. The perpetrators were young people, but that was little to go on. Youth in this town had their own considerable corner on crime.

But Tully had a gut feeling. And, with all his experience, he had learned to trust such feelings.

Tully had reconstructed the events thusly:

Sunday night some kids were out cruising, looking for thrills. There were several boys—different specimens of sperm were found on the woman. There may have been some girls also involved, cheering on their boyfriends—maybe masturbating them as they raped the woman. That was no flight of fancy; it was, indeed, a not unusual occurrence.

Tully didn't know why they had killed the woman, but if he had to guess—and he did—he assumed it was because they were afraid she might identify them later.

From the condition of the woman's car, the damage to her rear bumper, it looked to be a bump-and-attack scenario. So the perp's car likely was damaged—a broken grill?

The following morning, a deliberate hit-and-run—on Father Koesler, of all people. What a coincidence—if it was a coincidence. The best description of the car: a late-model black Jaguar with a damaged grill.

In the car, two young people, male and female. Two of Sunday night's group? Fantastic luck! With all those cops in that area of downtown, no police presence on that corner at that moment. Eyewitnesses, as usual, few and far between. No solid description of either occupant. And no one coming up with even a partial make on the license. Luck! Luck! Luck!

Just minutes later: armed robbery at a small convenience store. Proprietor shot and killed, seemingly for no reason. Perpetrators masked, but identified by terrified customers as young man and young woman from voice and demeanor. Once again, black, late-model Jaguar with crippled grill.

Luck holding.

That just may be their undoing, thought Tully. By this time they may be counting heavily on that run of luck.

None of the three crimes appeared to be planned, carefully or not. They were running on luck. Nobody could do that forever. They'd be back. Tully vowed he'd be ready for them.

While he was thinking this through and making notes, Sergeant Angie Moore entered the squad room and sat at her desk, which abutted Tully's. "You're thinking about those kids and their Jaguar, aren't you?"

Tully wasn't surprised. He'd grown used to her reliable intuition. He nodded.

"They're just achin' to park it for life in the slammer."

"We gotta bring 'em in," he said quietly.

"I keep thinking of that poor woman," Moore said. "What a horrible way to go! Humiliated to the dregs, then scared out of her wits, then a gun in her mouth. I mean, everything else they've done is bad enough, but . . ."

"Yeah, 'but.' I keep thinking, it could've been Anne Marie."

"She went through something like this, didn't she?"

"Uh-huh."

"I don't blame you for wanting them bad, Zoo. We'll get 'em."

"Uh-huh. Damn right!"

24

It was a command performance. Decreed by Dietrich Cardinal Schinder.

Schinder, in his late sixties, had been a very young man during Adolph Hitler's Third Reich. He had been conscripted into the German army. He never became a member of the Nazi party. He was in the Wehrmacht, the regular army. So he had no part in the monstrosities perpetuated by the Nazi high command. He participated neither in the Holocaust nor the execution of innocent civilians or enemy prisoners.

He was just a functioning soldier, but not for long. He was captured early. Fortunately for him, he was taken prisoner by U.S. forces and, as a bright young man, subsequently held a series of trustee jobs.

After the war, and once Germany began to recapture its peacetime purpose, Schinder entered the seminary, where he was evaluated as bright, talented, ambitious, and possessed of a piety that never got in the way of promotion.

He studied in Rome and, after ordination, became chancellor of the archdiocese of Cologne. His rise was rapid: auxiliary bishop of Cologne, then archbishop of Berlin, then Cardinal archbishop of Berlin. Before long, he was called to the Vatican, where he became a most trusted *eminence rouge*.

On a papal trip such as this one to Detroit, his was the ultimate responsibility for all things working as planned.

However, all things very definitely were not going as planned. The prime problem lay in this symposium, which was supposed to function as a natural segue to the pope's visit and his message. This symposium gave no indication that it was rigged. And it should have been. Something had gone wrong. Honest dissent was alive and well. It was supposed to be absent. Or at least that had been the plan.

It was Tuesday evening. The command performance was being held at the Lark, arguably the finest dining establishment in the metro Detroit area. Partly because their reservation had been logged in time and partly because the owners were Catholic, Cardinal Schinder had a private room for his ten "guests."

The clergymen had dined extremely well. The meal was now over; dessert had been downed and liqueurs served. An attentive Mary Lark had seen to it that the notables had signed her guestbook. Now the Cardinal was determined to get things straightened away for the pope.

The Cardinal tapped his glass with a spoon. Immediately silence reigned. Only the muted sounds of diners in other rooms could be heard. Even before Schinder had called for attention, there had been little conversation. While most of these priests had heard of each other, few of them had ever met.

Present besides Schinder were the conservative participants of each of the major panels of the symposium. Representing dogma was Father John Selner, S.S.; moral, William Palmer; canon law, Stanley Moser.

Also in attendance were the six moderators, including Father Koesler; and finally, representing the organizer, Monsignor Martin, was Father Paul Smith, who had eaten almost none of the excellent dinner. Nerves? Father Koesler wondered.

Conspicuous by their absence were the conservative spokesmen of the nonvital panels, and, of course, all of the liberal panelists.

Cardinal Schinder rose, very slowly. Since he was tall and he pulled himself erect so deliberately, it seemed he would just go on rising forever. It was the impression he wished to create.

Schinder was an imposing figure with his perfectly pressed black silk suit, the white-on-white clerical collar with its Cardinal red patch, his pale-to-the-point-of-colorless complexion, the white hair and eyebrows, the lips that seemed created to embrace an umlaut, and the dark eyes that penetrated all upon whom they fell.

"Gentlemen," the Cardinal intoned, "I need not dwell on what is my prime concern. Obviously, this symposium, particularly the way it is shaping up, is not, I repeat, *not* doing the job for which it was programmed."

Schinder's voice was deep. His English was perfect, with just the hint of a German accent. Clearly, any suggestion he might make would emerge as a command.

His listeners sat perfectly still. His opening statement required no response and none was offered.

"It is my understanding that the one in charge of organizing the symposium—particularly the one who invited the panelists—is not here this evening. Is that correct?"

There was a lingering silence before Father Paul Smith replied, "Yes, that is correct, Your Eminence."

"And you are . . . ?" It was impossible to ascertain the Cardinal's mood. He might have a solicitous thought for the missing monsignor. Or he might be contemplating sending Martin to the guillotine.

"I am Father Paul Smith."

"Oh, yes. I understand you assisted Monsignor Martin in setting up this symposium."

"Yes, I did, Eminence."

Schinder studied the floor.

It was a safe guess that he really wanted Martin and that he wasn't precisely sure of what to do with Smith. There was precious little he could do by way of punishing a retired priest. Organizing—or misorganizing—a symposium did not fall under any canonical law.

Over the centuries the Church had devised three basic forms of punishment aimed at getting her sons and daughters to do what the Church wanted them to do.

There was interdict, which affected a specific geographic or political region and denied sacraments to everyone in that district until the rulers or leaders of that area either did what they should or stopped doing what they shouldn't do. The reasoning harbored the hope that the residents of the district would so long for a return of the sacraments that they would force their leader to submit to Mother Church. It was not unlike what George Bush hoped would happen in Iraq. Since the Gulf War did not flush Hussein, Bush hoped the people would rise up and topple his regime. That didn't work nearly as well as interdict sometimes did.

Excommunication is a punishment that may entail a "shunning"— wherein the miscreant is isolated and virtually abandoned. Or it may be a penalty attached to a sin such as abortion, the forgiveness of which is reserved to someone higher than a simple priest—a bishop or a pope.

The object is to impress the "sinner" that this sin is so heinous that it cannot be forgiven in an ordinary confession to a priest. Eventually, of course, the person does go to a priest, since it is a matter of speculation whether bishops remember the formula for absolution. But it does impressively complicate matters.

Then there is suspension. This affects priests only, and the punishment is that the priest may not celebrate any sacraments while the penalty of suspension is in effect.

To attempt to suspend Paul Smith would be a bit redundant. He was retired, so he had no ordinary priestly duties. He had every Catholic's duty to attend Mass on Sundays and Holy Days, but he had no obligation of any sort to celebrate Mass, hear confessions, and so on. So for him suspension would be little more than an enforced vacation.

Indeed, there was not all that much Schinder could do to Monsignor Martin either.

Martin "belonged" to the archdiocese of Detroit. As such, he was the prime responsibility of Mark Cardinal Boyle. How far a Vatican functionary could go in meddling in diocesan affairs is, largely, unexplored territory. An earlier attempt to subdivide the authority and powers of Spokane's Archbishop Hunthausen concluded in messy failure.

Schinder and Boyle, as Cardinals, were prelates of equal rank whose unique function was to elect popes. As an archbishop and a Cardinal, Boyle presumably would answer to the pope alone. And the pope, of course, as far as ecclesial affairs were concerned, could do whatever he wanted.

Nonetheless, these were tricky waters.

For the moment, Schinder was in a bit of a bind. Disciplining Father Smith would serve only to highlight the Vatican's displeasure with the symposium. Penalizing Monsignor Martin, besides incurring the identical bad press for the symposium, would set up an awkward collision with the priest's local superior.

The obvious tack would be to seek Cardinal Boyle's cooperation. However, all the players in this power struggle knew what was going on. The pope sought to tweak Boyle for his intervention during the Council. Boyle, in his turn, was making the pope's mission difficult by giving free rein to Martin and Smith in their effort to make this an honest conference.

Clearly, Schinder would be more than able to block any further advancement for Martin, who would remain a mere monsignor into eternity.

But that was the future, and this was the painful present.

After weighing all these factors, Cardinal Schinder looked up and across the table at an attentive Father Smith. "Father Smith, this is the eleventh hour for the symposium. I would have thought Monsignor Martin would have cleared his calendar of whatever impediment to attending this meeting."

After a moment's consideration, Smith replied, in an ambiguous tone, "So would I."

Several present stifled an urge to laugh.

Schinder's cheeks gave indication there was blood beneath their pale exterior. "You will see him," Schinder said to Smith. Again, it was not a suggestion.

"Yes, Eminence."

"Then please tell him that I wish to see him before this symposium is concluded."

"I will tell him, Your Eminence."

"Good. Then, Father Smith, you are excused."

Even though he had eaten next to nothing, Smith felt he should express his gratitude for an invitation to a restaurant that he never could have afforded. But, staring at the Cardinal's fiery cheeks, he thought better of it. With no further remark, Smith left the room, gathered his hat and coat and departed. When he reached the isolation of his car, he laughed aloud.

The Cardinal's next words were for the six moderators. He noted that while the secular media very probably would give little coverage to the symposium's proceedings, the symposium would be carefully watched in and by Rome.

Without being overly specific, he implied that all the priest moderators were well aware of the "official" position of the Church in all the matters that would be discussed. He pointed out that these six priests as moderators would be well within their function to shift the balance of argumentation toward official and orthodox Church teachings.

If the moderators were to be conscientious in this role, the Church surely would record this effort and, sooner than later, reward it.

Koesler was disgusted that a responsible and distinguished churchman would stoop to not-so-subtle bribery.

He understood that many of the other priest moderators felt a like revulsion. But he said nothing. Of course he intended to conduct his panel discussion fairly. The Church had given him his priesthood; as far as he was concerned, there was nothing more to give or to receive.

The moderators were dismissed. They left without delay, saying nothing to each other. Koesler took this silence as a sign of embarrassment on the part of these men. He was proud of them.

Having concluded the meeting for the others, Schinder now spoke words of encouragement to the last remaining group—Fathers Selner, Palmer, and Moser, the panelists for dogma, morals, and canon law respectively. Schinder knew the weaknesses in the official Church position in those fields; he had further arguments that could help officialdom.

Having done all he could to shore up a bad turn of events, Schinder invited the remaining priests to share with him a nightcap. Selner, Palmer, and Moser pleaded exhaustion and, excusing themselves, left the Cardinal to drink up and pay up.

The Cardinal's lone consolation in this botched affair was that, in picking up the pieces, he was doing God's Holy Will.

Dave Wallace was not asleep. He hadn't fallen asleep at all.

He had arrived at Sally Forbes's apartment precisely on time. Being on time was one of his compulsions.

He'd brought some wine. It had been so long since he'd been invited to a woman's apartment he wasn't sure what to bring as a gift or, indeed, if any gift was expected.

Sally's social life in many ways mirrored his. Asked, she would have no answer as to the propriety of a gift. But she accepted the wine graciously.

At first their conversation was stilted, marked by long and awkward silences. In attempts to fill the dead air, each was guilty of inane attempts to find a fruitful topic.

Finally, they stumbled onto the obvious common denominator—music, specifically Church music. She loved it and dabbled in it. He was an expert. She had a spinet. After their meal, she asked him to play it. He was pleased that it was in tune and that all the keys worked.

She sat next to him on the small bench. He inhaled her delicate perfume.

After he finished playing, she turned on the CD player. Show tunes mostly, then ballads from Broadway shows.

They sat together on the couch. After a while, they held hands. They leaned closer. They kissed.

Nothing happened hastily. But slowly, as if carried by an alien force, they drifted into a quiet passion. He picked her up in his arms. It was as if she had no weight at all.

Very slowly, and with genuine affection, they made love. Sally was so relaxed that in a very short time she fell asleep.

This left him alone to think.

Had he blundered in his lengthy and encompassing grief for his late wife? He had shut himself away from any personal involvement, at least at any intimate level.

He too was so relaxed. He could hear—could feel—Sally's deep, regular breathing in a quiet slumber.

Easily, this could be his life now. It could have been his life for many years. He had set up the barrier.

He thought of all the women who had passed through and around his life. He was a fool—wasn't he?—not to have been sensitive to these good women and their honest interest in him.

He thought of Sally. He had been blind. As he remembered her special attention to him, he recalled the knowing smiles of others in his choir. Everybody knew. Everybody but him knew that Sally was his for the asking.

Tonight he had asked. Tonight she had given.

Why couldn't he build on this?

The question answered itself. All of his fearful emotions that revolved around his wife's death. He could not build a new life with Sally or any other woman.

He had not buried his wife.

Abigail—the martyr to a hierarchy's stubbornness. A pope had offered them a choice between a sterile, unnatural relationship and a dangerous and losing game of Vatican roulette.

A pope—any pope—could end this lunacy any time any one of them put a pen to paper. None of them did. None of them would.

One would pay for this unscrupulous malfeasance. This pope would pay before he had the opportunity to raise the stakes.

If this decision to block the pope eventually devolved upon him, so be it. He would not shrink from his responsibility.

He thought of how close he would be to the pope. He remembered pacing off the distance between his podium and the pope's pulpit. He could make it. Particularly if the security guards were induced somehow to back away from a tight encirclement.

There was a way.

Gently, carefully, he slid his arm from beneath Sally's head. Quietly, he dressed. Without disturbing her in any way, he let himself out of the apartment.

The night was dark. His breath was visible as he cursed the pope.

PART THREE

25

Seventy years ago, Bishop Michael J. Gallagher supervised the building of Sacred Heart Seminary on what were then vacant fields on the outskirts of Detroit. Today the area lies in the heart of the central city. It is bordered by Chicago Boulevard, Joy Road, Linwood, and Lawton. In 1967 it marked the northwest border of a deadly and costly riot that saw the mobilization of the National Guard and, eventually, the summoning of U.S. Army troops.

Tonight the building was quiet. Or, as quiet as old buildings get. Over the years, buildings stretch and sag and shift and speak their special and unique language. So it was tonight, with no sounds but the squeaks and moans of wood and brick.

The current crop of students, those few who lost themselves in buildings meant to house hundreds more young men, were out on Christmas break. Only caretaker personnel, security guards, and those in the entourage of the papal visitation now inhabited the vast, otherwise-empty corridors and rooms.

Clarence McAdoo, one of the security guards, walked his isolated rounds as he had so many times in the past. What made this evening different from all others was his nervousness.

Though he could not deny he felt jumpy, he would argue that it wasn't his fault; it was all this talk by everyone else.

At meals taken together, almost everyone on the staff exchanged rumors and gossip about the coming papal visit. Why was everyone taking on so? McAdoo had been around long enough to remember the previous papal visit. There was beefed-up security then, sure; that was only natural. Nor was it unique. Presidents and foreign leaders had been here. Always they drew huge crowds. They got plenty of security. That was expected.

And who could forget John Kennedy? Even with all that security, somebody reached him.

As McAdoo knew, and tried to convince the others, a pope is a chief of state—even if it is the smallest state in the world. So he automatically falls heir to all the protection the federal, state, county, and city agencies can provide.

But that's where the comparison ended. True, there was that incident in St. Peter's Square when the pope took a bullet. But that was, in modern times at least, unique. McAdoo was certain that the security that was trotted out for the pope was a mere formality. There wasn't going to be any trouble.

Then came all those worrywarts. According to them, this papal trip was not going to be any showcase wherein the pontiff would mouth pious platitudes—war was evil, so was abortion, so was premarital sex, so was euthanasia, so was divorce, and so on.

This time, according to them, he had a message that would have an effect on world population and definitely wasn't intended to hold down its growth. A message that would trouble the consciences of the world's Catholics.

This time there would be people disturbed enough that there well could be violence. And anybody—innocent bystanders, or, more likely, security personnel—could be in harm's way.

If there had been only one or two people acting like nervous Nellies, that would be one thing. But just about everyone had a rumor or slice of gossip that contributed to this doomsday feeling.

So, as he walked his dark and scary rounds listening to the familiar, but now foreboding, sounds of unease and ponderous movement, McAdoo's senses were overly acute.

Ordinarily he never called for or wanted company on his late-night rounds. Normally he liked being on his own, alone. Tonight he would have welcomed another presence. He wanted to talk. Right now, he felt, if only he could express his fears and misgivings to someone—anyone—they would go away.

Anyone would do—except that creep last night who wanted to know all about the routines and then gave him gratuitous hell over the security provided. McAdoo could survive without that guy.

He checked his watch. Almost midnight. Right on time for a tour of the building's second story, southeast corner. Take that, creep!

As he opened the door to the staircase, he knew something was wrong. He didn't know how he knew. He hadn't yet seen anything untoward. Was it an odor? Something!

He swung his powerful flashlight in a wide arc. Then he saw it. A body. Lying in a corner at the base of the staircase's first landing.

For an instant he thought it was last night's critic; how serendipitous that the priest would be rescued by the security about which he had complained so much.

But as he hurried down the steps, he knew it was not yesterday's busybody. Nor could anyone, security person or otherwise, be of any help.

The man appeared to be dead. McAdoo found no pulse. He shone his light first on the victim, then on the staircase.

There was supposed to be a light on at the top of this staircase. It was not lit. Probably burned out. By the shape the body was in, the man must've missed the first step in the darkness and hit just about every railing and stair on the way down.

McAdoo hurried to call the police. As he ran down the remaining stairs to the nearest phone, the thought occurred that at least this was an accident.

It would not be further fuel for the rumormongers.

At least it was an accident.

For thirty-some years they had lived with the phone. That was the principal reason Wanda Koznicki so valued their occasional vacation. If they were out of town, preferably out of the country, they were beyond the ordinary reach of the phone.

But now, as was true most of the time, they were not out of town. They were home. It was almost Christmas. And the phone was ringing.

Walter Koznicki had been asleep on his side facing the phone in their bedroom. On the first ring he snatched it up. He waited a moment to adjust to the real world, then he spoke, as quietly as possible, trying not to rouse his wife, although he knew she was awake.

He mumbled and listened for some time, then hung up. He did not need to turn on a light to get dressed. His long-standing habit was to place his clothes where he could reach and slip into them in the darkness.

All these were useless precautions in his attempts not to disturb Wanda. She never missed hearing the phone ring. His efforts were pro forma but he followed the routine faithfully. If nothing else, it made him feel better.

Wanda propped herself on one elbow. "What is it?" Her eyes were accustomed to the dark, yet she could barely see her husband.

"Trouble at the seminary." He stepped into his trousers.

"Someone hurt? At the seminary?" She was surprised. According to the dinner conversation Sunday night, there wasn't much concern for those billeted at Sacred Heart Seminary. Major security was concentrating on the pope and those closest to him.

"Someone is dead. But you should not worry. It seems to have been an accident."

"Then why? Why are you going out? It's the middle of the night." She picked up the clock on the nightstand and brought it close to her eyes. "Just after midnight! Can't this wait till tomorrow? After all, it's just an accident."

"You know how these things work, dear. We cannot take any chances. Not with the Holy Father coming in just a day. It is routine, but necessary. Try to get back to sleep, dear. Everything will be all right. There is no cause for worry."

She heard the mechanical sounds as he strapped his shoulder holster on. "Be careful now." Reluctantly she lay back down. It was unlikely she would get back to sleep. If her husband had to miss a night's sleep, then so would she. It was not a conscious decision, just something she knew from experience was going to happen.

Koznicki went from the bedroom directly into the study where he phoned Lieutenant Tully.

Anne Marie Tully by no means had become accustomed to the ubiquitous ringing phone, day or night. This particular ringing phone she ascribed to part of a nightmare. She groaned and turned over.

Tully recognized Koznicki's voice immediately and asked him to hold while Tully took the call on the kitchen phone.

"What?" Tully knew this was business, and their business was brutal.

"At the seminary." Koznicki, on his part, would be as direct as possible. "A security guard found a priest at the bottom of a staircase, dead. The staircase light was not working. So far the presumption is accidental death."

"You getting Moellmann in?"

"I shall call him immediately."

They were about to hang up when Tully said, "Walt, I think I'll try to raise Father Koesler. It may be a shortcut. And we'll want to wrap this up as quickly as possible."

After a moment, Koznicki said, "Good. We will meet at the morgue."

Tully found St. Joe's number and dialed, waking Koesler, who agreed to accompany Tully.

Since Tully lived so close to St. Joseph's rectory, Koesler had only a few minutes to get ready. As he dressed, he reflected briefly on all the emergency sick calls he'd responded to over the years.

Not anywhere near as many in recent years, what with people dying in hospitals and hospices rather than at home. Plus nowadays there was the prevalence of bestowing the sacrament once called extreme unction, now referred to as anointing the sick, long before imminent danger of death.

He was dressed, including overcoat and hat, and waiting at the rectory front door before it occurred to him that Lieutenant Tully had not mentioned the name of the dead priest. He wondered who it was.

Father Koesler sat with his back to the wall in the foyer on the main floor of the Wayne County Morgue. He would have been there alone but for the presence of Father Paul Smith. Koesler had suggested calling Smith, given the pivotal role the elder priest had played in preparing the symposium.

Although Smith had never attended an autopsy, he would not have minded being downstairs now. He thought he could handle the dissection. Unfortunately, his companion hadn't the stomach for it. So, rather than leave the poor man alone in this cavernous space, he decided to keep Koesler company. "Sort of brings back the old days, doesn't it?" Smith mused.

"How's that?"

"Oh, just sitting here. Not so much in a morgue, maybe a hospital. The faithful priest waiting for a doctor to deliver the bad news. Then guess who got to tell the family."

Koesler nodded. "You're right. I can remember times when the family had to be told and, by consensus, everyone would look to me to be the messenger. It doesn't take much imagination when a priest rings a doorbell at, say 2:00 in the morning, to figure that something's wrong. Something radical—like death."

"Nowadays the hospital staff pretty well shoulders that responsibility."

They sat in silence for a while. Each wishing he still smoked cigarettes.

"No family to notify now, is there?" Koesler asked.

Smith snorted. "A priest? At least no one close like a wife or kids. Matter of fact, I'm pretty sure his mother and father have passed. I don't know about sisters or brothers, nieces or nephews, that sort of thing."

"Time enough to get on to that a bit later, I suppose," Koesler noted.

Another quiet pause.

"Poor Father Hanson," said Koesler. "He seemed such a generous person. I just met him today."

"That's right. His conference is scheduled to begin in . . ." Smith consulted his watch. ". . . just a few hours."

"Good grief! In all the excitement, I lost track of that. The symposium! What will you do to replace him at such short notice? What can you do?"

Smith frowned in concentration. "I think I'm going to let Monsignor Martin worry about that. It *is* his ball game, after all."

Again silence.

"You know," Koesler said, "in all the years that building has been there, I don't remember a single fatal accident . . . until now of course."

"We were pretty young when we were introduced to Sacred Heart."

"That doesn't mean it couldn't have happened."

"I mean," Smith said, "just about everyone who lived in that building grew up there—even the ones who eventually became teachers there. When we were young we might easily have survived a tumble like Dan Hanson took. After being there a while, we knew how many steps there were in every stairway. We could travel confidently in the dark."

"Funny," Koesler said, "I don't mean it in any realistic way, but this just about answers Cardinal Schinder's prayer."

"Schinder's prayer? I don't . . ."

"Oh, that's right. You left his party early tonight."

"Well," Smith observed, "I was sort of dismissed."

Koesler smiled. "Yes, you were. But after you left, Schinder tried his best to influence the arguments of the liberal panelists. I think he'll be relieved when he learns that Dan Hanson will not be taking part in the symposium. But I'm sure he'll be shocked by the reason why."

Smith nodded. "That *will* be a blow to the liberal side of the dogma panel. And I don't see how Martin could possibly come up with someone to replace Hanson. Certainly not with someone of his caliber. Without Dan Hanson, the topic of infallibility will likely retain its status quo."

"And," Koesler added, "if papal infallibility goes unquestioned, the family planning and world population problems are just going to get worse. Especially if the pope protects present Church teaching in the cloak of infallibility."

"And that is going to have a spillover effect on the moral issue of birth control."

Koesler thought for a few moments. "What a time for the United Nations conference on population to be coming up! The Vatican is applying enormous pressure to keep birth control off the agenda."

"And they're succeeding."

"Yeah, a Dutch delegate was quoted in the paper just the other day as saying that a hierarchy of celibate men will continue to control the rest of the world's access to birth control."

"Ouch." Smith winced. "But I can't blame the protesters. We haven't shown much compassion when it comes to people in trouble over birth control. . . ." He thought for a moment. "Did you ever hear about the Irishwomen they called 'Magdalens'?"

Koesler shook his head and leaned back to rest against the wall.

"It happened," Smith continued, "around the middle of the nineteenth century and didn't end until just a few years ago, actually. Thousands of Catholic Irishwomen were made—well, slaves, with the approval of Church, state, and family. Their crime was having an illegitimate child or being orphans or prostitutes, or just being single. The Irish Church bunched them all together and called them 'Magdalens.'"

"What! I never heard of such a thing." Koesler was truly surprised at not knowing about such brutal and unfair—unchristian—treatment.

"It's true," Smith said. "Any woman who was . . ." He hesitated. ". . . inconvenient . . . was carted off to the parish priest. He would find a 'home' for her in one or another convent. If she was an unmarried woman, she'd be kept there until she had her baby and then the child would be taken from her and given out for adoption.

"Of course, in that super-Catholic country, they had no access to any means of birth control—or even knowledge that such a thing existed. They were lucky in the old days if they even knew what caused pregnancy. They wouldn't have known what to do with a condom or a diaphragm, or an IUD if you gave them one."

"No!" Koesler protested.

"Yes," Smith affirmed. "Then, since such an unfortunate woman was a shame and a scandal to her family, nine times out of ten she would have to spend the rest of her life in the convent. Not as a nun—more like a slave . . . doing laundry mostly."

"Wow! Makes you wonder what the Irish clergy were doing when they studied the Gospel story of the woman taken in adultery. Christ forgave and freed her. Sounds like the Irish Church condemned and imprisoned them."

Before Smith could reply, they heard steps coming up the granite staircase. First Lieutenant Tully came into view, then Inspector Koznicki and the medical examiner appeared. Koesler tried to read Tully's face to get some glimmer of what the autopsy had revealed. But as usual, the detective's expression was unfathomable. Koesler had known few to match Tully's ability to lock emotions inside.

The priests stood as the trio approached. "Now, we're working on a murder case," Tully said.

"Murder?!" Koesler was as confused as he was astounded. "But I thought Father Hanson simply fell down a flight of stairs in the dark!"

"More likely he was pushed," Dr. Moellman suggested.

"Pushed!" Smith flinched.

Koesler, brow knitted, looked at the inspector inquiringly.

Instead of responding to the point at hand, Koznicki nodded toward Moellman. "I don't know whether you gentlemen are aware that Dr. Moellman does not respond to emergency calls these days. His assistants handle them. He came this morning because I called him. Dr. Moellman knows that I would not have called if finding out what happened to Hanson were not a top priority."

"But *murder!*" Smith waved his hand in front of his face as if brushing away cobwebs. "How? Why?"

Thanks to the doc we know *how*. Now we've gotta find out why . . . and who."

"So," Koesler said, "how?"

"It looked like an accident. Or, it was made to look like an accident," Tully said. "Hanson tumbled down the staircase all right. Maybe more than one time."

"*More than . . . !*" Smith seemed thunderstruck.

"He hit everything that stairwell had to offer, and then some. He was covered with contusions—bruises. It looks like both legs were fractured, along with most of his ribs. Even his fingernails were broken."

"Is that it?" Smith asked. "Because the body had more injuries than were expected in a fall downstairs?" The tone of Smith's question, directed to the medical examiner, implied he thought this a fairly flimsy reason to suspect murder. "Is that why you think it wasn't an accident?"

"No." Moellman responded in the manner of one not accustomed to having his pronouncements questioned. "It would be easier to explain this if you're familiar with hanging."

"Hanging?"

"Yes, as in 'hanged by the neck until dead.'"

"Capital punishment!"

Moellman, at home in the arena, nodded. "Early on, when somebody was hanged, death came by suffocation."

Koesler knew he was not going to like this. Smith seemed to be taking it all in with equanimity.

"Sometimes that suited the purpose, and sometimes not. Like: 'It is the sentence of this court that you be taken from this place . . . and that you be there hanged by the neck *until* you are dead. With the emphasis on 'until.' Or, take the English custom of hang, draw, and quarter as a specialized punishment. The idea was to hang the victim by the neck, but not to kill him. Naturally, he fought death, and when his struggle was getting the best of him, the executioners would cut him down and put him on the rack and torture him by stretching him. But before he died of that, they'd cut him open—quarter him."

"I think we're familiar with that, doctor," Koesler said.

"That's why St. Thomas More was grateful to Henry VIII for commuting his sentence from being hanged, drawn, and quartered to merely being beheaded," Koesler added for Tully's benefit.

"Who?"

"Thomas More. He was the lord chancellor of England during the time of Henry VIII."

"Wait . . . they made a movie of that, didn't they?"

"A play *and* a movie: *A Man for All Seasons.*"

"Correct." The medical examiner was eager to regain the floor. "And then there came a time when people got a bit more humane. They still wanted criminals dead, but they changed their minds about the torture that went with hanging. They wanted the condemned to die quickly, instantaneously. That's when hanging became sort of a science."

"A science?" Smith was dubious.

"Yes . . . in a sense. Given a good strong rope, a lot depends on weight. The heavier the person, the farther he has to fall before he reaches the end of his rope—literally. Or if he weighs too much he could be decapitated when the body falls. Either way, death is about as instantaneous as anyone could want—"

"But," Koesler interrupted, "what does all this have to do with Father Hanson?"

"Yes, I was just coming to that. Hanson died of a broken neck. Of course that was obvious from the start. It was the way his neck was broken that made me think—"

"Of death by hanging?" Smith asked.

"Correct. The other part of the equation, besides the length of the drop, was where to place the knot. Originally, it was usual to tighten the rope around the person's neck with the knot at the rear. It took a long time and plenty of experience to decide that the knot had to be behind the ear so that when the rope was stretched full length, the neck was snapped to one side. Puts the head into hyperextension, back and to the side."

Koesler's face bespoke the queasy feeling in his stomach. Moellman realized he'd better get to the point. "The obvious cause of death was Father Hanson's broken neck. The assumption was that the fall caused it. But the fall didn't explain the damage to the neck. The first and second vertebrae were fractured. The second vertebrae was shattered and the bone transected the spinal cord. Reminiscent of the 'hangman's fracture.' And then I found what I was looking for at that stage."

"Not rope burns!" Smith said.

"No. Better. Fingertip bruises! The red flag. Fingertip bruises, the size of a dime—five indenting around the victim's jaw, and five in the rear of the neck." The medical examiner looked quite pleased with himself.

Inspector Koznicki picked up the thread. "The doctor is understandably cautious. He has listed the cause of death, officially, as a fracture of the neck in a manner undeterminable until such a time as the police investigate. That's official," he repeated.

"What we think happened is that Father Hanson was attacked at the top of the staircase. The killer probably came up behind him. He grabbed the victim with the right hand, cupping the chin, with the left hand on the back of his neck. Then the perp twisted his head to the right and downward, doing all that damage to the vertebrae and the spinal cord.

"Then he threw the dead body down the stairs. Maybe he even dragged the body back up and threw it down again. Either way, he wanted to make it look like an accident. And, if it weren't for the doctor's discernment that's just the way it might have gone."

Moellman attempted no expression of modesty. Possibly such an emotion was not in his quiver. He merely nodded and headed back down the stairs toward his favorite theater of operations.

26

Inspector Koznicki climbed the stairs slowly. Perhaps, he thought, he was a little old for this sort of thing. Or maybe he had just been at it too long.

He remembered early in his police career how excited and enthused he'd been by and about his work—solving crimes, unraveling mysteries, catching the bad guys. Now it seemed so senseless. Not his work, but the crimes. Yet they traveled hand in hand.

What could there be about a Catholic priest, a recognized theologian, that would motivate someone to commit murder? To break a man's neck?

These were some of his thoughts as he studied the marble stairs on his way up to the morgue's main floor.

Now Koznicki affected as much animation as possible. Despite Dr. Moellman's guarded official report, there was a murder to be solved, and these three people were vital to its solution.

He addressed the two priests. "You understand then what seems to have happened to Father Hanson?"

Both men nodded slowly.

Koznicki smiled. "So then, you know that we have a murder to solve. Now, can either of you tell me"—he looked from one to the other priest—"who would kill Father Hanson? Why would anyone want him dead?"

Silence.

"Well . . ." Father Smith hesitated.

"Go on, Father," Koznicki encouraged. "Say whatever comes to mind. Nothing is absurd when a murderer must be caught."

"Well, this may be absurd. But before you came along, Bob and I were talking about a meeting we attended this evening—or, I guess yesterday evening. Cardinal Schinder invited us and some of the symposium's panelists to a dinner meeting at the Lark."

"The Lark!" Like almost all Detroiters, Koznicki knew of the Lark at least by reputation. He was surprised that a priest, even a Cardinal, could afford to treat a bunch of people to dinner there. That a man of the cloth could afford anything beyond the basic of life amazed the inspector. He was old-fashioned in many ways. "What was the purpose of the meeting?"

"Cardinal Schinder seems displeased with some of the panel selections made for the symposium . . ." Smith looked at his watch. ". . . a symposium scheduled to begin in just a few hours. Father Hanson was supposed to be a panelist in the first of these sessions."

"What didn't he like—the Cardinal, that is?" Tully was pleased already that these two priests would be handy . . . though Father Koesler had as yet contributed nothing.

"He was dissatisfied with the spokesmen for the liberal opinions."

The creases in Tully's forehead asked the question.

Koesler attempted to explain. "There are six panel discussions that are supposed to stand as an introduction to what the pope will say at his Mass here in Detroit."

"Okay." Tully turned his attention to Koesler.

"The pope," Koesler continued, "holds fairly conservative views. In order for this symposium to be extremely helpful as an introduction to the pope's message, the conservative panelists should make a strong showing."

Rigged, Tully concluded. "Do the liberals stand a chance of winning—uh, or making a good showing?"

"That may be the problem," Koesler said. "They are not straw horses. They may make a very fine showing."

"And that would not help the pope's message?"

"Not by a long shot."

"So," Tully asked, "who chooses the speakers?"

Koesler turned toward Smith. "Monsignor Martin and I sort of collaborated on that," Smith said.

"Collaborated how?"

"He established the sort of theological outlook he wanted, and I indicated which experts might be the best interpreters of that school of thought."

"So," Tully said, "you think this Cardinal wanted Hanson out of the way."

"Not that he would be involved in any way with Hanson's death." Smith seemed shocked at the direction this conversation was taking.

"Lieutenant," Koesler said, "I was supposed to moderate that panel. Yesterday we talked our way through the presentation at a rehearsal. I can tell you that Father Hanson was about to drop a bombshell."

Koznicki rubbed his stubbled chin. "Bombshell? What sort of bombshell?"

"In effect, he was going to deny the Church's teaching on infallibility."

Tully was surprised. He had heard the gossip and rumors concerning the purpose of this visit and he'd been informed by his Catholic wife as to the global consequences if this infallible teaching were proclaimed.

Koznicki was stunned. His entire life had been steeped in Catholic doctrine. Part and parcel of this doctrine was the papal prerogative to teach the universal Church infallibly on matters of faith and morals. For Koznicki this doctrine was as unassailable as the law of gravity. "Do you mean that Father Hanson's position was that there was no such thing as infallibility? That it just never did exist?"

Gravely, Koesler nodded.

"Is that argument important enough to suspect it's a motive for murder?" Tully asked.

"I might have said no. I might not have considered it possible," Koesler said. "But now that the person whose contention this was has been murdered, I'd have to say yes. I think the opinion he was going to express and argue for could be considered important or disturbing enough to provoke someone to murder. At least to somebody who is staunchly conservative and prone to violence."

They looked to Koznicki to decide the matter.

"I agree," Koznicki said, after a moment's consideration. "There are any number of possible motives for Father Hanson's murder . . . motives we at present have no way of knowing. But this much is certain: He has been murdered. The killer tried to mask his deed by contriving a fall as the cause of death. Of all the possible reasons for this crime, we are presently aware of one very powerful motive: a significant challenge to a doctrine near and dear to most Catholics. Beyond that, should the questioning of infallibility cause widespread dissent, it could be a major blow to the Holy Father's credibility. In the absence of any better motive, for now we must assume, then, that Father Hanson was killed to prevent him from publicly arguing against and putting into question the doctrine of infallibility."

"One more thing we have to do," Tully said. "We're going to have to widen our loop of security. Father Hanson was not—and wasn't supposed to be—protected by our tightest security. We figured if there was going to be any violence, it would certainly be aimed at the pope. So, right now, there isn't any such thing as a functioning band of protection for the simple fact that the pope isn't here yet."

"Even if the Holy Father were here," Koznicki took up the point, "people on the level of Father Hanson would not have been specially protected. That must change! We must increase the periphery of security to include those who are even remotely attached to the Holy Father's visit. And that," Koznicki reflected, "will thin to some extent the strength of the protection we will be able to afford the Holy Father. But . . . there is no other way."

"You said"—Tully addressed Koesler—"that Hanson was supposed to be on the first panel discussion. How many panels are there?"

"Six."

"Okay, six. And Hanson's panel was a hot spot. Any others? Any panel discussions that could compare with the one on infallibility?"

"Maybe Father Smith would have a more informed answer. He set up the panels."

"Well," Smith said, "I wouldn't think there'd be an awful lot of controversy over stewardship or evangelization. There might be some disagreement on liturgy—there always is. But it doesn't tend to get virulent. However, when we get to the panels on morality and Church law, we are very close to the dogmatic discussion."

"And the setup is the same for those two panels? They both have very strong liberal arguments?" Tully asked.

"Definitely."

"Then that's the next periphery we've got to protect." He turned to Koznicki. "Walt, seems to me we got to give special cover to the liberal speakers on those two panels."

Koznicki nodded.

"Who are they?" Tully asked Smith.

"Father Rasmussen would be the liberal spokesman on morals. That's Norbert Rasmussen. And for canon law it would be Father Stanley Moser."

Tully jotted down the names.

Koznicki cautioned the two priests against sharing any of their conversation with anyone else, particularly the media, who would be hounding them for information. He then rehashed the new security measures that must be taken.

There would be no further sleep for any of the four men this night. The priests were too excited to relax. The two police officers had too much work to accomplish in a very small measure of time.

27

Pat Lennon sat at her desk cautiously sipping a steaming cup of coffee. Every so often she ran a hand through her hair. Crossed over her right leg, her left leg from just above the knee to the ankle presented a most attractive extremity. She was studying several clippings she'd found in the *Detroit News* library.

All of the articles had to do with the world's population crunch and the events and opinions that were adding to the problem.

One story noted a report from the National Academy of Sciences and the Royal Society of London: "If current predictions of population growth prove accurate and patterns of human activity on the planet remain unchanged, science and technology may not be able to prevent either irreversible degradation of the environment or continued poverty for much of the world."

That column concluded: "The world has quietly entered a new era, one in which satisfying the food needs of 90 million more people each year is possible only by reducing consumption among those already here. The only option may be an all-out effort to slow population growth."

An editorial in the *National Catholic Reporter* quoted Worldwatch president Lester Brown noting four major trends in what he termed this age of discontinuity: "(1) World population is expanding faster than the world's ability to produce basic foodstuffs. (2) The global economy appears to be chronologically sluggish. (3) The world energy economy is apparently 'on the edge of basic restructuring.' (4) The population boom is beginning to undermine world living standards."

The editorial stated: "We all have a stake in working to turn the many negative trends around, but—given that population growth is a basic part of the problem—the Catholic church has a special responsibility here.

"The world fertility rate is no longer declining. It ranges from an average of 1.3 children per woman in Italy (the Vatican's backyard, no less) to 6.7 in Pakistan. Worldwatch wisely notes that it is not enough simply to hand out contraceptives. Only 'fundamental changes that improve women's lives and increase their access to and control over money, credit and other resources' will finally lower the fertility rate.

"But contraceptives are a start."

Finally, in an article published in the Jesuit magazine, *America*, John C. Schwarz listed many of the world's problems concerning particularly poverty and overpopulation. He wrote: "A leading moral theologian of our time, Bernard Häring, a Redemptorist priest, who was himself a member of Pope Paul VI's special commission on the contraception issue, has continued to voice serious dissatisfaction with the Church's stand—on artificial contraception itself, and on the raising of this issue to a major point of Catholic orthodoxy."

Then Schwarz quoted Häring: "I hope our beloved Pontiff understands that we are dealing with a conflict of epic proportions, no less than the one at Antioch between Peter and Paul. . . . We are dealing with a question of maintaining a responsible and deliberate Christian ethic that will allow the Church to be a prophetic, believable voice in the effort toward peace, justice and the safeguarding of creation."

Then Father Häring added: "My most pressing concerns of these, my last years, are not disputes of sexual morality . . . but about the survival of the human race and life on our planet."

Lennon looked up but focused on nothing.

None of the articles Pat researched had been written as a preliminary to the present papal visit. Each of these articles feared that the Catholic Church's "official stand" on birth control was a definite contributing factor in the world's overpopulation and that it could lead to such a cataclysm that we might populate ourselves out of existence.

There was no sense of the hysterical in these articles. They were well reasoned. Overpopulation was not the only threatening statistic. Nor was the Church's persistent policy the only cause of this critical problem.

But the Catholic Church, in its insistence that the rest of the world conform to its teaching on family planning, was at the very least intensifying this coming crisis.

Adding to the weight of all this was the threat of the pope's next step. Realistically, this had gone well beyond the realm of rumor. As far as Lennon was concerned, the pope was damn well going to make Church policy, as set forth in Paul's *Humanae Vitae*, a doctrine protected by infallibility. Once he did that, things were going to get a lot worse. Fast.

As she was reaching these conclusions, she became conscious of someone standing on the other side of her desk. Bob Ankenazy smiled as he read the headlines of the clips she had been reading. "Glad you're doing some backgrounding," he said.

"Backgrounding? I'm not on this story."

"You are now." He covered her clippings with the *Free Press*'s morning final.

Her heart skipped as she quickly scanned page one. There it was: VISITING PRIEST SCHOLAR FOUND DEAD. The bug line: POLICE SUSPECT FOUL PLAY. Her practiced eye noted not only Joe Cox's byline, but also that the *Free Press* had copyrighted the report. That told her all she needed to know about that story.

There were plenty of caution words such as "alleged" and disclaimers such as "a source that wished to remain anonymous," or, "would not speak for attribution."

The inescapable conclusion was that one of the priest-experts who was to have spoken as part of the symposium was found dead about midnight at the bottom of a staircase at Sacred Heart Seminary. His neck had been broken. It might have been an accident, but police were investigating the possibility of murder. The priest, Father Daniel Hanson, had been a liberal scholar and was a professor at etc., etc., etc.

Pat looked up. "This is the first I've heard."

"It's on radio and TV . . . but they're all using Cox's story as their source. Evidently, they're unable to corroborate it. So, to protect their rears, they're attributing it to the *Freep*. If Cox gets burned, they don't want to go down in flames with him."

"Are we checking it?"

"Sure. So far we've got what Cox already wrote. The cops were called about midnight; the priest's neck was broken; it could have been an accidental fall or it could be murder. The cops give the impression their investigation is pro forma. It's a big story and they don't want to be caught bungling.

"It's pretty obvious they're playing this close to the vest. As usual, they want to investigate without us on their back. They wouldn't be giving us what they have so far without Cox's having broken the story. I'd have to say that even if what he implies is conjecture and may be false, he's got the essence. And there's no doubt he got it first. It puts the *Freep* way out front. That's why the boss wants you on this story. Yesterday."

"Oh, swell! The score's a hundred to nothing and he wants me to go in and win the game!"

"Just 'cause Cox got lucky doesn't mean we can't get this story back."

"Lucky! The dead priest was found about midnight, right?"

Ankenazy nodded. Secretly Ankenazy agreed with what he knew she was going to say. He was the messenger. And she was going to kill him.

"That means that he had approximately an hour and a quarter till the *Freep*'s final deadline. And he beat it. How the hell did he do that? Can you tell me?"

Ankenazy shrugged. "Give it your best shot, Pat."

"Yeah, I know. This wasn't your idea. Sorry I took it out on you."

With a brief smile, Ankenazy walked away.

How the hell did he do it? Cox's accomplishment almost defied logistics. One way he could've pulled this off . . . but she didn't want to think of it.

She tried to plan her strategy, or more exactly, come up with any strategy at all. But Cox and his scoop kept interfering with her thought process. Finally, she dialed a number.

"Cox," he said tersely after only one ring.

"Lennon," she said, in, to her, an amazingly calm tone.

"Howdja like it?" Unable to keep the gloat from his voice.

"Congratulations, sweetie. How'd you ever beat your deadline?"

"Uh-uh; mustn't tell all the family secrets."

"Okay—one thing. Tell me if I'm wrong: You're guessing on the murder angle."

"Okay, you win that one."

"You had to be." Pause. "I just wanted you to know: Simons put me on the story."

A longer pause. Then, "You're on! This really is the way to get back in harness, going against the best. See you at the finish line."

They hung up simultaneously.

She gave it another minute's thought before launching her own investigation of the story.

Cox had to have a source who was there at the seminary when the body was found. A source at the morgue couldn't have helped. By the time they got the body to the morgue it would be too late to call Cox in time for him to, first, clear page-one space with the night city editor and, second, write the story.

No, the leak had to be either with the uniforms that responded to the 911, or with the detectives that handled the scene, or with the EMS crew.

There was only one other possible explanation.

Cox wouldn't do that. He couldn't have done that.

But it would explain the scoop.

One room in Cobo Arena had been created and set aside for news conferences. No one had anticipated the room would be so full this early in the papal preliminaries. The media in general had not been impressed with the prelusive symposium. Generally, everyone was primed to glom on to the number one attraction: the pope.

About the only newsperson who took the symposium seriously was the *Freep*'s Joe Cox. And had that panned out for him!

He alone had perceived the structured dichotomy between liberal and conservative views on the various panels. These striking philosophical differences gave him an insight into Father Hanson's death.

Why might someone kill Father Hanson? Perhaps because Father Hanson was a crashing liberal. And crashing conservatives have a habit of not liking crashing liberals.

If this proved a false lead, at least it was not bad for starters.

In any case, Joe Cox was about the only first-string newsperson not at this early morning's news conference. This made some of the other top news gatherers somewhat nervous. So far this was Cox's story. In one mighty scoop he seemed to have regained the magic touch for which he had been famous before Chicago. The others did not know where Cox was just now. But quite a few of them secretly would have liked to be wherever Cox was.

But time and the news march on.

The sun guns cast a brilliance on the front end of the room. Grouped around those powerful and warming lights were the collected reporters from print, radio, and—the reason for the lights—television.

In the glare of the lights was the dais upon which stood two clerically garbed men: Dietrich Cardinal Schinder and Monsignor Frank Martin.

Schinder appeared refreshed. It was impossible to tell whether he'd had a restful night's sleep. It was a good bet that he had been awakened with news of Hanson's death. But he surely did not look it.

Monsignor Martin, on the other hand, looked rumpled, disheveled,

195

and tired. Sleep or no, Hanson's death had had an obvious effect on the monsignor.

As usual, the TV reporters started things off. Due to the lighting, neither Schinder nor Martin could identify who was asking questions. At best, they were able to ascertain the direction whence they came.

Voice: "Do you know for sure yet whether Father Hanson's death was accidental or murder?"

Schinder: "The police are still investigating."

Voice: "Which do you think it was?"

Schinder: "We're waiting for the police to say."

Voice: "This morning's *Free Press* said that Father Hanson's neck had been broken and that he had fallen down a flight of stairs. Doesn't that sound accidental to you?"

Schinder (with a smile that could at once be chilling or charming and a gesture that included Martin): "We are just simple priests. We cannot pretend to tell the police their business. We wait for them to complete their investigation."

Voice: "Now that Father Hanson is dead, what will happen to the panel on dogmatic theology?"

Schinder waved the question to Martin, who had been rubbing his eyes. He stopped when Schinder deferred to him. His eyes were red-rimmed. "There is no possible way we could go on with that panel. It is simply canceled. We will go forward with the rest of the program."

"However," Schinder added, "Father John Selner, the other dogmatic panelist, will offer his prepared paper to the conference. It will be part of the published report of the symposium."

Martin looked surprised and angry. Obviously this was news to him—something Schinder had neither cleared with him nor informed him of.

The questions and answers droned on. Realistically, there was not much the reporters could ask because there wasn't much the clergy-men knew. As the session continued—the reporters had to take some-thing home with them—the television crews dismantled their gear and departed. The radio and print people continued their questioning. It was always possible that someone would, willy-nilly, come up with something that was newsworthy. Woe unto the reporter who folded his or her tent and left before the elusive question had been asked and answered.

Pat Lennon had arrived at the news conference a bit late. But then she had received this assignment a bit late.

She too wondered where the hell Joe Cox was. She did not wonder about it nearly as long as had the others.

Early on, she noted Lieutenant Tully standing near the door directing a series of his detectives.

Both Lennon and Tully had lived in the Detroit area most of their lives. One reported for the most part on the local crime scene. The other spent most of his time catching criminals, mostly murderers. The lives of Lennon and Tully had touched several times over the years. Occasionally they had walked the fine line between friendship and an affair. The latter possibility had ended with Tully's marriage to Anne Marie. However the mutual trust that had developed between them was secure.

The parade of detectives receiving marching orders from Tully appeared to end. The news conference continued. Lennon made her way to Tully's side. Plainly he was pleased to see her.

After their affable greeting, Tully turned professional. "Did you catch Cox's story this morning?"

She nodded. "I've been wondering how he got it."

"So have we! Only we're not just wondering; we're trying to find the leak."

"You're sure it's a leak?"

"Gotta be!" His expression asked what else it could be. "His deadline had to be close to one A.M., no?"

Again she nodded.

"It just doesn't figure. The only ones who knew about the priest's death were the uniforms responding to the 911, our guys, and the EMS people. We've cleared the uniforms. We're looking at our guys now. But that story gave out way too much detail."

"The broken neck?"

"That's a big one."

She bit her lip. "If I'd had it, I would've used it."

Tully looked at her a moment. This is where they parted in adversarial ways. His job, in part, was to reserve information the sole possession of which could aid and expedite an investigation. Her task was to get all the information she could and communicate it—with some certain exceptions—to the public.

"The point is," Tully said, "that information should have been carefully protected and not released by anyone but a senior officer. The point is, we've got a problem and we've got to solve it."

"Is it murder?" she asked point blank.

"Doc Moellmann is not divulging the cause of death pending our investigation. But"—his tone was confidential—"I think it's safe to say that's probably where we're going."

Lennon recognized Tully's message. It was a cautious affirmation that he used with precious few, trusted souls. It meant that in his professional opinion, it was murder, but that Lennon should not write murder just yet. However, she would be safe in pursuing the story as if it were a homicide—because, in his expert opinion, that's what it was.

Lennon was aware that it had been some time since she had paid attention to the news conference. She glanced at the dais. Where there had been two clergymen fielding the questions, now there was one—Monsignor Martin.

"Where'd the other one go?"

"What?" Tully followed her gaze to the dais.

"There were two up there. The Cardinal's gone."

"Damn!"

Tully, followed by Lennon, strode to the arena guard standing near the only door to the room. "The Cardinal: Where'd he go?"

"He left."

"When?"

"Just a few, maybe five, ten minutes ago."

"What happened? Do you know what happened? Why he left?"

"He got a phone call." The guard pointed to the temporary hookup at the back of the room.

"Save me from pulling this information out of you," Tully said through tight teeth. "Give it to me from the top."

"Okay. This is my station. Me and Harry over there, we're supposed to check the credentials of everybody who wants to get in here.

"Like I say, about maybe ten minutes ago the phone rang. We've got it on low so we can hear the ring but it won't bother anybody else."

"And?"

"I pick it up. Somebody wants to talk to the Cardinal. I ask who's callin'. He says to tell the Cardinal it's about Father Hanson. So I go up to the dais and tell the Cardinal the message.

"Right away he gets up and I bring him to the phone. He listens for a couple minutes—make that seconds. Then he leaves."

"What did the caller's voice sound like?"

"Geez, it was real low. I could hardly make out what he was saying."

"*He*."

"Yeah . . . I think it was a guy."

"What'd he sound like? Give me everything you can remember."

"I think it was a guy. Yeah, I'm pretty sure it was a guy. Maybe kind of young. Maybe 'cause he sounded nervous is why he sounded young."

"And he said the call was about Father Hanson."

"Yeah. That's what I told the Cardinal."

"What did the Cardinal do then, after he took the call?"

"He left."

"He just walked out?"

"Well, he got his hat and coat from the rack and he went."

Tully, still trailed by Lennon, hurried out the door where they found a uniformed officer. "You know who Cardinal Schinder is, right?" Tully said.

"Yeah, right. He left maybe ten, fifteen minutes ago."

"Where'd he go?"

"I don't know."

"You're supposed to be with him everywhere in this building and get the next officer if he leaves the building."

"I tried. I tried. He refused. Said he had something important he had to do, and he had to do it alone. Honest, Zoo, there wasn't anything I could do about it. He flat out refused to have anybody go with him."

Tully turned when he saw the arena guard approaching. "What?"

"I just remember something the Cardinal said . . . before he hung up, I mean."

"What?"

"He said, 'This time, no murder.'"

28

Christmas vacation had begun for Anne Marie Tully's school. That was one of the reasons Wanda Koznicki had invited Anne Marie for a leisurely luncheon.

They met at Meriwether's on Telegraph Road just before noon to anticipate the luncheon crowd. Jim McIntyre, restaurant manager, knew their husbands as frequent diners. And he was acquainted with Mrs. Koznicki. So he seated the women in a secluded booth and later would offer them a complimentary wine.

The abundant Christmas decorations seemed strangely inappropriate to the two women.

For just about everyone else in the metro area the beautifully unique feast of Christmas was about to begin again. That plus a most rare visit by the pope himself created a special feeling of importance. No other place on earth—with the exception of the Vatican to which the pope would return following this visit—would have the pope as guest.

But for Wanda and Anne Marie there was no room for a papal welcome mat. Their husbands were involved. Already their lives were complicated by a murder investigation—an investigation that was somehow related to the pope's coming.

And they did not even know that now the various law enforcement officers were searching for a missing Cardinal.

They studied the menu briefly. Wanda wanted a salad. There were plenty. Anne Marie looked for a fish entrée. There were lots. When their waitress returned they ordered.

Wanda tore off a piece of her teacup bread for which Meriwether's was famous. "It's so unfair," she said, "the way the news media treat a thing like this when it happens in Detroit. Murders happen in other cities. They happen in Detroit too. But when someone well known is killed in Detroit, it's as if the city is to blame."

"I hadn't thought about it that way." Anne Marie was still a novice as Detroit policeman's wife. But she was willing to learn. And there were few teachers more qualified than Wanda Koznicki.

"For quite a few years now," Wanda said, "the city has taken this all too much to heart. We've become overly sensitive about our reputation, if you ask me."

Following Wanda's lead, Anne Marie started to tear off a piece of her bread, but found it too warm to handle just yet.

"Actually," Wanda said, "we have one of the best police forces in the country. But"—she shook her head as if admonishing a child—"while the news media go to great pains to report the incidence of murder here, you very seldom find them telling their customers how many of these crimes we solve."

"That's true." Anne Marie had only to reflect on her husband's pride in his work.

"And no one—*no one*—works harder to uphold this record than our husbands," Wanda said almost defiantly. "And that is something we, particularly, have to take into account and make allowances for—their dedication, I mean."

Anne Marie began to see where this near-monologue was going. She reached across the table to touch Wanda's arm reassuringly. "I know what you mean, Wanda. Zoo and I talked about this even before I knew he didn't mind being called 'Zoo.' I know he's lost a wife and family, as well as a significant other. He doesn't blame them for a moment. Those women may have gone into their relationship with him with their eyes wide open. But what they failed to grasp was Zoo's complete dedication to his job—catching the bad guys, as he puts it."

"That's what I meant, dear," Wanda said. "That's exactly what I meant. I've known Zoo almost as long as Walt has. And that goes back about thirty years. So I knew his wife and his kids. And I knew Alice. They are both good women.

"I suppose I have a special understanding here because Walt is something like Zoo. But the emphasis is on 'something.' Our kids have turned out pretty well, all things considered. But one of those things was that their father missed a lot of their childhood. The usual things, like a crucial basketball game he couldn't attend—not even after promising. Like that.

"We've been blessed, I believe, by having the children understand—more or less.

"The point is, dear, do not ever underestimate Zoo's dedication to his work. Walt may have unexpectedly missed a crucial game or a recital, but whenever there was a genuine crisis, he was there." Wanda's pause was on the pregnant side.

"And Zoo?" Anne Marie asked tentatively.

"He missed the birth of one of his children."

Anne Marie's spoon halted en route to her mouth. "That I didn't know."

"That may have been his worst mistake . . . although there surely were extenuating circumstances. But I thought it was important for you to know."

"You're probably right." Anne Marie seemed thoughtful as she finished her soup. "Look, Wanda, no one knows the future. I can't possibly predict what Zoo and I will go through together. All I know—and I do know this—is that we love each other and we're aware of the ground rules. I don't know whether we'll survive. All I know is we're going to give this our best shot."

They silently agreed that all that needed be said about Zoo's commitment to work and home had been expressed. They turned their attention to lunch and the topic that seemed to occupy everyone's conversation this day: the death, possibly by homicide, of Father Hanson.

"Speaking of our husband's careers . . ." Anne Marie savoringly sampled her entrée. ". . . I can't make head or tail of what happened to Father Hanson."

"Nor I. Nor anyone—yet. The first thing I thought of when I heard how the poor man died was that at least it was fast." Wanda smiled almost apologetically. "I'm sorry; I guess it happens when you reach a certain age; you start thinking of your own mortality. And when you do . . ."

". . . you don't want to linger."

Wanda chuckled self-consciously. "I'm afraid that's right. I find myself reading the obits religiously. Of course, I'm not preoccupied with death—my death. But more and more, friends and acquaintances are dying. It does make you think. The thought that occurs to me occasionally is 'how?' A long bout with cancer? Alzheimer's?"

"Or a broken neck. I see what you mean. I guess I don't think that much about death. It's going to happen, of course. I just don't center on it much."

Wanda shook her head. "I didn't either when I was your age. But with the years, something happens."

Anne Marie nodded. "I know you're right. You put me in mind of a movie I saw last year. I think it was *Grumpy Old Men*."

"I know the one—Jack Lemmon and Walter Matthau . . . and Ann-Margret, wasn't it?"

"Yes. There were these elderly men. One died of a heart attack—suddenly—just keeled over. And when the others discovered how quick the death was, they shook their heads and murmured, 'Lucky guy.'"

"Uh-huh. That's one feeling I have about Father Hanson: It was quick. I like to think he was dead even before he fell down all those stairs. So . . ." Wanda sipped her coffee. ". . . everyone is wondering why he was killed. I think it's clear as ice. Somebody wanted to prevent him from attacking that doctrine of infallibility. I can tell you that Walt was completely surprised to hear that called into question."

Anne Marie laughed. "Even Zoo—even *he*—was surprised. I'm not positive he'd ever heard of the doctrine before your dinner Sunday evening. But, evidently, he was impressed."

"I can understand that a successful demythologizing of that particular doctrine would upset a lot of applecarts. Even though it wasn't used much—maybe only once—it was like a hydrogen bomb held in reserve. Like the final weapon or a final argument. Of course, all men think they're infallible. At least some of the time."

Anne Marie chuckled. "So you think that—who?—some dedicated conservative did it—killed the priest before he had his chance to destroy the concept of infallibility?"

"Seems likely to me. Of course, at this stage, the way Walt or Zoo would look at it, no possibility would be overlooked. It could be that Father Hanson had an enemy, an enemy nobody knows about." She shook her head. "It could be anything."

"Then there's the problem of killing him in the seminary."

"Oh, but the security was not all that tight there. There were lots of ways of sneaking in undetected. That won't happen anymore. Now they've extended the first-rate security—the personnel and resources they were holding in reserve for the pope—to include virtually everyone taking part in this event. I think they called it 'widening the circle of security.'"

"Oh, but that development hasn't been made public yet, has it?"

"No," Wanda assured. "That's at least one area where the police have stayed one jump ahead of the news media."

Anne Marie urged Wanda to order dessert. After all, she'd had only salad. It was not the most logical of suggestions. Wanda had been calorie conscious through lunch. Now she was teetering on a compromise she surely would regret.

While she consulted the dessert menu, the manager approached the table. He seemed slightly discomposed. "Did you know"—he addressed Wanda primarily—"that the visiting Cardinal—I think his name is Schinder—did you know he was missing?"

Wanda and Anne Marie looked at each other, unsure of the question's portent.

"Yes," Wanda replied. "His name is Schinder, and, no, we didn't know that he was missing."

"Apparently," McIntyre said, "it happened this morning, during a press conference at Cobo. He left midway through the conference."

"And?"

"Well, it seems he's been found dead. Your husband is making a statement and answering questions right now. The TV set is in the bar. I thought you might want to see it."

Apparently there was nothing wrong with her husband. Yet Wanda felt a little weak in her knees. McIntyre had tried to break the news as gently as possible, but the death of a Cardinal linked with her husband's name filled Wanda with dread. But Walt was all right. He was just holding a news conference.

She struggled out of the booth.

Yes, she wanted to see Walt on TV. And no, she had lost all appetite for dessert.

29

There was almost no need for refrigeration in the Wayne County Morgue this day. The furnace wasn't working. The chill was not only felt by Dr. Wilhelm Moellman; he also communicated frost.

As this emergency autopsy began, Moellmann was breathing hard, emphasizing the fact that everyone's breath was visible.

Standing near the metal table were Koznicki and Tully. On the table was the unclothed body of Dietrich Schinder. Positioned near the door were Sergeants Mangiapane and Moore, ready to carry out any mission on which they might be sent.

Koznicki and Tully leaned in toward each other so they could communicate in whispers and not unduly disturb the already agitated medical examiner.

"Any break in that leak?" Koznicki asked.

"We've cleared all our people," Tully said. "It just has to be one of the EMS guys."

"What about the seminary?"

Tully wiggled his fingers to make sure they could still move. "Prints all over. It looks like the place hasn't been dusted since it was built."

"Witnesses?"

"No one. Not a thing. It's hard to imagine that building was ever filled. But they tell me it was packed some thirty years ago. Now even when the students are there, it's mostly empty. And it's Christmas break. The few who are there now are mostly the ones who're going to take part in the pope's visit."

"None of them can be helpful?"

Tully shook his head. "They've been impressed with the kind of neighborhood they're in. After supper, it's mostly into their assigned rooms and lock up for the night. Some go for a snack before bed. But it's pretty solitary."

"So . . ." Koznicki blew into his cupped hands. ". . . we do not know what brought Father Hanson out of his room and to that stairway?"

"Not a clue. He could've been going for a snack. He could've been taking a constitutional. My guess is he was called out of his room by someone or something. I don't see the guy who killed him just waiting patiently for him to come out of his room and conveniently go to the stairwell so he could be thrown down the stairs."

"Or . . ." Tully looked thoughtful. ". . . maybe he just happened along and saw something somebody didn't want him to see . . . and he was killed not because of who he was, but because of what he saw. . . ."

"There was a phone in his room?"

"Uh-huh. But no one who roomed in that vicinity can recall hearing a phone ring. Of course, no one was paying any attention. Still, it's so quiet in those halls that a ringing phone might knock you out of your chair."

"A knock on his door?"

"Possible . . . but why would he go with someone he didn't know?"

"Why wouldn't he? Why would it enter his head that anyone—especially anyone in the seminary—would want to kill him?" Koznicki tipped his head toward the body that was being autopsied. "The late Cardinal may have gone with someone he did not know. . . ."

"That was an odd thing he said on the phone: 'This time, no murder.'"

"Yes. It is almost as if the Cardinal had something to do with what happened to Father Hanson . . . short of murder, that is."

"Well, Koesler and Smith said as much." Tully wiggled his toes; he felt as if they might break. "They tell me it would've been fine with Schinder if Hanson had turned out to be a no-show."

"That does not mean he wanted Father murdered. Just that he preferred that Father not deliver his paper or take any part in the symposium."

"Think that might be it, Walt? Maybe Schinder contracted with somebody. They didn't necessarily need to know each other. Schinder wanted Hanson out of this conference. Somebody fouls up. Maybe they're trying to kidnap Hanson from the seminary. He puts up more of a fight than they counted on. Somebody gets carried away and breaks the guy's neck. Then they throw the body down the stairs to make it look like an accident."

Koznicki nodded slowly. "In that case, perhaps they called the Cardinal this morning to arrange a meeting. The Cardinal, in this scenario, is eager to meet with them. There were those besides Father Hanson that the Cardinal would wish silenced, yes?"

"Yes. Just about every liberal speaker on every panel."

"So," Koznicki continued, "the Cardinal could think there was a breakdown in communication. And that is why he might say, 'This time, no murder.'"

They stood in silence now, stamping their feet quietly.

"Sadly," Koznicki said finally, "our scenario does not lead us to this." Again he nodded at the corpse.

Tully nodded. "Why would they kill him?"

"Why would they break his neck?"

"A disagreement? He wouldn't pay? He wanted to call the whole thing off?" Tully enumerated possibilities as they came to him.

"But why a broken neck? Not a popular method of murder by any means."

Running low on theories, they stood again in silence.

Dr. Moellmann cleared his throat, his traditional signal that while the autopsy was not completed, there might be something the investigating officers should know.

Koznicki and Tully moved to the table. The late Cardinal looked the worse for wear.

"Just for a moment, and not for the record, I will deal in a comparison between the deaths of the priest early this morning and the Cardinal here."

Exactly what Tully and Koznicki wanted to hear. Moellmann could with every justification have dealt with the two deaths as two separate entities. The police wanted—needed—the comparison.

"First of all," the M.E. said, "cervical fracture was the cause of death in both cases." He looked up and over his glasses at the two officers. "But, there is a slight initial difference. The priest's neck was broken to the right as if the killer were right-handed. This neck was broken to the left . . . as if, in this case, the killer was left-handed. However, this does not mean all that much."

Nothing much so far. The first question on the officers' minds was whether this was a copycat murder or perpetrated by the same person who killed Hanson. And Dr. Moellmann knew that. He enjoyed toying with people—to a point.

"Look! See this . . . at the crown of the head. See this depressed fracture leaving a semicircular mark?"

The two officers were leaning over the body, carefully following the M.E.'s directions.

"Now, see beneath this fracture, the bone fragments lie inward. I would say a blunt instrument, perhaps a small hammer."

"That the cause of death?" Tully sounded disappointed.

"No. No, the fractured cervix is the cause of death. Just as with the previous victim . . . what was his name?"

"Hanson."

"Yes, of course. Both died of a broken neck."

"Unusual?"

"Unusual? Yes, I would say so. But with Schinder here, his assailant rendered him unconscious before breaking his neck. However, in striking the victim as he did, the perpetrator removes all doubt about the cause of death.

"Remember, Hanson had fallen, been pushed, thrown down the stairs. There was an effort to confuse the issue, to mislead us. Did the priest accidentally fall down the stairs and in the process break his neck? Or was his neck snapped and then, to try and fool us, was he hurled down the stairs?"

At this point, the doctor paused a moment so everyone could recall that, far from being misled, he had discovered the telltale marks of the killer.

"In this case"—the doctor indicated Schinder's body—"there is no effort to disguise the cause of death."

"Maybe," Tully ventured, "Schinder started struggling—fought back. And the perp clubbed him. Then he broke his neck."

"Perhaps. That is for you to decide. But, one last thing that may interest you. See, the ring finger on the right hand is missing. As is . . . a ring."

"Where do you see that, Doc?" Tully asked.

"The marks on the finger stump. There is the indentation made by a ring that fitted tightly. It looks as if someone tried to remove the ring and did not succeed. But he wanted the ring badly enough to amputate the finger to get it."

"Maybe in a hurry."

"Perhaps. But it is interesting, is it not, that the earlier victim, Hanson, was wearing a ring. I distinctly remember that. It struck me as odd that a priest would wear a ring. I didn't think they did that. Now a bishop . . ."

"Manj . . ." Tully spoke without taking his eyes from the corpse. "Hop over to headquarters and get the Hanson evidence bag."

"Right!"

Moellmann returned to the autopsy.

"Angie," Tully said to Sergeant Moore, "stay with this in case something else comes up."

Tully and Koznicki started up the stairs. "I must return to my assignment, Alonzo," Koznicki said. "Keep me apprised of your progress. And let me know should you need help."

Actually, Koznicki could have continued with this investigation. But he was confident of Tully's ability and the inspector wanted to demonstrate that confidence.

Waiting in the lobby were Fathers Koesler and Smith. Pat Lennon also was there. There was no law that said she couldn't be. Tully's option, should he want to get away from a media representative, was to consult with the priests behind closed doors, probably at headquarters. But an instinct told him Pat might prove useful. And he knew that should anything need to be kept secret, he could depend on her—as long as the need was authentic.

With nothing to distract them, not even an autopsied body, the three waiting people felt near frozen. Koznicki continued out the door, leaving Tully to continue the investigation.

"The subject is rings," Tully said. "Do priests or bishops wear rings on their fingers?"

Koesler and Smith looked at each other, wondering which would address the question.

"There is an old Latin aphorism," Smith said. "I won't go into the Latin, but what it means is, 'He who wears a ring is either a bishop or a fool.'"

"I take it then," Tully said, "that priests normally don't wear rings."

"First," Koesler spoke, "I'm sure the aphorism Father Smith quoted is not directed at married people wearing engagement and wedding rings. It does apply to priests. For a bishop, his ring is part of what he wears—like his clerical suit, a pectoral cross, or, during a liturgy, his vestments. And it's worn on the right hand. It used to be a Catholic custom when greeting a bishop to genuflect and instead of shaking hands, kiss the bishop's ring."

"'Used to'?" Tully said.

"Not many bishops expect or want that sort of homage. Certainly Cardinal Boyle did away with that practice as far as he was concerned a long time ago. And that goes for the Detroit auxiliary bishops as well."

"It gets to be confusing when greeting a bishop for the first time,"

Smith added. "You never know whether he wants that sort of fealty."

"But," Tully said, "bottom line: Bishops wear rings . . . right?"

The two priests nodded.

"And priests?" Tully asked.

Neither Koesler nor Smith jumped on that question.

"I guess," Koesler said finally, "the answer is yes and no."

"I think," said Smith, "that the 1917 *Code of Canon Law*—that's Church law published in 1917—permits the wearing of a ring by a priest to commemorate the earning of a doctoral degree. I assume the latest version of church law—1983—gives the same permission."

"But generally," Koesler said, "priests *don't* wear rings."

"According to Doc Moellmann," Tully said, "Father Hanson wore a ring. And"—he turned his head to look at a somewhat out-of-breath Mangiapane—"here it comes now."

Mangiapane handed Tully a small package. Tully opened it, pulled out a ring, and showed it to the priests. Lennon studied it also.

"During the autopsy," Tully said, "the M.E. removed this from Hanson's finger."

"Oh, yes," Koesler said. "There's an inscription on the inside. 'To Father Dan—a Doctor at last. Mom.' It would have been a commemorative gift from his mother on the occasion of his getting a doctorate. And on either side of the stone: 'C.U. Theo.' From Catholic University, in Washington, D.C. Probably a doctorate in theology."

"Pretty stone," Lennon said. "Looks expensive."

"I think so," Tully said. "We'll have it appraised. Now, the late Cardinal Schinder wore a ring?"

"He was a bishop," Koesler said. "I think certainly he wore a ring—"

"Any idea what Schinder's ring looked like?" Tully cut in.

"Yes," Smith said. "I remember because it was different. Well, let me put it this way: Lots of bishops own a ring like Schinder's, but few wear it. It was a ring given to each of the bishops of the world who attended the Second Vatican Council. It was a plain gold band—no stone. The front, or top, of the ring was shaped sort of like a miter. And on the front was a kind of imagery—the Apostles and a dove, the Holy Spirit.

"There was an inscription too . . . something like *Concillio Vaticano Secundo*. It was a little thicker than a wedding ring.

"As I say, all the bishops in the world who attended Vatican II were given these commemorative rings. Most everybody keeps them in a safe place, I suppose. Very few ever actually wear them. Cardinal Schinder was one who did. At that dinner last night, I noticed it."

"But," Koesler observed, "you asked whether the Cardinal had a ring and wore it. Does that mean it's gone? Somebody took it?"

"Exactly." Tully decided not to go into the manner in which it was removed. "It's one of the circumstances that makes us think Hanson and Schinder were not killed by the same person. We had to know what Schinder's ring looked like. I think if we find the ring we'll find the perp.

"Manj . . ." Tully turned to Mangiapane, who, despite the cold building, was perspiring freely from his speedy round-trip to headquarters, "get Angie from downstairs, then meet me at headquarters. We gotta get everybody we can looking for that ring."

30

Pat Lennon was obsessed with Joe Cox. She did not know what to make of the direction this story was taking.

At the outset he had made it clear that if this papal visit could not qualify as page-one news of itself, he might steer it there.

She understood that Cox, in returning from his discredited position in Chicago, faced an enormous challenge to regain his premier position on the Detroit news scene. Based on her rather intimate knowledge of him before Chicago, she had once considered him above manufacturing news. Now . . .

Incontestable was his provoking an actual fight during rehearsal of the symposium. And he owned that story.

In their latest conversation, Cox had bragged about how he'd been able to get an interview—one on one—with Cardinal Schinder. He had allowed as how, *if something happened to Schinder*, the importance of that interview could be inflated.

And now, Cardinal Schinder was dead—murdered.

She did not want to even consider the possibility that a man she once loved could become a cold-blooded killer. But she could not turn away from that possibility. Not now. When someone found that missing ring, if it was found in the possession of Joe Cox . . . well, so be it.

She had to force herself away from this preoccupation with Cox. Thinking about him was not going to get her job done. And as far as she could see, her job now was to try to come up with the Cardinal's ring. It had been good of Tully to let her in on the briefing on the ring. If she were to be the one to find it, she would cut him in. In their present relationship that was a given.

Tully had part of a major police force to search for the missing ring. She, for her part, could count on a few of the reporters she worked with. But she decided first to try to go it alone. And she was not without resources.

Seated at her desk in the city room of the *News*, she flipped her Rolodex, dialed, and spoke urgently and rapidly to a series of possible sources, with no luck. The only bright spot in this endeavor was the rare quality of the missing ring. It wasn't as if she had to go into long and vague descriptions. This ring, while by no means unique, was unusual enough to need only a few words for identification. As far as she knew there were only a few rings matching it in this whole area. And those were the commemorative rings sometimes worn by the Detroit bishops who had attended the Council.

That much made her quest easy. The rest was difficult.

She assumed—correctly, as it turned out—that the police were centering their efforts on pawnshops and jewelers in and closely around Detroit proper. It made no sense to duplicate what was already being done. So she concentrated on the far suburbs. Although if she had a last dollar, she would have bet it on the cops.

Her initial efforts were directed at people she knew personally and professionally. Now she had just about exhausted those contacts. This was like searching for the needle in the haystack with the added discouraging possibility that there was no needle. After all, whoever had taken the ring may simply have wanted the ring, and had no intention of pawning or selling it.

It was with tired finger and voice that she tried still another number. This was an elegant woman who did business from her home in Clawson, a northern suburb near the opulent Birmingham-Bloomfield area. "Nancy, Pat Lennon here. I'm looking for a ring."

"I've got it, sweetie. About time you tied the knot."

Lennon smiled despite her frustration. "It's not for me. And I'm not getting married."

"Doesn't matter. I've still got the ring."

"God, I hope so. This one's a man's gold band. The front flares out into a shape like a bishop's miter. It's engraved with a picture—some men and a dove . . ."

". . . and some Latin words."

Lennon was instantly energized. "My God, I think you've got it! Have you? Have you got it?"

"No."

"What? But you just came up with a perfect description!"

"I don't have it. But I was offered it. An hour or so ago."

"What happened?"

"Kid came in with it. Never saw one like that before. The two didn't go together . . . you know: the kid and that ring. Anyway, I didn't want any part of it. It looked like trouble, and believe me, I've seen trouble."

Lennon felt a wave of relief. A kid! That very definitely did not come close to describing Joe. So, for the moment at least, she didn't have to be concerned about him. "What happened?"

"Well, as I said, there was this kid and a ring that went together like the Rolling Stones and Mozart. No way was I going to do business with him. But I didn't want any trouble. He looked real nervous. I could see him pulling a gun or something. So I told him it was a real nice piece but that I didn't have the kind of clientele that would be interested in it. At best, all I could give him was what the gold was worth—maybe thirty, thirty-five, forty dollars tops. I told him the ring was worth lots more than that. And I gave him the name and address of Mannie's, down Livernois in Ferndale. Fortunately, I had made him an offer he could easily refuse. And he left. But I don't think he was going to try any further."

"Why's that?"

"He left without bothering to take Mannie's address."

"Oh, great! So he just disappears."

"No, I got his license. He was driving an old rattletrap, but it moved pretty good."

"You got his license? Great!"

"It was one of those personalized plates. I'll spell it out: H-A-R-P-O."

"Harpo like in the Marx Brothers?"

"You got it."

"Nancy, if I ever do get married, you'll get all the business for all the rings."

"Thanks, honey." *As good as she looks,* thought Nancy as she hung up, *I'm not going to plan my retirement party to immediately follow her wedding.*

For Alonzo Tully, Christmas had come just a bit early. But he was more than satisfied with the gift.

The Golds had been presented gift-wrapped by Pat Lennon. All that was needed was some by-the-book police work. Tully had felt remiss that he could give her nothing but a scoop. But that scoop had been his premature present to her.

The *Freep* was now ahead by only one. Two for Cox, one for Lennon.

It seemed silly, almost juvenile, but that was how the investigative-reporter game was played. More importantly, in that context, this story of violence surrounding the pope's visit had belonged to the *Free Press* with Cox's story of the explosive outburst at the symposium rehearsal. No matter that the story had been virtually created by Cox.

The *Freep* had gained a further grip on the story with Cox's scoop on what had turned out to be the murder of Father Hanson. Two for the *Freep*.

Enter Lennon. Her story would be in the early morning edition of the *News* and she would continue to develop it as the day—and editions—progressed. One for the *News*.

Meanwhile, Tully was allowing himself and his squad to savor the satisfaction of a good tight arrest. This was particularly gratifying to Tully. Because Anne Marie had been victim of a similar assault, Tully had desperately wanted this one. And he got it on a silver platter.

Now, Tully, Mangiapane, and Moore were standing around a coffee machine in Homicide, on the fifth floor of headquarters.

"That kid Harpo comes by his nickname honestly," Moore said. "For a while there I thought he was a mute."

"Andrew Watson"—Mangiapane used Harpo's real name—"just needed a little of the right stimulus. Like his parents and the promise of life without parole."

"Just the same . . ." Moore dropped the Styrofoam cup in the wastebasket. ". . . I don't think he'd have opened up without the deal."

"For him it was a bargain that was just too good to pass up," Mangiapane said. "He gives us the gang, 'specially that sleazebag Vanderwehl, and he skates."

"We had Harpo for conspiracy. And we could've made it stick without much trouble. But he didn't actually pull the trigger," Tully said. "He didn't even rape the woman. He just held her down. Which was bad enough," he added grimly.

Angie again felt nausea at the thought of what the gang had done to that poor woman.

"Harpo sang good," Mangiapane said, "but then so did Bonnie. Although they both held out longer than I thought they would."

"It was that goddam loyalty they thought they owed Rick Vanderwehl," Tully said. "He was the linchpin of the gang. One of those rare birds completely without redeeming value."

"I gotta admit, Zoo," Mangiapane said, "it does my heart good to see the 'tough guys' when the veneer shatters. I'm glad the other kids saw him crying and sniveling."

"So much for 'the leader,'" said Moore. "God knows how long it would have taken us to crack this if it hadn't been that Harpo was the misfit of the gang. He came from the other side of the tracks . . . the middle-class kid in with the rich kids."

"Yeah," Mangiapane said. "Harpo happened to be a first-class mechanic and none of the rest of them could—or would—turn a screwdriver. Add to that, he's a curiosity who says a word every century or so whether he needs to or not."

"The boys, when they dumped the body," Moore added, "didn't know that Harpo had stayed behind to get the ring. And when it wouldn't come off, the Cardinal's finger did. Getting to know these kids more than I ever wanted to, I'm really quite sure none of them would have objected to taking the ring—even to the point of hacking off the finger. But, of course, none of the others would have tried to sell it. Harpo was the only one who didn't get enough pocket money to keep up with them."

"It's odd," Tully said, "what a strange way the media played into these kids. They were after the pope, but they wanted us to widen the loop of security so they'd have a better shot at him. And that's why they took out the Cardinal: to force us into that broader defense. But we were already committed to that move after the murder of Father Hanson. Only the kids didn't know that because this time there was no leak.

"The leak the *Freep* got told the public the method of execution was a broken neck. That's why Schinder ended up with a busted neck: The kids were trying for a copycat killing."

"But he'd have gotten murdered in any case, don't you think?" Moore asked.

"I'm sure of it," Tully said. "Although I've got to wonder why he thought he could handle whoever was on the phone all by himself." Tully shook his head. "Probably says something about the guy's arrogance . . ." Tully wondered if maybe something like that came built in with the position. But on further thought, he'd never heard anything like that about Cardinal Boyle. Boyle had the reputation of being a gentleman. Reserved, but never, to Tully's knowledge, arrogant.

"All the same," Tully said, "if Schinder had told us about the call, it would've at least given us a chance to send a tail along, or some backup . . . and he'd probably still be alive today."

It was quiet as the three officers again thought back over these events. "Just strange the way the media got tangled in this case," Tully reiterated. "Not to mention how lucky Pat Lennon got in finding that jeweler. At the very least that saved us a ton of time."

"But," Moore said, "there's still a killer loose out there."

They knew it.

There had been a cap on this celebration from the start. Certainly everyone was both happy and relieved to close a really messy, multiple case of three counts of assault as well as three counts of murder in the first degree. One very bad actor was certain to be off the streets for the rest of his life. And a bunch of easily led kids would be doing a variety of time behind bars. One would walk away in exchange for cooperation. But Andrew Watson, alias Harpo, was deeply impressed and thoroughly shaken.

In addition, a possible "series killer" was proven a sham—thanks to an extraordinary medical examiner, good, solid police work, and a resourceful and obliging reporter.

Which, when all was sorted out and filed, put the police back at square one: Who killed Father Hanson and why?

Lieutenant Tully led his two sergeants into their squad room where most of the squad had already gathered. Shortly the rest of the team came in; the full complement was now on hand.

Tully smiled at them. "Well, we've done what we think the killer wants us to do: We've expanded the circle of security. Short of the feds, who won't get involved until the pope arrives tonight, there's a full house—practically the entire Detroit force and a beefed-up segment of county and state law enforcement.

"Whoever it is that wants the pope is banking on our having to protect just about everybody who has any part in this papal visit. Well, we can't protect everyone in the world. But we'll concentrate on the people the killer seems to have singled out: the participants.

"So we've got almost all of the seminary covered. I don't think anyone from the outside can penetrate that security.

"The kids—the Golds—had what they thought was an effective plan to create a major diversion after the pope lands on the seminary grounds. They figured that when we checked out the disturbance, they'd hit the man. The one thing wrong with their plan was that the feds would never have responded to that. They would depend on us to take care of the periphery. They would have just closed tighter around the pope.

"Still and all, with a good portion of security diverted, it was more possible—particularly since it will be dark out there—that one or another of them might've gotten in range to fire on the pope.

"The one thing they didn't figure is that anyone getting close and attempting an assassination would be dead. But dead perps are small consolation when the main man gets hit.

"So we owe the Golds one. We've talked the Church guys out of having the outdoor reception. We'll sweep the pope from Metro to the Cardinal's home in Palmer Park.

"But we shouldn't think for a minute that any of these measures will discourage the perp. The assumption is he wants the pope, and he'll go to any extreme to get him.

"We know what we've got to do to protect the pope. What we've got to figure out is how to keep this guy from working his way up to a better shot at the pope by picking off innocent bystanders—namely, the participants, like the guys in the symposium.

"Which brings us back to Hanson—the one guy already killed. Any thoughts?"

Silence.

"Geez, Zoo," Mangiapane said finally, "the next guy on the list—if there is one—could be . . . anybody."

More silence.

Tully looked around the room. There seemed no other response forthcoming. He stepped to the squad room door and motioned someone to come in. Father Koesler entered the room.

Even though most of the squad was acquainted with the priest from past cases, Tully wanted to impress upon his people that Koesler had been called in as an expert resource person. He wanted the squad to consider carefully what the priest would be telling them.

Koesler, Tully announced, would bring the squad up to speed on the peculiarly Catholic aspects of this murder investigation. So far, excluding the copycat killing of Cardinal Schinder, one priest had been murdered as an adjunct to this papal visit. There was the possibility if not the probability of more killings.

"There's always an element of danger when the pope is around," Koesler began. "But you know that better than I. The only time, so far, a pope was shot was in his own backyard—St. Peter's Square. He's in more danger when he travels, of course, because each setting is different from all the others. So each requires different precautions, and each must be safeguarded and secured differently.

"Which introduces the elements of unfamiliarity and surprise. And there's still a kind of mystique whenever the pope travels because for lots of years he didn't. He was called 'The Prisoner of the Vatican.' Even now, because his trips are relatively few and far between, there is something special about them. And that special quality can attract dangerous nuts. So there's always that element of danger.

"This visit is also somewhat different than the others because of the message he is expected to deliver. Actually, it seems no one in authority can verify what that message is going to be. But that doesn't matter; it's been newsed about so much that everybody is taking for granted the rumor is the fact.

"So whether he actually does it or not, he might just as well state—infallibly—that artificial birth control is wrong for everybody, all the time, no matter what the circumstance.

"This is no change whatsoever from what has been Church teaching for a long time. But in recent years very few people have paid any attention to his teaching. Still, even though the vast majority don't take the doctrine seriously, it causes problems. There are some Catholics—many, even though a small percentage overall—who still follow Church teaching no matter how many others say it's silly.

"There's an even greater impact on world population. The Vatican is one of the states that formulates world policy on lots of matters, one of which is whether overpopulation is a serious, world-threatening condition. The Church's doctrine on artificial birth control is an impediment to a unified and more forceful position. Population control would be simpler, more effective if the Vatican would add its voice to that of all the other nations. The Vatican presents its stand on this question as 'truth.' It's a little difficult to buck that.

"Still and all, people around the world—everybody from individuals to nations—can and do reject Catholic policy.

"That might change dramatically were the Church to claim this doctrine was not just its ordinary teaching authority, but that it was protected by the considerable power of infallibility.

"If this were to happen, nations would be put on warning that this Catholic position was definitely not going to change or even be compromised—maybe forever. And Catholics who had rejected this teaching in practice would have to reevaluate their conduct. Perhaps they would have to leave the Church. For priests, the choice of conformity or continued disobedience would be a matter of deciding whether to leave the priesthood.

"And this radical disaster I just described touches only the surface. It would be the first in a series of shocks that would challenge choices.

"Now, in the face of all this, we have a symposium that is supposed to lead into—contribute to the Holy Father's statement. But, for reasons not really relevant here, this symposium is delivering a mixed message.

"The presentation that was supposed to have been delivered this morning was not. And that was due to the murder of the presenter, Father Hanson. And, since I was supposed to be the moderator of that session, I know what point Father Hanson would have made. He would have denied on historical as well as on theological reasons the doctrine of infallibility."

"Lemme get this straight, Father," Mangiapane said, "the special reason so many people are mad—upset—whatever, is because they expect the pope to say that the Catholic Church teaching on birth control is infallible. And Father Hanson was gonna claim there ain't any such thing as infallibility?"

"That's about it."

"Then one kind of hypothesis we could make," Angie Moore said, "is that Hanson was silenced so he would not publicly state that the pope doesn't have this special power."

"I guess so. . . ." Koesler felt he was beginning to infringe on the realm of police affairs. And he certainly didn't want to do that. He was comfortable only in doing what Tully had asked him to do: be a resource person who could guide these officers through the maze of Catholic teaching, customs, dogmas, beliefs, whatever.

"What did we used to call this in the military," one of the officers said, "a preemptive strike?"

"Yeah," another chimed in.

"In this hypothesis," Moore added to her original observation, "the killer would have to be in agreement with the pope on the issue of infallibility, no?"

Koesler nodded. "And there are millions who fit that description . . . probably thousands right here in the Detroit archdiocese."

"Wait a minute!" Mangiapane was obviously perturbed. "Are you saying maybe the pope took out a contract on the priest?"

Tully chuckled softly. "No. But I'm glad you put that question on the record. We're brainstorming and anything that comes to mind is good."

"Father Koesler," Moore said, "since Vatican II, almost everything and everybody is labeled conservative or liberal . . . tell me if I'm wrong."

"No . . . generally, I'd say that's true."

"Then let's say the pope's belief in infallibility is a conservative statement. Whereas Father Hanson's opinion on infallibility would be in the liberal camp. Right so far?"

"Right."

"Okay, then from what you know of the rest of this symposium, is there another setup like the one on infallibility? Conservative versus liberal?"

Koesler set his jaw, then said, "Some more than others.

"That's the way it was set up by Monsignor Martin, who is a pastor here and was in charge of putting together the symposium. It's not— very definitely not—what the Holy Father or the Vatican had in mind. As a matter of fact, last night, Cardinal Schinder arranged a dinner meeting for just the conservative presenters plus all the moderators. So I was present. He had it in mind to bolster the presenters and . . . well . . . influence the moderators to tip the scales as much as possible toward the conservatives.

"So, earlier today, when I first heard of the murder of the Cardinal— even before we were told about the broken neck—I would not have been surprised to learn that someone in the liberal camp had done it."

"Well . . ." Moore hesitated as if searching for the next logical avenue of thought. "Let me ask you this, Father: Is there any other session scheduled for this symposium that is comparable to the one on infallibility? One that, maybe, could have a similar impact?"

"Oh, sure. That, as far as I can judge, would be the one on moral theology."

"What?" Many of the officers were confused. One confessed to his confusion.

"There were two main concerns about the pope's statement. One had to do with infallibility—we've already discussed that. The other was the topic that was going to be the subject of this infallible statement. That would be the Church's teaching on family planning and birth control. Well, that—this Church teaching—is the subject of one of tomorrow's sessions."

"And," Moore asked, "is there the same radical clash between the conservative and liberal schools?"

"I'll say! The conservative speaker, a Father William Palmer, will present the standing Church policy: that being that the only licit way to limit conception is abstinence, rhythm, or a slightly more reliable form of the rhythm method called natural family planning.

"The liberal presenter, a Father Norbert Rasmussen, will dismiss any concern as to method. He will argue that the only moral choice is between having or not having a child. Once that choice is made, the method of preventing conception is completely the choice of the couple—with no moral sanction on any method. With the exception of abortion—if abortion were used simply as a method of birth control."

"So," Moore concluded, "it's just as big a problem for the pope, isn't it? I mean, instead of running into a challenge to infallibility, he'll be confronting an argument against the Church's teaching on conception and contraception."

"Uh-huh." Sergeant Moore, thought Koesler, was proving herself a most logical detective.

"So," Moore continued, "the pope can say this doctrine is protected by his infallible statement—without being publicly challenged, since that priest is dead. Only to have another priest expert claim the protected doctrine isn't even a doctrine."

"That's about it." Koesler felt that his value to this brainstorming session was about over. The detectives had learned from him all they needed to formulate whatever police response would be appropriate. However, he felt it would be impolite simply to walk out. To signify that he was finished, he found a chair in a corner of the room and sat down.

Tully again took over. "Okay. I think we've got as good a bead on this thing as we're gonna get—thanks to the good Father here. Any ideas on the best course to take from here?"

Silence. Everyone had an idea but they all hung back, waiting for somebody else to step forward.

Finally, Mangiapane, fearless, ran with the ball. "Like I said before, whoever's gonna get it next—if it isn't the pope—is anybody's guess. But this Father Rasmussen seems to be an odds-on favorite. So how 'bout we pull in tight around him? Dare the perp to try to get at him?"

"That's a step," Tully said. "Anybody else got any idea?"

"Yeah," Moore said. "This is just a slightly different approach to what Manj said. But what if, instead of beefing up security around Rasmussen, what if we hang him out there like bait?"

"Dangerous," Tully noted. "Gives us a much better chance to nail the perp—but dangerous."

"Sure it is," Moore said. "We'd have to explain it to Rasmussen—get his cooperation and consent. But we'd be way ahead on protection for him and, if we're dealing with some twisted mind, the pope too maybe. And that's tomorrow. In effect, we got till tomorrow to get this guy or we're gonna have a real big problem. Whatever the killer's motives in taking out a priest, I've got a creepy feeling his bottom line is the pope. Maybe he hits on liberal theologians to throw us off his ultimate target. Either way we catch him with Rasmussen as bait."

Tully looked at his detectives and read general acceptance of Moore's plan—the same plan that had been in Tully's mind even before Moore expressed it.

"Okay, let's go with it. Now, where do we set Rasmussen up? Someplace where we can bait the trap and still protect him?"

"How about that downtown parish," Mangiapane said. "St. Aloysius. It's not that far from the seminary."

Once again, Koesler had to take the floor. "St. Aloysius would be ideal, except that it's in the same building as the Chancery—headquarters for the archdiocese. And the Chancery, actually, would be a great place to put somebody if you *really* wanted him to be protected. That building has a great security system."

"Then where?" Moore asked.

"Well . . ." Koesler gave the question some thought. "How about the archbishop's residence in Palmer Park? It's in a well-populated but prosperous section. Not all that challenging to someone who's good at breaking and entering. And there are plenty of places to conceal officers throughout the mansion."

"Sounds good," Tully said. "Let's get cracking. Oh, and wait a minute: So it doesn't look too much like a setup, let's see if we can get another liberal panelist in there with Rasmussen." He looked at Koesler. "Who would you suggest?"

"Somebody else from the liberal side . . . ?" Koesler reflected. "Okay. I'd suggest Father Duncan. He's the liberal on the liturgical panel. I know him. I'm sure he'd go along with this."

"Okay." Tully signaled a halt to further discussion. Time to move. "Make sure information on who's staying where is readily available. Now, let's set our little trap and see who out there is hungry."

As his squad got busy, Tully reflected on how he and the squad had originally been exempted from papal duty to pursue the more pressing homicide cases that would undoubtedly occur during these several days. What Inspector Koznicki could not have known was that the papal entourage would open the door to Detroit's most pressing homicide investigation in memory.

31

Tomorrow he'll be here.

Tully lay on his back in bed, hands behind his head.

And tomorrow night he'll be gone. He can't get out of town too soon for me.

Anne Marie lay with her back toward him. He could tell from her deep, regular breathing that she was fast asleep. Why not; he had reassured her that all was well and that everything was taken care of.

It could be true.

The trap was set. If all went as planned, by morning the perp would be in custody, Rasmussen would be alive and well, and security would get back to its single-eyed purpose of protecting the pope. He could say whatever the hell he wanted and then split.

It was not Tully's practice to be distractedly concerned with world population or overpopulation. He was obsessed with homicide within the corporate limits of the city of Detroit.

The title of an old film came to mind. *Death Takes a Holiday.* That surely was not true in Detroit. Just because the pope was coming to town didn't mean all that hatred and vengeance was going to turn into brotherly love. Matter of fact, possibly *because* he was coming, the homicide rate might well increase as word got around to those who couldn't read that the cops would be busier protecting the pope than sweeping the 'hoods.

Tully regretted—he sincerely regretted—that he was not part of the surveillance at the archbishop's mansion. But he wanted his detectives to know that he had confidence in them. For he had.

Nonetheless, he wished he were there.

For certain sure he would get no sleep tonight. How could he?

Had they figured this correctly? Was the setup foolproof? There had been so little time. Had they thought of everything? Was there anything even at this late hour that should be done? That could be done?

It was no use; he was going to lie here and torture himself with nagging doubts, second-guessing himself totally unnecessarily, all night, without sleep.

He might as well give up on sleep. That way he wouldn't miss it as much.

Tomorrow he'll be here.

Father Koesler was trying to read himself to sleep. It wasn't working any which way. He found himself rereading sentences, paragraphs, over and over. And sleep was nowhere near.

Now that he was away from the theologians and the police, Koesler could revert to the way he had traditionally regarded whoever happened to be the Holy Father, the heir to the throne of St. Peter, the vicar of Christ on earth. This traditional attitude of Catholics to the reigning pope was something Koesler could not simply shrug away.

People who held on to this belief were becoming an endangered species.

The line of demarcation seemed to be drawn at the point where Paul VI, ignoring his own study committee, published his *Humanae Vitae*. At which point, untold scores of Catholics changed course. Catholics who had grown up believing completely and without the slightest misgiving that the pope never erred whether speaking infallibly or not, suddenly were faced with a most uncomfortable conclusion: Their pope, the one who would lead them unswervingly to the truth (and, by extension, thus to Heaven) every single time, had made a mistake. A very big and radical mistake.

With the publication of that encyclical, Catholicism split. Some gloried in the pope's fearless stand in the face of popular opposition. Some were discouraged but decided to hang in there with a crack left open to disagree with the pope if conscience so dictated. And some left without looking back.

Somewhere in that middle ground was Koesler.

And he gave little thought to infallibility. Why should anyone get upset about a function that arguably had been used exactly once in a nonvital doctrine?

The rumored subject of the pope's upcoming message was something else again. Koesler himself would be forced to reevaluate his priesthood. After forty years! How could he be forced to acquiesce to something his carefully formed conscience—his Church-formed conscience—judged to be incorrect?

Koesler's only hope was that somehow this intensifying rumor was mistaken.

He was convinced the law enforcement agencies could protect the pope from violence. But could anyone protect the Church from the pope?

Tomorrow he'll be here.

Walt Koznicki, giving up on the possibility of sleep, was sitting in front of the television in the den. A movie was showing, a Western, the sound barely audible. He paid it no mind.

It was bad enough that the Cardinal, as well as two other innocent people, had been killed by maniacs. Some kids intent on becoming "somebodies" by murdering prominent people. Far more dangerous, because he had not made any mistakes and gave no indication he would make any, was someone who was quite probably intent on killing the Holy Father.

Actually, there was no demonstrable reason why there should be a link between the murder of a priest, Father Dan Hanson, and the pope. The connection was based on what the police would admit was an educated guess. There seemed to be rampant antipathy to His Holiness. There was reason, more than sufficient reason, to suspect that someone might want to kill the pope. There was no discernable motive for the murder of Hanson.

One opinion had it that whoever had killed Hanson wanted the protective loop around His Holiness to be enlarged to include all those who might be attacked—thereby weakening the ring of protection around the presumed main target. Hypothesis had it that perhaps another murder would have this effect.

Who might be the next victim? Would there be another victim? There was no way of telling. Looking now for a connection not with the pope, but with another participant in connection with the papal visit, the finger pointed at Rasmussen as a liberal theologian of the same stripe as the previous victim, Hanson.

On top of all that was Wanda's fear of what effect the Holy Father's statement would have on one of their own sons.

Wanda had not expressed her deepest feelings. Koznicki knew her well enough to understand that she was holding back. He did not have to search for her reason: She was ashamed to admit to her most Catholic husband that she wished the Holy Father dead.

Probably she was ashamed to admit such a wish even to herself. Probably she considered it a mortal sin. Thoughts could be sins as well as deeds, he knew.

As the movie droned on, he innocently drifted into a world of make-believe.

How is this for a scenario? Supposing the Holy Father was walking down the aisle of Cobo Arena . . .

In his mind's eye, Koznicki could see it clearly. He was replaying a similar procession in Pontiac's Silverdome some years back. There is the panoply of vestments. A sea of black and white, highlighted by magenta, deep reds and purples, and the incomparable crimson of the Cardinals. Thousands in the stands are roaring a welcome. The choir and orchestra are making faintly heard music.

In Koznicki's fancy, he is walking in step with His Holiness. Now Koznicki sees a hand come level with someone's shoulder. The hand is pointing a gun. Koznicki moves toward the gun. The crack of the weapon can be heard even above the roar of the crowd.

Koznicki looks back to see a red stain spreading over the Holy Father's white robe. Resigned anguish suffuses the pope's face as he slowly sinks to the floor.

Koznicki jerked back to reality. Though the house was cold, he was perspiring. It was a fantasy; of all the people in the world, outside of his wife or children, the Holy Father would be the first for whom Koznicki would take a bullet.

Then why did the gunman hit his target?

Did Koznicki move too slowly? Deliberately? So that his wife would no longer anguish over the possible effect a papal pronouncement would have on her son?

A fantasy. It could not happen.

But he could not erase the vision.

Tomorrow he'll be here.

In some perverse way, Dave Wallace saw himself as a knight about to embark on a noble but perilous crusade. In spite of Sally's fervent urging to spend a second consecutive night with her, he decided he needed this night at home, by himself. He needed to purify himself. He needed to rededicate himself.

There was no use kidding himself: The responsibility for preventing the pope from causing unending damage was pointing at him.

The late news reported that a gang of mindless young people had been arrested for several murders, including that of Cardinal Schinder. Their killing spree was supposed to have culminated in the assassination of the pope when he landed in a helicopter at Sacred Heart Seminary.

Damn! That would have preceded his planned attack, thus rendering his own action unnecessary.

It appeared that the gang's motive was mere notoriety. What the hell difference did it make? Their motive could have been literally anything. What counted was that they would have prevented the pope from elevating that ugly doctrine to the rank and protection of infallibility.

Wallace had hoped, but had never realistically believed, that anyone but himself would carry out this mission. The kids' action was a surprise not only to him but to everyone.

Wallace could hope, he could pray—but he would have to be prepared. His soul was in turmoil. But there was nothing he could do but wait. He knew what he had to do and how to do it. He found it difficult to pray; how does one *pray* for the courage to commit murder? To kill a pope?

Tomorrow he'll be here.

Father John Selner felt just awful. He had agreed to a scholarly debate, nothing more. He respected Dave Hanson. He had excitedly looked forward to doing battle with this wrongheaded but likable liberal.

Selner had been disappointed in Cardinal Schinder, the number two man in the Vatican—and a dedicated conservative, as was Selner. He was embarrassed and distressed by Schinder's interference in the symposium.

Now both these men were dead.

There would be no threat or meddling on Schinder's part. Perhaps more tragically there would be no debate with Hanson.

How many times had the two of them engaged in verbal battle in the past! Yet neither had budged the other in the slightest. Nonetheless, they had remained good friends, even though, by this time, each had abandoned all hope of scoring a single uncontested point in debate— even in simple conversation.

Still they were able to laugh, pray, drink, and prize each other's priesthood.

Gone!

The Church had lost a charismatic figure in Dietrich Cardinal Schinder. The Church had lost a brilliant scholar and Selner had lost a good and dear friend in Dave Hanson.

In his charity, Selner would now pray for both deceased priests. And then he would sleep and be ready to greet His Holiness late tomorrow.

Tomorrow he'll be here.

But it won't be just the usual cosmetic visit where he rides around in the popemobile waving at and blessing people. It won't be a run-of-the-mill trip where he makes bromide statements like war is bad, peace is good, women belong either in the bedroom or the delivery room, or birth control is a no-no. Tomorrow the pope will be greeted by a crowd that is at least partially hostile.

And all of this the result of Joe Cox's ability to stir things up! He had pretty well been in the catbird seat from the very beginning. And—a tribute to his experience and ability—it had been easy.

Of course, in the spirit of fair play, he had to tip his hat to this Monsignor Martin who had set up the symposium. It was Martin who had stacked dynamite and fire in every one of those panels. All Cox had to do was make an intelligent selection and then goad the participants and there was sure to be an explosion.

And Cox had made a good choice in igniting the discussion on morals. The pope had a habit of utilizing almost every possible occasion to condemn birth control. And the "faithful" answered him every time with a resounding, "You're nuts!"

The only other comparable panel that Cox might have torched was the one on dogma. But how was he to know that one of the panelists would deny infallibility?

He was equally pleased with himself for having lightly romanced that EMS gal, Emily. Although he'd had to allow for luck; after all, the driver might've been a guy. But when you're on a roll . . . It hadn't taken long to recruit Emily. Some tenderness, feigning a genuine interest in her job, promising to investigate some of her gripes . . . She'd asked Cox to do some pieces on something like police harassment or breach of contract. He had promised her he would try—knowing full well that Nellie Kane would never go for it. Promises, promises, promises.

Emily probably could have handed him his scoop under most any condition. But that her wagon had been the one responding to the attack on Father Hanson! How lucky can you get!

Luck was running a little thin now, Cox had to admit. Emily and her whole crew had been suspended pending the continuing investigation of the leak. Damn cops! They've cleared their own people so they'll keep the pressure on till they find the source—Emily.

Then there was his exclusive interview with Cardinal Schinder. It had printed up better than it had actually been. So, okay, Schinder didn't quite say what Cox had quoted him as saying. Schinder was no longer around to object or set the record straight.

What was the harm?

Just put a spin on a few of Schinder's statements and the Cardinal becomes a bit of a prophet. So he could foresee the threat to his own life! Probably advance his cause for canonization some day. Cox had done Schinder a favor in giving him larger-than-life quotes. And Schinder had returned the favor by giving Cox an exclusive that would be page one in the *Freep*—and, undoubtedly, in lots of other papers.

But no way could Cox get around Lennon's coverage of Schinder's murder. She had scored big on that. And after coming late into the story!

No doubt about it, Lennon was good. Damn good. A smile spread on Cox's face as he recalled and savored all the many ways in which Lennon was good.

Every time his memory traveled this well-worn path, Cox would begin to get a craving for Lennon. It just happened.

The phone rang.

"Tomorrow he'll be here, you know." Lennon didn't bother to identify herself.

"I know that." ESP at its best! Here he had just finished composing the image of Pat Lennon's body. All it needed was a voice. And here it was.

"I'm worried about you, Joe."

"That's nice. I've been thinking about you too."

She disregarded the personal intimation. "Look, Joe, you and I have been on a load of stories over the years. We've covered a bunch of them together, even if it was for competing papers. But . . ." She paused. He waited. Finally she plunged in. "Joe, I've never seen you develop a story like you did this one."

Cox scrunched down in his easy chair. He wasn't sure where this conversation was going. He didn't really care; he was just enjoying her voice, the only part of her he had not composed earlier. "What do you mean, lover?"

Again she would overlook the endearing term. "You know what I'm talking about. We touched on it earlier. You're managing this story, Joe."

"Jealous?"

"Come on!"

It was definitely the wrong thing to say. He knew it as the word escaped his mouth. Lennon didn't have a jealous bone in her well-crafted body. "Sorry," he said. "But where do you get off accusing me of that?"

"You don't expect me to believe all those quotes in your interview with Schinder. . . ."

"Why not? What makes you think Schinder didn't say what I wrote he said?"

"He's Nostradamus? He came here to prepare the way for the pope. What made him think his own life could be in danger, for instance? There was controversy here, okay. But not murder. Hanson hadn't even been killed yet. And there's a whole bunch of other quotes in there that are pretty good stuff, but strictly off the wall."

"What are you getting so worked up about, Pat? It's not like nobody ever juiced up an interview before."

"It's the whole damn thing, Joe. You goaded those guys into a fight at the rehearsal. And how in hell did you get the story on Hanson—and the method of murder? It was like you were there!"

"The lady who told me about it was there."

Lennon wanted very much to believe that last statement. In her heart she harbored a doubt. Would . . . could Joe Cox actually kill somebody just to create a sensational story? She didn't want to believe that. She wanted to believe what Cox had just told her. "I know what you're trying to do, Joe," she said at length. "But manipulating this story is not a real great way to regain your status here."

"Let me worry about that. Hey, gal, when this is over—when the pope goes home—what say we get together? Not like before," he added hurriedly before she could turn him down out of hand. "Just, say, a date. A legitimate date."

A long pause.

"Maybe. We'll see how tomorrow goes."

Tomorrow he'll be here.

When the pope gets here, he won't have us to worry about, thought Ronnie Albright.

It was all Rick Vanderwehl's fault.

No. Check that.

Ronnie had made a resolution some hours before. He couldn't guarantee he would never break his resolution. But he would try to keep it.

It was, simply, to take responsibility for what he did.

He hadn't been aware of it till today. Rick habitually blamed everyone but himself. The woman had to be killed. It was her fault. She shouldn't have recognized Ronnie. The grocer had to be killed. It was his fault. He didn't move fast enough for Rick.

To top it off, Rick came by it honestly. Ronnie had just spent a considerable time listening to Rick's parents blame everybody else for what their son had done. And what had all that gotten everyone? The Golds were on the ninth floor of police headquarters, locked up. With the exception of Harpo—who apparently learned to sing before he learned to talk—the Golds were going to be away from civilization for a very long time. Rick and himself? Maybe forever.

Ronnie could and did deeply regret he had ever thrown in with the Golds and Rick Vanderwehl. If he could change anything in his life, it would be that decision.

Now he would have to live with that—and maybe die for it.

Lieutenant Tully glanced at his illuminated digital wristwatch. Just past midnight.

The day had come. Today the pope would arrive in Detroit.

According to the original plans, Tully was not supposed to have had any participation in the papal visit. He was supposed to have anchored Homicide particularly from just before the pope's arrival until his departure.

But oddly, it was Homicide investigations—one closed, the other still perhaps involving a threat to the pope—that now drew him to the core of the pope's visit.

The phone rang. Tully lifted it from the cradle before the first ring ended. "What?" he snapped.

"We got another murder, Zoo."

"Who?"

"Palmer, Father William Palmer—the guy who was supposed to be on that panel with Rasmussen."

"Damn!" Tully had never felt lower.

32

It was early in the morning, and bitterly cold. But Dr. Moellmann, having been apprised of what had happened to whom, eagerly drove down the curving Jefferson Avenue.

Jefferson originally had begun at about the spot where Cadillac and his settlers got out of their canoes and founded Detroit. Now, Jefferson spread east and west like an ancient parent with open arms. Moellmann lived in the Pointes section of Jefferson, some miles from downtown Detroit.

Moellmann worked quickly but meticulously over the remains of Father William Palmer. There were special things he was looking for. And he found them.

The victim's neck was fractured in almost the exact location as Father Hanson's. Also nearly identical was the pattern of bruises on the neck, as well as the dime-size hemorrhages on and around the chin and the nape.

The only actual difference was that Palmer's body had not been hurled down the stairs. Palmer had not been wearing a ring. But if he had, everyone was certain it would have been left untouched. These killings definitely had nothing to do with robbery.

This was not a copycat killing. It was a serial killer. Moellmann danced around that conclusion pending the police investigation. But, again, no one doubted that Moellmann believed the serial-death theory.

By this time the techs were done at the scene and the Homicide detectives were on the street at an hour they considered ungodly early.

As the sun rose on a clear, frigid morning, the city and, indeed, the world, learned what had happened during the night. Those who were interested in what had been going on in "Murder City" became decidedly more interested. Those with a stake in the event were approaching dismay.

"He went through our security like the Indians through Custer," Tully said.

Tully and Koznicki sat in the latter's office, where they had been licking their metaphorical wounds before getting actively involved once again.

"It is humiliating," Koznicki allowed. "But I think it should not be."

Tully looked up, hoping for whatever balm his superior could apply.

"By now," Koznicki said, "this has turned into a guessing game. We made an educated guess—an extremely educated guess—and we guessed wrong."

Tully rubbed a palm with his fist. "It had to be Rasmussen. He was the odds-on favorite. He was about to deliver the second-most provocative speech. And he was from the left. Almost a carbon copy of Hanson. It had to be him."

"But it was not. Now we have no alternative but to regroup and start over."

Tully shook his head helplessly. "But Walt, if we start over, we're trying to get inside a crazy man's head. Okay, he wants to hit the pope . . . or so we assume. Okay, if that's the case, he wants to force us to thin out our blanket coverage of the pope. Okay, so we've got to do it to some degree. But now it seems like there's no rhyme or reason to it.

"Okay, I understand that Catholics have this black and white thing they call conservatives and liberals. But he hasn't picked one *or* the other. It's almost like he's picking victims at random. Far as I can see, there's no way in hell we can forestall that."

Koznicki said nothing. All that Tully said seemed true. But Koznicki tended to see their job in terms of demanding priorities. The first responsibility was to shield His Holiness from any harm. Then, to the remaining best of their ability, they had to protect everyone participating in or attending this event.

Through it all, they had to try to catch a killer. So far, there definitely was only one. The kids, the Golds, were an anomaly. They were akin to a deadly mosquito that had been swatted.

Now the police were up against a clever and effective killing machine who, so far, had limited himself to murder with his bare hands, the most elemental method of all.

And while there was no doubt in anyone's mind that the two priests had been murdered by the same person, there was no way anyone could guarantee that this perp was the only one who wanted His Holiness.

So what if, please God, they should find this bare-handed killer before he had the opportunity of killing again? Were there more—how many?—waiting to assume the task?

Walt Koznicki's thoughts were somber. They had every right to be.

There was a knock at the door. Mangiapane entered at Koznicki's bidding.

"Inspector . . . Zoo . . . I just checked with the feds. The Holy Father apparently hasn't changed his mind . . . about coming here, I mean."

Koznicki's surprise was evident. "Was he expected to have a change in plans?"

"I guess there was some talk. He really got shook up about Schinder."

"That is understandable," Koznicki said. "To be expected. After all, Cardinal Schinder was the Holy Father's right-hand man. It must have been a shock. But I would expect His Holiness to keep his commitments. Who doubted that?"

"I don't know whether there was a doubt involved," Mangiapane said. "I think it was the special agent in charge. He just wanted it checked out. After all, like he said, the Holy Father don't show here we got a lot of dismantling to do." He smiled. "It would also be a lucky break for us."

Tully said nothing. There was no way he would be happy to call off this investigation. There was a killer out there who needed to be put away. It didn't help that the perp had left a very capable and experienced Homicide Division with egg on its face.

"Wait," Tully said, "you got that handbook our people put together for this papal visit?"

"Yes, of course." Koznicki, in one hand, picked up from the windowsill an enormous loose-leaf notebook and handed it across the desk. Tully had to use both hands to receive the massive document.

Tully seldom thought of it, but now was one of those moments when he was impressed. Walt Koznicki was a large, powerful man, even at his age.

Tully searched the table of contents, then began to page through the handbook seemingly at random.

Koznicki turned his attention to Mangiapane. "When is the Holy Father slated to arrive from Rome?"

"Let's see . . . about 7:30 this evening."

"That means we have . . ." Koznicki studied his watch. ". . . about eleven hours to wrap this up and prepare for his arrival."

Mangiapane shrugged.

Koznicki glanced absently at Tully who had found the photos of the clerical participants.

"Have they cut back on any of the scheduled activities?" Koznicki asked.

"Well," Mangiapane responded, "after touchdown at Metro, he was supposed to go by chopper directly to the seminary, and then by limo to the archbishop's home to rest up." Mangiapane shifted his weight to his other foot. "But now, after what happened, they've cut just about everything to the bone. They've eliminated the side ceremonies and they're concentrating on Cobo Arena."

Without looking up from the handbook, Tully said, "Walt, you're the most official Catholic I know."

Koznicki smiled.

"Don't these guys have a uniform of the day? I see vestments and clerical collars and chains and beanies—all in different colors. And then I see business suits and ties—like Madison Avenue. Real neat. But all these guys have 'Reverend' and 'Right Reverend' and 'Very Reverend' and 'Most Reverend.' They should all look the same, no? I mean, they do have uniforms, don't they?"

"They used to," Koznicki said. "Before the Council, you would have seen all these clerical gentlemen in what is now the occasional dress. They would all be wearing black, and clerical collars. There would be some color, but only from the monsignors and bishops and, of course, the Cardinals.

"But after the Council, a number of priests did not want to be separated from the laity in what they considered a caste system. This is particularly true of the scholars and experts who are meeting here this week. And that, Alonzo, in somewhat abbreviated form, is why they are not all dressed alike."

Tully said nothing in response. It was not even clear that he had listened with full attention. He continued to flip through pages of photos.

From his absorbed attitude toward the pictures and the question he'd raised, Koznicki had a hunch that Tully was onto something.

Koznicki turned back to Mangiapane. "Then, the Holy Father's only public appearance here will be in the arena?"

"That's the way it shakes out, Inspector. He's due to arrive at the arena at 8:30 by motorcade from the airport."

"At 8:30," Koznicki repeated. "That should work out well. The downtown office workers will have left for the day. So the motorcade should have clear sailing."

"Hmm . . ." Tully mused as he repeatedly flipped a couple of pictures back and forth. Now Tully had Koznicki's complete attention.

Mangiapane, unaware that Koznicki had tuned him out, continued his review of what had been planned for the papal visit. "When the motorcade gets to Cobo, plans are to take him, and as many cars as will fit, right into the hall through the underground entrance. They've got a secure room for him and the other clergy to get vested. It's simple, Inspector. But along the way to keeping it simple, there won't be any popemobile. Which is too bad, 'cause that's bulletproof. It means the Holy Father is gonna have to walk the length of the arena to get to the altar. That'll be tough to secure. But I think we can do it."

Tully was shaking his head. Koznicki was watching him. "What is it, Alonzo?"

"Um . . . oh . . . nothing."

"Something," Koznicki insisted.

"Well . . ." Tully turned the handbook around to face Koznicki. "Look at these two pictures." He flipped the pages back and forth.

Koznicki took the pages from Tully's hand and turned them more slowly. Koznicki slowed even more until he was able to study the pictures more deliberately. After several moments, he looked across the desk at Tully. The silence became the unspoken question.

"You don't see it?" Tully seemed unsure of himself and wanted a corroboration from Koznicki that wasn't being offered.

Koznicki studied the designated photos again. Finally, he looked up. "They are the two victims of our serial killer."

"Look at them again. Aside of the fact that they're both priests and they're both wearing business suits, anything else strike you about them?"

Koznicki tried again. This time he knew what he should be trying to find: something in common besides their vocation and style of apparel.

The furrows on Koznicki's brow smoothed. "They resemble one another. Faintly. But there is some resemblance. Is that it?"

Tully nodded. "Now you know why I said I didn't have much."

But Koznicki would not let it drop. "You think it possible they were killed because they resembled one another?"

"No. That's hardly likely. That's almost out of a joke. It's impossible . . . isn't it?"

"Alonzo, we are out of theories. There seems no rhyme or reason for these killings. Where can we go with this theory?"

"Well, keeping in mind there isn't any foundation to this theory at all, I kept rummaging through these photos. Hanson, remember, was tall and thin, about six feet, with an oval head, and bald except for a white fringe, and he wore glasses.

"Palmer was tall and thin and had that same sort of elongated head.

He had white hair too, but he combed it over a bald spot. And he wore wire-rimmed glasses.

"So what am I looking for in this look-alike contest that's going nowhere? Tall, thin, glasses, bald or balding, and maybe something that argues for a resemblance that we'd recognize when we see it." Tully paused for effect. He had the complete attention of Koznicki, and of Mangiapane, who had long ago recognized that he was the third wheel.

Slowly, Tully turned the page till he found what he was looking for: a picture of a priest—younger than the other two, but very much in the running in the resemblance race.

"Yes," Koznicki said, impressed. "Who is he?"

Tully referred to the caption beneath the photo, which he was viewing upside down. "Father Gregory Ward. Age forty-five. Got a degree in music and theology. He teaches at . . . Witten/Herdecke University. And he's a panelist on the sacred-music program of this symposium. And there it is." Tully was not elated. "That's it. I didn't find anyone else in all of these people who vaguely had any resemblance to these three. But it's dumb . . . I wasted your time even telling you."

"Thus far," Koznicki said at length, "we have followed hypotheses that had the killer selecting controversial priests or liberal priests. And we have been wrong. Now we face the possibility of priests who look alike." He raised both hands in a gesture of futility. "What are we to conclude? That the first killing was a case of mistaken identity? That the killer was after Father A and killed Father B by mistake because it was dark? And when he discovered his mistake, he struck again at his original target? Or is it that he is just killing look-alikes? And if so, is Father Ward next in line to be the next victim on the killer's path toward the pope?"

"Ridiculous, right?"

Koznicki shrugged. Tully and Mangiapane let the obviously rhetorical question lie.

"What do you wanna do, Inspector?" Mangiapane finally asked.

"The least we can do, it seems, is go talk to this priest. See if he can shed any light on this. Perhaps he knew the other two priests. Perhaps he can tell us something that will bring all this together—connect the murders. It would be wise, in any case, to provide Father Ward with special protection. For all we know—and at this stage we do not know much—Father Ward may be an intended victim. This is developing into a case of 'Why is this happening?' rather than 'Who is doing it?' We may have to determine why this is happening before we can find out who is doing it."

"Let's get on it." Tully stood. "Manj, come with us."

33

The three detectives, Koznicki, Tully, and Mangiapane, waited on the fifth floor of Police Headquarters for an elevator. The elevators at 1300 Beaubien undoubtedly were not the slowest in Western civilization, but they ranked.

Finally the doors slid open, revealing a clearly surprised Father Koesler. No one made a move either to get on or off the car.

Tully was the first to speak. "What are you doing here?"

Further surprised, Koesler said, "You asked me to come."

"That's right. I did. Sorry." For Tully, it seemed that he had made that phone call to Koesler days ago, so much had happened in the meantime. "We've got to go on a run now. But I'd like you to stick around, if you don't mind."

"Not at all. I think I'll just drop over and see if the library's open."

With that, the officers, and a secretary who also had been waiting, boarded the elevator.

"Sorry about Father Palmer," Koznicki said. "We did everything in our power to prevent that."

Quite automatically, Koesler said, "Thank you." It seemed the thing to do, though on reflection, he wondered why anyone should express condolences when Koesler scarcely knew Palmer. It must have been that they both were priests.

As the elevator began its interminable descent, Koesler said, "I've just been over to Cobo Hall. Seems it's business as usual. I'm surprised. I thought they would cancel the remaining panels of the symposium. Matter of fact, I am surprised that the Holy Father hasn't canceled his visit."

"No," Mangiapane said, "I checked, and, so far, the trip's on."

The elevator traveled several more inches.

"As a matter of fact," Koesler resumed, "somebody—I guess Monsignor Martin—got the panelists to issue their papers in advance of their meetings, which seems strange. It's as if the verbal, live debate wasn't expected to take place. Very strange."

No one seemed eager to pick up the verbal ball. So, to fill the vacuum, Koesler continued talking.

240

"I thought it particularly odd that the liturgy panel hadn't finished the program for tonight's Mass until now. After all, the choir has to rehearse. And they need to know what the program will be. It's all very last-minute stuff. Not very considerate."

Koesler paused as the elevator neared the second floor. Still no one filled the conversational gap. So he plowed on.

"I ran into Dave Wallace in the corridor over there. He's the music director for this evening's liturgy," he explained, parenthetically. "He was fuming. Seems whoever's in charge of that panel made out a program of really rotten music. I looked it over and I had to agree with Dave. I mean, since the Council and the change to the vernacular, a lot of people have contributed some really awful music to the liturgy. And the worst of that is on tonight's program."

The secretary exited on the second floor. No one entered. Next stop, the main floor. Sometime.

"You know," Koesler now was having no trouble filling the void. He was warming to his subject. "We had achieved such a marvelous treasury of music down through the centuries. That was one of the tragedies of Vatican II: that it marked virtually the end of those Church classics by Palestrina and Perossi and the like.

"Maybe the strangest part of this whole thing is the person who programmed tonight's liturgy. Actually, I've never met Greg Ward, but I do know his work. He is one of the few active classicists left. How could he ever have submitted a program like tonight's? It's almost as if it were done by a different person."

Main floor.

Father Koesler moved to exit the elevator, but stopped when he realized he was the only one moving.

"What did you just say?" Koznicki asked.

"What?" Koesler had not been paying much attention to himself. He had to play his monologue back in fast reverse.

Before he could recall anything of importance he'd said, Koznicki spoke again. "What was the name of that priest you just mentioned?"

"Uh . . . Greg Ward . . . Father Gregory Ward. But I don't really know him. Just of him—his work."

"You said the program he wrote was unlike his work?" Koznicki pressed.

"Yes! That I am quite sure of. And if I had any doubts, they would be dispelled by Dave Wallace's agreeing with me."

"And"—Tully pushed the UP button—"what did you say last . . . the last thing you said?"

"Uh . . . I forgot."

"Something about, 'It's almost as if it were done by a different person,'" Tully supplied.

"Yes . . . I guess that's it." The others just looked at him wordlessly. "Well, it is," Koesler said somewhat defensively. "There's no way I could have imagined Greg Ward submitting a program like that. Unless, perhaps, he's not well . . . all the excitement and all . . ."

"We have another possibility," Koznicki said with some animation.

The ride returning them to the Homicide Division seemed much faster than the trip to the main floor.

Koznicki and Tully looked at each other with barely suppressed excitement. "Perhaps, Alonzo, the killer did *not* penetrate our security."

Tully nodded. "Maybe he was inside it all the time."

"Huh?" Father Koesler offered.

Once in the Homicide section, word got around that they were on to something. One by one, then in clusters, detectives crowded around the inspector's office.

Koznicki flipped the handbook open and showed the photo of Father Ward to Koesler.

He looked at it briefly, then said, "Yes. This is Father Ward. Though, as I said, I never actually met him. But I have seen him around. This is he."

"Manj," Tully said, "where did our guys get these mug shots?"

"Geez, Zoo, I think the priests brought them. When they got here our guys put the photos and the idents—which they also gave us—in mounts on these pages. That's one of the reasons it's loose-leaf: We kept getting this stuff in dribs and drabs."

"Okay," Tully said to Koesler, "take a look at the ident. You know this place where he's a teacher?"

"Herdecke? I've heard of it. It's not a major university, but good quality."

"Where is it?"

"Germany. The Rhineland area, if I'm not mistaken. Around Cologne."

"Manj," Tully said, "get this place on the phone, now, I don't care what the local time is. We want, we need some information about Father Gregory Ward. Press all the buttons!"

"Got it!" Mangiapane enlisted the aid of everyone, particularly officers with some foreign-country phone experience. In a relatively short time, he had one of Father Ward's colleagues on the line.

Inspector Koznicki was connected with a befuddled priest. After a brief introduction and explanation, Koznicki had the priest describe Father Ward. With growing signs of concern, Koznicki wrote, "medium to short build . . . full head of dark hair with usual heavy shadow . . . always claimed that he took after his Italian mother . . . explained his swarthy features and coloring . . . good eyesight, never wore glasses." And last but by no means least, the colleague remembered that Father Ward's flight was scheduled to either stop over or change over in Ireland and in Boston.

Next stop, the officers who had contacted Herdecke were rattling the connection with Dublin. There, they tracked down Superintendent Sean O'Reardon, who was most willing to provide information.

Koznicki explained the situation as it now had developed in Detroit. There was the possibility of a switch of identities either in Ireland or in Boston. Koznicki was putting his next to last buck on Ireland.

It rang a bell.

It could not be otherwise. On the day in question the body of an unknown male without any identification was found in Dublin Airport.

O'Reardon recalled that he had not believed the dead man to have been a tramp.

And, oh, yes: The cause of death was a broken neck.

Yes, O'Reardon would contact Herdecke and through them locate Father Greg Ward's family and arrange for a positive identification.

There it was.

Now only the package needed to be tied.

Not only was the bogus priest their murderer, he had killed before. He was dangerous and, even though to date as far as they knew he had killed only by hand, he might very well be armed. Chances of getting a firearm of some sort through Irish airport security was remote. Getting one in the states? In Detroit? He would have no problem.

Mangiapane drove; Koznicki, Tully, and Koesler were quietly thoughtful passengers. Plenty of backup followed. Koesler was ordered to remain in the car once they reached the seminary. This would be a dangerous situation, they explained.

Many of the uniformed officers called in for this duty were those whose previous assignment had been security for the seminary. They were familiar with the building and, on arrival, they closed off all entrances and exits.

Mangiapane checked with the security guard at the main entrance. He reported that, while there had been some traffic in and out this morning, no Father Ward had checked out.

Anything was possible. The bogus priest might have attempted flight dressed in civilian clothing. He might be in some remote area of the seminary. He might be . . . anywhere. Then, again, he might be in his assigned room. After all, he had no reason to suspect that anyone had broken his cover.

First, the police would try the obvious.

Koznicki, Tully, and Mangiapane, along with several other officers, took the stairs toward "Ward's" room.

Silently they positioned themselves along the walls of the corridor on either side of the door. A door that seemed to have taken on a silent menace.

Through a series of signs the officers made sure each knew what his or her responsibility was.

Convinced they were ready, Koznicki, standing to one side of the door, pounded on it. The force of his hammering shook the old but sturdy door in its frame.

"Police!" Koznicki said in a loud, commanding voice. "Open the door!"

No sound came from the room. Was it empty? Impossible to tell. They were certain only that there was no way out of that room other than through this door. Outside the windows was a drop of more than thirty feet to a cement and tile pavement. And there were officers waiting down there, just out of sight of the windows.

Koznicki looked at his assembled officers. They returned his gaze. He nodded, indicating he would try again.

"Police!" Koznicki shouted more loudly as he hammered the door. There could be no possibility that anyone in that room would not hear and understand. "Open the door and you will not be harmed!"

The police, weapons at the ready, waited.

This time they did not have to wait long.

An earsplitting blast came from within the room. Bullets splintered the door. The first volley was followed by two more. They had to be coming from a large-caliber semiautomatic weapon.

After the third burst, there was a moment of silence. Mangiapane spun from the right and Tully from the left. Mangiapane kicked the now all-but-destroyed door and it collapsed. Both officers now were in the center of the door space, crouching low and firing salvo after salvo.

Finally there were only echoes.

Either the impact of their bullets had carried the man out of one of the windows or he had jumped, taking shards of glass to the ground with him.

The sound of gunfire continued to reverberate through the ancient corridors.

The scene, in and out of that room, became the growing center of attention of nearly everyone within earshot of the gun battle. It seemed as if every window in that area of the second floor was filled with officers staring at the body crumpled on the ground.

People—workers, guards, guests—stepped tentatively from various parts of the building. All were shocked. Slowly the growing circle advanced toward the body with an attitude of near reverence.

It seemed much longer than it actually took for officers to take charge and secure the scene for the tech experts who were even now being contacted.

Father Koesler, obediently self-confined to the car, had waited with anxiety, not knowing what to expect. All he knew was that something he said had started all this. He felt some responsibility for what might happen.

When the shooting began, he was so startled he hit his head on the roof of the car. It seemed the noise would never end.

Then came the body through the window as if it were being pulled on a wire. Although logic told Koesler otherwise, events seemed to be taking place in slow motion; he knew he would never lose the image in his mind. It would be indelibly etched there.

Koesler would have left the car but for two considerations: He had promised to remain inside, and he did not want to enhance the memory of what he had just witnessed.

In time, Inspector Koznicki emerged from the building. Slowly, thoughtfully, he came to the car in which Koesler sat. He got behind the wheel but didn't switch on the ignition. Both men sat in silence.

Finally, Koznicki looked at Koesler and smiled—not an untroubled smile. But it unlocked the door. "Where are Lieutenant Tully and Sergeant Mangiapane?" Koesler asked.

"They will go in another car. There are reports to be made."

"Oh, thank God! I was afraid one of them had been hit."

Koznicki glanced sharply at Koesler, as though the thought of the danger they had shared had not occurred to him until this moment. "No. Thank God. They were the ones who answered fire. That is why they must submit reports. Routine. No, thank God! No one was hurt except the man who so far has no name."

Koznicki started the car, but had to wait in position as other police vehicles entered the seminary grounds. Koesler was grateful the car heater had been turned back on.

At last Koznicki was able to move out. He suggested dropping Koesler at St. Joseph's. That was acceptable.

Koznicki, as usual, was lavish in his praise of Koesler's help in breaking this case. Koesler realistically minimized his role. All he had done was to recognize that a Church music program did not much reflect its presumed programmer. Lots of people could have done that. In fact, the very same point had been made by Dave Wallace who was complaining about it. Very probably Wallace would have concluded that it was, at best, strange that what was chosen was not only such poor music, but also that there was a total absence of any classic composition in the program.

And, Koesler added, he certainly would never have gone into detail concerning these matters if that elevator ride had not been so long and everyone else had not been so quiet.

But Koznicki insisted on heaping credit on Koesler's reluctant shoulders.

Then Koznicki went on to fill in some gaps. About how Tully had noticed the physical similarities between the two priests who were victims of the serial killer. And the striking resemblance that mirrored the physical characteristics of the man calling himself Father Gregory Ward.

During this explanation, Koesler was particularly attentive.

"Unfortunately," Koznicki said as they neared St. Joseph's, "we have no identification for the alleged murderer. However, the Irish police now have a tentative identification of a man found in the Dublin airport last Sunday. Their John Doe was found with his neck broken and totally bereft of any identification. Once we exchange faxes with Ireland, we can move on to an ID for our man. For our man must surely have come from Ireland.

"But, the motive! The motive! If he wanted to kill the Holy Father—

and we assume he did—why would he kill two priests who were panelists in the symposium? To create a diversion? Why two who bore physical resemblance to each other? And to him? Or is that merely a coincidence? Did he have any other intended victims? And if so, would they have shed light on this resemblance?"

As Koesler was about to leave the car, an announcement came over the police radio.

"Did you hear that!" Koznicki exclaimed. "Now that changes everything."

Absently, Koesler exited the car, thanking Koznicki for the ride.

For a few moments, Koznicki wondered at Koesler's casual reaction to a major news bulletin. Perhaps it was a reaction to all that had gone on during this uniquely busy morning. So Koznicki continued on toward headquarters.

Koesler had heard the news all right. But he was too preoccupied with other thoughts for it to register.

Continuing in his distracted state, he began walking toward the church rather than the rectory. He lowered himself into a pew at the rear of the church. He knelt and thought and prayed. He sat and thought and prayed. He walked the aisles and thought and prayed.

Finally, he seemed to come to a private and unsatisfying conclusion.

As he walked to the rectory, his expression was clouded but resolute. Several phone calls later, he had located a priest who would fill in for him at the noon weekday Mass.

And then he began a purposeful walk. He did not seem a bit happy.

PART FOUR

PART FOUR

34

Father Koesler paid little attention to the slow-paced chaos of the anthill that was Cobo Hall. Long before his arrival the wrap-up and the take-down had begun. Things were being dismantled and stored. Maintenance men were everywhere doing busy things. Behind the scenes, lawyers for the city and lawyers for the Church were arguing over rental deposits.

Through all this he walked resolutely toward the room that was to have housed the liturgy panel. They hadn't yet taken the sign down.

Inside, workers were folding, packing, and storing everything but the walls. A few of the folding chairs were still standing. On one of these sat a lone figure in a black overcoat and hat. He seemed to be contemplating something that transcended all the activity about him.

Koesler walked over and sat down sat beside him.

After several moments, Father Smith turned to look at Koesler. Smith's eyes were red-rimmed. He had quite obviously been crying.

"Have you heard the news from the seminary?" Koesler asked.

Smith nodded.

"And have you heard the news from the Vatican?"

Again Smith nodded.

"This is no place for us," Koesler said. "C'mon."

As if he had nothing to say about the suggestion, Smith rose slowly and, it seemed, painfully, and followed Koesler. They made their way to the main door. Koesler hailed a cab, and they entered for the brief ride to St. Joseph's.

As they entered the rectory, they passed the Jesuit who had agreed to take Koesler's place at the noon Mass. His look said: There are two of you! So why did you need me? Koesler knew the question would never be addressed, let alone answered.

They went up the stairs to Koesler's room. He shut the door behind them and took Smith's hat and coat and put them with his own.

They sat opposite each other. Nothing was said for several moments. Smith's eyes teared again. He made no move to wipe the tears away.

"So," Koesler opened, "you know the Holy Father has canceled his trip at the very last minute."

Smith shrugged. Suggesting that he knew but didn't much care.

"And you also know about the death of . . . your son."

Smith bowed his head and said nothing.

"You tried to tell me in so many ways—" Koesler stopped. "This is going to be pretty heavy and I'm not entirely sure where it will end. Would you like a drink?"

Smith shook his head.

Koesler was about to pour himself some port, then thought better of it. He gazed at Smith. Finally he spoke.

"It started," Koesler said, "at the Koznickis' party. You made a pointed reference to a wake you'd attended where one irrepressible mourner remarked that the deceased was a dead ringer for her father. If I'd been a lot more insightful, I might have looked at the men who were panelists at the symposium, as Lieutenant Tully did much later. At least three of the panelists were physically similar. The youngest of the three was pretty nearly a dead ringer for you. I assume Lieutenant Tully did not include you in the group of look-alikes because your picture was not in his handbook.

"I should've been more attentive to your double meaning of dead ringer when you made it clear early on that you were responsible for the selection of the panelists. Monsignor Martin may have set the philosophical groundwork for the symposium but you selected the people. And among those you selected were at least two who completed the resemblance circle.

"Then you made a point of telling the story of the Detroit Gulf War veteran who was murdered here after surviving the war . . . the special angle being that his wife arranged for someone else to commit the crime.

"There was no particular reason to tell the story in my presence. I was familiar with all the details. You wanted me to know that just as she was responsible for what went on while doing nothing herself, so you were responsible for what went on with the panel while doing nothing yourself."

"Well," Smith said, "of course I didn't know—had no way of knowing—that Dermot was going to murder anyone. I only wanted you to be able to know that even though Martin issued the invitation, it was I who was responsible for the makeup of the panel."

Koesler nodded. "And finally, unless I missed some other clues you were dropping, there was the matter of the Magdalens. I had never heard of them. But you told me of this custom in the recent history of Ireland that took . . . what was the word you used? . . . *inconvenient* females and shipped them off to select convents where if they were pregnant out of wedlock they stayed for the delivery and compulsory adoption of their babies. And, since for whatever reason they were confined there they were a serious social disgrace to their families, they regularly were kept in the convents at menial work.

"That's what happened to your child's mother, isn't it? Is she still there?"

A long pause.

"She died in the convent long ago." This simple statement was the first indication that the conclusions Koesler had reached were correct.

"One more sign you did not contribute," Koesler said, "came when Inspector Koznicki mentioned that on the day 'Gregory Ward' arrived here, a man with no identification was found with his neck broken in the Dublin airport. The present hypothesis is that the person we know as Father Ward murdered the real Father Ward and assumed his identity. They're checking into that now."

Smith slowly raised his head until he was looking straight into Koesler's eyes. "He killed in Ireland!" Smith agonized. "Oh, God! Oh, God!"

Koesler allowed time for this unexpected and unwanted new information to sink in.

Then he said, "When Inspector Koznicki mentioned Ireland, another peg fell into the proper hole.

"From his picture and from what I was able to see of him, your son appeared to be in his mid-forties. Which would place his birth at about the time you were ordained. But you were not ordained here in Detroit, your diocese. You were one of the brilliant students sent abroad to study. You studied the last few years in the seminary and were ordained overseas. My guess? In Ireland. That's when all this started, isn't it?"

Smith's rigid visage relaxed markedly as his memory focused on "the beginning of it all."

"As you said"—Smith's voice was unsteady—"some of us were sent away to study. Some before ordination, some after, some both before *and* after.

"We were young. We were younger than our years. You know that as well as I. In our early twenties and still asking permission for everything from making a phone call to staying up 'after hours,' to having a cigarette. Maybe, in foreign countries, we were a bit more autonomous than you. We, the special study people, were in Louvain or Rome or Ireland or lots of other places for study in greater depth. I was at UCD in Dublin.

"I was twenty-four when I met Moira. She was five years older. We were virgins, of course. Neither of us knew much about the opposite sex. We took long hikes through the countryside. We invented a series of excuses for our respective superiors—my rector, her parents. We fell in love with each other's mind. We fell in love with each other's otherness. Moira introduced me to what it was like being a woman. And I returned the favor. Slowly, but, I guess, inevitably, our love became physical. We were delighted to experiment with each other, learning how to give and accept pleasure.

"That was marvelous. That was magnificent. That was excitement, playfulness, joy. That was pleasure other people our age were enjoying in marriage. They were in bedrooms, in beds. We were in hay in cowsheds. But that was a small price we were more than happy to pay.

"That was the end of what might be called our innocence."

Koesler felt he was listening to the plot of some standard Grand Opera. Everything bright and cheery was about to turn tragic and deadly.

He was right.

"Moira may have been ignorant of male physical response before me, but she was well aware of her reproductive system. She knew what to expect when she missed several periods.

"Not unlike many our age, we gave little or no thought to pregnancy. That was something that happened to other people . . . people who were not beloved and favored by God. We were dedicated to God. Especially me. I was going to be a priest!

"Strange . . . all the time we were making love—savagely, tenderly—we never squarely faced the fact that I was going to be a priest. And that that vocation did not include Moira.

"But now, she was pregnant. And we were scared stiff—with good reason. Like most seminarians of that era, I had always wanted to be a priest. All my life to that point had been directed toward being a priest. My dalliance with Moira had been just that: amorous play.

"But now the game got serious.

"I offered to do 'the honorable thing' and make 'an honest woman' of her. But it was a halfhearted offer at best. I did not want to turn away from the priesthood. However, especially with that offer on the table, Moira was in the driver's seat. She could've accepted my offer no matter however lukewarmly it was made.

"But Moira was too insightful for that. She knew if I had given up my vocation for her, I would never be happy. In time, I probably would've grown to resent her, the impediment to my life's goal.

"But, dammit, then reality sticks its ugly head into my life. She refused an insincere proposal. What I should've done was make it sincere. I should've insisted that we build a life together. I should have been man enough to take responsibility for what I'd done. After all, I had been 'man enough' to do it. I should have married the girl—happily.

"That's what I should have done. What I did was the cowardly thing."

Smith did not look at all well. He had been animated enough when narrating his early courting of Moira. Now it was as if he were dying little by little. "Are you all right?" Koesler asked. "You don't look well."

Smith waved him away. Once started, Smith seemed determined to lay the entire story bare.

"So," Smith continued, "we decided not to marry. Others had done that and survived.

"Little did either of us anticipate what was coming.

"I had never heard of the Magdalens. Hard as it is to believe, neither had Moira. It is a testimonial to just how disgraced these women were that few Irish people knew of their existence. People brought laundry to the convents and it was cleaned. It was washed and ironed by Magdalens who appeared in uniform and only in the company of nuns. If anybody ever gave any notice to these women, it was assumed they maybe were novices or postulants of that religious order.

"Moira pregnant was the ultimate disgrace to her family. Moira, about to be an unwed mother, would not tell who the father was. For that she was beaten. But she would not speak.

"As far as I was able to tell, there was only one person beside ourselves who knew. A Mr. Reidy, who owned one of the three pubs in Moira's village. He had chanced upon us once and, God knows why—probably because there are decent people in this world—promised to keep our secret.

"We were apprehensive for a while after that, waiting for the sword to fall. But Reidy was as good as his word. He kept our secret. I think he felt sorry for us. He wasn't much older than we were—and in after years I sometimes wondered whether maybe he had had a love affair that didn't work out . . . or maybe the girl he loved died; as far as I know, he never married—" Smith winced, whether from mental or physical pain Koesler had no way of knowing. After a minute he seemed to recover. He went on with his story.

"I was ordained in Dublin for service in Detroit. I left Ireland without knowing what had happened to Moira. I didn't see her. I thought she might have attended my ordination. I thought she had been sent away. I didn't know she had disappeared into a bottomless prison that was the 'charity' system.

"By this time, Reidy and I had come to be friends. As I said, I think he felt sorry for me. He was never judgmental, and I was grateful for that.

"Before I left Ireland, I reached an agreement with him. He would be my conduit for contact with Moira—if he could find her. I would send money, as much as I could, for Moira and the child—and for himself for his trouble.

"Shortly after I returned to Detroit, Reidy informed me that I might just as well stop sending letters to Moira through him. She was in a convent. He knew where she was, but couldn't get any letters to her without having them taken by the nuns.

"And then the boy was born. Moira never saw him. Nor did she have any choice in the adoption. Because Reidy had a sister who was a nun, he was able to find out about the boy and keep track of him. But Moira became lost to the world behind a series of convents that I could only liken to a Russian gulag."

Smith paused, seemingly lost in thought, then continued.

"Right then, I think, Robert, I should have chucked it all—my priesthood, my future—and found her and our child and tried to create a happy ending. Or as happy an ending as fate would allow.

"But . . . I was a coward. I decided to continue as I was. I continued my arrangement with Reidy, now only as far as the boy was concerned. Moira was lost to me.

"Robert"—Smith seemed to be losing strength—"it is very much like the traditional crucial lie. Tell it and it sets you on a path of lying. One lie begets the next, and so on. In this case it's an act of cowardice. One leads to the next until it reaches such proportions it has a life of its own.

"That's what it was with me. I made one cowardly decision. Then another. Soon it was the story of my life. At least the secret life I had with Reidy and eventually, with my son, Dermot."

Smith paused. He seemed to have run out of energy.

"You really don't look well," Koesler said.

"I think I'll take that drink you offered."

Koesler poured two glasses of port.

"We were surprised about you," Koesler said. "I was about five years behind you in the seminary. All of us knew you had been sent abroad to finish up. We also knew that guys like you were headed for special jobs: teaching in the seminary, Chancery work, maybe later on becoming a bishop. You didn't do any of those things. You sort of melted into the crowd. Then, as the years passed, you didn't invest in anything, like a summer cottage or a boat. You didn't take any of the more showy vacations."

"And now you know why."

"You were all torn up about Moira. That sort of explains why your career went into the dumpster."

"I was so embarrassed about what had happened. And I feared being found out. There was always a chance that someone, someone I hadn't known about, would blow the whistle. I thought that by keeping a low profile that would help. If I didn't stick my head up, nobody would hit it. So I turned down a series of the 'special' jobs."

"And the money you kept sending to this Reidy—that's why you didn't indulge in any of the luxuries."

Smith nodded, and sipped the port.

"But Reidy . . ." Koesler continued, ". . . how could you trust him? I mean, what was to stop him from keeping the money you sent and not doing what you wanted with it?"

Smith shrugged. "Robert, let's put it this way: I could not *not* try to help. Sending the money to Reidy was my only chance to do what I could. If he did with it what I wanted, God bless him. Nothing was certain; he could have died, emigrated to Australia. If he kept it for himself, well, he may have to answer for that. But then so will I. That will be a long line."

"And Moira?"

"Ah, Moira!" Even now, Smith spoke her name as one who loved her very much. "Eventually Reidy was able to help her a bit. He couldn't get her out of that system. But he was able to locate her—and even visit her from time to time. He was able to give her some of the money I sent. Or"—he looked purposefully at Koesler—"so he said. He was able to send me word when she died. Some twenty years ago. A young woman. But an old woman."

"And Dermot?"

"Dermot Hanrahan," Smith completed the name. "Hanrahan was the first family to 'adopt' him. The first of four 'adopting' families." Smith shook his head. "My luck must have rubbed off on him. Of all the marvelous, generous families in Ireland, it was Dermot's fate to be taken in by people who demanded everything of him from slave labor to doglike obedience.

"Dermot ran away a lot. This I am pretty sure is true: Reidy looked after the boy as best he could. Eventually he hired Dermot, though God knows in that little village the pub didn't need any more help. Reidy used the money I sent to pay Dermot's 'wages.'

"He sent me pictures of the boy as he grew. In many ways, he was the image of me." Pride showed briefly. "Only thing . . ." The pride gave way to despair. ". . . he hated me. He hated me without even knowing me."

"What did he know?"

"Not a lot—but too much." He smiled crookedly. "A classic case of a little knowledge being a dangerous thing.

"The families that had 'taken' him had made sure to berate him about his illegitimacy—that his mother was a 'hoor,' that his father was a good-for-nothing, that he would never amount to anything more than a barnyard heap—and that he ought to get down on his knees and be grateful they were giving him a roof over his head and putting food in his mouth—since that was more than his father would do for him.

"Real Christian folks," he said bitterly.

"The problem was, I guess, that Reidy was too good-hearted . . . too soft-hearted. He couldn't stand seeing the boy being beaten down so, and one night, when he'd had a few pints too much—or at least this is what he told me—he told the boy that his father was not all those rotten things that people were saying, that Reidy had known his father, and that his father was a good man.

"Naturally, the boy wanted to know why his father hadn't acknowledged him and taken care of him. And here . . . oh, God! . . . here is where the trouble started: Reidy told him that the reason his father couldn't acknowledge him was that his father had been a seminarian from the United States—that his father was a priest." He shook his head sadly. "It would've been better if he'd told Dermot that his father was dead.

"It didn't matter that Reidy told him that I had been sending money for him all along. It didn't matter that he told him that I'd been a superior student and that that's how I had come to be in Ireland—because I had been sent there to study—but that I'd had to return to the States after I was ordained.

"None of that mattered. All the boy could see was that I'd deserted his mother and thus him, and left them both to make their way—and a miserable way it was.

"Reidy was sick over it all, but there was nothing he could do. He'd spilled the beans and that was it. He tried to do the best he could after that. When Dermot wanted to know my name and where I was, Reidy wouldn't tell him. The boy was furious. He wept and ranted and raved, but Reidy wouldn't tell him.

"He was angry at Reidy, but he was confused too. Reidy was really the only father figure he had, so while he was angry at Reidy for keeping his father's name and whereabouts from him, he also, I think, in his way, felt an attachment for him.

"But, as for me . . . well, Reidy told me that Dermot's hatred for me grew until it became not only an obsession, but almost his raison d'être. He lived for one thing: to get even with his father . . . me."

Smith paused, and sipped his wine. But he needed to continue his story.

"Dermot squirreled away much of his money. Reidy didn't know why until quite recently. He knew that eventually Dermot would tell him what was going on." He shook his head. "Reidy had the kind of relationship with him that I would have wanted.

"Well, it seems Dermot read in the *Irish Press* about this papal visit to Detroit and the symposium. He didn't give a damn where the pope was going or why. He was attracted by the symposium because it featured priests who were experts in their field and all of them would be Americans. Dermot thought it possible that in his group he might find his father. All that he knew of his father was that the man was a priest, an American, and smart enough to have been singled out to study overseas. And since all this was taking place in Detroit . . .

"Something else he had wheedled out of Reidy: that he and his father looked a lot alike. And, since Dermot was forty-five, he knew his father would have been studying in Ireland some forty-five years ago."

Smith paused and sipped a bit more of the port. He seemed exhausted, but determined to complete his story.

"Well," Smith continued, speaking more slowly and carefully, "as it

259

turns out, Dermot had quite a crop to chose from. Actually, it's no surprise to anyone that there are lots of Catholic colleges and universities in Ireland where seminarians as well as priests can study. Besides UCD, there is St. Patrick's Maynooth, All Hallows, Clonliff, Milltown, and St. Dominic's.

"All Dermot needed to do was visit these schools and study the enrollment and class pictures for the years, roughly, 1948 through 1950. Then he could compile a list of bright young seminarians who were there from the States. All he had to do then was wait for the release of a roster of American priest experts who would take part in this symposium.

"As soon as Reidy informed me of what Dermot was doing, I volunteered to help Martin plan the symposium. I knew the guys who were studying in Ireland at the same time I was. On strictly American holidays—like Thanksgiving or July Fourth—we would all get together. It wasn't that tough to find a couple of guys who superficially resembled me and, therefore, Dermot. They didn't have to be clones, just have the general characteristics: tall, thin, balding, glasses. As it turned out, two of the fellows fit the bill quite well: Hanson and Palmer."

Koesler was unable to hide his revulsion. "You chose Hanson and Palmer deliberately! You sent them to their deaths in your place!"

Smith gazed at the floor. "I had no idea . . . Reidy had no way of knowing either. Outside of Reidy's telling me that Dermot was preparing for some sort of confrontation and that he planned to attend the symposium, I didn't know who Dermot was. I had seen photos of him as a young man, and I knew he looked enough like me so that I thought I'd be able to spot him if he showed up at the symposium. But it never entered my mind that he would come disguised as one of the panelists . . . or, God forbid, that he had already killed the real Father Ward!"

Smith paused to think through what he'd just said. "That's true as far as it goes. But I'm rationalizing, as I've done for most of my life. The whole truth is . . . once again, I was a coward. I was afraid to face Dermot after the life I left him and his mother. I figured he would just dump his pent-up anger on Hanson or Palmer. And that would be that. Or, so I hoped."

"Why would Dermot exclude the possibility that you were his father? The criteria fit you as well as the other two."

"Except for one thing: While I was in Ireland at the right time and the right place, I did nothing with my life. *His* father was headed for big things—like being an acknowledged expert in one or another ecclesiastical field. *His* father would not have ended up, as I did, a simple parish priest.

"And of course since I wasn't staying at the seminary I never came face to face with him anyway. Maybe if I had . . ." His face filled with anguish. ". . . Hanson and Palmer would be still be alive—and God help me—so would my son. . . ."

He pulled himself together somewhat.

"And, while we're at it, Robert, about my recounting what happened to that Detroit soldier who survived the Gulf War only to be murdered by his wife's brother, at her behest: The example was not meant to be taken literally. Just that her brother stood in for her. Just as Hanson and Palmer would stand in for me . . . Again—I had no idea Dermot had murder in his heart."

"But," Koesler pressed, "after Dan Hanson was killed . . ."

"Why didn't I warn Bill Palmer? A couple of things . . . maybe three. I didn't know whom to warn Palmer about. How could I know that Dermot actually did this? Who was Dermot? And, still playing the coward, I was afraid to let anyone know I had anything to do with this whole affair. Besides . . ." He shivered. ". . . it was just then that I got my death sentence."

"You what?!"

"I've been feeling really bad for about a month now. Afraid to go to the doctor. Afraid of what he might say." A brief smile. "A coward yet again. A few days ago I couldn't stand it anymore. Between the pain and the fear of what was causing it, I couldn't sleep. I lost my appetite and some weight—suddenly. So I finally went to the doctor. He put me through some tests." He winced. "I've got cancer of the pancreas."

He didn't need to amplify. Koesler had known people with pancreatic cancer. He knew how swiftly and terrifyingly it usually progressed. He felt deeply for Paul Smith—a man he'd grown close to only very recently. "Paul . . ." Koesler leaned toward him. ". . . how . . . long . . .?"

"How long have I got? They say a month or less. But I can tell you, I think it's less . . . lots less."

So much had been revealed in so brief a time, that an interval for silent reflection seemed necessary.

"Just as a matter of curiosity," Koesler said after a few minutes, "why all those clues—like the 'dead ringer' comment, and the Magdalens—and why me? Why did you pick me to dump all this on?"

"Could I say it seemed a good idea at the time? No. Well, I had no idea what was going to happen or how this was going to turn out. What would Dermot do? How would he relate to Hanson and Palmer? And, by the time of the Koznickis' dinner, I was feeling so rotten. I knew something was very, very wrong inside me. I wanted someone to know what had happened to me. To Dermot. Someone had to be able to tell the story—maybe to Dermot. But I couldn't just come out and tell *anyone*. So I devised the clues and gave them to you because . . . oh, I guess I was still rationalizing—thinking that maybe if somebody could figure things out . . . and . . . well, you're good at piecing things like this together. I had confidence you could do it. And you did.

"But I felt somebody had to know . . . that I had to tell somebody."

Smith cradled his downturned head in his hands. "Bob . . . such a mess. I've made such a mess of my life. And not only *my* life. Moira and Dermot and Dan Hanson and Bill Palmer. And, God help me, Father Ward. And I'm supposed to be a priest! With all this baggage, I've got to face God, in just a little while." He paused. "If you have anything to say about it, see if you can get an epitaph that says 'Coward.'"

"Paul, do you believe anything you've been saying over the past forty-five years?"

"What?"

"You've told people how Jesus came for sinners, not only the just. The story of the Good Shepherd. He has a hundred sheep. But at day's end he has ninety-nine in the fold. So he goes out searching till he finds the one that's strayed. The poor woman who loses a coin and cleans everywhere till she finds it. Always, it is a source of joy when a penitent sinner comes home.

"So, okay, you could have been—you should have been more responsible. Moira should never have been incarcerated in the Magdalen program. Dermot should not have had to grow up as an abused orphan. Our two priests needn't have died. Father Ward needn't have died. Dermot needn't have died. It all seems overwhelming when you pile it up in one indictment.

"The opposite of a devil's advocate could make a pretty good case for the defense. To have taken the opposite course from the one you chose would have called for an almost heroic decision.

"I know what it's like wanting the priesthood more than anything. I can imagine how you felt when you stood to lose it due to an irresponsible affair. But neither you nor Moira knew—could have known—what she was getting into by being an unwed mother.

"But, I agree with you on this: Now is no time for rationalization and excuses. Now is a good time to shoulder responsibility and come with sorrow and contrition to our God."

"I . . . I don't know if I can."

"Of course you can. What you think is that you're unworthy. But you've spent forty-five years telling sinners like us that none of us is *worthy*, yet God welcomes us anyway. Can't you believe for yourself what you've consoled others with over these many years? There will be more joy in heaven over one repentant sinner than over ninety-nine just.

"I'm sure I don't have to ask you whether you're sorry for all the mistakes you've made, the blunders, the selfish decisions, the cowardice."

Smith shook his bowed head as he wiped away tears.

"You've told me everything," Koesler said. "Why don't we make what you've told me your confession."

Abruptly, Smith raised his head and met Koesler's gaze.

"No, not again!" Smith said, almost defiantly. "I make this my confession and I seal your lips forever. One more act of cowardice. I can't do that again! I wish to God I'd never done it. But I can't do it again."

"You don't have to, Paul. Let me give you absolution. Let me give you the forgiveness of Jesus. And then let me make an appointment for you with my friend, Inspector Koznicki.

"You can open up to him, Paul. You can help the police. It's what a brave person would do."

Smith relaxed and smiled genuinely for the first time. He nodded solemnly. "It is," he said, "isn't it? What a brave person would do."

35

He was confused. He shook his head. That hurt.

Imagine! After all these years—his first hangover. Lucky he had asked John Andrews to cover for him in the parish this morning. John was retired, but he was a top-notch organist and choir director, and always willing to help out.

It was so quiet and dark and warm, especially warm. He hadn't thought about turning down the heat or opening a window. Which was why, on this morning of January 1, he was overwarm even though his only covering was a sheet.

He lay motionless. Then he moved his head slowly, very slowly, from side to side. His clothing lay in a pile on the chair.

Dave Wallace slid out of bed and into his clothes. His mouth tasted like a parade of prelates had been marching through it. He could only guess at how bad his mouth smelled.

He sat in the chair and lit a cigarette. It had been years since he'd smoked. As it happened, he'd picked up a pack at last night's party. It had been years since he'd drunk this much. And God knew how long it had been since he and Abigail had made love.

Then into his life had come Sally Forbes. Had it really been less than a month ago? The rehearsal for the Papal Mass. Then practically every night thereafter. He had been so relieved that the pope had canceled his visit. With that cancelation all the rumors regarding the ban on artificial contraception died away. Apparently it would remain as Paul VI put it in *Humanae Vitae*—a noninfallible teaching, still open to question. And while that was not really satisfactory to either left or right wing of the Church, it was vastly preferable to what the liberals feared the present pope would do.

Wallace looked at the form in bed. Sally slept on her side, back toward him. Her shoulder-length red hair contrasted beautifully with the pillow's whiteness.

Then, as if she somehow became conscious of his studying her, she wakened and turned over on her back. She rubbed her eyes, then looked at him. She stretched like a cat. "All dressed up?"

"Force of habit," he said.

She threw the sheet off and stood. She was nude. She walked to the door of the bathroom and took a robe from the hook.

Once more Wallace was reminded of a conviction he had never really forgotten: The curve that runs from a woman's waist to her knee is, arguably, the most beautiful line God ever drew.

She walked directly to him and sat on his lap. "Wasn't that a nice New Year's Eve party the choir threw last night?"

"I'm not sure," he said. "You'll have to fill me in."

"But . . . you were the life of it!"

"I was?"

"Oh, yes. You played every tune they suggested. If they could hum it, you could play it. Even transpose it up or down on request."

"I did? That's pretty good."

"And just think, we've got the Holy Father to thank for it."

"Huh?"

"If he hadn't scheduled a visit here in the first place, we wouldn't have gotten that diocesan choir together again. And you wouldn't have—finally—noticed me."

"I suppose that's true. I was blind, really blind, not to have singled you out ages ago. But now, with no pope on the horizon, I can appreciate you like mad. There's only one thing."

She drew back from him in surprise. "What's that?"

"Do you think we could date for a while? I mean, just regular, everyday old dates?"

She smiled and snuggled against his shoulder. "Of course we can. Mother always used to say that I had a habit of leaving out the middles."

"This is the day of football madness," Joe Cox said, cradling the phone on his shoulder. "So I thought what I'd do is get some carryout chicken from Dad'Z. I've got plenty of booze and maybe we could spend a quiet holiday together."

"What? No deadlines, no scoops today?" Pat Lennon also cradled the phone as she touched up her nails.

"No plans for anything like that. But hell, this is Detroit; anything can happen anytime."

Her more thoughtful reaction was identical to her initial response to his invitation: She found it depressing. There was nothing attractive there. She was pretty sure he felt the same way, but was reluctant to admit it even to himself.

"Sort of makes you want to stay close to the phone . . . just in case something breaks," she added.

He sensed her negative reaction. "Pat, you're not sore about the way I covered the story on the pope, are you?"

"Why should I be?"

Actually, she had been relieved when it turned out that he wasn't intimately involved in the case. "Look, Joe, I know the pressure you've been under since you got back from Chicago."

"Wouldn't you feel the same if you were in my boots?"

"I honestly don't know, Joe. I don't think I'd be quite as intense."

"And what does that mean?"

"Why go into that again?"

"You think I steered the story . . . manipulated it."

"That's what I said. And I've got no reason to change my opinion. But, like I said, Joe, I don't know what I'd've done in your place. You had a lot of territory to reclaim." She sighed mentally. "Why don't we let it drop? It's over."

"Okay. Then what about my original invitation? You didn't go either way."

Lennon hesitated. "Joe . . . I could make up lots of dandy excuses. But you're too good a newshound to fall for any of them. I think you and I are past tense. If we fool around with our relationship—try to give it CPR—we're going to end up not liking each other very much. And I wouldn't want that to happen."

"No chance, huh?"

"If there is, it's not now."

Cox's inclination was to press. He had trouble believing that any woman—even the redoubtable Pat Lennon—could shrug off his full court press.

On the other hand, he knew Pat. She didn't suffer fools gladly. And a fool was somebody who didn't take her seriously. So before she could close the door permanently, he would back off. Pat Lennon, alone of every woman he knew, could get him to do that.

"Okay, Pat. I don't want us not to be friends either. So, although it's not starting very well for me, Happy New Year."

"Same to you, Joe. Enjoy the football."

Cox replaced the receiver. He felt very much alone. Well, he thought, you can't put the toothpaste back in the tube. If he had to start from scratch in this town—and he did—why not a new woman to go with the territory? The more he considered that, the more attractive this prospect was. On second, or maybe third, thought, playing the field would be just what the doctor ordered.

Suddenly he was grateful Lennon had backed away. Old love affairs were for old people. And Joe Cox would always be young in spirit. And that was what was most important.

But he wouldn't force it. Romance tomorrow. Football today.

He got a beer from the fridge and popped the top. He turned on the TV. It was some sort of bowl parade. Orange, or Rose, or who cared? For just a second there was a stabbing pain. It was the spot in his heart formerly occupied by Pat Lennon. Then it was gone.

Or was it?

Wanda Koznicki served coffee and cake to her husband and their New Year's guest, Father Koesler.

"Another marvelous meal, Wanda," Koesler said.

"Nothing fancy, Father," Wanda said. "Just plain food."

Koznicki beamed. "Prepared with love."

Walt and Wanda smiled at each other. Theirs, Koesler reflected, was a genuine marriage. They have grown in their relationship. It had weathered many a formidable storm. They were closer to each other now than when they began. And that, Koesler thought, was the real proof of marriage. Not a notation in a book or a collection of documents.

"Why don't you fellows go into the living room while I finish clearing the dishes?" Wanda said.

"How about I help?"

"Not on your life, Father." Wanda's smile said she appreciated the offer but, as previous guests in her house could testify, Wanda wanted no one in her kitchen. "Into the other room with you both!"

Obediently, the two balanced their dessert and coffee and carefully made their way to comfortable chairs and settled in.

The holiday decorations were very much still present in the house. In silence the two men let the colored lights sweep over them.

"Do you hear anything about the Holy Father's health?" Koznicki asked.

"Just what I read in the papers—no, wait: There's always the clergy scuttlebutt—for what that's worth. It's all speculation really. The official diagnosis, according to new reports, is that it was a bad case of the flu. And, due to the Holy Father's age and delicate health, they think it better that he rest . . . et cetera, et cetera, et cetera."

"And local opinion disputes that?"

"Not exactly. But we're counting in all the violence that prefaced his aborted trip. Specifically, the murder of Cardinal Schinder. The Cardinal was the Holy Father's right hand. The word is that Schinder tried to talk the pope out of introducing infallibility into the birth control controversy. But, like a loyal soldier, once His Holiness insisted, the Cardinal went to prepare the way. So . . . the hypothesis is that the pope took Schinder's murder as an omen. So much so that the pope is content to leave birth control in the status quo."

"Remarkable." Koznicki tasted the coffee which now had cooled to a drinkable temperature. "One is tempted to see God's hand in this. Yet I cannot think that God condoned, much less caused, this violence and these murders."

"Neither can I. I suppose we might think that while God does not condone murder, yet He can draw good from evil." Koesler was somewhat surprised that Koznicki apparently was opposed to the rumored infallible doctrine. Else why would the inspector think God had a hand in preventing that escalation? Until now, Koesler hadn't viewed Koznicki as having very many liberal ecclesial bones. But Koesler, of course, had no way of knowing about Koznicki's son and his near crisis with birth control.

"Or," Koesler continued, "perhaps it's as Dietrich Bonhoeffer told a German soldier as the two watched Allied bombers practically obliterate Berlin. The soldier said, 'How could a loving father let this happen?' And Bonhoeffer replied, 'How could we let this happen to a loving father?'"

"Yes." Koznicki seemed to want to tuck that away for future meditation.

"However," Koesler said, "as far as the media is concerned, the pope's 'almost' visit and the murders are yesterday's news. And the majority of our fellow citizens are vaguely regretful that the Holy Father didn't come. But they can empathize when it comes to the flu. So the whole strange story is behind us . . . except, I suppose, for the murders."

The utensils Koznicki used—cup, saucer, plate, and fork—were standard size, but they appeared as children's toys in his huge hands. "The murder of Cardinal Schinder is both before and ahead of us," he said. "Everyone in that Golds gang is eager to talk to us despite the urgings of their lawyers. Convictions are pretty much assured, although the court is not my province. Whatever sentences are passed, we can be quite sure of one thing: That young ringleader, Rick, will be spending the rest of his life in prison."

"We won't miss him at all."

"Then"—a look of concern crossed Koznicki's face—"there is Dermot Hanrahan, as we now know him. His death precluded a trial, but we can be certain among ourselves that he murdered Father Ward in Ireland, as well as Fathers Hanson and Palmer here. But, except for a very few people, Hanrahan's motive will have died with him." He shook his head. "And Hanrahan would not be dead if he had not been able to procure a weapon...."

The statement was left unfinished as the police inspector and the priest pondered the last day of Dermot Hanrahan's life. How, where did he get the gun ... the semiautomatic that he had fired through the door of his seminary room, drawing the answering fusillade of police bullets that killed him?

Koznicki sensed Koesler's unspoken question. "Where did he get the gun? Where does anybody get a gun? You know as well as I that all he had to do was walk down any street in almost any part of Detroit with money in his pocket and he would have little or no trouble in buying a weapon, no questions asked." Kosnicki shook his head again. "But a semiautomatic ..."

Again both men were silent, thinking of the many innocent lives that had been taken because of the easy availability of all manner of deadly weapons.

"Something still puzzles me," Koesler said finally. "How did Dermot know about Father Ward? And he'd have to know—how *did* he know which flight he'd be on?"

"There again," Koznicki said, "like his motive, his methods died with him. But we have pieced together what probably happened.

"We know that Ireland—at least the Republic—is, by anyone's description, a Catholic country. There was extensive newspaper coverage of the pope's planned trip. Along the way, the participants in the pilgrimage and the program were identified. Several priests coming from

Europe would have touched down in Ireland, particularly if nonstop flights were sold out. Unfortunately for him, this was the case with Father Ward.

"Probably Hanrahan selected Father Ward because taking his place would require only a brief masquerade on Hanrahan's part. And undoubtedly he thought he could carry off being an expert in Church music more easily than in the field of theology or church law."

"And the flight?"

"Ah, yes, the flight. The records show that Hanrahan made a phone call to Herdecke. We can only guess—but it is a reasonable supposition—that he learned thereby which flight Father Ward would be taking. He may even have made some arrangement to meet the priest, possibly pretending to be some sort of official—perhaps a Church representative, or a guide, or a reporter or some such.

"Of course, if Father's itinerary had not called for a change of planes in Ireland, Dermot would have been forced to try for another participant, or even another plan. Here, his luck was good. Later, it would turn on him."

"So," Koesler said sadly, "there it ends. With a lot of bad luck for everyone . . . the truly tragic figure being Father Smith."

Kosnicki nodded. "Father Smith may have been guilty of poor judgment, and perhaps even sin," he said thoughtfully. "But there was little reason to pursue the matter. That he was guilty of a crime, even technically, could be hotly debated. And when the prosecuting attorney learned of his physical condition, it was clear there was no time for a trial in any case. But"—he looked at Koesler stolidly—"his confession seemed to relieve his conscience."

"Confession will do that," Koesler noted pointedly.

In their shared glance Koznicki correctly read that Koesler was the first to have heard that confession. The law had granted Father Smith freedom. The sacrament promised him forgiveness.

"Father Smith's burial was out of the country?" Koznicki asked.

Koesler nodded. "About a year ago, the ashes of some of those poor women, the Magdalens, were gathered and interred in blessed ground in Dublin. We were able to have Paul's ashes, along with his son's, buried there. That tortured 'family' is together at last."

Koznicki went to the fireplace, stirred up the embers, and deftly added a couple of logs. Without turning to Koesler, he said, "I am sure the Holy Father is indeed ill, and we pray for his full return to health . . . but is it not strange that none of the murders had anything to do with him?

"Cardinal Schinder was the victim of some rich bored young punks. Of course their ultimate target was the Holy Father, but we got them long before they would have had a chance at His Holiness.

"Then there was the troubled, tormented Dermot. The media led the world in speculating that he too intended eventually to kill the Holy Father. Only a very few people know Dermot's motive. And those few people are not talking."

"A little mystery is good for the soul," Koesler suggested.

With that, Wanda entered the living room carrying a cup of coffee. "What? No football? Don't they play umpteen games on New Year's Day?"

Koznicki chuckled. "We were savoring the last of Christmas—and good friends."

"Well," Wanda said, "I'll drink to that!" and she sipped the steaming coffee. "By the way, Father, I meant to tell you how beautiful your eulogy for Father Smith was."

Koznicki looked up sharply. Could she have overheard their just-completed conversation? No, the dishwasher had been going full blast. Wanda knew nothing of the relationship of Father Smith and Dermot Hanrahan. There were few secrets between Koznicki and his wife. She did not need to know the complexities that linked that father and son. Better, Koznicki figured, that Father Smith retain his unblemished reputation as far as Wanda was concerned.

"Thank you," Koesler replied to Wanda's compliment. "Father Smith was a very special man . . . friend . . . priest. I must admit I didn't know Paul intimately until . . . well, actually, not until your party here a few weeks ago. But, in this brief time, we grew quite close.

"Well . . ." Koesler stood. ". . . these have been very busy days. I'm sure you're tired, and I know I am."

The Koznickis' protests about ending the evening were pro forma. They *were* tired. One of the many nice things about Father Koesler was that he never overstayed his welcome.

There were words of farewell at the door. Koesler pulled the collar of his coat up to cover his ears. It was bitingly cold. Thank God his car started.

He drove away with kind and prayerful thoughts about the Koznickis.

And then his thoughts turned to Paul Smith.

What might he, Koesler, have done had he been in Smith's moccasins? What if he had met the curious, giving, loving Moira? How would he have handled the news that he was to be a "father" in the essential meaning of the word? At that moment, as a seminarian not yet a priest, he would have needed no dispensation. He was a layman then. Perfectly able to marry. It would have meant losing his lifelong ambition.

But it was clear. This entire story had to do with accepting responsibility.

If Paul had shouldered his responsibility to Moira, probably all three—Paul, Moira, and Dermot—would be alive now. And Fathers Hanson and Palmer, and Father Ward as well.

Dermot had a responsibility to himself, to build a life for himself. Or, as he did, he could live for revenge alone. As a result he and three priests were dead.

Now, dear Lord, let them be at peace. No one but you could understand all, forgive all. Give them your peace. At long last, let them rest in peace.